THE
PROCESS
READER

THE
PROCESS
READER

RICHARD E. RAY
Indiana University of Pennsylvania

GARY A. OLSON
University of South Florida

JAMES DeGEORGE
Indiana University of Pennsylvania

PRENTICE-HALL
Englewood Cliffs, N.J. 07632

Library of Congress Cataloging-in-Publication Data

RAY, RICHARD E.
  The process reader.

  Includes index.
  1. College readers. 2. English language—Rhetoric.
  I. OLSON, GARY A., 1954-   II. DEGEORGE,
  JAMES, 1936-   III. Title.
  PE1417.R32 1986   808'.0427   85-25668
  ISBN 0-13-723586-0

On the cover:
Jean Arp, *Mountain Table Anchors Navel* (1925)
Oil on cardboard with cutouts. 29⅝ × 23½".
The Museum of Modern Art, New York.

Editorial/production supervision and interior design: Virginia Rubens
Cover design: Bruce D. Kenselaar
Manufacturing buyer: Harry P. Baisley

Printed in the United States of America

10 9 8 7 6 5 4 3 2 1

ISBN 0-13-723586-0   01

PRENTICE-HALL INTERNATIONAL (UK) LIMITED, *London*
PRENTICE-HALL OF AUSTRALIA PTY. LIMITED, *Sydney*
PRENTICE-HALL OF CANADA INC., *Toronto*
PRENTICE-HALL HISPANOAMERICANA, S.A., *Mexico*
PRENTICE-HALL OF INDIA PRIVATE LIMITED, *New Delhi*
PRENTICE-HALL OF JAPAN, INC., *Tokyo*
PRENTICE-HALL OF SOUTHEAST ASIA PTE. LTD., *Singapore*
EDITORA PRENTICE-HALL DO BRASIL, LTDA., *Rio de Janeiro*
WHITEHALL BOOKS LIMITED, *Wellington, New Zealand*

ACKNOWLEDGMENTS

Isaac Asimov, "The Scientists' Responsibility," reprinted with permission from *Chemical & Engineering News,* April 19, 1971, 49 (16), pp. 3, 7. Copyright 1971 American Chemical Society. By permission of the author.

F. Lee Bailey with Harvey Aronson, "Alone," from *The Defense Never Rests* by F. Lee Bailey. Copyright © 1971 by F. Lee Bailey and Harvey Aronson. Reprinted by arrangement with New American Library, New York, New York.

Russell Baker, "From Song to Sound: Bing and Elvis," copyright © 1977 by The New York Times Company. Reprinted by permission.

Sharon Begley (with John Carey and Mary Bruno), "How Animals Weather Winter," copyright 1983 by Newsweek, Inc. All Rights Reserved. Reprinted by permission.

Sharon Begley (with Mary Hager), "Victims of Mount Vesuvius," copyright 1982 by Newsweek, Inc. All Rights Reserved. Reprinted by permission.

Joseph L. Braga and Laurie D. Braga, "Foreword" to *Death: The Final Stage of Growth,* ed., Elisabeth Kubler-Ross, general editors, Joseph L. Braga and Laurie D. Braga (Englewood Cliffs, N.J.: Prentice-Hall, Inc., 1975), pp. x-xi.

Maury M. Breecher, "The Secret Attraction of Kissing," from *Focus,* II, no. 34, July 15, 1984, 6. By permission of Maury M. Breecher.

Alexander Calandra, "Angels on a Pin," from *Saturday Review,* 51, December 21, 1968, 60. By permission of Alexander Calandra.

Truman Capote, "The Festivities," from *In Cold Blood* by Truman Capote. Copyright © 1965 by Truman Capote. Reprinted by permission of Random House, Inc.

Bruce Catton, "Grant and Lee," from *This Hallowed Ground* by Bruce Catton. Copyright © 1955, 1956 by Bruce Catton. Reprinted by permission of Doubleday & Company, Inc.

Norman Cousins, "Dr. Brand." Selection is reprinted from *Anatomy of an Illness, As Perceived by the Patient,* by Norman Cousins, by permission of W. W. Norton & Company, Inc. Copyright © 1979 by W. W. Norton & Company, Inc.

Harry Crews, "The Car," copyright © 1975 by Harry Crews. Originally appeared in *Esquire* Magazine, December, 1975. Reprinted by permission of John Hawkins & Associates, Inc., 71 W. 23rd St., NY, NY 10010.

Joan Didion, "Many Mansions," from *The White Album,* copyright © 1979 by Joan Didion. Reprinted by permission of Simon & Schuster, Inc.

Jo Durden-Smith and Diane DeSimone, "Is There a Superior Sex?" From Jo Durden-Smith and Diane DeSimone, "Men and Women: Part Five," *Playboy,* 29 (May 1982), 159+, as printed in *Readers' Digest* as "Is There a Superior Sex?" 121, no. 727 (November 1982), 263-270. Originally appeared in *Playboy* Magazine: copyright © 1982 by *Playboy.* Reprinted with permission from the November, 1982 *Readers' Digest.*

Paul R. Ehrlich, "North America After the War," with permission from *Natural History,* vol. 93, no. 3; copyright The American Museum of Natural History, 1984.

Bruce Feirstein, "Are You a Man or a Wimp?" from *Real Men Don't Eat Quiche* by Bruce Feirstein. Copyright © 1982 by Bruce Feirstein. Reprinted by permission of Pocket Books, Inc., a division of Simon & Schuster, Inc., and *Readers' Digest,* December, 1982.

Paul Fussell, "Notes on Class," from *The Boy Scout Handbook and Other Observations* by Paul Fussell. Copyright © 1982 by Paul Fussell. Reprinted by permission of Oxford University Press, Inc.

Dick Gregory, "Political Dogs," excerpts from "Lesson Twelve: Techniques of Persuasion," pp. 223-226, from *Dick Gregory's Political Primer* by Dick Gregory and edited by James McGraw. Copyright © 1972 by Richard Claxton Gregory. Reprinted by permission of Harper & Row, Publishers, Inc.

Susan Jacoby, "Battering Back," from *The Possible She* by Susan Jacoby. Copyright © 1978, 1979 by Susan Jacoby. Reprinted by permission of Farrar, Straus and Giroux, Inc.

Carl Jensen, "Censorship and Junk Food Journalism," *Wilson Library Bulletin,* 58, no. 7 (March 1984), 483-485.

Suzanne Britt Jordan, "That Lean and Hungry Look," copyright 1978 by Newsweek, Inc. All Rights Reserved. Reprinted by permission.

Henry Kendall, "Second Strike," September, 1979. Reprinted by permission of *The Bulletin of the Atomic Scientists,* a magazine of science and world affairs. Copyright © 1979 by the Educational Foundation for Nuclear Society, Chicago, IL 60637.

Martin Luther King, Jr., excerpt from "Pilgrimage to Nonviolence" (pp. 101-107) in *Stride Toward Freedom* by Martin Luther King, Jr. Copyright © 1958 by Martin Luther King, Jr. Reprinted by permission of Harper & Row, Publishers, Inc.

Barbara Lawrence, "Four-Letter Words Can Hurt You," from *The New York Times,* October 27, 1973 Op-ed. Copyright © 1973 by The New York Times Company. Reprinted by permission.

Jessica Mitford, "Parting the Formaldehyde Curtain," from *The American Way of Death* by Jessica Mitford. Copyright © 1963, 1978 by Jessica Mitford. Reprinted by permission of Simon & Schuster, Inc.

Donald Murray, "The Maker's Eye: Revising Your Own Manuscripts," from *The Writer,* October, 1973. Reprinted by permission of the author. Copyright © 1973 by Donald M. Murray.

Patricia O'Brien, "Where Has Childhood Gone?" in *Notre Dame Magazine,* 10, no. 3, July 1981, 22-23. By permission.

Vance Packard, "The New (and Still Hidden) Persuaders," from *Readers' Digest,* 118, February, 1981. By permission of Vance Packard.

John Aristotle Phillips and David Michaelis, "How I Designed an A-Bomb in My Junior Year at Princeton," from *Mushroom* by John Aristotle Phillips and David Michaelis, as it appeared in *Readers' Digest,* November, 1979. Copyright © 1978 by John Aristotle Phillips. By permission of William Morrow & Company.

Neil Postman, excerpted from "Euphemisms," from the book *Crazy Talk, Stupid Talk* by Neil Postman. Copyright © 1976 by Neil Postman. Reprinted by permission of Delacorte Press.

William J. Rewak, S.J., "Universities Must Not Remain Neutral in the Moral Crisis over Nuclear Weapons," reprinted from *The Chronicle of Higher Education* XXV, no. 23, Feb. 16, 1983, 64. Copyright 1983 by *The Chronicle of Higher Education.* Reprinted with permission.

Andrew A. Rooney, "Sound and Noise" and "Trust," from *And More by Andy Rooney.* Copyright © 1982 Essay Productions, Inc. Reprinted with the permission of Atheneum Publishers, Inc.

Mike Royko, "Making Money," from *Boss: Richard J. Daley of Chicago,* copyright © 1971 by Mike Royko. Reprinted by permission of the publisher, E.P. Dutton, a division of New American Library.

Carl Sagan, "The Ice Age and the Cauldron," from *The Cosmic Connection* by Carl Sagan. Copyright © 1973 by Carl Sagan and Jerome Agel. Reprinted by permission of Doubleday & Company, Inc.

Carl Sagan, "Who Speaks for Earth," from *Cosmos,* by Carl Sagan. Copyright © 1980 by Carl Sagan. Reprinted by permission of Random House, Inc.

Diane K. Shah (with Ronald Henkoff), "Nightclub Cowboys," copyright 1979 by Newsweek, Inc. All Rights Reserved. Reprinted by permission.

Diana Shaw-McLin, "We Lay Waste Our Powers." This article first appeared in *The Humanist* issue of March/April 1984 and is reprinted by permission.

Judy Syfers, "Why I Want a Wife," *Ms.,* 1 December 31, 1971. Reprinted by permission of Judy Syfers.

Carol Tavris and Leonore Tiefer, "Everything You Ever Wanted to Know About The Kiss," copyright © 1979 by Carol Tavris and Leonore Tiefer. Originally appeared in *Redbook.*

Richard Taylor, "Late Summer 1756," from *Girty* (Turtle Island and Berkeley, California: Netzahaulcoyotl Historical Society, 1977). By permission of Netzahaulcoyotl Historical Society and Richard Taylor.

Alexander Theroux, "How Curious the Camel," *Readers' Digest,* 122, February, 1983. By permission of Alexander Theroux.

Lewis Thomas, "Computers and the Human Mind," from *The Youngest Science* by Lewis Thomas. Copyright © 1983 by Lewis Thomas. Reprinted by permission of Viking Penguin Inc.

Lewis Thomas, "Notes on Punctuation," from *The Medusa and the Snail* by Lewis Thomas. Copyright © 1974, 1975, 1976, 1977, 1978, 1979 by Lewis Thomas. Originally published in the *New England Journal of Medicine.* Reprinted by permission of Viking Penguin Inc.

Kurt Vonnegut, "How to Write with Style," reprinted by permission of International Paper Company.

Ellen Willis, "Memoirs of a Non-Prom Queen," from *Rolling Stone,* August 26, 1976. By Straight Arrow Publishers, Inc. © 1976. Reprinted by permission.

Tom Wolfe, excerpts from *The Right Stuff,* copyright © 1979 by Tom Wolfe. Reprinted by permission of Farrar, Straus & Giroux.

William K. Zinsser, "Clutter," from *On Writing Well,* third edition, 1985. Copyright © 1985 by William K. Zinsser. Reprinted by permission of the author.

CONTENTS

THREE
DESCRIBING
61

FOUR
COMPARING AND CONTRASTING
91

FIVE
DEFINING
143

SIX
CLASSIFYING AND DIVIDING
193

SEVEN
ANALYZING A PROCESS
245

EIGHT
ANALYZING CAUSE AND EFFECT
303

NINE
ARGUING YOUR CASE
AND
PERSUADING YOUR AUDIENCE
363

The famous scientist tries to convince us that understanding climatic changes on earth is extremely important and that exploring outer space is one way to add to this understanding.

GLOSSARY
421

SUBJECT INDEX
433

PREFACE

Surely it would be ridiculous to think that the speaker in Ecclesiastes had college readers and composition students in mind when he said, ". . . of making many books there is no end, and much study is a weariness of the flesh." Yet these words from the Bible might still be regarded as a caution to writing instructors and students alike—the former because of the proliferation of writing textbooks and the latter because of the labor of studying them.

However, we do not offer *The Process Reader* as simply another addition to the already crowded bookshelves of instructors or as a weight to be added to the labor of students. Instead, we believe this text represents a positive contribution to the "making of books," and we bring it to you believing that its features will make both teaching and writing less arduous and more effective. We believe this book to be the most thoroughly process-based reader available today.

The Process Reader is a writing process text, with the processes keyed to eight rhetorical modes ranging from narration to argument. The fifty-two modern essays are intended to fulfill the reader's expectations of a good college reader: The essays are not only interesting to read, but also show the variations a particular rhetorical form will yield under the imaginative direction of accomplished writers.

However, the instructional materials accompanying the essays are what make this book valuable and unique. These materials are designed to guide students through the writing process while keeping them aware of the existence of a reading audience beyond their instructor and classmates. This is achieved, in part, by including audience-related questions among those that follow each essay and, in part, by alerting students to the concept of "audience" in the guides for planning, writing, revising, and proofreading that conclude the discussion of each rhetorical mode.

Incorporating audience awareness into the questions on the essays and the heuristic guides prepares students for the audience-based writing cases that appear at the end of each chapter. These "Writing Scenarios" establish realistic composing situations and identify purposes and audiences. Thus, they are multipurpose, giving students the opportunity to write in a particular rhetorical mode on a clearly defined topic while at the same time directing their writing to a specified audience or audiences. We know of no other reader that does this.

These writing cases have been designed to meet varying classroom needs, and they range from relatively complex, idea-based cases to the objective and highly practical. We believe the writing cases, along with the heuristics ("Prewriting Questions") and audience-related questions accompanying the essays, will encourage students to think of their instructors as writing editors rather than composition readers who represent single-member audiences.

Each essay is followed by three groups of questions. The first of these, "Questions on Meaning and Content," ask about the ideas and purpose underlying the writing. The second, "Questions about Rhetorical Strategies," focus attention on the writing at the whole-essay level and ask students to examine the writing in relation to the particular mode, to matters relating to audience, and to various structural principles at work in the essay. The third, "Questions on Language and Diction," direct attention to the writing strategies appearing at the sentence level—strategies that often go unnoticed by students. Many of these questions have a recursive effect since a variety of sentence-level devices recur from essay to essay and from rhetorical mode to rhetorical mode. As students progress through the book, they are presented with new sentence-level strategies and, at the same time, are reacquainted with those that appeared in earlier essays.

We believe *The Process Reader* applies writing process theory in a very practical way. We have tried to construct the book so that its practical features appear with constancy throughout rather than in bunches within sections. We think this constant emphasis on the practical will reduce the frustration that a great many students experience while learning to write effectively. We hope this will be the case. If it is, then the book will make teaching more satisfying and writing more effective and less laborious.

We would like to thank the following teachers and scholars for reading versions of the manuscript and for providing detailed comments and suggestions: Professor Laurie Bowman; Professor Duncan Carter, Boston University; Professor Betty L. Dixon, Rancho Santiago College; Professor Jay Jernigan, Eastern Michigan University; Professor John Hagaman, Western Kentucky University; Professor Kathleen Hart, Bowling Green State University; Professor Eileen Lundy, University of Texas at San Antonio; and Professor Ralph Voss, University of Alabama.

Much of what appears in this book was made possible by the research of such authors as James Britton, Charles Cooper, Edward Corbett, Janet Emig, Linda Flower, Lee Odell, Frank O'Hare, James Raymond, Nancy Sommers, and Ross Winterowd. We do not imply that any of these people have endorsed this text. They have not. But anyone who produces a modern writing text owes a debt to these people and to many others in the field, and we wish to acknowledge that debt here.

In addition, Marlyne Olson deserves special recognition for her expert copy-editing and word processing services, as do Phil Miller, our acquisitions editor, and Virginia Rubens, our production editor.

Finally, we wish to thank Marlene Ray, Marlyne Olson, and Frankie DeGeorge for their support.

INTRODUCTION

THE ORGANIZATION OF THIS BOOK

Fifty-two modern essays, grouped according to rhetorical modes, provide the writing models for *The Process Reader*. The eight rhetorical modes we focus on in this text are *narration, description, comparison-contrast, definition, classification and division, process, cause and effect,* and *argument and persuasion.*

For each rhetorical mode, we have tried to select model essays that are interesting to read and that show various approaches to the modes themselves, since no description of a rhetorical mode can ever completely cover the variations that it will exhibit in the hands of skillful writers. The essays also vary in length, tone, style, and organizational strategies, and we have included essays that emphasize ideas, as well as those that deal with practical matters.

The first chapter of the book introduces students to the concept of rhetorical modes in general and to reading and composing strategies. Each subsequent chapter introduces a specific rhetorical mode and presents a detailed discussion of the characteristics associated with it. Special sections in these chapters advise students on prewriting activities and on organizing, writing, revising, and proofreading for the mode.

The questions following each essay are divided into three sets. The first set examines essay content; the second focuses on organization and writing structure; the third concentrates on sentence-level writing strategies and various devices that are valuable to know about but which are often over-looked by the inexperienced. These questions also ask students to check the meanings of words that may fall outside their own working vocabularies.

THE GUIDING PRINCIPLE

The principle guiding *The Process Reader* is that achieving mastery in writing is remarkably similar to achieving mastery in any other complex activity. The first step is always to *look,* to *see,* to recognize the signs that guide writers or other artists and craftspeople as they move through a process which takes them from an idea to a finished product.

The signs cannot be absorbed all at once, and, in writing, they will vary from mode to mode just as they do for the painter moving from oils to water colors to acrylics. The principle, however, remains constant: Practice in any art or craft must be disciplined practice. It must be based on something; otherwise the uncertainty will never disappear, and the product will improve only slowly over long periods of time as the apprentice struggles to invent or discover techniques that already exist and could have been learned by noticing.

The signs that students need to recognize and then practice are presented in the writing-support materials in each chapter. Many items in these materials are recursive, looking back and touching on principles and techniques introduced in earlier sections. The purpose is to reinforce the techniques that students should practice in their own writing, eventually as a second-nature response.

Here and there in the Prewriting Questions, the checklists, and the discussions, we ask students to account for what they do as they write, to be ready to explain, for example, why they have presented their ideas in a certain order, or to show what they have incorporated into an introduction to prepare the reader for the body of the paper, or to point to features that were put there because of a concern for audience. We have done this as a means not only of reinforcing the principles learned from section to section, but also as a way of reminding students that writing is a problem-solving and decision-making process and that they must learn to take charge of what they are doing and be aware of how they have molded and fashioned their finished products.

A CASE APPROACH TO WRITING ASSIGNMENTS

We have carried the process approach into the Writing Scenarios included with each chapter. These are writing cases, not the general writing assignments traditionally found in college readers. The writing cases, which carefully define a writing situation and name a specific audience, place controls on student writing, controls relating to purpose, situation, and audience—the same controls operating on the professionals whose essays appear in the book.

In these writing cases, we have used the concept of audience in a practical way. We realize that audience as it applies to writing is a slippery term, one impossible to define to everyone's satisfaction since writers—unlike speakers—are not looking out over a physical audience as they write, and unseen audiences are always difficult to identify with exactness.

Whether experienced writers create or invoke their own audiences, as one group of researchers maintains, or attempt to identify audiences based on various criteria, as another group insists, is not highly pertinent to composition students. Real reading audiences do exist and do react to what they read, and students must learn to relate their prose to such audiences. At times in the writing cases, we name specific audiences, and we believe that students will readily see the logical relationship between the writing situation and the named audience. At other times, we name primary and secondary audiences; and, on occasion, we refer to broad, general audiences, since such audiences exist, even if they cannot be precisely defined according to their composition. Sometimes, we also ask students to invoke their own audience, one they believe would be appropriate to the topic and situation.

A FINAL WORD

We believe *The Process Reader* will help students compose with confidence and a sense of purpose. We hope that not only will students learn to internalize the kind of problem-solving techniques necessary to good writing, but that they will also come to understand many of the complex relationships between reading and writing.

THE
PROCESS
READER

ONE

PREPARING
TO
READ AND WRITE

Reading and writing are essential skills. It would be very difficult to be successful in today's complex, technological world without having at least an adequate command of language. In a writing class your most important objective should be to develop these skills fully. This chapter will help you achieve that goal by providing some basic information about how to read and write more effectively.

HOW TO READ ESSAYS EFFECTIVELY

Thorough reading is not simply a matter of glancing at every word in a document. Although surface reading is important, it is only the beginning. Good readers look at more than the words on the page; they look for hidden *and* obvious meaning, relationships between various aspects of the article, and whether the author supplies enough support for what he or she has said. In other words, good readers become intimately involved with whatever they are reading. Practically everyone has experienced the feeling of having read a book or chapter and afterwards not remembering any of the materials. Often this happens because readers have not become *involved* with the document; instead, they have simply let their eyes passively scan over the words.

1

Becoming engaged with a piece of writing means that you carry on a type of conversation with the author. For example, the author may make a point and you may ask yourself, "Where is the evidence to support that point?" Then, if the author supplies enough convincing evidence, you may say to yourself, "Ah ha, I see you *do* have a good point there." In other words, as you are reading you should be testing, weighing, examining, questioning. Good readers do not believe something simply because it is written down. They do not approach a document passively, letting the words flow unquestioned. Good readers ask questions, look for answers, demand support. They challenge the author.

When you read in this active way you are a critical reader and a critical thinker. The word *critical* in this sense does not mean easily finding fault with something. This is a common misunderstanding. A *critic,* for example, is not someone who watches movies, views plays, and reads books *in order to find fault with them.* The word *critic* comes from the Greek word *kritikos,* which means a person with the ability to discern things clearly and to separate fact from fiction. The critic then, is one who analyzes something, who reads (or views) something analytically and carefully. Perhaps one of the most important reasons for attending school in general is to become a critical thinker—a person who is able to analyze things and discern fact from fiction.

Whenever you read, you should especially be a critical thinker. You should be analyzing, questioning, weighing the facts, finding what is true and what is not. If you read in this way, you are much more likely to understand and remember what you have read than if you were not actively involved with the piece at all. Also, as you become a critical reader, you will find that you will become much more careful with your own writing; you will make sure your own statements are reasonable and are supported by sufficient evidence.

Learning to be a critical reader and thinker is not extremely difficult, but it does take practice. You must know what to look for, what to question, what constitutes evidence. Perhaps it would be helpful for you to think of the reading process as the writing process in reverse. Instead of devising a thesis statement and then finding convincing support for your thesis, you are trying to find someone else's thesis and trying to evaluate whether that author supplies enough convincing support for the thesis.

When you read an essay, it is a good idea to make notes on the page as you are reading. Of course, you would never write in a book that does not belong to you, but you should not be afraid to write in your own books. In fact, making notations in your text is one of the most important ways of becoming an effective reader. Reading with pen in hand helps you maintain an active involvement with the text.

There is no "right" way to mark a book, but we will give you one strategy that may help you in the future. First, you may want to ask yourself *why* you are reading the text. What is *your* purpose? Entertainment? To obtain information? To prepare for a test? Depending upon your reason for reading a text, you may want to mark different things as you read. For example, someone reading Lewis and Clark's journals may be interested only in the *historical content* of the document, while another reader may be interested in the *literary qualities* of the journals, and a third reader might be interested in what the authors reveal about the *psychology* of the early settlers. Your purpose helps you determine exactly what to mark. In other words, all essays are not read the same way by all readers.

Regardless of your purpose in reading an essay, however, you will want to know what the thesis of the essay is. Usually, your author's thesis will appear somewhere in the beginning of the essay, often in the first one or two paragraphs; it is important to underline this thesis and perhaps write the word *thesis* in the margin next to the statement. As you read through the essay, try to locate the major points that the author uses to support the thesis. Underline these statements and place a number in the margin next to each major point. In other words, if the author discusses four major points, you would number each one consecutively throughout the article so that when you reread the essay in the future you can easily locate the thesis statement and the four major points. In discussing each major point, the author is likely to have supplied a certain amount of evidence or support for that point. Of course, you do not want to underline *all* of this evidence, or most of the essay will end up being underlined. However, you may want to place some kind of notation next to the various pieces of evidence so that you can locate them easily. Some readers place consecutive letters (A, B, C, . . .) next to the points in each section of the essay. Other writers will circle the key word of each point or use different color inks to distinguish main points from evidence. The exact format that you use is not important. What is important is that you devise some kind of system for marking your text and stay with that system while reading the text. As you develop as a reader, your marking system is likely to evolve. For example, you will find that you use one type of system for certain kinds of texts—textbooks, for example—and another system for another kind of text—essays, perhaps. Don't hesitate to experiment with your text marking.

After you have marked an essay, you should have, in effect, an outline of that text: the thesis will be clearly marked; the major points will be highlighted and numbered; and the major evidence will be indicated. Another reader should be able to understand the gist of the essay by reading what you have marked instead of the entire essay. This procedure also makes it very easy for you to reread a text in a short amount of time and remember the important factors about the text.

The greatest advantage of marking a text you are reading is that it helps you become actively involved with the text. Because you are actively searching for key points and evidence, you are less likely to read passively and allow the words to rumble by without making any impression. Finally, marking a text in this way will be particularly helpful when taking an essay exam based on readings. The markings will help you refresh your memory of the many facts put forth in an essay or chapter.

Below is a sample page from one of the essays in this text. The page contains underlinings and notes similar to those suggested above. As you become an experienced reader, you will develop your own system for marking a text, but this sample page will give you an idea of how some writers mark a text.

Embalming is indeed a most extraordinary procedure, and one must wonder at the docility of Americans who each year pay hundreds of millions of dollars for its perpetuation, blissfully ignorant of what it is all about, what is done, how it is done. Not one in ten thousand has any idea of what actually takes place. Books on the subject are extremely hard to come by. They are not to be found in most libraries or bookshops.

In an era when huge television audiences watch surgical operations in the comfort of their living rooms, when, thanks to the animated cartoon, the geography of the digestive system has become familiar territory even to the nursery school set, in a land where the satisfaction of curiosity about almost all matters is a national pastime, the secrecy surrounding embalming can, surely, hardly be attributed to the inherent gruesomeness of the subject. Custom in this regard has within this century suffered a complete reversal. In the early days of American embalming, when it was performed in the home of the deceased, it was almost mandatory for some relative to stay by the embalmer's side and witness the procedure. Today, family members who might wish to be in attendance would certainly be dissuaded by the funeral director. All others, except apprentices, are excluded by law from the preparation room.

THE WRITING PROCESS

In your college writing classes your instructors will probably go into depth about the writing process. We would like to discuss the process briefly in order to give you an indication of how to go about composing an effective essay. Varous writing specialists will divide the writing process into different parts, and it is difficult to say whose discussion of the process is more valid than others. What is important, however, is that you approach your writing in a systematic manner.

We like to think of the writing process as involving five main activities: **prewriting, organizing, writing, revising,** and **proofreading.** You should not think of these five activities as rigid steps frozen in this sequence, as if once you were finished with one you could never go back to it. Instead, think of these elements as five major *activities* that every good writer engages in when composing an effective piece of prose. Often, you will have to move back and forth between the various writing activities. For example, while revising your paper you might discover that you need additional information in a certain paragraph. You then would want to do some additional prewriting. In other words, view the parts of the process as flexible, not rigid. Below we define these five activities and show how they fit into the general concept of the composing process.

Prewriting

Prewriting is an extremely important part of the writing process, but unfortunately it is often ignored by many writers. As its name implies, prewriting refers to activities that you usually engage in *before* you begin writing a draft of your essay, although you can come back and prewrite at any time in the writing process. Specifically, prewriting means gathering information for your essay and evaluating that information before writing a draft. Prewriting is an important part of the composing process because having sufficient information about your subject before you begin to write about it enables you to compose much more effectively than if you try to think of all your ideas *while* you are writing. Certainly, you will also want to think of ideas while writing your draft; but if you have already gathered most of your details before you begin, you will find that producing an effective first draft is much easier than if you had not.

There are many techniques for gathering information for your composition. *Brainstorming* is perhaps the easiest prewriting technique to use whenever you must compose a paper. Brainstorming simply means thinking of every possible detail about your subject and jotting these details down in your prewriting notes. In other words, rather than rushing right into a draft without thinking about your subject first, sit down and spend some time contemplating your subject and the various details that you probably will need to include in your paper. Make a list of these details. Brainstorming is certainly a simple method of gathering details for your paper, but it is nonetheless quite effective, especially if you spend enough time thinking about your subject.

Below is a sample brainstorming sheet we used in prewriting for the Prewriting section of this chapter. Notice how the sheet is informal and even sloppy; we quickly wrote down all ideas that came to us in whatever order.

How To READ Effectively

Reader's _purpose_ is important   define CRITIC

Read. + Writ. = essential skills

＊ CRITICAL READER ＊

Reading = more than glancing at words
must become intimately involved
real reading = type of conversation
PASSIVE   VS   ACTIVE   "KRiTiKos"
always look for evidence
Give a strategy for marking books
(Maybe a sample Page!)

After you have brainstormed as completely as possible, you may want to ask yourself the *5-W questions*. The 5-W questions (who? what? when? where? and why?) help you gather *factual* material about your subject. Journalists ask the 5-W questions when reporting on an important incident, because these questions help supply some of the most important information about a subject. When you are prewriting, remember to ask these questions and to jot down on your prewriting notes any information that you have not already recorded. For example, if you are writing about how you helped win an important basketball game, first use the five Ws to ask yourself the obvious, more general questions:

Who was our opponent?

What made the game so important?

When did the game take place? (not just the date, but *when* during the season schedule)

Where was the game played? (whose court?)

Why were my efforts central to winning the game?

Then use the five Ws to draw out more specific information about the game itself:

Who else played key roles in the game?

When during the game did victory look doubtful?

Why did it look doubtful?

What event(s) turned the game in our favor?

When did this/these event(s) occur?

Why did they occur?

What was my role at this/these time(s)?

You can also use the five Ws to help sketch a basic picture of any individual part of the game. These key questions will help you add additional information to your notes.

Another method of gathering information for your prewriting notes is called *freewriting*. To freewrite, time yourself for five or ten minutes and write as rapidly and spontaneously about your subject as possible. During this timed period, you should not stop to think about what you are writing. Instead, keep your pen to the page and continue writing for the full period *without stopping*. Write down every thought about your subject that comes to your mind. Your objective is to keep writing, no matter what. Once you have completed this quick freewrite, read through the page, extract any information not already included in your prewriting notes, and add these details to your notes. The advantage of freewriting is that it helps draw from your subconscious details about your subject that you might not have remembered when you were consciously brainstorming. Also, it is a good warmup exercise before you actually begin writing your essay, and it often helps writers overcome "writers' block." Remember that the freewrite is not your first draft or the beginning of the paper itself; it is part of the process of gathering information for your paper. Of course, you may also find that you can use some sentences from your freewrite in your draft.

Below is a sample freewrite one of our students used in prewriting for a paper on her home town. Notice that the thoughts have flown out in random order. After freewriting our student examined the sheet and extracted pieces of information that were not already included in her prewriting notes.

- Waterbury -

I've always loved Waterbury -- its quaint houses, nice parks, and trees. Especially those trees! Waterbury has the nicest trees. Big, old oaks, real tall pines, and lots of white birch. Most houses have _some_ trees around them. I guess the only thing I don't like abt. Waterbury is the factories. Way too many factories! Especially the two big ones downtown. So, I guess W. isn't an _ideal_ place. But I still love it.

Another method of gathering information is to use a *heuristic:* a list of specific questions about a subject that help you remember items of information that might be of use in your paper. There are many types of both formal and informal heuristics. In fact, the 5-W questions are a type of informal heuristic. The text includes a specific heuristic, called Prewriting Questions, in each section to help you write papers for that section. Remember to refer to these lists of questions when you are prewriting, and they will help you gather details for your composition.

It is difficult to stress to beginning writers how important prewriting is to good writing. Certainly, a business person would not want to make an important decision without having sufficient information to help make the decision a wise one. The same is true for a writer. In most instances you do not want to plunge into a draft without first having thought about the many details that you should or should not include in your paper.

Organizing

Certainly, no experienced football player would begin a play without first stopping in the huddle to receive instructions about how to organize the next play. Having a plan ahead of time allows the football team to focus its energy in an ordered and productive way. The same is true about writing. It is very important to devise some kind of **organizing** scheme *before* you begin to write your first draft; this will help you write a more effective essay than if you had begun with no plan at all.

Often, when students hear the word *organizing,* they immediately think of the formal outline, which assigns captions and Roman numerals to the major sections of a paper and letters or Arabic numerals to the subsections. Although outlines may be helpful to some people, many experienced writers do not need to begin something as short as an essay with an outline. Many writers feel that such outlines are a waste of time, while some other writers find that outlines add discipline to the act of writing. If you are uncomfortable with formal outlines and your instructor has not asked you to write them, you can still organize your material effectively without the formality of an outline.

We suggest that after you have prewritten thoroughly, you take your prewriting notes and try to determine the order in which you want to discuss details in your paper. The information throughout this book gives you specific advice about how to organize papers in each rhetorical mode for purpose and audience; generally, however, you will want to think about the most effective way to present the material listed in your prewriting notes and then number these items in the order that you think they should appear in the composition. If you are especially conscientious, you might even recopy your prewriting notes in their new order, but even this is not necessary. What is necessary is that you devise some logical order for your material so that you do not present it in a chaotic way and thereby confuse your readers.

Unless you are writing a formal outline, the organizing part of the writing process should not take long at all, *but you should not forget this important activity.* The small amount of time spent in devising an organizing scheme will pay off later when you are writing your draft. It is much easier to write any kind of paper once you have spent time prewriting and organizing. This is why we believe that you should always spend time on these important activities; the writing of the draft is bound to be much easier than it would have been otherwise. Of course, your concerns with organization do not end when you begin your draft; often you will need to come back and make adjustments. But beginning with a plan will give you a sense of direction.

Writing

One reason that some writers experience difficulties in writing effective prose is that they try to do too much at one time. They try to prewrite, organize, revise, and proofread *while* they are writing. This practice is very inefficient. It stands to reason that if you try to do too many activities at once, you are not likely to do well at any of the activities because you are dividing your time and energy. This is why we suggest approaching writing as five main activities. The **writing** part of the process is one in which you compose the first draft of your paper. You may be surprised to discover that writing the first draft can be one of the easiest and least time-consuming aspects of producing your paper. In fact, we suggest that you write your first draft as rapidly as possible. If you have done a thorough job in prewriting and organizing your paper, you already will have a good idea of how your paper will proceed and what information it will contain, thereby making your writing task much easier than if you have not done these activities beforehand.

There is no need to worry about composing perfect prose while you are writing your first draft; you will have plenty of time to rework your prose during the revising and proofreading stages. For example, don't puzzle over how to end a particular sentence or over what exact word should go in a particular place. If you run into these types of difficulties, draw lines and then fill in the blanks later. Your main purpose while writing the first draft should simply be to get a draft on paper as quickly as possible. Of course, while you are writing you should be following closely your prewriting and organizing notes. The main reason you should not worry about how your first draft sounds is that you will spend plenty of time in revising it after the draft is complete. Now, however, simply try to express your ideas as accurately and quickly as possible.

Revising

We suggested that you write your first draft quickly because the real work has yet to come. The bulk of your time and energy in writing any worthwhile document should be invested in **revising** your prose. Too many inexperienced writers believe that once they have written a first draft, they are done with their assignment. This simply is not the case. Even the best writers rewrite a draft several times before they are satisfied that their document says exactly what they want it to say in exactly the right way.

Revising does not mean correcting spelling and superficial errors in your prose; these activities will come after you have finished revising. Instead, revising means totally reworking your draft several times. As an analogy, think of a potter making a clay vase. The potter first gathers all the materials he or she needs (prewriting); conceptualizes how the vase should look when it is completed (organizing); then places a blob of clay on the wheel and forms it into the general shape that the vase will eventually take (writing). After you have written a first draft of a paper, you simply have a blob of clay in the general form of the finished product; much work remains. The revising process is similar to that used by the potter who takes the blob of clay and forms it slowly and carefully into a finished vase. This is why we have said that you should try to write your draft rapidly. You still will be spending much of your time in reshaping your prose into a meaningful, finished product. Certainly, you do not want your paper to be a formless blob, like a crudely shaped vase lacking the finishing touches. Instead, you want to rework it until you are proud to put your name on the finished product.

Generally, good writers will revise their papers several times. Revising refers to large-scale changes in your prose. You may eliminate a paragraph, move a paragraph from page two to page four, add two new paragraphs, completely rewrite paragraph three, go back and do additional prewriting, even change the organizing plan that you originally started out with. These are the types of activities that should go on while you are revising.

Perhaps the most effective way to revise your prose is to first make sure that you have a clear thesis statement and that the organizing plan you started out with is effective. Once you are satisfied with the general makeup of your prose, you should go through the text sentence by sentence. Carefully read a sentence to yourself and then aloud. Play with the word order. Think about alternative ways of rephrasing what you have said in the original sentence. Ask yourself what changes would make the sentence better. Once you are satisfied with the sentence, *rewrite* it on a blank piece of paper. Do the same for the next sentence, the sentence after, and all of the sentences until you have gone through the entire text, rewriting each sentence from your original draft to the new piece of paper. Once you have done this you have revised your text one time. We suggest that you revise your paper at least two or three times, following the same procedure.

Now that word processors are becoming very accessible, you may have the opportunity to write and revise your papers on one of these useful writing tools. They make it quite easy to rearrange paragraphs and totally restructure an essay. They help eliminate the tedious part of revising. If you have the opportunity to use a word processor, you might even discover that revising can be fun.

Remember the importance of revising. Along with prewriting, revising is one of the most important aspects of writing effective prose. Unfortunately, too many writers leave this *essential* activity out of their writing process. The more time you spend in revising, the more likely it is that you will end up with a polished, effective piece of writing—one that you will be proud to place your name on.

Proofreading

In the analogy mentioned above, the potter forms the clay from a blob to a satisfactory vase during the revising process. There is, however, one final part of the process left. After you are satisfied that your finished product has taken the exact form that you want, you still will want to *polish* the piece so that all of the rough edges are smoothed over. This is the **proofreading** stage. Proofreading means paying attention to the smaller, but no less important, aspects of your prose. During proofreading you should be concerned with correcting all your spelling and grammatical mistakes, making sure that your punctuation is accurate, and finding any words that you have misused. As with revising, you will want to approach the proofreading stage systematically. Read through your text several times, sentence by sentence, looking at each sentence individually. Perhaps it is best to separate your proofreading activities: Read through once for punctuation, once for spelling, once for grammar, and so on. Separating the activities in this manner will help you to concentrate on the exact things you are looking for.

Many writers find that an effective way to proofread is to read your text backwards, reading first the last sentence, then the second-to-last sentence, then the third-to-the last sentence, and all the way through to the first sentence. The reason for this seemingly strange procedure is simple. When you have spent time writing a paper, you have programmed the text into your mind. Although you may not have consciously memorized your paper, it nonetheless is etched in your subconscious. When you read through the paper in its correct order, it is likely that you will read by several mistakes simply because you know how a word *should* be spelled and you take it for granted that it is spelled correctly. In contrast, when you read the text from the back to the front you help to deprogram the text from your mind, and you are more likely to spot misspellings and other errors than you would have by reading the text in its natural order.

The proofreading stage should not take much time at all. Most of your writing time and energy should be invested in prewriting, writing, and revising. Proofreading, like organizing, should go by relatively fast.

Budgeting Your Time

The discussion of the writing process above is only a brief outline of how to approach your writing tasks. We hope that it gives you a general idea of how to write effective prose. If you are not familiar with looking at the writing process in the terms we have discussed, it may seem at first that we are asking you to spend much more time in writing than you may have done otherwise. This may not be the case, however. What we are discussing above is a *redistribution* of your writing time. In other words, we are asking you to spend a certain amount of time in each of these activities, rather than to try to lump all five activities together at one time. For example, imagine that your friend Jerry is an inexperienced writer. Instead of engaging in all five activities of the writing process, he rarely prewrites and revises. Generally, his writing process and the time he spends in it looks like this:

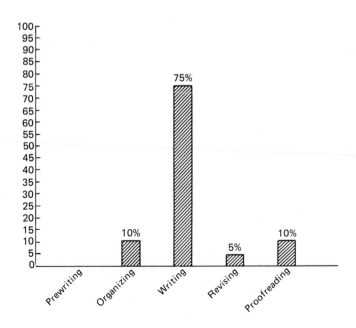

Clearly, Jerry spends most of his time *writing* a draft, and while doing so he tries to prewrite and revise.

In contrast, suppose your friend Natalie is an experienced writer. She makes sure that she remembers all five activities in the writing process. Natalie spends about the same amount of time on her paper as Jerry does on his, but Natalie budgets her time. Natalie's writing process might look something like this:

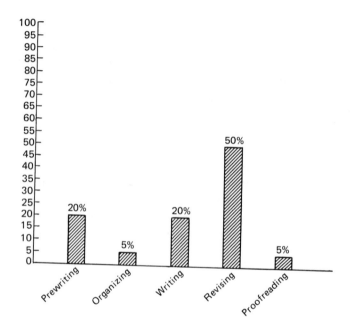

Notice that Natalie spends a substantial amount of time *prewriting* and *revising*. Organizing and proofreading take up comparably less time. You may also have noticed that Natalie spends more time revising than she does writing a first draft. Of course every writing project is unique, as is every writer.

The graph illustrating Natalie's writing process is simply an example of how to distribute your time in the writing process; it is not a rigid formula that you must or should follow. However, we hope that, like Natalie, you will spread your time and energy across the writing process in such a way that all activities receive a fair amount of attention.

THE RHETORICAL MODES

You probably have noticed that this book is divided into chapters on subjects, such as narrating, describing, comparing, and contrasting, and so on. Each chapter discusses a specific **rhetorical mode:** a strategy for writing a particular kind of essay. We wish to make clear from the very beginning that in many ways dividing writing into these various modes is an artificial procedure. It is unlikely that when you have left the academic world anyone will ask you to write a "comparison and contrast report," or a "process analysis paper." Most often, writers mix several of these strategies in the types of writing that they do.

Although most often you will not find pure examples of one mode or another in the essays you read, it is very likely that an essay is dominated by a particular mode. For example, an essay *comparing or contrasting* the economies of the United States and the Soviet Union may also use *description* and *definition*. You will find that most of the essays in this text contain a mixture of modes but are *dominated* by one principal mode. Don't view a rhetorical mode as a restrictive and rigid blueprint that allows you no freedom. Instead, think of it more as a general design for expressing your subject to your reader. If your reader knows that you are setting out in an essay to compare and contrast two things, this information is likely to assist the reader in reading and understanding the essay.

It is perhaps best to think of the rhetorical modes as reflecting ways that humans think. When you go to the store and try to decide which of two competing products you should buy, you are *comparing* and *contrasting*. When you tell a friend an exciting story that happened on your recent camping trip, you are *narrating*. When you explain to someone how to tune up an automobile, you are *describing a process*. In other words, the rhetorical modes are strategies that people use to convey information; they are common ways to arrange thoughts. Practice in writing in one or more of the rhetorical modes is likely to help you to think in a more formal manner. When your instructor asks you to write a comparison and contrast paper about the difference between living in your home town and living on a college campus, that instructor is asking you to exercise the mental powers involved in weighing and evaluating two things. Such practice is likely to sharpen your ability to communicate.

Each chapter of this book discusses a single rhetorical mode. At the beginning of each chapter, we discuss strategies for writing papers in that mode. We also provide a heuristic (Prewriting Questions) for helping you prewrite for papers in that section. Following our discussion are several modern essays that are dominated by that particular mode. You can read these essays both for content and to see how other authors have used the rhetorical mode to convey their thoughts and ideas.

When writing a paper dominated by a rhetorical mode, you will want to decide during the prewriting and organizing processes exactly how you will arrange your material for that mode. The mode that you use will have a great bearing on how you present your material in your essay. It is a good idea to read fully the chapter on a specific rhetorical mode before you begin writing a paper in that mode.

TWO

NARRATING
A STORY

One writing strategy you can use to get your message across to readers is called **narration.** Narration is storytelling. When you are writing a *narrative,* you are "telling what happened"; you are providing a factual or fictional account of an event or events. Short stories and novels are the most familiar form of narration; however, it is also common to use narration, or storytelling, to make a point in an essay. As the writer of a narrative, you are the *narrator,* or storyteller.

Whether you have realized it or not, you use narration frequently in your everyday conversation. When you explain to a friend how you helped win the final game of the baseball tournament, or when you describe to someone the events leading up to an accident you were in, you are narrating—you are telling the story of what happened. Narration is a particularly valuable strategy because it is usually a firsthand account of some event and therefore makes the event seem that much more credible.

Often narration is used in the context of a larger speech or document. For example, as governor of California and then as president of the United States, Ronald Reagan frequently began important speeches with a short story that made a point about something. Clergymen often make use of narration in their sermons, and sometimes politicians and public speakers begin a speech with a short narrative. They might, for instance, discuss the subject of child abuse by first telling a brief story about a particular child who experienced a shocking tragedy. Similarly, proponents of handgun control might tell how misuse of a handgun in a particular instance caused a needless death or injury. Such stories help speakers and writers make their points much more forcefully than they would be without them. When you use a brief narrative as a part of a larger speech or piece of writing, it is often called an *anecdote*. Usually, an anecdote is only a part of what you have to say, a device to help you make a point.

A story has the tendency of making something much more *vivid* and *real* than a simple explanation might. For example, last year one of our students wrote a paper arguing that drinking and driving is a very dangerous habit that all people, young and old, should avoid. This student began her paper with a short narrative about how her sister had died in a tragic automobile accident on the night of her high school graduation. Her sister and three of her friends had been drinking heavily to celebrate their graduation and lost control of their car on a mountain road. This student's paper is particularly forceful because the readers begin by *seeing* a tragedy take place before they hear the writer's argument against drinking and driving. Because the readers *share* this tragedy with the writer, they are likely to be receptive to what the writer is going to say in the remainder of the paper. In her essay, our student used narration as a small part of the whole essay, as a device to make a point. Of course, she could have written a paper that was narrative throughout, in which she simply told the entire story of the accident.

Narration can be used simply to entertain, as in the case of short stories and novels; however, it is also an important strategy to use when you are making some point for your reader. Usually when you are writing a narrative essay for a freshman writing class, you have some main point to impress upon your reader.

PREWRITING

To begin **prewriting** for your narrative essay, it is important for you to gather as much information and detail about your subject as possible. Often, it is the amount of detail that separates a good narrative from a poor one. Perhaps it is best to begin your prewriting by brainstorming. Jot down as many facts, opinions, observations, sights, smells, and sounds about your subject as you can recall. At this point, you don't need to decide what items you will include in your essay and what you will not; instead, try to gather as much information as you can. Try to picture yourself back in the event or sequence of events you plan to discuss in your essay. You may even wish to close your eyes while you recreate the situation, and try to feel that you are actually taking part in the event right now. What colors do you see? What is the weather like? Does anyone say anything important to you? What is the event like? What do you feel? Why is this event taking place? What important sights do you see? Who else is there? What facts will best help your reader understand this event and its significance? Can you think of any *unusual* details that will impress your reader about your subject? In other words, ask yourself as many questions as possible about your subject and jot down every bit of information that may help you write your narrative. You may also wish to ask yourself the 5-W questions: who, what, when, where, and why. These questions will help you generate some *factual* information about your subject.

In addition, you may wish to *freewrite* briefly about your subject. Time yourself for perhaps five or ten minutes and write as rapidly and spontaneously as you can, paying no attention to spelling, wording, grammar, or any of the traditional values of good writing. Just try to record many of your impressions on paper. When you have completed your freewriting, look through the page to see if you have produced any additional facts that you can add to your prewriting notes. You may also wish to refer to the narration heuristic in this chapter to help you prewrite. These questions may help you generate additional details about your narrative.

Once you have gathered as much information as possible about the event, you are ready to read through this information carefully in order to determine what is essential to your narrative and what is irrelevant to the main point. There is a paradox involved in writing a good narrative. On the one hand, a narrative should be chock-full of good descriptive details about your subject. On the other hand, you do not want to bore your readers by recounting every single minute that was involved in a long event; instead, you want to choose the most important items and highlight them. In other words, selecting the right material from your prewriting notes is very important.

Below is a brief heuristic to help you prewrite for your narrative. Simply jot down answers to relevant questions on your prewriting notes. Be as specific as possible, but feel free to abbreviate and take shortcuts. Since no one will read these notes but yourself, you do not need to worry about writing in full sentences or with neat penmanship. Instead, you should be most concerned with generating as much specific information as possible.

Prewriting Questions for Narration

1. What is the *main point* of my narrative?
2. What is the *purpose* of my narrative?
3. Who will read my narrative and why?
4. What conclusions do I want my readers to draw about my subject?
5. What *point of view* should I adopt?
6. Exactly what happened during the event and in what order?
7. Who took part in the event?
8. When did it occur?
9. Where did it occur?
10. Is the weather or the time of day a significant detail?
11. *Why* did the event happen?
12. What specific sights, sounds, and smells can I remember?
13. What specific details will make my main point especially clear?
14. What *unusual* details can I remember?
15. Which details should I especially highlight?
16. Considering my purpose, which details are less important or irrelevant?
17. How should I *organize* my narrative?
18. Should I use chronological order?
19. Would a *flashback* be effective?
20. What verb tense should I use throughout my narrative?

ORGANIZING

After you have thoroughly prewritten, you will want to devise some kind of **organizing** scheme for your essay. There are many ways to organize a narrative. The most common method is to proceed chronologically, that is, from the beginning of the event to the end. Some writers, however, begin their narrative with a *flashback,* in which they recount some important or exciting incident that happened in the middle or end of an event and then return to the beginning of the story. Conversely, other writers may begin at a time in the present and then go back to tell the story and how it began.

To make a decision about how to organize your narrative, it is necessary to keep your *audience* and *purpose* in mind. *Why* are you writing this essay? Exactly who will read it and for what purpose? Are you an amateur surfer recounting for a surfing magazine your experience at a regional tournament?

Are you writing an essay for the student newspaper of your former high school in which you recount your first experience at college? Will your readers be familiar with the kind of experience you are narrating, or will your narration provide new insight into the experience? Many of the choices you will have to make while writing your essay will have to do with who your readers are. This is why it is important to know your audience before you begin to write.

After you have answered these questions to yourself, you may have a better idea about how to organize the narrative. Also, ask yourself what is your purpose in writing the narrative? For example, do you want your essay to entertain the reader, to thrill the reader with the near-disaster that worked out all right in the end, or to make the reader laugh or smile while enjoying the humor in the event you relate? Or do you want to emphasize a point (like drinking and driving don't mix)? Or are you writing the narrative to show the reader that you learned a lesson from something that happened to you?

There are many other possible purposes. The point is that you should know what your purpose is, what you want to convey to the reader through your narrative. Knowing the purpose will give you a good idea of which details are significant and which are not.

Knowing your audience and purpose can also tell you where to start the narrative. Since narratives tell about events that took place in time, knowing your purpose will help identify the most logical point to use as the beginning of the event. If your purpose is to explain to the reader that your encounter with a speeding driver running a red light left you so distracted that you could not concentrate on your studies for two days, then you probably do not want to start your essay with the alarm clock ringing and waking you out of bed that morning. Neither do you want to explain that you brushed your teeth, ate breakfast, and read the morning paper before walking to the corner to meet your ride.

But if your purpose is to show the reader how disasters can happen on what seem to be the calmest, most ordinary days, then you may want to begin with getting out of bed in the morning and mentioning events that went as expected and made you feel comfortable and immune to the world's problems.

In other words, you will want to decide which parts of the event are most worthy of being highlighted and which parts would simply be boring to the reader and do not need to be included in your narrative. What are major and necessary parts of your story and what are minor ones? There is no *rule* specifying how to select material from your notes. You must use your best judgment and your sense of purpose and audience. Perhaps the best way to make such a decision is to place yourself in the role of the reader. Ask yourself, "If I were reading this narrative, what parts would I *want* to hear and what parts would make no difference to me?" If you are honest with yourself when playing the role of the reader, you should be able to select the most important material to include in your narrative.

As you are searching your notes for ways to arrange your material, you may find that you have not done enough *prewriting*. If so, feel free to do some additional prewriting. Remember, the five activities of the writing process do not constitute a rigid, step-by-step formula in which you never return to an activity once it is done. For example, you may find that not only will you need to do additional prewriting while you are organizing, but that you have to return and do more later in the writing process.

After you have selected the material for your essay and devised some kind of organizing scheme, you may want to take your prewriting notes and place numbers next to the items according to how they should appear in your narrative. For example, there may be three items toward the end of your list that you may wish to include in the beginning of your essay and other items toward the beginning of your list that you may want to include in the middle of the narrative. Numbering the items in your prewriting notes will help you impose order on your essay and will help you stay by that order.

Many narrative essays contain an introductory paragraph or two in which the author reveals the *main point* (thesis) to readers. Why are you writing this essay? What conclusions do you want your readers to understand from the narrative? You will want to explain this information in your introduction. The body of the narrative contains the discussion of your subject in whatever order (often chronological) that you choose to tell it. The narrative's conclusion puts your story in perspective. It explains the significance of the events discussed in the body and shows how they support your main point. For example, let's say that our student mentioned above had written an entirely narrative essay. The main point mentioned in her introduction might be that drinking and driving proved fatal for her sister, and on the night of her long-awaited graduation from high school, too. The paragraphs in the body might discuss each phase of the fatal night her sister died, leading up to the tragedy itself. The conclusion might repeat her main point: that her sister's carelessness that night led to a horrible tragedy. All narratives will contain some kind of beginning, middle, and end; but it is up to you to decide exactly what material you should include in each of the parts of your essay. For example, you may decide that it is best with your particular subject to hold off mentioning the main point until the conclusion—where it will somehow surprise the reader. Again, you should base such decisions on your purpose and audience.

Before writing your narrative, you will want to choose a *point of view:* the perspective you will take as a writer. Should you tell the story yourself as if you are involved personally? In such a case you would use the first-person narrator: "I watched in disbelief as my girlfriend skied past the front-runner and won the state championship." Or perhaps you will want to remain detached from the event by using the third person: "To the disbelief of the spectators, Mary Gray skied past the front-runner and claimed the state championship." There are advantages and disadvantages to both points of view. First person allows you to describe events in a more personal and sometimes more forceful way. Third person, however, allows you to say what your characters are thinking and feeling, as if you could read their minds: "Mary grinned with pleasure as she conquered the final slope and sped past the front-runner; she felt that no one could stop her, and she was right." Again, *purpose* and *audience* should help you decide what point of view to adopt.

WRITING

Many writers spend too much time in the actual **writing** of the first draft of an essay. Usually this happens when inexperienced writers try to do too much in one sitting; they try to prewrite, organize, revise, and proofread while they are writing the first draft. Instead of trying to do so much at one time, try to spend sufficient time prewriting and organizing. This will make the writing part of the process go by much faster. You don't need to revise and proofread while you are writing unless you happen to catch some obvious flaws. Wait until you have completed your draft before you begin to rearrange it. Instead, write your narrative as rapidly as possible, referring to your prewriting and organizing notes as you go. There is no need to worry about spelling or punctuation at this point. If you can't think of the right word or if you can't decide how to complete a sentence, draw a line and go on to the next word or sentence; you can fill in the blanks later. Finally, don't feel that once you have prewritten or organized you can't come back to these activities again if necessary.

While writing, you will want to pay attention to your use of detail as you go along. Try to make your readers feel that they are experiencing the same event that you did. Of course, no reader of a narrative can experience the identical feelings and sensations that you did as the event happened, but by using clear and specific details you can make readers *feel* that they are participating in the event; this is what a good narrative is all about.

Finally, you may want to pay special attention to your verb tense as you are writing. It is important to keep your tense consistent—all present tense or all past tense, for example. Certainly, you will want to shift tense if there is a real reason. For example, you may wish to use present tense throughout your narrative but past tense in a flashback. However, you don't want to arbitrarily shift back and forth between tenses; such a practice will confuse your readers.

REVISING

Once you have written the first draft of your narrative, the real work begins. Don't fall into the common trap of believing that once you have completed a draft you are done with your essay. Even the very best writers must rewrite their drafts over and over before they are satisfied with them. Try to remember that **revision** is a normal and necessary part of writing and that it is something you automatically do when composing any document of value. In the revision part of the writing process, read through your draft quickly and try to get a sense of whether the *organizing* scheme you have chosen works well. In other words, look at the largest issues first. If you feel that your original organizing plan is ineffective, now is an excellent time to think of alternatives. Ask yourself: "What is the most effective strategy for presenting my material to particular readers?"

After you are satisfied that the narrative is organized in a logical way and that it effectively develops your main point, you can begin working on smaller issues. At this point, you may want to take each paragraph of the narrative separately and ask yourself if that paragraph is as effective as it can be. Does it convey the exact meaning that you are trying to get across to your reader? Should you add additional details to make it even clearer? Should you delete certain statements that do not help to get your point across? Does each paragraph contain adequate transitions between related but separate points? Do you need to go back and do some additional *prewriting*? When you are satisfied that each paragraph accurately portrays your message, copy it onto a new page, until you have rewritten the entire essay. Of course, while you are rewriting you can fill in the blanks of any words or sentences that you could not think of while writing your first draft. Your second draft, then, should be substantially better than your first.

Even now, your revision is not complete. You probably should rewrite your narrative at least one more time, following the same procedure described above. Between drafts, it is a good idea to take a break and engage in some other activity; this will give you a little *distance* from your essay and make your revising easier. We recommend that you revise in this way at least two times in order to produce a paper that you are proud to put your name on. Some writers revise their papers more than five times before they are satisfied.

PROOFREADING

During revision you are most concerned with content and the larger issues—in other words: does your narrative say what you want it to say? During **proofreading,** however, you are most concerned with the smaller issues. Have you misspelled any words? Is your punctuation correct? Have you used the right words in the right places? Is your writing grammatically correct? Certainly, you will want to correct any surface errors that you find at any time during the writing process, but you do not need to be too concerned about these issues while writing or revising. One way or the other, you do not want to ignore these issues; they are important to your narrative. After you have revised your narrative, remember to proofread it closely for any of these smaller, but nevertheless important, elements.

After you have completed your narrative, you may wish to refer to the Narration Checklist below. This checklist will help you determine if you have forgotten any important aspects of your narrative.

Narration Checklist

1. Have you made your main point clear enough?
2. Does your introduction contain sufficient information to orient readers to your subject?
3. Have you directed your narrative to your specific audience?
4. Is your narrative organized in a logical way?
5. Have you included every important detail about your subject?
6. Have you eliminated unimportant and irrelevant information?
7. Have you maintained a consistent *point of view?*
8. Have you inadvertently shifted tenses in the narrative?
9. Is your *exact* meaning clear in every sentence?

10. Does your conclusion put your subject in perspective for your readers?
11. Have you spent enough time revising your narrative?
12. Are your sentences grammatically correct?
13. Have you checked the punctuation of each sentence?
14. Have you checked your spelling?

Alone

F. LEE BAILEY, with HARVEY ARONSON

In this narrative, which forms the introduction to F. Lee Bailey's The
Defense Never Rests, *this famous defense attorney suggests a special kind
of training to prepare criminal lawyers for the courtroom. It is a kind of
training unavailable in law schools.*

The Carolina coast was below me: white and gleaming in the afternoon   1
sun. I leveled off about a mile above the earth and swung the Sabrejet
parallel to the coast, looking for a beach picnic to buzz or a pair of young
lovers to startle. Then I glanced at the instrument panel and saw the red
warning light flashing: FIRE.

There had been trouble with our Sabrejets—planes catching fire on take-   2
off and costing pilots their lives—but I hadn't worried about that when I left
the runway seconds before. I was a fighter pilot and chief legal officer for a
Marine unit based at Cherry Point, North Carolina. I was twenty-three years
old and I was punching holes in a sparkling sky; enjoying myself while
putting in the necessary time for flight pay. And I guess I was protected by
the rationale that enables any pilot to keep going after he's seen a buddy
killed in a crash—*it must have been pilot error, it could never happen to me.*

Only now, on a sun-splashed day in 1955, a red warning light was saying   3
that it could happen to me. I had to make a decision: I could use the ejection
seat and bail out, or I could shut down the engine and try for a dead-stick
landing.

If I bailed out, there was the possibility that the airplane might crash in a   4
populated area. True, the region was sparsely settled, and I could always
point the ship to sea. But there was no guarantee that it wouldn't turn and
come back to shore. And suppose the parachute was defective—the terminal
velocity of a free-falling human being is 125 mph. Then I remembered the
words of an old navy lieutenant who had been my instructor in all-weather
school. "A ground bum," he had said, "is a guy who points the nose down
the moment he gets in trouble, because he knows he doesn't belong in the
sky. A pilot climbs like hell, knowing that altitude is both time and insurance, knowing he'll never get hurt as long as his plane doesn't hit the
ground."

I grabbed the microphone and yelled "MAYDAY" as loud as I could. I   5 hauled back on the stick, turned toward the base, and yanked the throttle back to idle cut-off almost in the same instant. I had made my decision—a flame-out approach.

Essentially, a jet airplane is a flying gas tank powered by a blowtorch, 6 and I would have bailed out if the fire warning light had remained on when I cut the power. But it went out, and the air was silent. I had enough altitude, and the runway at Cherry Point is the longest in the world—I landed without difficulty. When I got out of the cockpit, I was soaked with sweat and figuring to myself that I had earned a full year's flight pay by saving the government a million-dollar jet fighter.

Later, after the plane had been towed into a hangar and checked, I talked 7 to an old maintenance chief. He said there had been no fire, just a short in the warning system.

"But I bet you thought about poppin' out, Lieutenant," he said with a 8 grin, "what with all the fire trouble we've been having lately."

"A passing thought, Sarge," I said in the best tradition of the fearless 9 fighter pilot. "Just a passing thought."

His reply was appropriate if not eloquent: "Horseshit." 10

I can still feel the excitement of that moment of decision a mile above the 11 earth. If I ran a school for criminal lawyers, I would teach them all to fly. I would send them up when the weather was rough, when the planes were in tough shape, when the birds were walking. The ones who survived would understand the meaning of "alone." If I understand anything, I understand that. I've been a pilot for seventeen years.

I am also a criminal lawyer. 12

QUESTIONS ON MEANING AND CONTENT

1. This essay serves as a preface to F. Lee Bailey's *The Defense Never Rests,* a book that describes a number of Bailey's most famous cases. What does this narrative offer that would be helpful to someone about to begin reading such a book?

2. Bailey makes his point in this narrative by analogy—by comparing one thing or experience with another to show that each is similar in some way. Here he suggests an analogy between flying a jet, especially during rough weather or when the planes have been having problems, to practicing criminal law; that is, a pilot alone in a jet is somehow similar to a defense attorney in a courtroom. Thus, flying a jet would teach future attorneys what being alone means. What meaning of *alone* does emerge from the essay?

3. As this essay defines the term, why would it be valuable for a criminal lawyer to understand what *alone* means?

4. Can you find other parallels in the essay between piloting a jet and conducting the defense of someone charged with a serious crime—murder, for example?

5. When Bailey looks back on the moment he decided to point the plane skyward instead of earthward, he says he had a feeling of excitement. Do you take his statement at face value? Based on other details mentioned in the narrative, what other emotion or emotions might he have been experiencing? What details tell you this? How would the old maintenance chief have responded if Bailey had told him about his feeling of excitement?

QUESTIONS ABOUT RHETORICAL STRATEGIES

1. This essay is patterned after a very old use of narrative to make a point, teach a lesson, or stress a moral. It is written in the fashion of the old fables and parables that made their points through analogy. Aesop's fables and the parables in the Bible are examples of the form Bailey is following. The narrative stands alone until the very end. Then the point is made or the point is so obvious it doesn't have to be stated. The narrative forms an analogy with the point revealed at the end. Can you think of experiences or happenings in your own life that are analogous to situations you have experienced in college? What point or lesson can be drawn from the earlier experience and applied to your life now? Could you write a narrative patterned after Bailey's to illustrate this?

2. Notice how Bailey concludes his essay with a single, short sentence set off as a paragraph. This, too, is roughly similar to the old fables, many of which ended with a single sentence stating a moral. In a way, these attached morals often provided a somewhat dramatic conclusion. Is this the effect of Bailey's short sentence? Would you prefer a conclusion that explained more fully why a criminal lawyer should understand the meaning of *alone* in the same way that a jet pilot should?

QUESTIONS ON LANGUAGE AND DICTION

1. In paragraph 4, Bailey remembers his flight instructor's talk about a "ground bum." What is a ground bum? Do you think other occupations have the equivalents of ground bums among their members? If so, offer examples and explain why these people would fall into a category similar to pilots who are ground bums.

2. In paragraph 6, Bailey defines a jet plane as "a flying gas tank powered by a blowtorch." This metaphorical definition emphasizes the hazards built into this piece of equipment and represents a way of redefining something dangerous, as, for example, when we refer to a building as a "fire trap." Notice, however, that Bailey thinks of the jet in this way *after* he is in danger. How much of a tendency is there for people to ignore the potential dangers in the mechanical contrivances that we must deal with in our lives? If we really defined things in ways that stressed their dangers, would this have an effect on our lives? Or would we soon become hardened to the definitions? Using Bailey's definition as a model, how would you define *automobile? Motorcycle? Elevator? Chain saw? Drunken driver?*

How I Designed An A-Bomb
in My Junior Year at Princeton

JOHN ARISTOTLE PHILLIPS and DAVID MICHAELIS

After the first semester of his junior year at Princeton, John Aristotle Phillips found himself on academic probation and facing a new semester in which failure in a single course would end his days at the university. His first good fortune of the new term was that his courses interested him. The second was that fellow students in one of his classes maintained that terrorists could never muster the intelligence or gain access to enough information to build a nuclear bomb. Phillips challenged this view and set out to show that a physics major suffering with grade average problems could construct plans for a workable atomic bomb. In this narrative, Phillips and his classmate, David Michaelis, tell how Phillips successfully met the challenge.

The first semester of my junior year at Princeton University is a disaster,   1
and my grades show it. D's and F's predominate, and a note from the dean
puts me on academic probation. Flunk one more course, and I'm out.

Fortunately, as the new semester gets under way, my courses begin to   2
interest me. Three hours a week, I attend one called Nuclear Weapons
Strategy and Arms Control in which three professors lead 12 students
through intense discussions of counterforce capabilities and doomsday
scenarios. The leader is Hal Feiveson, renowned for his strong command of
the subject matter. Assisting him are Marty Sherwin, an authority on cold-
war diplomacy, and Freeman Dyson, an eminent physicist.

One morning, Dyson opens a discussion of the atomic bomb: "Let me   3
describe what occurs when a 20-kiloton bomb is exploded, similar to the two
dropped on Hiroshima and Nagasaki. First, the sky becomes illuminated by
a brilliant white light. Temperatures are so high around the point of explosion that the atmosphere is actually made incandescent. To an observer
standing six miles away the ball of fire appears brighter than a hundred
suns.

"As the fireball begins to spread up and out into a mushroom-shaped   4
cloud, temperatures spontaneously ignite all flammable materials for miles
around. Wood-frame houses catch fire. Clothing bursts into flame, and
people suffer intense third-degree flash burns over their exposed flesh. The

very high temperatures also produce a shock wave and a variety of nuclear radiations capable of penetrating 20 inches of concrete. The shock wave levels everything in the vicinity of ground zero; hurricane-force winds then rush into the vacuum left by the expanding shock wave and sweep up the rubble of masonry, glass and steel, hurling it outward as lethal projectiles."

Silence falls over the room as the titanic proportions of the destruction begin to sink in.   5

"It takes only 15 pounds of plutonium to fabricate a crude atomic bomb," adds Hal Feiveson. "If breeder reactors come into widespread use, there will be sufficient plutonium shipped around the country each year to fashion thousands of bombs. Much of it could be vulnerable to theft or hijacking."   6

The class discusses a possible scenario. A 200-pound shipment disappears en route between a reprocessing facility and a nuclear reactor. State and local police discover only an empty truck and a dead driver. Two weeks later, a crude fission bomb is detonated in Wall Street. Of the half-million people who crowd the area during the regular business day, 100,000 are killed outright. A terrorist group claims responsibility and warns the President that if its extravagant political demands are not met, there will be another explosion within a week.   7

"That's impossible," a student objects. "Terrorists don't have the know-how to build a bomb."   8

"You have to be brilliant to design an A-bomb," says another. "Besides, terrorists don't have access to the knowledge."   9

Impossible? Or is it? The specter of terrorists incinerating an entire city with a homemade atomic bomb begins to haunt me. I turn to John McPhee's book *The Curve of Binding Energy,* in which former Los Alamos nuclear physicist Ted Taylor postulates that a terrorist group could easily steal plutonium or uranium from a nuclear reactor and then design a workable atomic bomb with information available to the general public. According to Taylor, all the ingredients—except plutonium—are legally available at hardware stores and chemical-supply houses.   10

Suddenly, an idea comes to mind. Suppose an average—or below-average in my case—physics student could design a workable atomic bomb on paper? That would prove Taylor's point dramatically and show the federal government that stronger safeguards have to be placed on the storage of plutonium. If I could design a bomb, almost any intelligent person could. But I would have to do it in less than three months to turn it in as my junior independent project. I decide to ask Freeman Dyson to be my adviser.   11

"You understand," says Dyson, "my government security clearance will preclude me from giving you any more information than that which can   12 be found in physics libraries? And that the law of 'no comment' governing scientists who have clearance to atomic secrets stipulates that, if asked a question about the design of a bomb, I can answer neither yes nor no?"

"Yes, sir," I reply. "I understand." 13

"Okay, then. I'll give you a list of textbooks outlining the general principles—and I wish you luck." 14

I'm tremendously excited as I charge over to the physics office to record my project, and can barely write down: 15

John Aristotle Phillips
Dr. Freeman Dyson, Adviser
"How to Build Your Own
Atomic Bomb"

A few days later, Dyson hands me a short list of books on nuclear-reactor technology, general nuclear physics and current atomic theory. "That's all?" I ask incredulously, having expected a bit more direction. 16

At subsequent meetings Dyson explains only the basic principles of nuclear physics, and his responses to my calculations grow opaque. If I ask about a particular design or figure, he will glance over what I've done and change the subject. At first, I think this is his way of telling me I am correct. To make sure, I hand him an incorrect figure. He reads it and changes the subject. 17

Over spring vacation, I go to Washington, D.C., to search for records of the Los Alamos Project that were declassified between 1954 and 1964. I discover a copy of the literature given to scientists who joined the project in the spring of 1943. This text, *The Los Alamos Primer*, carefully outlines all the details of atomic fissioning known to the world's most advanced scientists in the early '40s. A whole batch of copies costs me about $25. I gather them together and go over to the bureaucrat at the front desk. She looks at the titles, and then looks up at me. 18

"Oh, you want to build a bomb, too?" she asks matter-of-factly. 19

I can't believe it. Do people go in there for bomb-building information every day? When I show the documents to Dyson, he is visibly shaken. His reaction indicates to me that I actually stand a chance of coming up with a workable design. 20

The material necessary to explode my bomb is plutonium-239, a man-made, heavy isotope. Visualize an atomic bomb as a marble inside a grapefruit inside a basketball inside a beach ball. At the center of the bomb is the initiator, a marble-size piece of metal. Around the initiator is a grapefruit- 21 sized ball of plutonium-239. Wrapped around the plutonium is a three-inch reflector shield made of beryllium. High explosives are placed symetrically around the beryllium shield. When these detonate, an imploding shock wave is set off, compressing the grapefruit-sized ball of plutonium to the size of a plum. At this moment, the process of atoms fissioning—or splitting apart—begins.

There are many subtleties involved in the explosion of an atomic bomb. Most of them center on the actual detonation of the explosives surrounding the beryllium shield. The grouping of these explosives is one of the most highly classified aspects of the atomic bomb, and it poses the biggest problems for me as I begin to design my bomb. 22

My base of operations is a small room on the second floor of Ivy, my eating club. The conference table in the center of the room is covered with books, calculators, design paper, notes. My sleeping bag is rolled out on the floor. As the next three weeks go by, I stop going to classes altogether and work day and night. The other members at Ivy begin referring to me as The Hobo because of my unshaven face and disheveled appearance. I develop a terrible case of bloodshot eyes. Sleep comes rarely. 23

I approach every problem from a terrorist's point of view. The bomb must be inexpensive to construct, simple in design, and small enough to sit unnoticed in the trunk of a car or an abandoned U-Haul trailer. 24

As the days and nights flow by, linked together by cups of coffee and bologna sandwiches, I scan government documents for gaps indicating an area of knowledge that is still classified. Essentially, I am putting together a huge jigsaw puzzle. The edge pieces are in place and various areas are getting filled in, but pieces are missing. Whenever the outline of one shows up, I grab my coffee Thermos and sit down to devise the solution that will fill the gap. 25

With only two weeks left, the puzzle is nearly complete, but two pieces are still missing: which explosives to use, and how to arrange them around the plutonium. 26

During the next week I read that a high-explosive blanket around the beryllium shield might work. But after spending an entire night calculating, I conclude that it is not enough to guarantee a successful implosion wave. Seven days before the design is due, I'm still deadlocked. 27

The alarm clock falls off the table and breaks. I take this as a sign to do something drastic, and I start all over at the beginning. Occasionally I find errors in my old calculations, and I correct them. I lose sense of time. 28

With less than 24 hours to go, I run through a series of new calculations, 29 mathematically figuring the arrangement of the explosives around the plutonium. If my equations are correct, my bomb might be just as effective as the Hiroshima and Nagasaki bombs. But I can't be sure until I know the exact nature of the explosives I will use.

Next morning, with my paper due at 5 p.m., I call the Du Pont Company 30 from a pay phone and ask for the head of the chemical-explosives division, a man I'll call S. F. Graves. If he gives me even the smallest lead, I'll be able to figure the rest out by myself. Otherwise, I'm finished.

"Hello, Mr. Graves. My name is John Phillips. I'm a student at Prince- 31 ton, doing work on a physics project. I'd like to get some advice, if that's possible."

"What can I do for you?" 32

"Well," I stammer, "I'm doing research on the shaping of explosive 33 products that create a very high density in a spherically shaped metal. Can you suggest a Du Pont product that would fit in this category?"

"Of course," he says, in a helpful manner. 34

I don't think he suspects, but I decide to try a bluff: "One of my 35 professors told me that a simple explosive blanket would work in the high-density situation."

"No, no. Explosive blankets went out with the Stone Age. We sell [he 36 names the product] to do the job in similar density-problem situations to the one you're talking about."

When I hang up the phone, I let out a whoop. Mr. Graves has given me 37 just the information I need. Now, if my calculations are correct with respect to the new information, all I have to do is complete my paper by five.

Five minutes to five, I race over to the physics building and bound up the 38 stairs. Inside the office, everybody stops talking and stares at me. I haven't shaved in over a week.

"Is your razor broken, young man?" asks one of the department sec- 39 retaries.

"I came to hand in my project," I explain. "I didn't have time to shave. 40 Sorry."

A week later, I return to the physics department to pick up my project. 41 One thought has persisted: If I didn't guess correctly about the implosion wave, or if I made a mistake somewhere in the graphs, I'll be finished at Princeton.

A secretary points to the papers. I flip through them, but don't find 42 mine. I look carefully; my paper is not there.

Trying to remain calm, I ask her if all the papers have been graded. 43

"Yes, of course," she says. 44

Slowly I return to my room. The absence of my paper can only mean that 45
I blew it.

In the middle of the week, I go back to the physics-department office, 46
hoping to catch the chairman for a few minutes. The secretary looks up, then
freezes.

"Aren't you John Phillips?" she asks. 47

"Yes," I reply. 48

"Aren't you the boy who designed the atomic bomb?" 49

"Yes, and my paper wasn't . . ." 50

She takes a deep breath. "The question has been raised by the depart- 51
ment whether your paper should be classified by the U.S. government."

"What? Classified?" 52

She takes my limp hand, shaking it vigorously. "Congratulations," she 53
says, all smiles. "You got one of the only A's in the department. Dr. Wigner
wants to see you right away. He says it's a fine piece of work. And Dr. Dyson
has been looking for you everywhere."

For a second I don't say anything. Then the madness of the situation hits 54
me. A small air bubble of giddiness rises in my throat. Here I have put on
paper the plan for a device capable of killing thousands of people, and all I
was worrying about was flunking out.

QUESTIONS ON MEANING AND CONTENT

1. Phillips uses much ingenuity, applying strategies for learning or
gathering information that normally are not taught in the classroom. In
one of these, Dr. Tyson is asked to look at a figure Philipps knows is an
incorrect figure. What is Phillips trying to learn in this instance? What
other unusual strategies does Phillips employ?

2. Phillips' grades may have been below average, but he certainly was
not a below-average student generally during this term. He takes extraordinary pains and makes a number of personal sacrifices to piece together this
complex jigsaw puzzle. What are some of these?

3. Would this essay be as appealing if the narrator had made all A's
during his three years at Princeton? Why or why not?

4. "If I could design a bomb," Phillips says, "almost any intelligent
person could." Does his success prove his point that "almost any intelligent person could?" If this does prove his point, then what does "almost

any" mean? Describe the intelligent people who might be excluded by this "almost any" restriction.

5. Phillips knows his bomb will work because his plans are evaluated by a physicist who knows what will work and what will not. How would a terrorist who designed an A-bomb know?

6. In the final paragraph, Phillips says, "Then the madness of the situation hit me." Why hadn't it "hit" him earlier? When Phillips was in Washington, D.C., the woman behind the desk says off-handedly, "Oh, you want to build a bomb, too?" How does this episode relate to Phillips' reaction at the end of the essay?

QUESTIONS ABOUT RHETORICAL STRATEGIES

1. The essay is written in first person, present tense, a form about as close as a writer can come to talking to readers face-to-face and telling them about an experience or adventure. This offers the advantage of immediacy. If the writer handles first person, present tense well, probably no other method gives readers so strong a feeling that events are taking place as they read, and this form also offers many opportunities for creating suspense and conveying emotion. At the same time, however, writers who use this form, especially inexperienced writers, can get carried away in trying to create suspense or emotion, just as any of us can when telling a group of friends about an exciting experience. Our friends tend to smile and indulge us and go on listening, but readers are sometimes turned away by this and consider exaggerated suspense or emotions to be unrealistic. Point out places in this narrative that are particularly suspenseful or where the speaker is expressing emotions. In your judgment, are these presented with just about the right touch—neither too much nor too little emphasis? Which of these are intense enough that a writer might be tempted to overwrite in order to convey an extra degree of emotion or tension?

2. Suppose that Phillips had told his advisor a few weeks after the course the same basic story he tells us. Then assume that his project advisor wrote a narrative about the same event, using the conversation with Phillips and his experience as advisor as an information base. Assume also that his narrative was written in third person, past tense. What are some ways in which this second narrative would differ from the one you have just read? What advantages would the advisor have? What disadvantages? Which versions do you think you would prefer? Why?

QUESTIONS ON LANGUAGE AND DICTION

1. Throughout the essay, the authors explain one thing in terms of something entirely different. Such comparisons are a way of letting readers see or understand an unfamiliar subject. Examine the following comparisons and evaluate their effectiveness as a way of explaining something quickly and clearly:

   a. Paragraph 3—using the sun as a base for describing a nuclear fireball

   b. Paragraph 21—using the beachball-to-marble metaphor to show the structure of an A-bomb

   c. Paragraph 25—using the jigsaw-puzzle analogy to describe Phillips' progressing research.

2. In paragraph 25, Phillips' days and nights are "linked together by cups of coffee and bologna sandwiches." This is a type of metaphorical statement, since days and nights aren't literally "linked" together by food. How does this metaphorical statement differ from those mentioned in question 1 above? Is this description of passing time an effective one? If so, what does it add to the writing? Does it tell readers something beyond the fact that time seemed to be passing quickly for Phillips?

3. As an extension of questions 1 and 2, examine the third sentence in paragraph 54 and comment on the "small air bubble of giddiness" mentioned there. What sort of expression is this? What meaning does it have? Does it work for the authors; that is, do you, as reader, find it to be an effective way of describing Phillips' feelings at the time?

4. What are the meanings of the following words: *opaque, postulate, preclude, specter, titanic.*

Late Summer 1756

RICHARD TAYLOR

In this selection, Richard Taylor puts himself in the place of the notorious frontiersman, Simon Girty, while narrating events drawn from Girty's experiences. Simon Girty, who was well-known from the Ohio River north to Canada when the American frontier still lay well east of the Mississippi, was often considered villainous by the white settlers because of his activities with American Indian tribes.

My initiation to Delaware comes through a hole burned in the stockade at Fort Granville. This sad excuse for a fortification stands, or stood, between the Juniata River and Sherman Creek on the Susquehanna. A ramshackle square of cabins joined by logs laid horizontally, maybe 8 feet high. This flimsy wall and 20 militiamen are the only protection between us and about 100 Delawares and Shawnees led by some French. Us being my mother, my step-father John Turner, my three natural brothers and one step-, and some dozen or so neighbors, mostly Lacefields and Bartletts. 1

Burning the hole is easy, done almost before we see the smoke. The lay of the fort is such that a deep ravine runs from the river up to a few feet of the pickets. This ravine, overgrown with brush and saplings, gives them cover enough to fire it fast and secret, blue flames gnawing a 6 foot gap before we can dump our first bucket. The fighting quickly centers on this spot. From my window where I am crouching I see several Canadians and Indians shot as they rush through, cut down in our crossfire. But some of ours fall too, including Armstrong, who was left in charge when that simpleton Captain Ward took most of the men to guard the wheat reapers in Sherman Valley. Which is why, of course, they pick now to attack. As the fighting grows hotter, one by one those holding the gap are killed, beets sprouting out of their foreheads, chests filled with thimble-sized holes. 2

Then out of this confusion—the smoke, the gunfire, the women bellowing—steps the chief frog. Half-hidden behind a tree, a squat dandy wearing spotless white breeches shouts in fragile English for us to give up. There really isn't much choice since most of the men are either dead or dying. The Frenchman offers quarter and solemnly promises to hold off 3 his Indians. This decision is left up to my step-father John Turner, who inherited the command from Armstrong ten minutes before. One look around the fort, the litter of dead and bleeding, and he just throws down the gate, leaving us to their mercy. Which is not much. The instant our weapons are down, a dozen assassins dash in and tomahawk the wounded, including our nearest neighbor, an old man named Brandon. No one lifts a hand to stop the slaughter. The Frenchman is nowhere in sight. After this first furious cruelty, they become more select, singling out those too old or feeble for work, killing and scalping them also. The rest, those of us still with breath in our bodies, are turned into pack mules and loaded with nearly our own weight in plunder. I am forced to tote an enormous brass kettle. John Turner I remember staggering under a hundred-pound sack of salt. In one afternoon my whole family falls captive—John Turner, my mother, Baby John, my brothers Tom and George and James.

Three days later we reach Kittanning, a large Delaware town up the Alleghany. The whole village turns out for the homecoming, cheering their husbands, their fathers, their brothers, taunting and stoning the prisoners. Never have I see so many people in one place. Hordes of gawking onlookers dressed in knee-length leather frocks or near naked, menacing crow-black eyes set in skin the color of tobacco. There are 50 or so lodges, rude cabins mostly, and some tents made of hides. We are led to a clearing in the center of the village. Here we are tied to posts to be offered as sport to the squaws and urchins who stayed behind. Swinging willow whips and clubs, they beat us for a solid hour during a general holiday.   4

At Kittanning my mother is made a widow for the second time. Widowed from the man who murdered the Delaware named Fish, who made her a widow the first time. The triangle stretches into a square. It so happens the chief of this town is a one-eyed terror named Tewea, pronounced "Too-way." This Tewea, better known as Captain Jacobs, is the Fish's brother, and the last time he saw his brother alive he was setting out with a boodle of skins to trade with my father and John Turner, who were, in more ways than one it was said, partners. The question is whether Tewea remembers. He acknowledges that he does by smashing John Turner in the mouth and ordering a large fire.   5

So at Kittanning up the Alleghany my brothers and me are orphaned for a second time as our stepfather roasts before our eyes. We all expect the same treatment, but fortunately Tewea considers the score evened. And besides, he has other plans for us. No fool, he knows we are worth more to   6 him alive than dead. So after much squabbling among the tribesmen, we are parcelled out to separate villages for adoption, the idea being for us to replace those killed during the attack on Granville. We are split up because we will lose our white ways sooner, none of us being considered blood-poisoned enough (I, next to eldest, am 15) to be beyond correction.

Tom and George are sent to Goschachgunk, a Delaware village at the fork of the Muskingum River. James, my mother and her baby, to a Shawnee town on the Scioto ("Elk River") in the Ohio country. Me, to Cattaraugus in New York where the Senecas adopt me not long before I adopt them. Safe back on their homeground and fat with plunder, they leave me pretty much on my own. Once I know they mean to adopt me, I put aside Chambers' Mill and begin a life not so different from what I'm accustomed to. Indian ways come easy. The life is no harder, no crueler than life with my father. The food, better and more abundant. The free life suits me.

That spring, before the oak leaves are the size of a squirrel's ear, I am adopted into the tribe. This is a solemn event and the whole village turns out for the ceremony. How it is done. First, some old women strip and beat me with willow switches just short of drawing blood. This, to stir up the impure spirits in my body. Next they drag me to water where the white blood is scrubbed from my skin with sharp gravel and sand from the sacred bottom of the Allegheny River. Along the banks the whole tribe stands witness. The sachems look on from high ground, old men sucking their hollow clay pipes, some muttering and thumping a deerskin drum. When their chanting dies off, one old waster, toothless and drawn up in the face, pulls my ear to his face and whispers my secret name. He tells me I have become one of "The People."

So starts my first three years with the Senecas, the Maechachtinni, grandchildren of the Sun and the Moon. The white blood washes off easier than dirt. Most of the time I am free to hunt. When I am not hunting, I am eating or sleeping. The language comes slower. The words, which sound at first like the grunts of rutting brutes, break up at last into separate sounds and meanings. Though I pick up words soon enough, they are not under-stood when I try to speak until I learn to draw them from deep in my chest and pass them through my nose. The secret is in the breath. Soon I have the sounds for most things and know to point to others. From the time I can speak, my acceptance is complete. The rest comes easy. Wearing a loincloth, acquiring a taste for stewed dog and boiled mussels, an eagle feather tied to my scalplock, my white skin greased and gaudy, my career beginning. Rub a sheep against pitch, he gits up with tar.

QUESTIONS ON MEANING AND CONTENT

1. The author constructs the narrative as if it were being told by Simon Girty, an early American frontiersman. Why, in your opinion, does Richard Taylor succeed or fail in his efforts to make the narrative seem as if it does come from Girty's own mouth? What do you find in the nature of the descriptions and in the words, phrases, sentences, and grammar to show that Taylor has tried to portray a rough frontiersman speaking?

2. Consider the last sentence in the narrative: "Rub a sheep against pitch, he gits up with tar." What is the meaning of this sentence? Does it make a point for the narrative as a whole? How does it relate to the statement in paragraph 6 that says of the Girty children, "None of us being considered blood-poisoned enough . . . to be beyond correction"?

3. The mythology of the American frontier suggests that those captured by Indians behave differently from Simon Girty. In a typical scenario, a captive would pretend to adopt Indian ways but would, in reality, be constantly working out plans for escape. Girty converts to the Seneca way of life without resistance. At the end of paragraph 7, he offers reasons for accepting Seneca life so readily. Is he convinced? What effect, if any, do the first six paragraphs have on how you evaluate the reasons Girty offers in paragraph 7?

QUESTIONS ABOUT RHETORICAL STRATEGIES

1. This narrative is told in the first person and uses the present tense. Do you think the author chose wisely in presenting the narrative in this way? Why or why not? What would be the effect if this were told by a third-person narrative using past tense? (If you have trouble visualizing the difference, rewrite one of the paragraphs, using third person, past tense.)

2. The narrative has three settings: Fort Granville, Kittanning, and the Seneca village at Cattaraugus. Find the places where the narrative moves from one setting to another. How does the author handle these movements? What can you learn from this that you can apply to your own narrative papers?

3. Can you explain why the narrative begins where it does—with the burning of the hole in the stockade? After all, the French and Indians had been attacking for some time before the hole was burned in the wall. Did the author choose a good starting point? Why? Would starting at an earlier point strengthen or weaken the narrative?

4. At some point in most narratives, writers have to inject background information, usually referred to as *exposition*. The background information provides readers with details and facts that existed before the beginning of the narrative. Such information helps readers understand the narrative more fully. Most of paragraph 5 is devoted to background information. Why is the information in paragraph 5 necessary to the long paragraph that follows? Where else in the narrative does the author insert background information?

QUESTIONS ON LANGUAGE AND DICTION

1. In paragraph 3, the people in the fort give up and place themselves at the mercy of the French and Indians. Girty says that their mercy "is not much." The descriptive passage that follows shows that Girty is *understating* the case. What effect, if any, is achieved by this understatement? What would be the difference if Girty had said the "surrender leaves us helpless against their merciless brutality"?

2. Throughout the essay Girty speaks as a person who expects harshness and brutality as a matter of course. The understatement referred to in question 1 above is an example of this. He describes violence and hardship explicitly but frequently understates or refers to events in an odd way, sometimes taking us by surprise. How is the reference to "general holiday" in paragraph 4 consistent with the way Girty speaks throughout?

3. In paragraph 5 Girty raises the question of whether or not Tewea remembers John Turner. The answer to this question really is "Yes, he does"—but how does Girty answer the question? Can you find other examples in the essay of odd or unusual ways of expressing things?

Angels on a Pin

ALEXANDER CALANDRA

The systematic problem-solving methods of scientific and scholarly disciplines represent part of an inheritance passed down from generation to generation by dedicated scientists and scholars. It is this rich inheritance that permits the various disciplines to provide an orderly means of preserving old knowledge and creating new. However, in our reverence for this received knowledge, we sometimes forget that there are other ways to answer questions and solve problems. In this narrative, Professor Alexander Calandra, of Washington University in St. Louis, tells of a student with the courage to place his grade point average in jeopardy to show that many of the methods not honored in the classroom yield satisfactory results in solving a problem posed in his physics examination.

Some time ago, I received a call from a colleague who asked if I would be the referee on the grading of an examination question. He was about to give a student a zero for his answer to a physics question, while the student claimed he should receive a perfect score and would if the system were not set up against the student. The instructor and the student agreed to submit this to an impartial arbiter, and I was selected. 1

I went to my colleague's office and read the examination question: "Show how it is possible to determine the height of a tall building with the aid of a barometer." 2

The student had answered: "Take the barometer to the top of the building, attach a long rope to it, lower the barometer to the street, and then bring it up, measuring the length of the rope. The length of the rope is the height of the building." 3

I pointed out that the student really had a strong case for full credit, since he had answered the question completely and correctly. On the other hand, if full credit were given, it could well contribute to a high grade for the student in his physics course. A high grade is supposed to certify competence in physics, but the answer did not confirm this. I suggested that the student have another try at answering the question. I was not surprised that my colleague agreed, but I was surprised that the student did. 4

I gave the student six minutes to answer the question, with the warning that his answer should show some knowledge of physics. At the end of five minutes, he had not written anything. I asked if he wished to give up, but he 5 said no. He had many answers to this problem; he was just thinking of the best one. I excused myself for interrupting him, and asked him to please go on. In the next minute, he dashed off his answer, which read:

"Take the barometer to the top of the building and lean over the edge of the roof. Drop the barometer, timing its fall with a stopwatch. Then, using the formula $S = at^2$, calculate the height of the building."   6

At this point, I asked my colleague if *he* would give up. He conceded, and I gave the student almost full credit.   7

In leaving my colleague's office, I recalled that the student had said he had other answers to the problem, so I asked him what they were. "Oh, yes," said the student. "There are many ways of getting the height of a tall building with the aid of a barometer. For example, you could take the barometer out on a sunny day and measure the height of the barometer, the length of its shadow, and the length of the shadow of the building, and by the use of a simple proportion, determine the height of the building."   8

"Fine," I said. "And the others?"   9

"Yes." said the student. "There is a very basic measurement method that you will like. In this method, you take the barometer and begin to walk up the stairs. As you climb the stairs, you mark off the length of the barometer along the wall. You then count the number of marks, and this will give you the height of the building in barometer units. A very direct method.   10

"Of course, if you want a more sophisticated method, you can tie the barometer to the end of a string, swing it as a pendulum, and determine the value of 'g at the street level and at the top of the building. From the difference between the two values of 'g,' the height of the building can, in principle, be calculated."   11

Finally he concluded, there are many other ways of solving the problem. "Probably the best," he said, "is to take the barometer to the basement and knock on the superintendent's door. When the superintendent answers, you speak to him as follows: 'Mr. Superintendent, here I have a fine barometer. If you will tell me the height of this building, I will give you this barometer.' "   12

At this point, I asked the student if he really did not know the conventional answer to this question. He admitted that he did, but said that he was fed up with high school and college instructors trying to teach him how to think, to use the "scientific method," and to explore the deep inner logic of the subject in a pedantic way, as is often done in the new mathematics, rather then teaching him the structure of the subject. With this in mind, he decided to revive scholasticism as an academic lark to challenge the Sputnik-panicked classrooms of America.   13

QUESTIONS ON MEANING AND CONTENT

1. The author says that he was not surprised when his fellow physics professor agreed to a retest, but he was surprised that the student did. At this point, what assumptions was the narrator making about the student? About his colleague? About the original test?

2. Why do you think the student agreed to be retested? Does his willingness to retake the exam have anything to do with the point he was trying to make? What exactly was the point he was trying to make? Does the title of the essay offer any clues to help explain what the student wanted to demonstrate? Visit the library and learn what you can about Scholasticism in the Middle Ages. The Scholastic philosophers took seriously questions like "How many angels can fit on the head of a pin?"

3. In the second test, the student still does not give the "expected" answer, but he does use a barometer in solving the problem, and he does demonstrate some knowledge of physics. Do you think the author should have given the student full credit for the answer instead of "almost full credit"? Why?

4. Based on the way the author relates the narrative, how would you characterize his attitude toward the student and the whole episode generally? What can you point to in the essay to support your answer?

5. Originally the student maintained that he should receive full credit for the first test. His instructor thought he should receive a zero. The author, as arbiter, was called in to help settle the dispute. Who won the dispute—the student or the instructor? Or did all parties involved win, including the arbiter? Explain.

QUESTIONS ABOUT RHETORICAL STRATEGIES

1. Notice how the author uses two techniques to convey information to the reader. In most of the essay he describes or summarizes events to help carry the narrative forward. But in places he uses direct quotations—first the original test question and the student's answer. Then, after the second test has ended, he conducts a dialogue in which he has the student do most of the talking, letting the student fill in details and move the narrative toward a conclusion. Finally, in the last paragraph, the author takes over the narrative again and concludes the essay by summarizing the rest of the conversation with the student.

What does the narrative gain from the direct quotations of the test question and answers and from letting the student speak? How effective would this narrative be if the author summarized or described happenings throughout? In your view, does the author strengthen this piece by cutting off the dialogue with the student and returning to his summarizing voice to conclude this essay?

2. This narrative deals with two significant events: the first test and the retest. Although the author relates the narrative in the first person, past tense, he was not a participant in the first significant event. This means that he will have to begin the narrative at the point when he became a participant and then bring the reader up-to-date by supplying background information, or exposition. How and when does the author do this? What can you learn from the author's handling of background information that you can apply in your own narrative writing?

QUESTIONS ON LANGUAGE AND DICTION

1. What is meant by the "Sputnik-panicked" classrooms mentioned in the last sentence in the essay?

2. In the "value of 'g' " mentioned in paragraph 11, what does "g" stand for?

North America After the War

PAUL R. EHRLICH

Even though he uses past tense to relate his narrative, eminent scientist Paul R. Ehrlich has combined imagination and scientific knowledge to show the awesome chain of future events set off by foolhardy human conduct. The story he tells takes place near the close of the present century "when humanity's luck ran out" and the bombs fell.

It was almost the end of the century when humanity's luck ran out. Most   1
of the nuclear war scenarios had been optimistic. Three-quarters of the American and Soviet arsenals, more than 30,000 nuclear devices, exploded with power in excess of 9,000 megatons (9 billion tons) of TNT. The large cities of North America, Europe, Russia, China, and Japan, as well as huge areas of dense forest, fueled fire storms. Soot from these fire storms joined dust lofted into the stratosphere by thousands of ground bursts. Smoke from myriad smaller fires choked the lower atmosphere and darkness enshrouded the Northern Hemisphere from a few days after the early July war until October, when substantial sunlight again began to reach the earth's surface.

Soot and smoke absorbed large amounts of solar energy; dust reflected   2
more back into space. This plunged temperatures in all inland areas to below zero for virtually the entire dark summer. Except for small refugia on the coastlines, temperatures across the North American continent fell below 10° F for several months, going well below zero in many places for extended periods. No place in the Northern Hemisphere escaped severe frosts. Although far fewer weapons were detonated in the Southern Hemisphere, plumes of soot moved rapidly across the equator from the North, creating quick freezes in many places. Dusky skies, lower than normal temperatures, and radioactive fallout eventually covered the entire planet. The "nuclear winter" predicted by the world's top atmospheric scientists in late 1983 had come to pass.

By January, much of the debris had cleared from the skies, but lingering   3
smoke, stratospheric dust, and material from still-burning fires prolonged an unusually cold winter. Spring and summer were also colder than usual. Nitrogen oxides, produced when the thermonuclear fireballs burned

atmospheric nitrogen, had severely damaged the stratospheric ozone layer, which normally filters out ultraviolet rays harmful to plants and animals. This made the return of sunlight a mixed blessing.

Blast, fire, prompt radiation and delayed fallout, zero temperature, toxic   4
smog, and lack of food eliminated the vestiges of human life. Even in the warmer places—the coastlines where the cold had been ameliorated by the thermal inertia of the oceans—people could not survive. The few officials and military personnel in the United States and Canada whose deep shelters had not been "dug out" by Soviet missles, and who had passed the nuclear winter underground, starved soon after emerging in the frigid spring. Tropical peoples, even in coastal areas of Mexico, succumbed to exposure, radiation sickness, hunger, civil disorder, and epidemic disease. Starvation finished the Eskimo. Human beings were gone from North America—indeed, from the entire Northern Hemisphere.

But not all life was extinct. Scattered pockets of severely frost-damaged   5
chaparral along the coast had escaped the great fires that had swept most of California bare. Even after the erosion of bare slopes in the postwar rain, many seeds survived. The Olympic Peninsula and parts of coastal British Columbia and Alaska had suffered less than inland areas because, as in California, the adjacent sea had moderated the long cold period. Even in coastal areas many plants died from a combination of low light, toxic air pollution, high radiation (the last especially affected the sensitive conifers), and from the continual violent storms generated by the sharp sea–land temperature gradient.

Inland in the subartic and arctic North, virtually all of the growing plants   6
had died. Cold-resistant boreal trees, deprived of the normal environmental cues that induce cold hardiness, were not prepared for the nuclear after-math. Paper birches and aspens, which can tolerate temperatures of $-100°$ F when acclimatized, died when midsummer temperatures dropped in a few days to $-20°$ F. In the Rocky Mountains and sections of the East, substantial areas of forest had not burned, but most of the standing trees had succumbed to the extreme, unseasonable cold. Persistence of plant popula-tions in most parts of what had been the United States and Canada de-pended on the survival of seeds and roots (or other subterranean organs) in the frozen ground.

Due to vagaries in wind patterns, vegetation survived in a few enclaves   7
along the west coast of Florida, parts of Yucatan and Chiapas in Mexico, and the Osa Peninsula of Costa Rica. But in most of Florida, Mexico, and Central America, the devastation of growing plants was virtually complete. Sub-

tropical and tropical floras, unfortunately, had had much less evolutionary experience with extreme cold: only a very few relatively hardy seeds and subterranean parts survive outside of the enclaves.

Most of the higher vertebrates went the way of *Homo sapiens*. The cold alone killed many animals before radiation, thirst (lakes, rivers, and streams were covered with several feet of ice), and starvation could affect them. In the smoggy darkness, many had a reduced ability to find food, preventing them from adequately stoking their metabolic fires. Nearly every species of migratory land bird went extinct. But in places in the Northwest, a few warmblooded creatures—crows, ravens, starlings, ptarmigan, gulls, black bears, coyotes, rabbits, and rodents—managed to survive. So did some of the hardier denizens of the coastal chaparral pockets in California—but the extremely high radiation levels gradually pushed many populations to extinction.   8

In the continental interior, a handful of vertebrates survived the cold, mostly reptiles, amphibians, and fishes whose physiological plasticity allowed their body temperatures to drop to near freezing. Warmblooded animals that hibernate had no opportunity to build reserves for a normal winter, let alone a nuclear winter. The lower metabolic rates of the lower vertebrates permitted scattered individuals to survive in deep crevices, burrows, or beneath the ice of large lakes. Most of those few survivors starved the following spring.   9

The majority of insects were even less fortunate. In seasonal environments, insects normally pass the winter (or other stressful seasons) in a specific developmental stage—and virtually all were caught in the wrong stage. Only in arctic and alpine areas, where insects are adapted to summer frosts, did some insect fauna survive the freezing.   10

During the first postwar summer, seeds began to sprout in areas where fire storms had not sterilized the soil. Surviving perennials in coastal pockets also began to produce new growth. But continuing cold weather and strong ultraviolet radiation damaged the tender young plant tissues. Many desert spring annuals that depended on now-extinct insects for pollination failed to reproduce. In refugia where insect pollinators did survive, they often were disoriented by the ultraviolet light, which though invisible to mammals was visible to them. This not only reduced their capacity to pollinate but also to reproduce themselves.   11

In arctic and alpine areas, many surviving insect populations dwindled further or went extinct from lack of food. The growing season was extremely short and frosts frequently damaged plants struggling to recover. The abundant female mosquitoes had few vertebrates to feed on, and the males found little nectar in the few surviving flowers. Only a small fraction of the boreal   12 insect fauna that had survived the first winter went into diapause for the next.

Not only was spring silent over most of the continent that first year following the war, but summer was silent as well. In much of what had been the United States, no birds sang, no dogs barked, no frogs croaked, no fishes leaped. As they emerged into the desolation, most of the scattered lizards, snakes, turtles, and toads starved. Most areas were utterly devoid of organic motion beyond the wind-induced flutter of the leaves of scattered plants. There were exceptions, though. In mines, caves, and deep underground shelters, flies, roaches, rats, and mice had survived and in some had even thrived on the cadavers of people who had sought shelter there. When some of these survivors emerged at night, they found a similar resource in the abundant thawing cadavers of people and domestic animals. These scavengers built large local populations. But they soon crashed when they exhausted their grim resources.   13

All in all, life was in worse shape at the end of the first postwar summer than it had been in the spring. Only where substantial plant communities remained—on the northwest coast, in the coastal California chaparal, and in the tropical and subtropical pockets—did relatively diverse vertebrate and invertebrate populations survive. And even there losses were substantial. The last North American mountain lions, lynxes, large hawks, golden eagles, and other large predators went extinct; the refugia were not big enough to save the decimated populations of most animals that require large home ranges. Vultures did survive on the abundant carrion as did the once endangered bald eagle, outlasting—and even dining on—the species that had endangered them. Kestrels also made it, dining on grasshoppers. Most herbivorous insects that specialized on the less hardy plants were incapable of switching to plants with different suites of chemical feeding stimulants and toxic defenses. So they followed their plants into oblivion.   14

For several years after the war, dust from the partly denuded continents and smoke from lightning-ignited fires in forest remnants, smoldering peat bogs, coal stocks and seams, and burning oil and gas wells produced cool summers and unusually harsh winters. But gradually the climate returned more or less to normal, except that, in the near absence of vegetation, much of the central continent was more arid than before the war.   15

Over the next decades, plants began to reconquer the desolate continent. In the normally cooler latitudes many seeds in the soil were largely undamaged by cold and radiation. During each growing season for the first few postwar years, some prewar seeds germinated. And each year some of the seedlings survived.   16

Species adapted to disturbed areas did best. Kudzu vine, crab grass,   17 stork's bill, dandelions, and similar weeds quickly covered large areas, often choking out species that people had once considered "more desirable." In California, an impoverished chaparral community slowly reclaimed the denuded hillsides, aided to some extent by its natural adaptation to fire. A rare survivor in that community was the gypsy moth. In the subarctic and the arctic, grasses, sedges, and dwarf willows regenerated relatively rapidly in spite of the short growing season. Some of the growing herbaceous and shrubby plants, accustomed to summer frosts, had only been set back, not killed, by the nuclear winter and subsequent frosty summers.

Forests returned slowly, since many trees require more than a decade to   18
complete a generation. In the West, aspens from the coastal refugia and from surviving roots spread in a few hundred years to cover large portions of their previous range. Simultaneously, scrubby Gambel's oak reappeared and formed dense local stands. No significant herbivores took advantage of the oak's periodic years of heavy acorn production; concomitantly, relatively few animals were available to disperse the acorns until feral rat populations began to transport and store them. Then the oaks spread rapidly.

In the East, the turkey oak, a denizer of poor soils, underwent a similar   19
explosion. Several species of wind-pollinated pines also made a comeback. Widespread, previously common species—white and southern pines in the East, and piñon, lodgepole, and ponderosa in the West—were the most successful.

Vegetation recovered most slowly in the subtropical and tropical areas.   20
There, wherever intense cold had prevailed, virtually all the plants—like the animals—had been destroyed. Most species could not tolerate chilling even to a few degrees *above* freezing, and their seeds were not cold hardy. Those plants that survived in refugia began gradually to spread into the debris-littered wastelands, but progress was slow—especially for the many plants that depended on now-extinct animals to disperse their seeds. This was much more important in tropical than in temperate ecosystems.

The first animals to repopulate substantial areas of North America were   21
also "weeds." Roaches, rats, and houseflies suffered setbacks in the early years, but they persisted and increased, free of significant natural enemies and able to feed on a variety of plant materials and organic debris. Crickets and grasshoppers, both relatively generalized feeders, spread back fast from coastal refugia. Fire ants, having taken in stride massive attacks with pesticides before the war, survived the ultimate human assault in pockets along the Gulf Coast and spread once more over what had been the southeastern United States. As the flora recovered, snowshoe hares reinvaded much of their old territory, fanning out from surviving northwestern populations

and reaching the east coast in a few hundred years. They renewed their famous cycling behavior—population outbreaks followed by crashes. That they did so in the total absence of their lynx predators (long thought to have been a cause of the cycles) would have fascinated population biologists—if there had been any around.

The first predators to reoccupy the desolate areas were spiders, balloon- 22
ing in from refugia and emerging from underground burrows. Coyotes also thrived, learning to hunt the rats and following the spreading front of snowshoe hares. Wolves faded away: there were too few survivors. Because of the vagaries of fallout patterns, wolves had suffered more than most species from radiation effects, and they did not successfully adapt to a diet of rats and hares.

A casual observer might have missed the most significant change in 23
predator trophic levels: the near absence of predacious and parasitic insects. The impact of toxins from the war, together with the cold, was similar to spraying the entire continent with insecticides. In many cases, the smaller populations at the predator trophic levels died off even though their plant-eating insect hosts had survived. One result was huge outbreaks of locusts, gypsy moths, cutworms, and Japanese beetles, which decimated the foliage over large areas. Another was that some previously rare herbivorous in-sects, freed from natural controls, developed huge, destructive populations, just as new pests had often been created by the misuse of pesticides before the war.

Although most insectivorous birds were extinct, cattle egrets, dining on 24
the larger insects, gradually spread throughout North America. They were joined by ravens, crows, starlings, and gulls, all of which shifted their diets to a heavy emphasis on insects. Robins also reinvaded from refugia, but in the absence of lawns and with a severe shortage of earthworms, their populations grew with glacial slowness.

Some three thousand years after the war, the first human beings set foot 25
on what had once been the United States. A handful of people had persisted through the postwar chaos in the Southern Hemisphere; the scattered groups of survivors had not all dwindled to extinction as many biologists had feared they might. But all had reverted to subsistence farming, mostly with stone and wooden implements. Most libraries had been destroyed by the war or in the subsequent social breakdown; the few that remained decayed in the deserted cities. People had had no time to preserve cultural artifacts that were peripheral to the daily struggle for existence.

Almost three thousand years elapsed before human populations grew 26
large enough to form small, rudimentary cities and to begin exploratory

moves into the mysterious and devastated North. Both the knowledge and the implements of industrial civilization were long gone. The new pioneers came in simple sailboats, moving along the Gulf Coast into ex-Texas. Over the next several millennia, they repopulated the transformed continent, farming the primitive maize and potato strains they had brought with them; hunting rats, hares, muskrats, beavers, and coyotes; and gathering locusts. Deer had not survived in North America, and the few that did in South America had been hunted to extinction.

To its prewar residents, North America of the year 5000 would have   27
seemed a strange and unstable land indeed. Populations of the commonest organisms were still fluctuating violently. When grasshoppers had a good sequence of years, hordes of ravens, crows, starlings, gulls, and egrets made the vast plains a study in black and white. Then, as the foliage was exhausted, the grasshoppers died out, the birds succumbed or moved on, and dust storms swept the land—often leading to many decades of desolation before plants restored the ground cover.

Biologists transported in time would have been depressed at the low   28
diversity in forests, grasslands, and deserts, but they would have been astounded at some of the organisms in abundance. Eastern diamondback rattlesnakes were everywhere, having spread from their Florida refugia and adapted to colder climates while feasting on rats. Monarch butterflies and tiger swallowtails were nowhere to be seen. The most common butterfly on the eastern coast was *Cissia joyceae,* an attractive little wood nymph once known from only a single specimen from Costa Rica. With unusual rapidity, it had evolved the ability to pass winters as a caterpillar in diapause and now had several generations a year, thriving on a diet of grasses.

In the West, a tiny beige hairstreak butterfly, *Strymon avalona,* survived   29
the war on Santa Catalina Island, to which it had previously been restricted. The hairstreak crossed to the mainland after the war and became widespread and common. It too evolved a broadened diet, thriving on locoweeds, vetches, and other weedy plants, as well as on lupines, which had become extremely common as disturbances remained widespread.

Giant land snails and walking catfishes had become prominent features   30
of the warmer parts of the continent. These were not strange mutants but simply exotic organisms that had gained a foothold before the war. Such tough, competitive organisms had become dominant in the absence of many previous predators and competitors. Indeed, contrary to popular mythology, increased mutation rates due to high levels of ionizing radiation had not significantly speeded evolution. Prewar mutation rates and genetic recombination had provided all the genetic variability needed for evolution to

proceed rapidly under strong selection pressures. The genetic damage done by radiation-induced mutations only weakened populations; the mutations did not produce any "hopeful monsters" that rapidly replaced previous types.

Only minor evolutionary changes occurred during the time between the   31
war and the human reinvasion. Resistance to pesticides, for example, which had been common in the old days, disappeared. Some specialists broadened their niches. Camouflage and other protective mechanisms of many smaller insects declined because the previous great diversity of insectivorous birds—including most of the species that searched carefully for their prey—had been largely lost. Three millennia had not been enough time for North American ecosystems to make substantial evolutionary progress toward rediversifying the biota. That would require a thousandfold greater time.

Homo sapiens was barred from one cultural evolutionary course it had   32
once taken. The human groups that went through the first industrial revolution had thoroughly depleted the nonrenewable resources of the plant before they blew it up. No nearly pure copper lay around on the surface as it had in the Old Stone Age; it had to be extracted by the smelting of low-grade ores. Oil could no longer be had by drilling down a few feet; it could be obtained only by drilling several thousand feet. High technology was required to obtain the resources needed by technological civilization. And high technology did not exist in the postwar Stone Age.

The war and its aftermath had destroyed most of the stocks of resources   33
and much of the knowledge of how to use them. During the millennia that followed, while *Homo sapiens* barely hung on, remaining stockpiles of materials rusted away, decayed, and dispersed—and scientific knowledge was forgotten. Whether this was a blessing or curse might have been debated if there were time travelers, but the result was final. The technology that had produced automobiles, airplanes, television, computers, ICBMs, and thermonuclear devices would never be regained.

QUESTIONS ON MEANING AND CONTENT

1. Before you had read the essay, what would you have included in a list of the twenty or twenty-five most important things on this planet? (Don't include abstract things or forms of behavior—for example, a better understanding of each other. Save those for another list.) List only things you can see or touch. After reading the essay, how would you revise your list?

2. As you began to read the essay did you expect to find descriptions of the destruction of cities, factories, institutions, and so forth and more references to how people perished? Why do you suppose these are missing? What does their absence tell us about the author? If you had expected such descriptions, what does that tell you about yourself?

3. In paragraph 31, Ehrlich refers to the "new pioneers" coming to Texas by sailboat as "the human reinvasion." How do you react to his word choice, which suggests that when human beings first came to the North American continent, they were *invading* then also? Usually we use the word *invasion* in relation to enemies. Do you think Ehrlich chose the word consciously? If so, what does he mean? Had you written this piece, would the use of the word have occurred to you? Would you have used it? Explain.

4. At one point, the author says that biologists—had they been there to observe—"would have been astounded at some of the organisms in abundance." Are you surprised by some of the survivors?

5. Some plants, animals, insects, and so on, that humans have felt favorable toward do survive in Ehrlich's scenario. But they are outnumbered by the ones we have tended to scorn or tried to stamp out. How can you explain this?

6. Occasionally the author accounts for something that survived or disappeared by referring to "the vagaries of fallout patterns." Because fallout patterns would not be entirely predictable, the survivors and victims after an actual nuclear war might differ somewhat in places from the account offered here. How much would this affect the total picture? Explain.

7. One of the ironies in the essay is that all the products of modern technology that we had taken so seriously have disappeared from North America, and the people who migrate here from the southern hemisphere bring no modern technology with them. Yet they arrive in simple sail boats, a means of harnessing natural energy that had been preserved by our technological culture mostly as an expensive toy to be used for diversion, for play. Can you think of other primitive "toys" preserved by us for leisure and recreation that might be useful after nuclear devastation? Does the essay or its details suggest other ironies to you?

8. At the conclusion, the author says that the technology we had developed will never be regained. Yet human beings are already on the scene, busy with their primitive farming. Do you think Ehrlich is right? Why or why not?

9. The author begins by saying that "humanity's luck ran out," but beyond that he offers no interpretations, does not use emotional words like *terrible* or *horrible* or *tragic*. Do you think this is so because Ehrlich is taking an objective, scientific view? Or would a professional writer—after studying the likely effects of nuclear war—have done the same? Why or why not? To what degree does this objective presentation arouse your emotions?

QUESTIONS ABOUT RHETORICAL STRATEGIES

1. The author relates the narrative as an observer looking on from a distance, one able to see everything that has taken place. Since no one on the continent survived the war, it would be impossible to have a first-person narrator. Nevertheless, if one had survived and the essay covered less time, why would a first-person narrator still be a poor choice? Or, if you don't think this would be a poor choice, what limitations would first person impose on the writer?

2. The narrative begins by describing a catastrophic event and then is organized in a pattern following the passage of time—as you would expect in a narrative. The paragraph openings throughout the essay make the organizational pattern clear, with references to advancing time providing the transitions that move the narrative forward. Each transitional reference to time is followed by a paragraph or block of paragraphs describing conditions and noting the changes taking place during that time. However, notice how much space is devoted to the short time span immediately following the war. The first fourteen paragraphs carry the narrative only to the end of the first postwar summer. Then paragraph 15, which is short, covers several years; paragraph 16 begins, "Over the next decades." Soon the references are to thousands of years.

Why does the narrative move so slowly through time at first and then begin to leap foward, spanning much larger blocks of time in much less space? Could the author have handled his materials differently? Would you have wanted him to? Do you think a book length narrative on the same subject would follow this same pattern?

QUESTIONS ON LANGUAGE AND DICTION

1. What are the meanings of *ameliorated, boreal, decimated, denizens, diapause, fauna, feral, gradient, metabolic rates, mutants, rudimentary, sedges, vagaries, vestiges?*

WRITING SCENARIOS

1. Your best friend has moved to another state, but you have managed to stay in contact with one another through frequent letters. In fact, you often compete with one another, trying to write the most interesting letters. You have decided to write a narrative about an experience of yours, prefer- ably one that involved dangers and could have ended much more seriously than it did. You wish to emphasize the harrowing nature of the experience because you want to *entertain* your friend. (As an additional assignment, write about the same subject, but the audience for the second account is your father or mother, or both. Although you want them to know about the experience, you don't wish to alarm them or make them worry about you excessively. Thus, you will present the experience in a way that will inform but avoid any emphasis that would generate too much concern for your future safety.)

2. The editors of the student literary magazine on your campus are interested in publishing a few interesting narrative essays. You have de- cided to write an essay about some event that you knew was going to take place and which you had to wait for with some fear or apprehension. Ideally, the event would have the following stages: stage 1 in which you await the event; stage 2, in which the event begins and then takes place; and stage 3, in which the event ends. (Each stage may also have substages within stages.) A flood or a storm would frequently have these three stages, as would a confrontation between you and someone else. Organize your paper accord- ing to the stages, but modify the organization according to the event itself or the emphasis you wish to give the event. You want your narrative to create tension and then release the tension, roughly on the pattern of the piece on the A-bomb by Phillips and Michaelis. Thus, the most dramatic part of the experience will tell you what to emphasize. You may wish to emphasize that the anticipation was more fearful than the event itself; on the other hand, something like a flood would emphasize the event, and the tension release could come as the waters finally begin to recede. In any case, let the event and the emphasis determine organization. Your readers are students in- terested in a good story.

3. The department of health sciences at your college is sponsoring a "handicap awareness day" on your campus. The object of the event is to educate people to the problems and concerns of handicapped citizens. Your favorite professor, one of the organizers of the event, has asked you to participate because she is impressed with your writing abilities. First, she has asked you to spend at least five or six hours, preferably longer, as a handicapped person. (In some cases this will require the cooperation of someone else, preferably another class member who is working on the same assignment and who will need similar assistance from you.) You plan to spend time as a person without sight. This will require a blindfold and a helper to be with you at all times. You should try to do the things you ordinarily do, including fairly complex activities, such as eating, showering, brushing your teeth, getting into and out of a car, "listening" to a TV show, and so on. Your narrative, which will be published in the student newspaper, will recount the day's experiences, and your audience will be people who have sight. You will show how your "eyes were opened" by the experience, even though such a short experience may give you only a small sense of what it is like to be blind. Nevertheless, a small sense can fill a very large sensitivity gap.

4. A local historian is writing a book containing many of the legends and folk tales of your state. She has asked you to write a narrative that retells a legend well-known to your family, friends, or people in your community. Ideally, the legend should be considered true by most of the people who know it, and perhaps it is best if you believe it yourself. The legend may involve someone you know or are related to, or it may not. Many families, both rural and urban, pass down such legends because they involved relatives or allegedly happened in places where they had lived. Many such legends, especially the rural ones, have been recorded in folklore books. Recently, a large number of urban legends have been recorded by Jan Harold Brunvard in *The Vanishing Hitchhiker* (W. W. Norton & Co., 1981) and *The Choking Doberman* (W. W. Norton & Co., 1984). (If you choose to write on this topic, you might want to look through these books to see if your legend—or your version of it—appears there. This would be proof that the legend is widely known already.) Your legend need not be scary, although many are. It need only tell of something that someone did or something that happened to someone. Choose a topic that you believe readers would be interested in learning about. You can either assume a broad audience—since such legends are widely appealing—or you may assume a narrow audience, such as the residents of your state or community.

5. The editors of *People* magazine have decided to print in every issue a narrative about an exciting incident that happened to "ordinary people." To make this feature even more interesting, the editors have decided to ask "ordinary people" around the country to write the essays. You have been asked to select someone in your community who has had an interesting experience and to write a narrative about it. To prewrite for this assignment you will need to interview someone concerning a significant experience that person has had. Since you will want to generate reader interest, look for someone with an experience that was extremely puzzling, odd, or danger-

ous. (If you don't already know of someone who has had such an experience, you may ask friends or relatives about their experiences or whether they know of someone who has had such an experience. For example, you may decide to interview a police officer, a firefighter, a pilot, a doctor, a nurse, a cab driver, a paramedic, a Vietnam veteran, a World War II or Korean War veteran, a crime victim, or someone who has been arrested.)

Be sure to ask questions that will reveal highlights of how the person reacted to or sensed the experience as it took place. The sense experiences that stay in the memory after the experience is over can say something important about the nature of the experience. So, you will want to be sensitive to sight, sound, smell, and *kinesthetic* feeling (the feeling of movement, of being jarred around in an accident, for example).

Ask yourself questions about the experience, too. Is the experience sufficient by itself; is it sufficiently frightening or exciting to stand alone? If so, you may want to build your narrative toward the most dramatic moment of the experience. Most experiences, however, will illustrate some point. For example, F. Lee Bailey's experience in the Sabrejet is dramatic, but it also shows what being alone really means and suggests that criminal lawyers should "know" the meaning of *alone* before they begin to practice criminal law; and Simon Girty, the speaker in "Late Summer 1756" is relating the experience that changed his life. What does the experience you are writing about illustrate? An insight that came to the person as a result of the experience? A lesson learned? Some new awareness? A moral?

In general, your readers are those who read *People* magazine, especially that vast group who like to experience things vicariously. Also, though, you will be writing to readers who have a special interest in the person who has undergone the experience—that is, relatives and friends of the person. For these people, the experience you relate will have importance, but they will also have a very strong interest in the person. Thus, the person will be as important to this audience as the experience. For example, a reader strongly opposed to war would probably still be interested in reading about an experience drawn from war if the experience was that of a great-grandfather or other relative.

THREE

DESCRIBING

Description is probably the rhetorical strategy that you are most familiar with. Description is the act of using words to depict some person, place, or thing. The word *describe* means literally to "copy off" and to "sketch in writing or painting." You can describe concrete things, such as your new stereo and your favorite fishing hole, or abstract things, such as how you felt when you won the state beauty pageant.

We all use description in our everyday transactions. When you tell a friend about the beautiful beach that you visited last weekend and explain how the beach looks and *why* it is beautiful to you, you are describing. When you try to create for your children a verbal picture of your deceased grandmother, you are describing. In other words, description is the process of making something vivid for the reader or listener, of using words to help someone visualize something he or she is unable to see or experience in person.

You can describe just about anything. You can tell someone of the intense reds and oranges of last night's sunset, or of the silky brown hair of your newest date. In fact, description is such a common and important strategy that it is difficult to imagine a piece of writing containing no description at all. Often description is used as a prelude to other strategies. For example, you might decide to begin a narrative essay about your visit to the beach by first describing how beautiful the beach was. Or, you might begin an essay comparing and contrasting your home town to the town where your college is located by first *describing* the two locations. Description is particularly useful in such cases because it helps your reader understand something in the same way that you do. In other words, in describing you try to get readers to perceive a subject exactly as you do. For example, if you want to depict the beach as a very pleasant and peaceful place, you might tell the reader about the softly rolling waves, the pure white sand, and the frequent gentle breezes. On the other hand, if your vacation was not entirely enjoyable and you want to describe why, you might mention the candy wrappers littering the beach, the roasting sun, and the confusing chatter of portable radios all tuned to different stations. Clearly, you can use description to convey to readers your personal view of the subject you are discussing; this is why description plays such an important role in so many written documents.

While narration emphasizes actions and a series of events, description emphasizes what something looks, feels, smells, sounds, or tastes like. While narration emphasizes verbs and adverbs, description makes more use of adjectives and nouns. While narration is concerned with events happening in *time,* description is more concerned with how things are arranged in *space.* A good description captures your subject at one moment in time just as a good photograph might.

As with most of the rhetorical strategies discussed in this book, description can be used as a strategy within a larger piece of prose, or it can be the dominant framework for a single piece of writing. Generally, there are two types of description: objective and subjective. *Objective* description is prose in which your own personal feelings about a subject do not come into play. You use objective description most often in business, technical, or scientific reports in which you must provide detailed factual pictures of certain items. For example, a technical writer might prepare a manual for new employees that describes several pieces of machinery and then explains how to use the equipment. In such a case, the descriptions are purely factual and would not reveal the author's opinions or prejudices about the equipment. Or, a journalist might describe a huge inner-city fire without introducing his or her own feelings about the blaze.

Subjective description, on the other hand, is impressionistic, vivid, and personal. It depicts a person, place, or thing in such a way that the author's feelings about the subject are quite clear to the reader. For example, another journalist might describe the same downtown fire in a subjective way, writing about "a tragic and senseless blaze," and "the most terrifying fire" he or she "had ever witnessed." Clearly, the same subject can be treated in one or both ways. You base such a decision on the purpose of and audience for your particular essay.

In many ways, subjective description goes *beyond* objective description because it not only provides a factual perspective of a subject but also reveals the author's personal feelings toward that subject. In subjective description, you are most likely to use the most vivid words and phrases as well as language rich in emotion and connotation.

PREWRITING

Your objective in writing any type of descriptive prose is to get your reader to *visualize* and sometimes acquire a *feeling* for some person, place, or thing. In order to achieve this objective you will need to include a great deal of descriptive details so that your readers can form an accurate picture of your subject. As a result, **prewriting** is particularly important when describing.

A good way to begin your prewriting, is to examine your subject closely. If possible, take notes while you are looking at your subject, just as an artist might draw a quick sketch of a subject that he or she will later paint. This direction observation is important because when you are describing you are using one or more of your five senses to help you illustrate your subject to your reader. If you begin your prewriting by actually looking at your subject, you will be able to take down many visual and other sensory details that you might have forgotten if you simply had tried to remember what your subject looked like.

When describing you will want to pay particular attention to details that relate to the five senses. What shapes and colors do you see? What sounds do you hear? What texture does your subject have? Are there any relevant aromas or tastes associated with your subject? Jot down on your prewriting notes all the sensory data that you can. It is not necessary to make a judgment at this point about whether or not you should include certain items in your paper. Instead, simply jot down every fact and detail about your subject that comes to mind.

Of course, if you cannot examine your subject close up, you will have to try to visualize it with your mind's eye. Perhaps you should close your eyes and imagine yourself looking at your subject. Try to imagine yourself there for a full minute. Then, in your prewriting notes, record all of the data about your subject that you can remember.

Whether you are *brainstorming* or looking right at your subject, you should look especially for those features of your subject that are unique. What makes your subject stand out from other, similar things? The beach where you spent your summer vacation, for example, might have an impressive sand bar stretching far into the ocean. Or, the favorite teacher whom you are describing might have a unique mannerism that sets her apart from all your other instructors. Always try to locate the special features of your subject; they will help to make the subject especially vivid and recognizable to your readers.

Also, try to be as specific as possible in recording these details. For instance, it isn't enough to say that "the sunset was beautiful," when you can say, "the sunset was beautiful because of the intense red and orange streaks stretching across the horizon." In fact, it may be best to forget the word *beautiful* and emphasize the details that made it beautiful to you: ". . . intense red and orange streaks stretched majestically across the horizon." If you have described effectively, the reader will know the sky was beautiful. The key to good description is in finding exact and specific details that help the reader form a picture of your subject. The word *beautiful* in the first example above does not help a reader form an exact picture of anything because the reader must fill in the blank that *beautiful* leaves. However, when you mention the orange and red streaks stretching across the sky, the reader has a more precise picture of your subject and can begin to visualize it in a more accurate way. In other words, when prewriting for your descriptive essay, you are looking for the most precise, accurate, and vivid details. You do not want words that only portray a hazy, fuzzy image of your subject.

Besides observing your subject and brainstorming about it, you may also want to spend five or ten minutes *freewriting*. That is, while timing yourself, write quickly and spontaneously. Then, you can extract from your freewrite any additional details about your subject and add them to your prewriting notes.

Finally, you may be able to generate additional information for your essay by answering any relevant questions in the heuristic that follows. It should help you prewrite for your essay.

Simply jot down answers to these questions on your prewriting notes. You should be as specific as possible, but feel free to abbreviate and take shortcuts. Since no one will read these notes but yourself, you need not worry about writing in full sentences or with neat penmanship. Instead, you should be most concerned with generating as much specific information as possible.

Prewriting Questions for Description

1. What is the *main point* or *general impression* I am trying to convey to my readers?
2. What is the *purpose* of my descriptive essay?
3. Who will read my essay and why?
4. What do I want my readers to *feel* and *understand* about my subject, or do I want them just to see the subject as it is, objectively?
5. What does my subject *look* like?
6. What color is it?
7. What size is it?
8. What familiar thing is it like?
9. What does it *feel* like?
10. Does it have a unique texture?
11. If it is a *place,* where is it located?
12. If it is a *person,* what special characteristics or behavior distinguish that person?
13. If it is a *concept* or *feeling,* what concrete details will help readers understand it?
14. Are there any unique but relevant *sounds* or *tastes* associated with my subject?
15. Are there any unique but relevant *smells* associated with my subject?
16. What are the most important and unique *visual* aspects of my subject?
17. Which of these specific details will best help me convey my general impression or main point to my readers?
18. Which details *will not* help?
19. Which details should I place special emphasis on?
20. What words best describe the various parts of my subject?
21. How should I organize my essay?
22. Should I describe my subject as a *stationary observer* or as a *mobile observer?*

ORGANIZING

As in any good piece of prose, **organization** is an important factor. After you have prewritten for your descriptive essay, you will want to devise an organizing scheme that best gets your points across to your reader. It is advisable to avoid the type of organizing some writers attempt: They describe the subject by listing whatever details come to mind in whatever order. Instead, an effective descriptive essay has a clear and definite order.

While the typical organizing plan for a *narrative* essay is *temporal* (following some kind of order in time), the typical organizing scheme in descriptive essays is *spatial* (following some kind of order in space). Most often, writers of descriptive essays will describe their subjects by using some kind of geographical pattern. For example, if you were describing your college dorm room, you might begin at the doorway, discuss the objects near the right wall, mention the items near the back wall, and end with the objects near the left wall. In such a case, there's a clear order for the reader; it is as if the reader were standing in the doorway and his or her eyes were traveling from right to left. When you use this type of geographical organizing scheme, you are said to be a *stationary* (or *fixed*) *observer*. This term refers to the fact that an observer can take in the entire description by standing in one location and allowing his or her eyes to examine objects across the entire location.

A spatial description can proceed from any point to another point so long as it follows a clear pattern. You may move from right to left, from top to bottom, from back to front, or from important object to important object. The pattern you choose, of course, will depend on your subject and what point you are trying to get across to your readers. Try to describe your subject in such a way that your readers do not become confused with all the details. Having a clear spatial pattern will help readers understand the subject better than if you had no apparent order.

Sometimes you may decide to describe a subject as a *mobile observer*: an observer that moves from point to point around the subject that you are describing. For example, if you were describing your college campus, you might move from location to location as if you were walking or driving around the campus encountering the important points of interest. Neither format—describing as a stationary or mobile observer—is inherently better than the other. Generally, you will want to describe smaller places as a stationary observer and larger, open locations as a mobile observer. Your decision about which format to use should be based on your subject, the purpose of your essay, and who will read it.

Although you will be providing many details about your subject, you will want to make sure that your essay conveys *one major impression* to your reader. You probably will decide what this impression should be during your prewriting activities, but you will want to make sure that your organizing scheme helps to convey this particular impression. For example, if you are describing your dorm room, you may wish to convey the general impression that this room is warm and friendly and is a place you look forward to returning to after a hard day of classes. Or, you may wish to convey the impression that the painted cinder block walls and the one small window only produce a feeling of coldness and loneliness. Whatever the feeling you are trying to transmit, you will want to make sure that your details and the way that you arrange them help to make your readers feel or comprehend that impression. As a result, it is best to be particularly selective about which details you include in your essay and which you do not. For example, if you are describing your car as a vehicle that is dependable but not very fast, you may decide not to mention that occasionally it fails to start in the morning. Choose the details that most effectively help you transmit your main idea to your reader. Or, you may be writing a letter to your parents to describe the new apartment that you and your friend have just rented. Your general impression may be that the apartment is a safe and clean one; therefore you would not want to mention the fact that roaches conquer the kitchen every night and occasionally a field mouse scampers across the bedroom floor. Instead, you would want to concentrate on the sparkling bathroom, the modern sprinkler system, and the excellent security system in the building. Thus, in devising an organizing scheme, it is important to be selective; remember your purpose and audience.

WRITING

Once you are satisfied that you have sufficient relevant details about your subject and an organizing scheme that will help your paper effectively convey one general impression, you will want to begin **writing** your essay. As usual, try to write your first draft as rapidly as possible, paying close attention to your prewriting and organizing notes. If while writing your draft you find that your prewriting notes are incomplete or that your organizing plan is not appropriate, you may want to stop writing and do some additional prewriting or organizing.

Remember that your objective in writing a descriptive essay is to convey a major point to your readers. As you are composing, you will want to make sure that each paragraph contributes substantially to that point. Does the paragraph establish a point or discuss an aspect of your subject that clearly supports your main point? Are you including enough details and examples to make these aspects or subpoints clear? It is easy to forget that as the author you have seen and experienced your subject; don't presume too much of your readers.

The success of your essay will depend, among other things, on your understanding of your audience. It is important to determine how much and what kind of information your readers will need in order to understand your point fully. If you are describing your dorm room to other students who are familiar with the dormitories on your campus, you may wish to omit certain *general* details about your subject. If, however, your audience is wider, you will want to include such information. Ask yourself: "What does my audience already know about my subject? Am I discussing a subject that is commonly known [Christmas trees, for example], or one that is not so familiar [my favorite vacation hideaway]?" Having a clear concept of audience will help you compose more effectively during the writing stage.

Finally, while you are writing keep in mind that the most successful description is that which goes beyond *telling* readers what something looks like; it *shows* them. You don't want to *tell* your readers, "My grandmother's face began to show signs of old age" when you can *show* them:

> Distinct lines began to stretch across my grandmother's forehead. Her eyes were puffy and red, and wrinkles crisscrossed her loving face like highways on a road map. She was growing old.

You don't want to say, "My doberman is big" when you can show it:

> My doberman is so big that when she stands on her hind paws she can rest her front ones comfortably on my father's shoulders.

Every subject you describe will have its unique characteristics; your task is to accentuate them, show how your subject is special.

REVISING

As we have said and will continue to say many times in this text, the key to effective writing lies in large part with how well you **revise.** We urge you to spend sufficient time and effort in *rewriting* your descriptive essay several times after you have completed your first draft.

A good first step is to read through your essay carefully and determine whether your organizing scheme is an effective one. Is there a clear thesis statement that the paragraphs of your essay clearly support? Also, you will want to make sure your paper conveys one general point or impression about your subject. In other words, determine whether the larger aspects of your essay are adequate for your purpose and audience.

After you have read through your paper once, looking at the larger items, you are ready to proceed through your essay sentence by sentence, weighing and judging each sentence. Try to determine if the sentence (and the paragraph it is in) adequately describes the part of your subject that you are discussing. Are you presuming too much of your readers? Should you add additional information that will help the readers see or feel that aspect of your subject? Have you included details that are not essential or that do *not* help your reader understand a certain aspect of your subject? Does each sentence convey the *exact* message you had intended, or have you inadvertently phrased your sentence in such a way that readers can get meanings different from the one that you had originally intended? After examining and weighing each sentence, write each sentence onto a new page in the best possible language that you can compose until you have rewritten your entire essay. Remember to revise your essay in this fashion several times.

One of the most important devices for revising a descriptive essay is to try to imagine that you have never seen your subject before. Then, from the prose on the paper *as you have written it,* ask yourself, "Can I clearly visualize my subject *from the descriptions I've provided*?" In other words, will your readers be able to picture your subject exactly as you want them to. This procedure of switching roles is difficult to accomplish, but it will prove to be one of the most effective ways of improving your descriptive paper. You must, of course, be honest with yourself. If you honestly cannot visualize the part of your subject discussed in a certain paragraph, then you will want to add and delete material from that paragraph until your reader would get the proper message. This type of role playing takes practice, but once you have mastered it you will find that your revising will become much easier.

While you are revising, you will want to pay particular attention to how your essay conveys information from the senses. Have you been able to integrate any relevant sounds or aromas into the essay? If so, are these details specific enough to help your readers experience your subject? In other words, are you *telling* your readers or *showing* them? Have you said, "The mixture of aromas from the cafeteria confused my senses" when you could have said,

The pungent smell of sauerkraut and fish, mixed with the sweet aroma of apple pie and fudge brownies, and the smoky smell of hot dogs and baked beans confused my senses.

Have you said that "The crowd in the football stadium gave out a roar," when you could have said,

> The tumultuous screams and cheers of 50,000 Florida State fans combined to produce one deafening roar.

Remember to pay particular attention to *how* you have phrased such important descriptive details.

PROOFREADING

Despite the kind of essay you have written, your **proofreading** tasks will remain the same. By the time you begin to proofread, you should have already taken care of the largest aspects of your descriptive essay; you should have made sure it contains a clear thesis statement, an effective organizing plan, adequate transitions, and clear, vivid language. Now you will want to check your spelling, punctuation, and grammar. Of course, throughout the entire writing process you may have caught and corrected several surface errors, but now you will want to make a special effort to locate any remaining problems. Remember, you need not worry about these issues during the writing or revising stages. But do not ignore them: A well-proofread paper will help you communicate to your readers without distraction.

After you have completed your descriptive essay, you may wish to refer to the Description Checklist below. This checklist will help you determine if you have forgotten any important aspects of your essay.

Description Checklist

1. Does your descriptive essay clearly convey one main point or general impression?
2. Does your introduction contain sufficient information to orient readers to your subject?
3. Have you directed your essay to your specific audience?
4. Is your descriptive essay organized in a logical way?
5. Have you described your subject consistently as either a *stationary* or *mobile* observer?
6. Have you included every important detail about your subject?

7. Can your readers truly visualize your subject from what you have written?

8. Have you presumed too much or too little of your readers?

9. Have you included sufficient *sensory data* about your subject?

10. In describing each aspect of your subject, do you merely *tell* your readers or do you *show* them?

11. Have you eliminated unimportant and irrelevant information?

12. Is your *exact* meaning clear in every sentence?

13. Are your descriptions clear and vivid or fuzzy and hazy?

14. Does your conclusion put your subject in perspective for your readers?

15. Have you spent enough time revising your descriptive essay?

16. Are your sentences grammatically correct?

17. Have you checked the punctuation of each sentence?

18. Have you checked your spelling?

Nightclub Cowboys

DIANE K. SHAH with RONALD HENKOFF

Gilley's is a huge nightclub in Pasadena, Texas, described here by one patron as "real down-home" and by the authors, in reference to what takes place there, as "more soap opera than horse opera." This descriptive essay takes the reader on a tour of the make-believe world of Gilley's—a world where the busy bar and dance floor serve as backdrops for males testing and showing off their masculinity on the mechanical bull, with the punching bags, or at the pool tables, hoping to impress each other and the female patrons looking on.

Once again Wesley (Tanker) Wells mounts the notorious bull. He tucks   1
his jeans into his genuine cowboy boots, tugs on his ten-gallon hat and coolly leans back for a ride. Suddenly, the big black beast starts thrashing wildly about. "C'mon, cowboy, ride that bull!" yells Debbie Smith, his latest honey-blond girlfriend. Bravely, Tanker stays with the bull, right hand grasping the curved backbone, face still impassive under the tall brown hat. Then the animal lurches and spins and—*oh-oh*—Tanker tumbles to the ground. Grinning, he rolls onto his feet and walks wobbly-legged to the sidelines. "You done real good, Tank," coos Debbie, who doesn't seem the least bit mindful that it was nothing but a $2 ride on a mechanical contraption.

FOOT-STOMPIN': So it goes at Gilley's, a gridiron-size nightclub (capacity: 2
5,500) in Pasadena, Texas, 10 miles south of Houston. Named after co-owner Mickey Gilley, a popular country singer, Gilley's is pure, foot-stompin' honky-tonk—a 48,000-square-foot cavern with bands, a ballroom-size dance floor, bars, pinball machines, pool tables and, of course, that bogus bull. Right now, the club stands at the brink of national notoriety: John Travolta is trying to master the mechanical monster for his role in "Urban Cowboy," a movie that Paramount Pictures will start filming at Gilley's this month.

For all its nascent fame, Gilley's has long been home to a flourishing   3
breed of drugstore cowboys, all bent on mimicking the macho mannerisms of their vanishing, real-life counterparts. Seven nights a week, they come swaggering in by the hundreds to quaff some Lone Star beer, test their manhood on the bull and maybe corral a good old girl. For every reputation

made on the bull, there is an ego bruised—not to mention other bodily parts. But no matter. Women, meanwhile, come in search of Mr. Goodbull. "Three weeks ago, I saw him riding it," sighs 19-year-old Debbie of Tanker. "Now we're together most all the time."

The capital of urban cowboyland attracts a remarkably diverse clientele. A few are genuine cowhands; others are executive types who shuck their three-piecers for a chance to dance the cotten-eyed Joe and the two-step. But the mainstays are young men who work in nearby refineries, shipyards and grain elevators, and women who toil as clerks and waitresses. "Mostly, that's what we get in here," shrugs Sherwood Cryer, manager and co-owner of Gilley's. "They work every day at some damn job. Then they come in here to drink and fight and chase girls."   4

NO SALE: The pickup action starts right in the entranceway. There the men, dressed to their sideburns in fancy, tooled boots, cowboy shirts and Stetsons, try out lines on women who sport ultratight jeans, abundant makeup and Farrah Fawcett hairdos. "Hey, how y'all doing?" one lone stranger greets two female arrivals. "If I come after you later, will y'all dance with me?" No sale—but further along, weekend regular Thomas Jordan has better luck with: "Hey there, pretty lady, I like that embroidery on them jeans." The passing redhead smiles. Jordan, who's taken to riding the bull with a red rose stuck in this teeth, seems equally pleased. "I've got 25 girlfriends," he boasts, "and I met 'em all here. These women are foxes. On a scale of 1 to 10, I'd rate them all a 15."   5

Gilley's is big enough to accommodate almost any urge—or deter it. One cowgirl makes her feelings known by her T shirt. It sports two strategically placed circles and the warning: "I'm perfectly adjusted, so don't touch the knobs." Nearby, a cowboy slumps at a table, slowly dropping beer bottles to the floor; not far away, a couple lean against the stage, locked in a passionate embrace. His name is Teddy (it says so on his belt), hers is Debby—and both are gloriously drunk. Later in the club's parking lot, they will become involved in a bellicose ten-person argument. The following night Teddy will again be stationed near the stage, wearing the same red and white cowboy shirt—but without Debby.   6

The scene at Gilley's, in fact, seems to be more soap opera than horse opera. Tanker, a 20-year-old welder who moved back in with his parents after his pet cougar bit a hole in his waterbed, has both a roving eye and a rigidly proprietary attitude toward his woman. A tall, would-be rival approaches Debbie in the middle of a pool game and delivers honky-tonk's cruelest insult: "Hey there, girl, what're you doing spending your time with that Rexall cowboy?" Tanker slams down his pool cue and glares at the   7 offender, who, after some soul-searching, turns on his heels and stalks away.

To divert such aggressions into peaceful channels, the management has   8
installed mechanical punching bags. Each is hooked up to a large dial that measures how hard a punch is thrown. Three punches cost a quarter, and some cowboys stand around all night dropping coins and swinging fists— only to cause another headache. "When I first installed the bags," says Cryer, "the gals kept pulling out the cords because the boys wouldn't dance. I don't know what it is with some of these cowboys. They just stay bunched up most of the time and leave those old girls alone."

WAR WOUNDS: The life-size mechanical bull is a more formidable ad-   9
versary; unlike a bucking bronco, it never tires. It has thirteen speeds and its movements are controlled by a single lever, which is mercilessly operated by former rodeo champ Steve Strange. Very few people ever achieve higher than a 7 speed, and almost everyone finally falls off. A second, less spirited bull has recently been added, but injuries from the first are not uncommon, and are displayed as if they were war wounds. Tanker once landed on his head—before they put down enough mattresses—and suffered a concussion. He came away from another spill with two broken ribs. Two nights after breaking her foot, a girl named Becky Walker was back on the bull wearing a cast. Recently, Jessie LaRive, a determined-looking lady with short hair and green eye shadow, rode the bull right up to its top speed. Jessie was eight months pregnant. "That baby's gonna be tough." she predicts.

Like the country ballads that infuse it, the life of a drugstore cowboy is a   10
series of abrupt ups and downs—each absorbed with an unflappable fatalism. Marion Dulin, a Gilley's patron for three years, found her car tires slashed one night, and suspects it was done by some cowboy whose invitation she had refused. But to the pretty flower-shop clerk, a slashed tire here and there is not too big a price to pay. "Other clubs are commercial," she shrugs. "But this place is real down-home."

QUESTIONS ON MEANING AND CONTENT

1. In the opening paragraph, the authors describe riding the bull as "nothing but a $2 ride on a mechanical contraption." But doesn't riding the bull represent something more to Gilley's patrons than "a $2 ride on a mechanical contraption"? What? Which do you consider the more accurate view, the authors' or the patrons'? Why?

2. The supreme insult at Gilley's is to call a male patron a "Rexall cowboy." Since many of the men there are drugstore or urban cowboys, why would they be so sensitive about this name? Or is this kind of sensitivity simply a necessary ingredient for anyone indulging in illusions? As the authors describe Gilley's, to what extent is it real? Or is Gilley's a pure fantasyland?

3. Tanker Wells seems to be hard, masculine, and capable. He works as a welder. He continues to ride the bull despite having suffered a concussion from one spill and two broken ribs from another. To drive a rival away from Debbie, he merely "slams down his pool cue and glares." He keeps a cougar as a pet. Yet when the cougar bites through his water bed, he moves back home with his parents. This seems out of character, ironic, almost pathetically contradictory. Offer an explanation for this. What other contradictions are suggested by the descriptions in the piece?

4. If you have read Harry Crews' descriptive essay, "The Car," in this section, consider this question: With what are Gilley's patrons confusing themselves?

QUESTIONS ABOUT RHETORICAL STRATEGIES

1. The authors' descriptions express an attitude toward Gilley's and its patrons, an attitude that establishes the tone of the essay. What is the tone of the essay? Point to details that create and illustrate the tone.

2. In the essay the authors frequently quote what various patrons have said. This allows the people to describe themselves, both through the language they use and what they say. What pictures of the patrons do you get from the quotations? What do these quotations contribute to the overall picture that emerges of Gilley's?

QUESTIONS ON LANGUAGE AND DICTION

1. There is much evidence in the essay to show that the authors enjoy playing with words—"bogus bull," "mimicking the macho mannerisms," for example. What are other examples? Do these expressions add either to the descriptive qualities of the essay or to its tone? How?

2. What is meant by the phrase "unflappable fatalism," used in the final paragraph?

3. What are the meanings of *bellicose* and *proprietary*?

Victims of Mount Vesuvius

SHARON BEGLEY with MARY HAGER

This essay combines objective and subjective description to show the historical and scientific importance of the excavations of a city buried by volcanic eruptions, and offers glimpses of people caught by sudden catastrophe while going about their daily activities.

The ground had trembled for four days along the shore of the Bay of   1
Naples, but when the sun rose over the meadows of Mount Vesuvius on
Aug. 24, A.D. 79, none of the 4,000 residents of Herculaneum suspected that
it would be a fateful morning. In a sumptuous house near the forum, a slave
began unpacking a crate of glassware nestled in straw; on a business street,
baker Sextus Patulcus had just set our loaves of bread, pizzas, and pastries
imprinted with his initials. Suddenly, with a blast 10 times more powerful
than the explosion at Mount St. Helens two years ago, Vesuvius erupted. By
the next day Herculaneum and Pompeii, a city of perhaps 25,000, were dead
and buried in volcanic ash.

Although debris preserved both cities like flies in amber, Pompeii has   2
always attracted the most archeological attention. Now Herculaneum is
catching up. Two years ago archeologists uncovered four skeletons outside
the town. Last week the National Geographic Society announced that an
expedition had unearthed the largest cache ever of Roman skeletons—80 in
all—and with them a fossilized chunk of history. "Who says dead men
don't talk?" asked anthropologist Sara Bisel, who is analyzing the bones.
"These bones have something to say about the people's everyday life."

Preserved: The skeletons suggest that the citizens of Herculaneum were   3
short by today's standards: the average height for men was about 5 foot 7, for
women just under 5 foot 2. Their teeth were in good shape, and only four
skeletons showed signs of even mild arthritis. Bisel, who has removed 36
skeletons (20 men, 6 women, 10 children) and preserved them in acrylic,
reports that five had suffered traumatic injuries such as broken bones, blood
clots and sword wounds. She has also determined how physically fit the
victims were: the skeleton of a soldier has enlarged arm bones, probably
from lifting a shield and hurling a javelin, and its knee joints reveal the
musculature of a horseman. After scientists analyze the chemical content of
the bones, they will be able to piece together a typical Roman diet: meat and

vegetables leave different traces of the metals strontium and calcium in bones.

In a letter to the historian Tacitus, Pliny the Younger gave a vivid account   4
of the eruption from which modern volcanologists, studying the debris overlying Herculaneum, have reconstructed the events of that fateful August. The first eruption sent a column of ash and pumice 12 miles high, says Haraldur Sigurdsson of the University of Rhode Island. Winds carried it southeast toward Pompeii, which was buried under nine feet of debris. Herculaneum, although closer, was on a different slope, and initially received only a few inches. But the next day, the towering column of material collapsed and a mud avalanche, preceded by a burning wind, roared into the town. "It must have extinguished all life," says Sigurdsson. Temperatures rose as high as 750 degrees, and the town was buried under 60 feet of mud and ash.

Torrent of Ash: The positions of the skeletons gave poignant evidence of   5
the fury of Vesuvius. One skeleton, apparently a sailor's, clutches an oar as he lies beside the hull of his 27-foot vessel. The remains of a woman, her finger bones still bearing gold rings set with gems, lies in an archway near the shattered skeleton of another woman; scientists suspect that the second woman was blown by the volcanic wind from the terrace above. Nearby they found the remains of a servant girl clutching a baby in her arms. Volcanic debris overran the town in five minutes, flowing at 60 miles an hour, and there was no escape. A soldier, his sword still beside him, lies face down on the beach, suggesting the force with which the torrent of ash and the searing wind hit those desperately running away from it. On another part of the beach, excavators found a group of six adults and six children, huddled together in a futile search for safety. Giuseppe Maggi, director of the dig, calls the find "a masterpiece of pathos."

Archeologists have excavated only one-third of Herculaneum, most   6
recently the old beachfront 500 yards inland from today's shoreline. Although only one-fifth the size of Pompeii, and more representative of a typical Roman provincial town populated by ordinary Romans—clerks, tradesmen, administrators—Herculaneum nonetheless boasted monumental architecture and unusual grandeur. The decor of the public buildings— marble statues around a theater stage, heroic paintings on a basilica—demonstrates the populace's civic devotion. Personal touches in the modest homes—including shrines to household gods and tiny gardens nourished with well water—reflect ageless middle-class values. Herculaneum, like Pompeii before it, has become a storehouse of history in freeze frame.

QUESTIONS ON MEANING AND CONTENT

1. The opening of the essay informs us that "none of the 4,000 residents of Herculaneum suspected that it would be a fateful morning." How do the authors know this?

2. In paragraph 2, anthropologist Sara Bisel tells us that bones do, indeed, talk. What kind of information have the bones revealed to the excavators? What other excavated items had stories to tell?

QUESTIONS ABOUT RHETORICAL STRATEGIES

1. The opening paragraph contains background information, or exposition, so that the details in the essay can be related to the total disaster. Yet the paragraph is also descriptive. What details in the description here show that the authors wanted to emphasize the awesomeness of the event? How do the details in the second sentence of paragraph 1 add to the effectiveness of the description?

2. The authors provide many details to show us why the excavation is of historical and scientific importance. We know, for example, something about the average size of the people, their occupations, and their civic interests. But the essay also contains a strong subjective element with some descriptions having a potential to arouse our feelings for these people. What are some of the descriptive details that do this?

QUESTIONS ON LANGUAGE AND DICTION

1. In paragraph 5, what does Guiseppe Maggi mean when he refers to the adults and children "huddled together" as "a masterpiece of pathos"?

2. What are the meanings of *basilica, forum, pumice?*

How Curious the Camel

ALEXANDER THEROUX

The people who use camels have found them impossible to live with comfortably and simply impossible to live without. In this essay, Alexander Theroux explains this paradox while revealing many of the other contradictions characteristic of this unpredictable creature of opposites.

It is a beast of great mystery, an ancient enigma—the camel, according to   1
legend, alone knows the 100th name of Allah. It is the ultimate paradox of
whole parts: a mode of transportation, of exchange, of sustenance, indeed,
of survival itself. The Bedouin call their country "the mother of the camel"; it
would perhaps be more accurate to say that camels mother their country.
Like the benevolent schmoos invented by cartoonist Al Capp, they are a
self-contained welfare system, able to turn themselves into food, garments,
anything a person might need. The Arabs eat them, beat them, ride them,
race them, bet on them and sleep in their shadows. They do everything but
marry them. They drink their milk, wash in their urine, and cut them open
for water. Camel hair is used for everything from clothes to tents. Their
droppings provide fuel.

Arabian camels have one hump. This is the famed dromedary, the   2
runner. Many nomads might be astonished to see the two-humped Bactrian
variety of central Asia, a slow, plodding beast of burden. The distinction,
like that between stalactites and stalagmites, has confounded schoolboys for
ages.

A camel has been described as a horse planned by committee. It has a   3
comic munch of a face—loony, serene and disgusted all at once—with liquid
eyes that shine bottle-green at night. Its eyelashes are as long as Ann
Sheridan's. Its large nostrils can close against blowing sand. A ruminant, it
chews its cud, and its floppy lips, seemingly insensitive to thorny plants,
cover teeth long enough to eat an apple through a picket fence. You can
almost chin yourself on its bad breath.

It is a large creature, reaching lengths of ten feet and standing about   4
seven feet at the shoulder. Its smooth padfeet, each with two toes united at
the sole by a web of skin, serve long, pistonlike legs able to gallop at up to 15
m.p.h. (though it much prefers to walk). It can live 40 years, spits, can travel
untold miles of waterless desert. Its stomach contains a wet cud—the half-

chewed slop that the animal sucks back up to its mouth with a slobbering sound as it plods along, all the while gurgling as if to remind the rider of the liquid inside its body.

Camels come in a variety of colors—reddish-brown, brown, yellow,   5
skewbald and white (the most favored). It is simultaneously a living well, a woolbag, a winch and a windbreaker. Camels are wealth. To possess 50 is to be considered rich.

The camel is called the Ship of the Desert, its habitat. It survives on   6
guddha—leaves, dried plants, grass and withered tribulus. It relies on its humpfat, as well, which is stiff and upright when in top condition but decreases in size when the camel is overworked.

A cry of *wolloo-wolloo-wolloo* lures the beasts. Try it, but be careful. A   7
camel may attack without provocation—kicking backward and forward— and can inflict appalling injuries. It is irascible, often scarred. It sometimes makes sucking sounds as it grolches and grizzles. It bites whatever is in reach—a kneecap, a shoulder, a man's belly.

If you want to ride a camel, the first challenge is to persuade it to kneel.   8
Then, approaching the beast from behind, lean forward and catch the saddle tree with the left hand, placing your left knee high. As the camel starts to rise, a process that flings you heavily backward and forward, you swing your right leg over and sit astride. The traditional *"Hut!"* urges the camel forward. And then it's on down the yellow brickless road, those vast, empty expanses of sand where the moon at night looks cut from paper and the temperature drops with the sun almost to arctic degrees.

As a pack camel begins walking—about 40 short steps a minute—you   9
have to aim him; he will not walk straight by himself. And just as often you have to walk yourself, hand-hauling him by headrope. Characteristically, the camel seems to take no heed of its rider and is rendered serviceable by stupidity alone. Once resigned to moving, it lopes dopily along with half-lidded eyes as if in a kind of brain-out.

While not tame, the camel is never exactly wide-awake enough to be   10
called wild. Its occasional docility even allows it to be of use in lifting heavy things. It usually makes no sound when it walks—Bedouin have taught it not to whine because of night raids—but when infuriated, its bellows can be heard more than two miles away.

Distances are measured by the day's journey of camels, at the end of   11
which they are usually hobbled lest they wander off. During the hottest part of the day—when desert temperatures soar to 130 degrees Fahrenheit and more—camels rest. Habitually, they crouch facing the sun, exposing the least amount of body surface.

Camels have been known to die of suffocation in the hot winds. They 12
also succumb to thirst and overwork, staggering and falling stiffly, with a
sob, upon their knees. Bedouin dependent on the beast fear this more than
the desert's impossible extremes of heat and cold: it means being marooned.
Pouring water down the camel's nose may revive it. But often, once a camel
collapses, it's good-by. The caravan can only pass on, leaving it a lonely dot
behind. The camel faces west. And then it waits. And waits.

My brother Paul once saw a camel collapse in Afghanistan. Someone cut 13
its throat, and in seconds a crowd fell upon it with knives, serving collops of
meat from the carcass. A camel is good only when eaten young—even then
its meat is rank and very tough. Exhausted camel is truly poor food.

Camels carry their young for a year, can drop a foal every three years, 14
and may have 12 calves in a lifetime. Cow camels are often kept for milk.
Slightly salty in taste, the milk, fermented, is also the basis of a mild liquor.

Finally, there's the matter of water. The camel, as we all know, needs 15
rarely to drink. It can average 250 miles between drinks, even longer under
duress, and travel for up to 30 waterless days. Then it can gulp up to 28
gallons in a single haust of say ten minutes. When the Bedouin are in dire
straits, the camel is killed for its water. The camel's fate, it seems, recapitu-
lates Islam—to give, to yield, to submit.

It is indeed an intricate equation, the camel a beast of binaries: wild but 16
domesticated; savage yet submissive; vile and vulnerable; patient as well as
perverse, walking down the long centuries over vast wastes in the very
directions of mystery that man himself feels he needs to follow. It is impossible to say whether the camel can go through the eye of a needle. And yet this
can proudly be said: it bears its load.

QUESTIONS ON MEANING AND CONTENT

1. In many places the author speaks scornfully of the camel. "You can
almost chin yourself on its bad breath," he says at one point and at another
suggests that the camel "is rendered serviceable by stupidity alone." What
are other such insults in the essay? Is the author's attitude toward his subject
merely one of scorn? Or do other details offset the scornful remarks? How
would you describe the author's attitude toward the camel?

2. In paragraph 1 camels are said to be a "self-contained welfare system,
able to turn themselves into food, garments, anything a person might
need." The camel, however, exacts a price for providing this welfare. What

are the benefits and what are the hazards that accompany this welfare system?

3. The author presents the camel as a creature with one quality or characteristic seemingly canceling out another similar characteristic or quality. For example, in describing the camel's face, he says that it is "loony, serene, and disgusted all at once." What are other contradictions mentioned in the essay?

4. Juxtaposed with descriptions of the camel are descriptions of the desert. What specific characteristics of the camel fit it for this environment? In what ways are the camel's temperament and the nature of the environment similar?

QUESTIONS ABOUT RHETORICAL STRATEGIES

1. This essay opens with a summarizing description of the camel's usefulness to people, and the closing paragraph offers a summary description of the camel based on its behavior, thus providing a frame for the essay. How well does the opening summary prepare the reader for the diversity of details that come in the body of the essay? Does the body of the essay make clear the contradictions listed in the final paragraph?

2. The essay is a mixture of objective and subjective description and even contains descriptions of processes. Examine several paragraphs, and then explain how the author goes about blending the objective and subjective descriptions. Which paragraph contains a fairly detailed process description?

QUESTIONS ON LANGUAGE AND DICTION

1. What is the source of the analogy and play on words in paragraph 8 where Theroux refers to the desert as "the yellow brickless road"?

2. In paragraph 5, the author refers to a camel metaphorically as a "woolbag," a "winch," and the like. What are other metaphors or similies (comparisons using *like* or *as*) used in the essay?

3. Using a good dictionary, look up the following words: *collops, enigma, haust* (Hint: If you can't locate *haust* in your dictionary, check *haustellum*), *skewbald*.

The Car

HARRY CREWS

In this essay, Harry Crews describes the first three cars he owned, shows what they meant in the context of events in his own life, and comments on the influence cars can have on all our lives.

The other day, there arrived in the mail a clipping sent by a friend of   1
mine. It had been cut from a Long Beach, California, newspaper and dealt with a young man who had eluded police for fifty-five minutes while he raced over freeways and through city streets at speeds up to 130 miles per hour. During the entire time, he ripped his clothes off and threw them out the window bit by bit. It finally took twenty-five patrol cars and a helicopter to catch him. When they did, he said that God had given him the car, and that he had "found God."

I don't want to hit too hard on a young man who obviously has his own   2
troubles, maybe even is a little sick with it all, but when I read that he had found God in the car, my response was: *So say we all.* We have found God in cars, or if not the true God, one so satisfying, so powerful, and awe-inspiring that the distinction is too fine to matter. Except perhaps ultimately, but pray we must not think too much on that.

The operative word in all this is *we*. It will not do for me to maintain that I   3
have been above it all, that somehow I've managed to remain aloof from the national love affair with cars. It is true that I got a late start. I did not learn to drive until I was twenty-one; my brother was twenty-five before he learned. The reason is simple enough. In Bacon County, Georgia, where I grew up, many families had nothing with a motor in it. Ours was one such family. But starting as late as I did, I still had my share, and I've remembered them all, the cars I've owned. I remember them in just the concrete specific way you remember anything that changed your life. Especially I remember the early ones.

The first car I ever owned was a 1938 Ford coupe. It had no low gear and   4
the door on the passenger side wouldn't open. I eventually put a low gear in it, but I never did get the door to work. One hot summer night on a clay road a young lady whom I'll never forget had herself braced and ready with one foot on the rearview mirror and the other foot on the wind vent. In the first few lovely frantic moments, she pushed out the wing vent, broke off the

rearview mirror and left her little footprints all over the ceiling. The memory of it was so affecting that I could never bring myself to repair the vent or replace the headliner she had walked all over upside down.

Eight months later I lost the car on a rain-slick road between Folkston, Georgia, and Waycross. I'd just stopped to buy a stalk of bananas (to a boy raised in the hookworm and rickets belt of the South, bananas will always remain an incredibly exotic fruit, causing him to buy whole stalks at a time), and back on the road again I was only going about fifty in a misting rain when I looked over to say something to my buddy, whose nickname was Bonehead and who was half drunk in the seat beside me. For some reason I'll never understand, I felt the back end of the car get loose and start to come up on us in the other lane. Not having driven very long, I overcorrected and stepped on the brake. We turned over four times. Bonehead flew out of the car and shot down a muddy ditch about forty yards before he stopped, sober and unhurt. I ended up under the front seat, thinking I was covered with gouts of blood. As it turned out, I didn't have much wrong with me and what I was covered with was gouts of mashed banana.   5

The second car I had was a 1940 Buick, square, impossibly heavy, built like a Sherman tank, but it had a '52 engine in it. Even though it took about ten miles to get her open full bore, she'd do over a hundred miles an hour on flat ground. It was so big inside that in an emergency it could sleep six. I tended to live in that Buick for almost a year and no telling how long I would have kept it if a boy who was not a friend of mine and who owned an International Harvester pickup truck hadn't said in mixed company that he could make the run from New Lacy in Coffee County, Georgia, to Jacksonville, Florida, quicker than I could. He lost the bet, but I wrung the speedometer off the Buick, and also—since the run was made on a blistering day in July—melted four inner tubes, causing them to use with the tires, which were already slick when the run started. Four new tires and tubes cost more than I had or expected to have anytime soon, so I sadly put that old honey up on blocks until I could sell it to a boy who lived up toward Macon.   6

After the Buick, I owned a 1953 Mercury with three-inch lowering blocks, fender skirts, twin aerials, and custom upholstering made of rolled Naugahyde. Staring into the bathroom mirror for long periods of time I practiced expressions to drive it with. It was that kind of car. It looked mean, and it was mean. Consequently, it had to be handled with a certain style. One-handing it through a ninety-degree turn on city streets in a power slide where you were in danger of losing your ass as well as the car, you were obligated to have your left arm hanging half out the window and a very *bored* expression on your face. That kind of thing.   7

Those were the sweetest cars I was ever to know because they were my   8 first. I remember them like people—like long-ago lovers—their idiosyncrasies, what they liked and what they didn't. With my hands deep in crankcases, I was initiated into their warm greasy mysteries. Nothing in the world was more satisfying than winching the front end up under the shade of a chinaberry tree and sliding under the chassis on a burlap sack with a few tools to see if the car would not yield to me and my expert ways.

The only thing that approached working on a car was talking about one. 9 We'd stand about for hours, hustling our balls and spitting, telling stories about how it had been somewhere, sometime, with the car we were driving. It gave our lives a little focus and our talk a little credibility, if only because we could point to the evidence.

"But, hell, don't it rain in with that wing vent broke out like that?" 10

"Don't mean nothing to me. Soon's Shirley kicked it out, I known I was 11 in love. I ain't about to put it back."

Usually we met to talk at night behind the A&W Root Beer stand, with 12 the air heavy with the smell of grease and just a hint of burned French fries and burned hamburgers and burned hot dogs. It remains one of the most sensuous, erotic smells in my memory because through it, their tight little asses ticking like clocks, walked the sweetest softest short-skirted carhops in the world. I knew what it was to stand for hours with my buddies, leaning nonchalant as hell on a fender, pretending not to look at the carhops, and saying things like: "This little baby don't look like much, but she'll git rubber in three gears." And when I said it, it was somehow my own body I was talking about. It was *my* speed and *my* strength that got rubber in three gears. In the mystery of that love affair, the car and I merged.

But, like many another love affair, it has soured considerably. Maybe it 13 would have been different if I had known cars sooner. I was already out of the Marine Corps and twenty-two years old before I could stand behind the A&W Root Beer and lean on the fender of a 1938 coupe. That seems pretty old to me to be talking about getting rubber in three gears, and I'm certain it is *very* old to feel your own muscle tingle and flush with blood when you say it. As is obvious, I was what used to be charitably called a late bloomer. But at some point I did become just perceptive enough to recognize bullshit when I was neck deep in it.

The 1953 Mercury was responsible for my ultimate disenchantment with 14 cars. I had already bored and stroked the engine and contrived to place a six-speaker sound system in it when I finally started to paint it. I spent the better half of a year painting that car. A friend of mine owned a body shop and he let me use the shop on weekends. I sanded the Mercury down to raw metal, primed it, and painted it. Then I painted it again. And again. And then again. I went a little nuts, as I am prone to do, because I'm the kind of guy who if he can't have too much of a thing doesn't want any at all. So one day I came out of the house (I was in college then) and saw it, the '53 Mercury, the car upon which I had heaped more attention and time and love than I had ever given a human being. It sat at the curb, its black surface a shimmering of the air, like hundreds of mirrors turned to catch the sun. It had twenty-seven coats of paint, each coat laboriously hand-rubbed. It seemed to glow, not with reflected light, but with some internal light of its own.

I stood staring, and it turned into one of those great scary rare moments   15
when you are privileged to see into your own predicament. Clearly, there were two ways I could go. I could sell the car, or I could keep on painting it for the rest of my life. If twenty-seven coats of paint, why not a hundred and twenty-seven? The moment was brief and I understand it better now than I did then, but I did realize, if imperfectly, that something was dreadfully wrong, that the car owned me much more than I would ever own the car, no matter how long I kept it. The next day I drove to Jacksonville and left the Mercury on a used-car lot. It was an easy thing to do.

Since that day, I've never confused myself with a car, a confusion   16
common everywhere about us—or so it seems to me. I have a car now, but I use it like a beast, the way I've used all cars since the Mercury, like a beast unlovely and unlikable but necessary. True as all that is, though, God knows I'm in the car's debt for that blistering winning July run to Jacksonville, and the pushed-out wing vent, and finally for that greasy air heavy with the odor of burned meat and potatoes there behind the A&W Root Beer. I'll never smell anything that good again.

QUESTIONS ON MEANING AND CONTENT

1. Since Crews describes three cars he once owned, why does he title the essay, "The Car," instead of "The Cars"?

2. In paragraph 3, Crews says that he remembers cars "in just the concrete specific way you remember anything that changes your life." How did cars change his life?

3. Crews decides to sell his 1953 Mercury during a sudden insight. He calls the experience "one of those great scary rare moments when you are privileged to see into your own predicament." What does he mean? What was his predicament? Has anything ever happened to you that caused you to see into your predicament? If so, was the moment "scary," or would you describe it in another way?

4. Since the sale of the Mercury, Crews says, "I've never confused myself with a car." What passages from the essay illustrate his earlier confusion between himself and a car? What do you think the essay is saying about the effects of such confusion? What happens to people so affected—by cars or anything else?

5. Do you think Crews' statement about confusing himself with a car relates to his remarks in paragraph 2 about people finding God or something God-like in cars? If you think so, can you explain the relationship?

6. By the end of the essay, has Crews demonstrated that he once loved cars but now scorns them? Or is his attitude more complex than that? Please explain.

QUESTIONS ABOUT RHETORICAL STRATEGIES

1. Crews describes his first two cars rather generally. The Ford was a coupe, the passenger's door wouldn't open, and so forth. The Buick was "square, impossibly heavy, built like a Sherman tank" and "could sleep six." He becomes more specific, however, when describing the Mercury. Is this shift to more specific details in keeping with the point he makes in the final paragraph?

2. You could explain this essay by saying that Crews is really describing himself and his passage through a series of experiences that caused him to grow. You can see this quite readily in the case of the 1953 Mercury. What do the earlier cars and the A&W Root Beer stand contribute to the image of what the author was or was becoming?

3. Can you think of something in your own life that absorbed you intensely but eventually caused you to change? If so, try writing a descriptive paper explaining what happened to you.

QUESTIONS ON LANGUAGE AND DICTION

1. What does Crews mean when he says in paragraph 12 that "It was *my* speed and *my* strength that got rubber in three gears"? Why are the two uses

of the word *my* in italics? How does this sentence reveal some of Crews' confusion?

2. What kind of afflictions are *hookworm* and *rickets?*

WRITING SCENARIOS

1. For the last few years, you have been involved in a "pen pal" program, in which you exchange letters with someone in a foreign country. Your pen pal, who has never visited America, has asked you to describe something specific about America. The "something" may be anything that is uniquely American or something that has a counterpart in other countries but which has a somewhat different form in America. You may use as a subject anything that would be unusual enough to be asked about—anything from a "tourist trap" to a "supermarket" to a "high school assembly program." Try, however, to select a topic that in addition to its concrete details will be highly interesting to your reader.

2. Your former elementary school is sponsoring a reunion of your graduating class. Your former classmates have asked you to give a brief, personal presentation at a luncheon. You have decided to talk about a *place* that is (or was) important to you. Choose a place that was important to you and most others of your age group as you grew up. Your audience will be the people you grew up with and who may share your feelings for this place. You can also make a point about the place, showing the importance it had in your life, but you will also want to capture the essence of the place for the benefit of your readers who will be able to nod their heads in pleasant agreement as they listen to your presentation.

3. The editor of your campus newspaper has asked you to write a character sketch of someone you know who is noticeably unique or unusual. The purpose of the essay is not to present an insulting or degrading picture of someone, but to show that this person makes your campus community more interesting. Your essay will have a dual audience: a general audience that would be curious enough to read a human interest piece, and readers who know the person about whom you are writing.

4. You are an important member of your student government, and school authorities have asked you to write a description of some part of your college campus. This may be a building, an interesting or attractive part of the campus (something you might point out to a visitor), a dining hall, a student hangout—anything that forms a part of your school. You are producing a document that will show what this particular part of your school was like while you were an undergraduate student. Your description will be placed in a time-capsule, to be opened in the year 2050. At that time, your description will be read, along with those of others, and your essay will be printed in the school newspaper. In other words, your audience is a future audience made up of the students at your school in the year 2050, all living alumni, and anyone else with an interest in the school. In the narrative, you will want to be accurate and at the same time capture the feeling that students now have for whatever part of the school you are describing.

5. You are thinking about majoring in communications, and so you have joined your college Communications Club. During monthly meetings, club members make presentations about various aspects of media, and then everyone discusses the subjects over refreshments. For your presentation you have decided to write a character sketch in which you label a fictional character according to a type and then describe the traits which show that your label makes good sense. (A fictional character could be a character in a play, novel, short story, comic strip, movie, or television show.) First, you are answering the question, "Who is so and so?" (Don't answer by saying that so and so is a character in a comic strip, etc. Be more specific; your label should say, for example, that Beetle Bailey is a "likeable, unambitious loser.") Next, you will want to answer the followup question: "What do you mean, a 'likeable, unambitious loser' "? In answering this you are providing the descriptive details that will make this general descriptive label clear and show *who* and *what* the character is. Your audience is made up of students who are interested in how characters are presented by media.

FOUR

COMPARING
AND
CONTRASTING

Probably not a day goes by that you do not use **comparison** and **contrast.** Virtually every time you make a choice, you do so by comparing and contrasting at least two things. Depending upon the subject you are analyzing, the thought you devote may be slight and the choice quickly made, as, for example, when you examine the menu in a restaurant or when you decide which television program to watch. On the other hand, you may have spent weeks or months comparing and contrasting before you chose the college or university you now attend.

Comparison and contrast is a method for examining two or more things of the same general class in order to understand each of them more clearly. Comparing tells you how two or more things are similar; contrasting tells you how they are different. But using either alone is of limited value since the picture you get is incomplete. Thus, you would rarely use either by itself, although people frequently talk about making comparisons or comparing things when they are really applying both processes. Comparative shopping is an example of this process. The shopper actually looks for differences in prices, quality, and features of similar goods as well as at the similarities.

Sometimes, however, one part of the process becomes more important than the other. If you are examining two subjects that are very similar, then you will want to examine differences closely, since the differences, once identified, will help you to distinguish between the two. This is the principle underlying fingerprinting. Experts are able to tell one fingerprint from another because of slight differences that appear in the similar patterns of the prints.

On the other hand, when two things are quite different, then you look for similarities, evidence to show that the two are the same in some respects. If you were comparing submarines with surface ships, then you would be searching for similarities to show that all sea-going vessels share certain common characteristics. The same would be true if you were comparing lighter-than-air dirigibles with heavier-than-air airplanes.

Writing that uses the rhetorical pattern of comparison and contrast frequently leads to a recommendation or conclusion. For example, a study of prices at two grocery stores might lead to the general recommendation that price-conscious customers will want to consider shopping at Store X because its prices of 100 different items are from 2 to 8 percent lower than prices of the same items at Store Y. A broader study of the two stores might break the recommendation into parts: Cost-conscious shoppers may want to take advantage of the lower prices at Store X, but shoppers should keep in mind that Store Y carries a wider variety of fresh fruits and vegetables, more brand name products, and more specialty items than Store X does. Both the narrow study of prices and the broader study offer evaluations of the two stores and serve as aids in making shopping decisions.

Comparison/contrast does not always lead to recommendations or conclusions. Often the purpose is to bring new information to readers, to make readers aware of some change, or to explain or illustrate something. In such cases, one base of the comparison/contrast will likely be something the reader already knows something about. A fashion writer, for example might place last year's spring fashions beside the new spring fashions and compare and contrast the two in order to explain or describe the designs for the new season. It isn't crucial that readers know the details of last spring's fashions; a good comparison/contrast essay makes these details clear. Although it is convenient for readers to understand one of the subjects being compared, it is not always necessary. An engineer might explain through comparison/contrast how combustion takes place in both gasoline and diesel engines. If the audience knows very little about either engine, then the engineer would first have to explain how combustion takes place in one engine and then go on to point out the similarities and differences of achieving combustion in the other. If, however, the audience is familiar with the combustion process in the gasoline engine, then the comparison/contrast could, after a brief introduction, begin at once.

Placing something similar but not well understood next to something the reader does understand is one way to explain the unfamiliar subject. This can sometimes even enhance the understanding of the familiar subject because of the additional perspective offered by examining the second one. Apprentice mechanics who understand how combustion takes place in a gasoline engine can broaden their understanding of internal combustion engines by reading a comparison/contrast explaining combustion in both gasoline and diesel engines.

Often readers are already familiar to one degree or another with both subjects, but comparison/contrast can still be a handy tool for making some point clear to readers. A sports writer might explain a baseball manager's game strategy with a heavy-hitting but slow team by comparing it with the strategies common to lighter-hitting but faster teams.

Comparison and contrast can also illustrate to readers how to identify or tell similar subjects apart. This kind of writing is usually done by experts and directed toward an audience of interested nonexperts. (Remember, most of us through our work experience, education, or hobby and leisure interests are experts at something.) Thus, a botanist might use comparison/contrast to show amateur naturalists how to distinguish a Norway maple from a sugar maple. Such comparison/contrasts can be very useful. Consider, for example, the inexperienced fisherman who cannot tell a northern pike from a muskellunge, two fish of the family *Esocidae* that, to the inexperienced, look strikingly alike. Yet even inexperienced fisherman must be able to identify each fish if they are to abide by varying rules governing seasons, minimum length, creel limits, and so on. The expert provides a helpful service by teaching identification through comparison/contrast.

PREWRITING

Before you begin writing your comparison/contrast paper, you should know what details you will use to show how your subjects are similar or different. You should also have a clear understanding of your purpose—that is, what you want your essay to tell your readers. Finally, the **prewriting** should lead to a strategy for organizing your paper.

As usual, you will want to make sure you know who your readers will be before you begin to generate information for your essay. Once you know who your readers are, you will be able to determine what details are essential and what are not, what kind of tone you should adopt, what level of vocabulary you will use, and so on. Are you writing an article for the student newspaper of your former high school, in which you compare and contrast attending college and high school? Are you writing an article for a ski magazine in which you compare and contrast two new brands of skis? Or, are you writing a letter to your parents in which you compare and contrast your dorm room with an off-campus apartment you would like to rent? Certainly, each audience would require you to make different choices as you write.

Ideally, you should determine your purpose in making the comparison and contrast before you begin to generate a list of similarities and differences. However, you won't always know your purpose, except in a very general way, until you have examined the details that make up the similarities and differences. For example, if you planned to compare prices at two stores, you would know at the outset that your paper would offer an evaluation based on the price of goods and that your paper would make recommendations to shoppers. But you could not make recommendations until you had collected and studied the data on pricing.

Comparison/contrast papers that explain or illustrate a point rather than evaluate often present the same problem. If you were asked to write a paper comparing and contrasting high school and college classes, you would still have to answer the questions, "to show what?" and "to whom?"

One way to answer these questions is to compile a list of similarities and differences in order to see what possible answers suggest themselves. Even the more general details would soon suggest a focus as they begin to accumulate. Naturally, in analyzing classes in two schools, the details would vary from high school to high school and college to college, but a quick inventory might produce something like the following:

High School	College
Classes meet daily	Classes meet 2 or 3 days per wk.
Classes continue all year	Classes continue for a semester
Full yr. to cover a subject	Much material covered in a short time
Final exams once per yr.	Final exams each term
Most work done in class	More work done at home
Class size of about _____	Class size of about _____

These few details offer a possible focus for your paper. For one thing, they suggest that you might use your paper to tell readers that it is easier to fall behind and harder to catch up in college classes than in high school classes. You now have a point to make, which will serve as a control for your paper. You not only know that you will be emphasizing differences, but by knowing your purpose you will be better equipped to select or reject details as you continue to brainstorm for similarities and differences.

Brainstorming to compile a list of similarities and differences is the basic prewriting activity for comparison/contrast. If you know the purpose of your paper, the point you want to convey to your readers, your brainstorming will have direction from the start, making your job easier. If, on the other hand, you are searching for a focal point, the brainstorming can guide you toward it, as in the above example.

Once you have a comprehensive, carefully compiled list of similarities and differences, a great deal of your work toward producing a good comparison/contrast essay has been done. However, you will want to be careful not to approach the task too casually. Sloppy analysis will almost surely produce an ineffective paper, one that looks as if it were done casually, and it is the chief trap set for inexperienced writers of comparison/ contrast essays. The casual approach often results from knowing your subjects well. You begin by deciding to compare two people—friends, perhaps, whom you have known for a long time. Being familiar with the two subjects gives you a sense of security, and you quickly jot down a few details and then set off to write a paper explaining that these two people seem to be very similar but are actually different, or vice versa. The resulting paper will likely be loosely organized and leave readers scratching their heads about what you were trying to demonstrate. Readers already know that any two people are similar in ways yet quite different, or vice versa. It is the exact details you use what will make the real difference between an effective and ineffective paper.

Your main task while prewriting is to study your subjects as a careful observer. Remember that saying two things are similar yet different or quite different yet similar is not enough. Your purpose must be more finely tuned than that. If a realtor described two houses as "very similar but really quite different," you would find this statement to be inadequate. You would probably ask something like, "What do you mean, 'very similar but quite different'?" The realtor might answer, "Well, both are red-brick, ranch-style homes with the same outside dimensions, but the interior layout of House A would appeal more to a large, active family while the interior of House B was designed for a couple or small family that entertains frequently." The question forced the realtor to provide a focus for the similarities and differences, and you can now ask questions that will draw out the specific differences in the interior layouts of Houses A and B. The above statement is the kind you need to lead readers into a comparison/contrast and to keep your own writing on track in the paper.

After careful observation of your subjects, you will want to formulate a statement similar to the one about the two houses, and use this as a focus for your essay. To find such a statement, study your list of similarities and differences. The statement will still be general. You will want it to be. But it will point in a specific direction. It will tell readers why you are making the comparison/contrast. In addition to telling readers what to expect in your paper, it will also give you direction in organizing your materials.

Next, test your statement by asking the same question put to the hypothetical realtor above: "What do you mean by quite different? (Or quite similar?)" If the answer requires another statement to provide direction, then you are still one step away from a focal point for your essay. Here's another example to illustrate the point. You have decided to compare your two supervisors at the Big Hamburger franchise and have begun with a statement of purpose like this: "Both Ms. Smith and Ms. Jones supervise in a way that gets the work done, but their techniques for accomplishing this differ radically." Ask the same question here that you asked of the realtor: "What do you mean, 'differ radically'?" The answer will lie in your brainstorming list and should lead to a rephrasing on this order: "Although the staff members at Big Hamburger work hard for both Ms. Smith and Ms. Jones, Ms. Smith makes us feel like mere employees while Ms. Jones makes us feel like worthwhile people who are doing important work."

Below is a heuristic for helping you generate information to add to your prewriting notes. Answer any question that relates to your paper.

Prewriting Questions for Comparison/Contrast

1. What is my purpose in this essay? What point or recommendation do I want to make by comparing and contrasting my subjects?
2. Do I really understand my purpose? Can I make a general statement of purpose that is still specific enough to alert my readers to my main point?
3. What are my subjects like? With what do they share pertinent characteristics?
4. What are my subjects similar to that my readers might be familiar with?
5. How do my two subjects differ?
6. What pertinent characteristics do they not share?
7. Which of two things is better than the other?
8. Which is more desirable?
9. Which do most people desire?
10. Which is more valuable?
11. Which is more costly?

12. What groups of like details on my brainstorming list will work toward making my main point clear to my readers?
13. Does each group of like details relate to the point or recommendation I intend to make?
14. Are there groups of like details that I should eliminate because they will not help to illustrate my point or recommendation?
15. Are any groups of like details long enough to suggest a full paragraph devoted to illustrating the details for one subject and a following paragraph showing the other subject in the light of these similarities and differences?
16. Which groups of like details contain few similarities and differences and suggest using the details to talk about both subjects side-by-side in a single paragraph?
17. How much do my readers know about the subjects of my comparison/contrast?
18. What examples or terms will have to be explained or defined for readers?

ORGANIZING

If you have carefully produced a list of similarities and differences and know what you want the comparison/contrast to tell your readers, you are now ready to **organize** your paper. First, you will want to study your list again, looking for the details that you can place into similar groups that will illustrate the subpoints you will need to explain your purpose statement. If you have arrived at your purpose statement by studying your list, then you know the groupings will be there. To illustrate let's pursue the hypothetical case of the two supervisors at Big Hamburger, Smith and Jones. Assume you have gleaned the following similar details from your freewriting and brainstorming list. (Keep in mind that these details may not have appeared in the same order on your lists but would represent details you had pulled from the list because they were similar):

Ms. Smith

- Almost never calls anyone by name. Says "you" or "you there" to get our attention.
- Goes through periods when she calls all males "Clyde" and all females "Janie."
- When she does use a name it's our last name.

- She is likely when angry to say "Rublowsky, if you can speed up enough to finish mopping the grill room before the shift is over, go out back and help Smeltzer hose down the patio."

- Says "I" and "me" a lot: "I'll have to see to that"—when actually she will order someone else to see to it.

- Says, "That's another problem I'll have to work out," or "You let me worry about that. When I've decided what to do, I'll let you know."

- When she makes a mistake and everybody knows it, then she doesn't use a pronoun at all—says something like, "That shouldn't have happened."

Ms. Jones

- Calls us by first names. When she gets a name wrong, as she sometimes does with a new worker, she apologizes—"I'm sorry; I'm not good with names, but I'm working on it. I'll get it right next time."

- Uses "we" when she talks about work that has to be done: "This is not going to be easy, but we'll just have to do it."

- When something goes wrong, she refers to herself—"I should have thought of that beforehand," or "I should have known that wouldn't work."

These details suggest that one subpoint which will explain the differences between working for Smith and Jones has to do with the way each uses language in talking to workers and in referring to herself. Your prewriting list will provide groupings that you can bring together and use to make a point that will help make the purpose of your comparison clear. These similar items may be scattered here and there among other details, but you can easily glean them from the list since they will form a single subpoint. If it appears at this point that you have insufficient details, you may want to prewrite further.

Once you have identified groups of details that will explain your purpose, you can then think about arranging them in your paper. There are two common ways of organizing comparison/contrast papers, but each demands that you use the same general points of comparison for each subject. If you were comparing two kinds of sailboats and are talking about bow and stern configurations, mast location, and number and types of sails for one, then you would be expected to cover the same points for the other.

The Block Method

A simple method of organizing a comparison/contrast essay is to present all the points of comparison for one subject and, when that is completed, go on to present the same points for the other. This *block method* can be efficient and effective if the entire comparison is short and not very complex. The method does not work well, however, for longer pieces since readers must remember all the important details about the first subject while reading about the second subject. Thus, the block method loses its effectiveness as the comparison lengthens. The writer organizing in this way also loses the immediacy that comes from keeping subjects together as the similarities and differences are pointed out. The effect of showing the two subjects together is the same as you would achieve by showing two paintings to an audience as you compared and contrasted the techniques of the artists. To hold up one painting and talk about it and then put it down and pick up the other would be less effective than standing between two easels and pointing first to one painting and then the other with the audience always able to see both.

Below is an illustration of the block method.

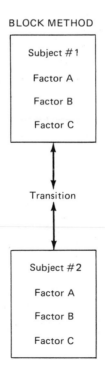

BLOCK METHOD

Subject #1

Factor A

Factor B

Factor C

Transition

Subject #2

Factor A

Factor B

Factor C

The Factor Method

The second and more common method of organizing comparison/contrast papers is the *point-by-point* (or *factor) method.* Here you take up the similarities and differences one at a time, first for one subject and then for the other. Sometimes this is done by devoting a paragraph to one point, explaining how one of the subjects reflects this point. This would then be followed by a paragraph on the same point but showing the similarity or difference for the other subject. Most often, however, you will want to handle one point about both subjects in a single paragraph. Much depends on the amount of details or examples you have to illustrate each point. A single point could require more than one paragraph for full development whether you were discussing one subject in a single paragraph or referring to both subjects in one paragraph. No matter how you arrange your details and subjects in the paragraphs, the important consideration for point-by-point organization is still to present your points of comparison so that each one adds meaning to the focus or purpose controlling your essay.

On the next page is a graphic illustration of the factor-by-factor method.

Finally, if your essay emphasizes similarities, then you should acknowledge differences, either at the beginning or end of the essay. If the paper emphasizes differences, then the reverse is true—introduce the similarities. This is frequently done at the beginning of a paper, just after the introduction, but can be put off until the end. Putting these details elsewhere can destroy the organization and coherence of your paper. Placed at the beginning, such details serve as background for readers to take into the essay with them. At the end, they round out the picture you are presenting.

WRITING

Your prewriting and organizing activities have given you sufficient details for developing your essay and a plan for arranging them. You know what it is you want your comparison/contrast paper to tell your readers and in what order you will present your details. You are now ready for the actual **writing** of the paper.

As we advised in earlier chapters of this book, write the first draft of your paper as quickly as you can. Producing a full first draft is important. Once you have it, you can add, delete, rearrange, and fine tune individual sentences much more effectively than you can if you try to do any of these while

FACTOR METHOD

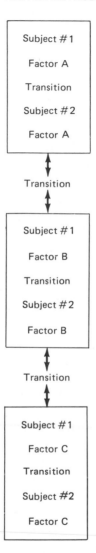

the first draft is in progress. Don't hesitate, however, to do additional prewriting or organizing if necessary.

Writing your draft quickly has two advantages. First, it gets you over the psychological barrier that frequently keeps writers laboring over the opening sentence of the paper, the introductory section, the opening sentences of each paragraph, or minor items. Tell yourself that you will worry about these concerns later, when you have the whole, albeit rough, product before you. This will allow you to see how your tinkering in one place affects something in another part of the essay. Much of the revising that writers do along the way while producing a first draft has to be reworked later when the completed draft gives the writer a clearer view of the entire piece.

Your main concern in the first writing is that your details and examples make clear the purpose of your comparison, and good prewriting will make this a minor problem. You also will want to think about your audience as you write. How much do those who will read the paper know about your topic? If you are comparing two friends, you may need to include many descriptive details. If you are comparing mountain climbing with scaling the face of a tall building, then you will have to present the details about these specialized activities very carefully, knowing that an example that is clear to you may not be clear to your reader. You won't want to assume that readers will know the vocabulary of mountain or building climbing.

It is important to keep your audience in mind as you write the rough draft, but also remember that you can key your revisions to the needs of your audience. So keep audience in mind as you write, but don't allow concern for audience to slow you too much at this stage. You can come back and tailor your prose to the audience after you have completed a first draft.

REVISING

Usually, you will want to spend much more time **revising** than you have spent in producing your first draft. If you have the time available, you may wish to put your rough draft aside for a day or two before you begin to revise. This will help you to see more clearly what you have produced. When revising, be prepared to rewrite as often as necessary, particularly individual sections of the essay.

As a first step in revising, read through your essay carefully to be sure that your organizing strategy has worked effectively. Will you need to go back and reorganize? Is your purpose in making the comparison/contrast clear to your readers? Do you make the purpose clear in the introduction so that readers take this information along as they proceed into the body of the paper?

Do your paragraphs point back to your reason for making the comparison; that is, does each paragraph help support the main point (thesis) you are making in your comparison/contrast essay?

Next, you will want to make sure that each sentence in the essay specifies exactly what you want it to say. Have you used terms that should be defined for the benefit of your audience? If you are writing about something that may be unfamiliar in any way to your readers, then you will want to be especially careful. People who are expert at something too often assume that other people know all but the most complex aspects of what they are expert in. And this is just as often not true. If you ski, sail, hike, or climb, to cite only a few examples, you can become so familiar with the processes and equipment that you come to think of the words and phrases used to describe these activities as parts of everyday language when, in fact, they are not. The same is true if you are comparing ideas or things related to your college major or your work experience. While revising you will want to make sure that you have written so that your audience will understand everything you have to say. For instance, if you have written about sailing, you may wish to ask a friend who doesn't sail to read your current draft, looking for examples, phrases, or terms that may not be clear.

As a final precaution, you may wish to make sure that you have used transitions at critical points along the way to help keep readers in close touch with the topic. Some transitions common to comparison/contrast essays are *likewise, similarly, unlike, on the contrary,* and *on the other hand.*

PROOFREADING

Proofreading remains the same for any type of essay your write. During the **proofreading** process, you should eliminate small items that may distract your reader—errors in grammar, punctuation, or spelling. Many of these errors you will have found and changed while writing and revising, but now is the time to identify and eliminate any that remain. A good technique is to read each paragraph from the end to the beginning. Read the last sentence first, then the next to last, and so on. This lets you see each sentence in isolation and tends to make misspellings and other small errors stand out.

Below is a checklist that will help you make sure that you have not eliminated important parts of your comparison/contrast essay. Read the questions and examine your paper carefully.

Comparison/Contrast Checklist

1. Does my comparison/contract essay make a point about my subjects clearly and express my recommendations clearly?
2. Does my introduction present my point and give readers enough background to allow them to read the body of the paper intelligently?

3. Is my organizing pattern (*block* or *factor*) effective given my particular subjects?

4. Have I considered what my audience doesn't know about my subjects?

5. Have I presented similarities and differences in an order that logically develops and makes clear the purpose of my essay?

6. Does every similarity or difference presented for one subject have its counterpart for the other subject of comparison/contrast?

7. Have I eliminated all discussions of similarities or differences that really do not help to illustrate the point or recommendation I want to make?

8. Have I provided enough details for each point in my essay?

9. Does each sentence express the exact meaning I intend?

10. Does my conclusion put my essay into perspective for my readers?

11. Have I included transitions between each new point throughout the essay?

12. Does this checklist suggest that I have not spent enough time revising my essay?

13. Have I carefully proofread for grammar, punctuation, and misspelling?

That Lean and Hungry Look

SUZANNE BRITT JORDAN

Suzanne Britt Jordan maintains in this essay that fat people have more fun than thin people and that they are also more realistic and a good deal brighter. Fat people know how to relax. They would never punish themselves during their leisure time by jogging, and they understand the futility of always preparing for tomorrow. Unlike thin people, they know that happiness can't be achieved by setting a goal and then working toward it. Even more importantly, she says, fat people are smart enough not to believe in logic, a way of thinking that thin people could never achieve because they are always looking for simple answers.

1   Caesar was right. Thin people need watching. I've been watching them for most of my adult life, and I don't like what I see. When these narrow fellows spring at me, I quiver to my toes. Thin people come in all personalities, most of them menacing. You've got your "together" thin person, your mechanical thin person, your condescending thin person, your tsk-tsk thin person, your efficiency-expert thin person. All of them are dangerous.

2   In the first place, thin people aren't fun. They don't know how to goof off, at least in the best, fat sense of the word. They've always got to be adoing. Give them a coffee break, and they'll jog around the block. Supply them with a quiet evening at home, and they'll fix the screen door and lick S&H green stamps. They say things like "there aren't enough hours in the day." Fat people never say that. Fat people think the day is too damn long already.

3   Thin people make me tired. They've got speedy little metabolisms that cause them to bustle briskly. They're forever rubbing their bony hands together and eyeing new problems to "tackle." I like to surround myself with sluggish, inert, easygoing fat people, the kind who believe that if you clean it up today, it'll just get dirty again tomorrow.

4   Some people say the business about the jolly fat person is a myth, that all of us chubbies are neurotic, sick, sad people. I disagree. Fat people may not be chortling all day long, but they're a hell of a lot *nicer* than the wizened and shriveled. Thin people turn surly, mean, and hard at a young age because they never learn the value of a hot-fudge sundae for easing tension. Thin

people don't like gooey soft things because they themselves are neither gooey nor soft. They are crunchy and dull, like carrots. They go straight to the heart of the matter while fat people let things stay all blurry and hazy and vague, the way things actually are. Thin people want to face the truth. Fat people know there is no truth. One of my thin friends is always staring at complex, unsolvable problems and saying, "The key thing is . . . ." Fat people never say that. They know there isn't any such thing as the key thing about anything.

Thin people believe in logic. Fat people see all sides. The sides fat people   5
see are rounded blobs, usually gray, always nebulous and truly not worth worrying about. But the thin person persists. "If you consume more calories than you burn," says one of my thin friends, "you will gain weight. It's that simple." Fat people always grin when they hear statements like that. They know better.

Fat people realize that life is illogical and unfair. They know very well   6
that God is not in his heaven and all is not right with the world. If God was up there, fat people could have two doughnuts and a big orange drink anytime they wanted it.

Thin people have a long list of logical things they are always spouting off   7
to me. They hold up one finger at a time as they reel off these things, so I won't lose track. They speak slowly as if to a young child. The list is long and full of holes. It contains tidbits like "get a grip on yourself," "cigarettes kill," "cholesterol clogs," "fit as a fiddle," "ducks in a row," "organize," and "sound fiscal management." Phrases like that.

They think these 2,000-point plans lead to happiness. Fat people know   8
happiness is elusive at best and even if they could get the kind thin people talk about, they wouldn't want it. Wisely, fat people see that such programs are too dull, too hard, too off the mark. They are never better than a whole cheesecake.

Fat people know all about the mystery of life. They are the ones ac-   9
quainted with the night, with luck, with fate, with playing it by ear. One thin person I know once suggested that we arrange all the parts of a jigsaw puzzle into groups according to size, shape, and color. He figured this would cut the time needed to complete the puzzle by at least 50 percent. I said I wouldn't do it. One, I like to muddle through. Two, what good would it do to finish early? Three, the jigsaw puzzle isn't the important thing. The important thing is the fun of four people (one thin person included) sitting around a card table, working a jigsaw puzzle. My thin friend had no use for

my list. Instead of joining us, he went outside and mulched the boxwoods. The three remaining fat people finished the puzzle and made chocolate, double-fudged brownies to celebrate.

The main problem with thin people is they oppress. Their good inten- 10
tions, bony torsos, tight ships, neat corners, cerebral machinations, and pat solutions loom like dark clouds over the loose, comfortable, spread-out, soft world of the fat. Long after fat people have removed their coats and shoes and put their feet up on the coffee table, thin people are still sitting on the edge of the sofa, looking neat as a pin, discussing rutabagas. Fat people are heavily into fits of laughter, slapping their thighs and whooping it up, while thin people are still politely waiting for the punch line.

Thin people are downers. They like math and morality and reasoned 11
evaluation of the limitations of human beings. They have their skinny little acts together. They expound, prognose, probe, and prick.

Fat people are convivial. They will like you even if you're irregular and 12
have acne. They will come up with a good reason why you never wrote the great American novel. They will cry in your beer with you. They will put your name in the pot. They will let you off the hook. Fat people will gab, giggle, guffaw, gallumph, gyrate, and gossip. They are generous, giving, and gallant. They are gluttonous and goodly and great. What you want when you're down is soft and jiggly, not muscled and stable. Fat people know this. Fat people have plenty of room. Fat people will take you in.

QUESTIONS ON MEANING AND CONTENT

1. Readers often won't tolerate writing that attacks a group of people when the individuals in the group can be easily identified. We can write about bigots or vicious people, for example, because readers can assume, rightly or not, that they themselves are not bigots or vicious people. But thin people know they are thin people. Why is Jordan able to write about thin people as she does? Do you find the essay offensive? Do you think thin people would find the piece offensive? Is she really "attacking" thin people? Explain.

2. What does Jordan mean when she says in paragraph 5 that "Thin people believe in logic. Fat people see all sides?" How are these statements similar to the statements in paragraph 4: "Thin people want to face the truth. Fat people know there is no truth"?

3. What stereotype of thin people do the first two sentences of the essay suggest? If you have trouble answering this, drop into the library and find out what the allusion to Caesar means.

QUESTIONS ABOUT RHETORICAL STRATEGIES

1. What is the tone of the essay—that is, the feeling that comes through and suggests what Jordan's attitude toward thin people really is? After you have answered this question, then reverse your answer. How would the language in the essay change if her tone were the opposite?

2. The body of this comparison/contrast essay can be separated into three sections. Jordan first contrasts how the two groups behave, then moves to how the two think, and later comes back to how they act or behave. Where does each movement begin and end?

3. Jordan's primary method of handling the points of contrast is to show both groups, thin and fat, in the same paragraph, rather than to devote a paragraph to one and the next paragraph to the other. Look closely at some of these paragraphs. Can you see the advantage of this kind of development for this subject? Explain.

4. Why are paragraphs 7 and 8 each devoted to only one group? Offer a rationale for why the author might have done this. For example, wouldn't these two paragraphs fit together well to form one paragraph? Is there some advantage in using two paragraphs here?

5. Look closely at paragraph 9. Rhetorically speaking, how is the example presented there different from the other examples in the paper? Don't answer this question in terms of the content of the example. Instead, show the difference in how the example is presented—the rhetorical mode.

6. Study the paragraph endings in the essay, using the following principle as a guide: In writing that strives for wit, paragraph endings (also beginnings) can be especially important since the end position is one of emphasis. What is said at the end of a paragraph lingers in the mind during the momentary pause as the reader moves to the next paragraph. A writer engaging in wit can use this paragraph ending spot to say something catchy, to make a rapier thrust at the opponent, or to say something complimentary about his or her own side. The process is similar to getting your two cents in and then walking out the door. To what degree does your examination of Jordan's paragraph endings show that she is following this pattern?

7. Evaluate the opening and closing paragraphs of the essay. How effective are they? Why?

QUESTIONS ON LANGUAGE AND DICTION

1. Can you visualize and describe the different types of thin persons named in the next-to-last sentence in paragraph 1?

2. What are the meanings of *expound, machinations, prognose?*

Sound and Noise

ANDY ROONEY

Andy Rooney compares sound and noise to show that each has something to do with our day-to-day comfort or discomfort. He also shows that one person's sound may be another person's noise.

They're tearing down a nine-story building just outside my office window. It doesn't look as though it's going to be a short job either, because when they finish jackhammering this to the ground, they're going to start riveting up a new one. Obviously I've either got to get used to it or move. 1

I think the trick is to get thinking of it as a sound instead of a noise. The difference is hard to define, but a noise is mindless and irritating, while a sound can be soothing. I've known people who live in the city who can't sleep when they go to the country because of the crashing silence. 2

I like the sound of someone whistling on his walk to work, but if someone starts whistling around the office, my mind comes to a halt and I can think about nothing except how irritating the noise is. I start psychoanalyzing the whistler, trying to think why it is he or she feels compelled to make this noise by forcing a stream of air through pursed lips. 3

On the other hand, I've worked in newspaper city rooms filled with people moving, yelling and typing and I can continue to work, absolutely oblivious to the pandemonium around me. 4

A horn honked unnecessarily or more than once for any reason is noise. Every time someone behind me blows his horn the instant the light turns green, I turn red. 5

A ringing telephone can be a welcome sound or an irritating noise, depending on the circumstances. I've gotten over that feeling that it may be someone wonderful calling me every time the phone rings, but there is still a sense of anticipation we're all programmed to have when we hear the phone. Even when I know it's not for me, I can't stand to have a phone ring without answering it. 6

A barking dog is a noise, not a sound. There are almost no times of day when I can stand to hear a dog bark. Part of it is that you have the feeling the dog wants something it isn't getting and if you like dogs, that bothers you. It's like a crying child. 7

One of the most inexplicable noises is a soft one. It's the one each of us 8 hears when we're staying alone in a house at night. Who *are* those people we always hear creeping up the stairs to our bedroom? The house never makes a noise when there's someone else in it with us.

There are good sounds and bad noises everywhere. Bullfrogs in the   9
distance down by the pond are a great sound; so is Dave Brubeck, Segovia, Pavarotti or Horowitz. Even Frank Sinatra is a good sound if you're in the mood for him. The most intrusive sound being inflicted on most of us by a few of us these days is the loud radio or stereo tape player blaring out rock music.

Sounds are important in a war. In 1944 the 1st Infantry Division, the Big   10
Red One, was our most warwise fighting force. It didn't panic. It did what it had to do. At one point in the move across France, a green infantry division was moved in on the 1st Division's flank. One company of that division ran across an arsenal of German weapons. When the 1st Division found German weapons, they destroyed them. These inexperienced soldiers were intrigued with the handy little German Schmeisser machine guns and, during a brief fire fight in the middle of the night, started using them against their former owners. Hearing that familiar sound on their flank and assuming the presence there of the enemy, a mortar unit from the 1st Division calmly turned its weapons in that direction and dropped shells until there was silence. Tragedy of war.

Everyone should think twice before making a noise.   11

QUESTIONS ON MEANING AND CONTENT

1. Do most people classify certain things they hear as sounds and others as noises? Is Rooney right when he says that circumstances can determine whether something is a sound or a noise?

2. How many specific examples cited by Rooney do you think are shared by a large number of people? Do you share any? Which ones don't you share? Can you explain why? Circumstances? Some other reason?

3. Consider the example in paragraph 2 in which city people can't sleep in the quiet of the country. What are the city people missing: sounds or noises? Both? In the example, what does "crashing silence" mean? Have you ever been bothered by the absence of sound or noise? If so, what were the circumstances? How do TV and movie producers use the absence of sound to get reactions from their audiences?

4. Explain why the Schmeisser machine guns mentioned in the long paragraph near the end were apparently noise to one group and sound to another.

QUESTIONS ABOUT RHETORICAL STRATEGIES

1. This essay was originally written as a newspaper column. Can you tell that? How? Does Rooney's vocabulary provide a clue? Do the sentences and paragraphs? How? Or do you simply associate the author with newspaper columns?

2. How do you account for the last paragraph, which is one short sentence? Do you think that sentence appears because of Rooney's long career as a newspaper writer? Or does the sentence achieve something that might work well in writing found in other sources? In what way does that sentence relate to the meaning of the piece? Or does it just relate to the preceding paragraph? Notice that the sentence is expressed as a moral.

3. Consider Rooney's opening paragraph and the long paragraph on the infantry at the end. How do these paragraphs illustrate the same or a very similar point?

4. Assume that you have been assigned a comparison/contrast essay on sound and noise for your composition class. Would the structure of your paper differ from Rooney's? If you think it would differ, explain why. How is Rooney's piece organized?

QUESTIONS ON LANGUAGE AND DICTION

1. What is the meaning of the word *green* in the "green infantry division" mentioned in paragraph 10?

2. Identify Segovia, Pavarotti, Horowitz.

Is There a Superior Sex?

JO DURDEN-SMITH and DIANE DE SIMONE

Jo Durden-Smith and Diane De Simone use the findings of modern research into sexual differences to explain the vulnerabilities and strengths of being male or female. The authors show that understanding these strengths and weaknesses can go far toward defusing the issue of which sex is superior.

Science is just beginning to understand why the bewildering strengths and weaknesses of each sex seem to come packaged together. Why a woman's immune system is more complex than a man's but more likely to attack the body it's supposed to protect. Why men, in general, are superior in math reasoning but are much more likely to be sexual deviants or psychopaths. Why women are strong in areas of communication but more often suffer from phobias and depression. And why there are more males at both ends of the intellectual spectrum—more retardates as well as more geniuses.   1

A full explanation of why men and women tend to be differently gifted and protected, and differently at risk, has yet to be developed. But some important components are already known for sure.   2

Affair of the Heart. Let's start with heart disease. Forty-two million Americans have some form of heart or blood-vessel disease. This year about 1.5 million will have heart attacks; the majority will be men. "Aha!" men might say. "That's environment. Just wait until the same number of women start pulling the same weight we do. They'll soon be dropping like ninepins from the effects of stress, just as *we* are."   3

Sorry, guys. That's untrue on three counts. First, women in the work force are healthier in general than their non-salaried sisters. Second, women appear to be protected against the most common form of heart disease by their natural sex hormones, the estrogens. And, third, they seem to respond to stress—chemically and behaviorally—differently from men.   4

So-called Type-A people—who have a chronic urgency about time and are hard-driving, competitive, extroverted and aggressive—are said to be particularly at risk from the damaging effects of stress. Studies show, however, that Type-A females, when solving work-related problems, don't show the increase in heart rate, blood pressure and adrenalin flow Type-A   5 males do. Even when their overall health picture is the same, they don't have as many heart attacks.

Women tend to be put into stress by the emotional coloration of their lives—not by paper problems but by people and communication problems. When they experience setback, failure or emotional pressure, they respond emotionally or become depressed.   6

Why should there be that overall difference? Perhaps it has to do with the different evolutionary pressures. Men, the hunters and competitors for sex, were more likely to need elaborate stress mechanisms in the presence of danger; women, the nurturers and centers of social groups, were more likely to need fine-tuned emotional responses and skills.   7

Scientists working with male laboratory animals have shown that domi-nance (sexual success and the maintenance of a large turf) is associated with high blood pressure and hardening of the arteries—telltale signs of stress. But they've also found that the animals at the top of the heap have high levels of testosterone, the main male sex hormone. And testosterone tends to increase harmful low-density-lipoprotein cholesterol, leading to harden-ing of the arteries—a problem in human males.   8

Math Gene. Let's move to an area in which *women* seem to be at a disadvantage: mathematical-reasoning ability.   9

"*That's* environment," women may say. "Girls are taught that math is for boys. They're given no encouragement." But in a December 1980 report and a follow-up in April 1981, two psychologists at Johns Hopkins Univer-sity, Camilla Persson Benbow and Julian C. Stanley, suggested that there might well be biological differences in math-reasoning ability between males and females. "You have to understand," Benbow says, "that we didn't start out looking for sex differences in mathematical ability. The Johns Hopkins Study of Mathematically Precocious Youth conducted six talent searches between 1972 and 1979. We were looking for seventh- and eighth-graders with aptitude for mathematical reasoning.   10

"We found about 10,000 children, but we also found something that rather shocked us: far more boys than girls among our high scorers. We studied the boys and girls on many of the significant variables that might account for the discrepancy—preparation and a liking for math, encour-agement and so on. We could find no appreciable differences—except the one in math-reasoning ability. Since 1979, we've looked at another 24,000 children and have found the same sex difference in this ability."   11

Benbow would love to find an environmental difference that has been overlooked. But she cites a follow-up study completed on a group of girls   12 specially taught and specially encouraged. And even *that*, she says, seems to have made little difference.

"All this," says Benbow carefully, "suggests that biological influences   13
may account for part of the difference between the sexes in math-reasoning ability after all. If so, then it's likely because females tend to use their superior verbal skills [abilities governed primarily by the brain's left hemisphere] in their approach to problems. Males seem less dependent on context. They're more abstract, more adept at visual-spatial tasks [abilities controlled by the brain's right hemisphere]. Human males like to manipulate *things*—from Tinker-toys to the cosmos," She laughs. "Females are more dependent, more communicative, more sensitive to context and more interested in people." Such differences, linked to brain organization, may help explain why members of one sex or the other are over-represented in certain professions.

Precarious Existence. For every strength, there is a weakness. Men tend   14
to be better at visual-spatial tasks, women at verbal tasks. But both are comparatively weak in the skill in which the other is strong.

If you've ever given a kids' party you know that girls develop faster and   15
are more mature than boys. In fact, the very existence of males is more precarious than that of females right from the beginning.

Between 120 and 140 males are conceived for every 100 females. From   16
there on in, it's downhill all the way. More males are spontaneously aborted during pregnancy, and although they retain a slight edge at birth—106 to 100—the decline continues. More males than females are born dead. Thirty percent more males than females die in the first month of life. And 33-percent more major birth defects are associated with males. By adulthood the ratio of men to women has become about equal—at a considerable cost to males.

One reason for this is that males have to go through more elaborate   17
transformations in the womb. More can go wrong with them, and they are born less sturdy than girls. For example, the slightest brain damage—occurring during or after birth—can have a more debilitating effect on boys. Also, damage often affects their language skills in the left hemisphere, where boys are more at risk and in which they're less well organized. Boys are four or five times as likely to suffer from language disabilities as girls; more likely to stutter (five to one); to be autistic (four to one); to suffer aphasia, or extreme difficulty learning to talk (five to one); and to have dyslexia—extreme difficulty with reading and writing (four to one).

Men commit almost all the violent crime. In the criminal psychopath,   18 something may have gone wrong with the way the left hemisphere governs behavior. Scientists have recently found a constitutional predisposition, a *genetic* element, for several generally male disorders; hyperactivity, alcoholism and early-onset schizophrenia.

"The genetic studies have looked at what happens in adoption," says   19
psychiatrist Pierre Flor-Henry, clinical professor at the University of Alberta, Canada. "Is there an increased risk that a child, even if adopted early, might follow the pattern of his real parents instead of that of his adoptive parents—in crime, hyperactivity, schizophrenia, and so on? The answer is yes. Nature, a predisposition, is at work in some way we don't yet fully understand."

Flor-Henry believes that the right hemisphere of the human brain de-   20
veloped in such a way that visual-spatial skills were linked in it to mood and movement, and the organization of the male right hemisphere became particularly pronounced. Flor-Henry thinks that violent, antisocial males lack control of the verbal and social left hemisphere.

Females evolved in a more balanced way and developed verbal skills and   21
controls in both brain hemispheres. That somewhat explains why women tend not to become psychopaths and violent criminals. Women, remember, tend to become depressed when under stress.

Phobic Females. Women are, in fact, at risk—just where males are   22
strong. Every year, up to 20 million Americans suffer from depression; 60 percent of them are women. Of course, there *are* real environmental causes for depression. But that doesn't explain why so many more women than men are afflicted by a disorder that affects mood, movement and sex drive. Or why phobias—about heights, closed spaces, snakes and so on—cripple women at least twice as often as they do men.

"Depression and phobias often hang together," says Flor-Henry. "They   23
attack the hemisphere in which the organization of the female brain is more precarious—the right hemisphere. And both seem to involve a genetic predisposition, just as many predominantly *male* disorders do."

Then there's premenstrual tension. British gynecological endocrinolo-   24
gist Katharina Dalton believes that premenstrual tension affects four out of ten women to some extent, and at some time in the eight days before and during menstruation, it *seriously* affects the life of one of those four. Symptoms include increased incidence of asthma, epilepsy and migraine-headache attacks, as well as tension, memory lapses and loss of emotional control, and an increased inclination to crime.

Fine-Tuned Immunity. While men are not as subject as women to mood   25
afflictions, it may be that they're generally more at risk from the whole sea of

viruses and bacteria in which we swim. Certainly they don't produce as much immunoglobulin M—a blood protein important to the body's defenses—as women do.

The female's immune system is more complex than the male's in any 26 case. Why? The answer is babies. For nine months, a pregnant woman has to support inside herself, and *not reject,* as she would a graft, a bundle of tissue that is antigenic to hers, because of the father's contribution to its genetic makeup. At the same time, she has to protect herself *and* this bundle of tissue against any infections. To do it, she must have inherited a more sophisticated immune system than any man's, one capable of finer tuning.

This advantage, too, has a disadvantage. Sometimes the female immune 27 system becomes *over-*efficient and attacks the body it's supposed to be protecting. Women suffer much more than men from certain so-called auto-immune diseases—from such well-known ones as rheumatoid arthritis and lupus to even more mysterious ones, such as Graves' disease, in which the glands, the hormones and behavior can be affected.

Twentieth-century science is uncovering unexpected news about our 28 separate inheritances as men and women. The news is that who we are today is simply the current expression of our long history. Women are still protected for the purpose of motherhood—whether or not, as individuals, they want to have children. Men are still geared to be hunters and sex seekers—whether or not, as individuals, they hunt or seek sex. Men are also less stable, more various than women.

Pluses and minuses—they belong together, making men and women 29 complementary and necessary to one another. Neither is better, neither is worse. It is not a competition. We have to learn to understand that.

QUESTIONS ON MEANING AND CONTENT

1. How knowledgeable or how ignorant are we about sexual differences? What did you learn about your own sex from reading this essay that you didn't know before? About the opposite sex?

2. Does the authors' account of sexual differences conflict with views you had before reading the essay? If so, which ones in particular? If you had held different views on certain issues, has reading the essay changed your mind? Why or why not?

3. In their conclusion, the authors say of the two sexes that "Neither is better and neither is worse." Does the information in the essay support that conclusion?

QUESTIONS ABOUT RHETORICAL STRATEGIES

1. Would you say that this essay was written for a broad, general audience or a more specific kind of audience? If you think the latter, identify the specific audience, examine the characteristics of the authors' words, sentences, and paragraphs, and show how they support your conclusions about the intended audience. Does the information content of the essay, the amount of detail in explanations, and so forth, also tell you something about the intended audience? What?

2. People sometimes adopt defensive or aggressive attitudes about their own sex: "No, mine is not the inferior sex." "Yes, mine is definitely the superior sex." Does the authors' treatment of the subject take this into account; that is, do they write so as to make both sexes comfortable with the way the piece is written? If so, what can you point to in the essay to show that the authors were conscious of this potential audience problem? Do these instances show a stronger concern for what was being said or how something was being said?

3. How does the essay present the comparisons and contrasts? What is the pattern of development? Why is the organization effective?

4. In your view, are the authors trying to write in a way that would make the essay interesting for the audience at the same time they are conveying information to the audience? If so, where do you find evidence of this?

QUESTIONS ON LANGUAGE AND DICTION

1. What do the terms *better* and *worse* in the final paragraph mean? What does the word *superior* in the title mean? If you were asked to find substitute words for all three, what words would you choose? Do your prefer your substitutes over those used by the authors? What difference would your choices make?

2. What are the meanings of *antigenic, nurturers, precocious?*

3. Look up the following words in a good dictionary: *autistic, aphasia, dyslexia,* and *phobia.* How do the authors employ these terms effectively in the essay?

Bing and Elvis

RUSSELL BAKER

Here, Russell Baker reflects on the careers of Bing Crosby and Elvis Presley, placing them in the context of their generations and explaining how different times and the different emotional needs of the people accounted for the immense popularity of these two vastly different singers.

The grieving for Elvis Presley and the commercial exploitation of his death were still not ended when we heard of Bing Crosby's death the other day. Here is a generational puzzle. Those of an age to mourn Elvis must marvel that their elders could really have cared about Bing, just as the Crosby generation a few weeks ago wondered what all the to-do was about when Elvis died.   1

Each man was a mass culture hero to his generation, but it tells us something of the difference between generations that each man's admirers would be hard-pressed to understand why the other could mean very much to his devotees.   2

There were similarities that ought to tell us something. Both came from obscurity to national recognition while quite young and became very rich. Both lacked formal music education and went on to movie careers despite lack of acting skills. Both developed distinctive musical styles which were originally scorned by critics and subsequently studied as pioneer developments in the art of popular song.   3

In short, each man's career followed the mythic rags-to-triumph pattern in which adversity is conquered, detractors are given their comeuppance and estates, fancy cars and world tours become the reward of perseverance. Traditionally this was supposed to be the history of the American business striver, but in our era of committee capitalism it occurs most often in the mass entertainment field, and so we look less and less to the board room for our heroes and more and more to the microphone.   4

Both Crosby and Presley were creations of the microphone. It made it possible for people with frail voices not only to be heard beyond the third row but also to caress millions. Crosby was among the first to understand that the microphone made it possible to sing to multitudes by singing to a single person in a small room.   5

Presley cuddled his microphone like a lover. With Crosby the microphone was usually concealed, but Presley brought it out on stage, detached   6 it from its fitting, stroked it, pressed it to his mouth. It was a surrogate for his listener, and he made love to it unashamedly.

The difference between Presley and Crosby, however, reflected genera- 7 tional differences which spoke of changing values in American life. Crosby's music was soothing; Presley's was disturbing. It is too easy to be glib about this, to say that Crosby was singing to, first, Depression America and, then, to wartime America, and that his audience had all the disturbance they could handle in their daily lives without buying more at the record shop and movie theater.

Crosby's fans talk about how "relaxed" he was, how "natural," how 8 "casual and easy going." By the time Presley began causing sensations, the entire country had become relaxed, casual and easy going, and its younger people seemed to be tired of it, for Elvis's act was anything but soothing and scarcely what a parent of that placid age would have called "natural" for a young man.

Elvis was unseemly, loud, gaudy, sexual—that gyrating pelvis!—in 9 short, disturbing. He not only disturbed parents who thought music by Crosby was soothing but also reminded their young that they were full of the turmoil of youth and an appetite for excitement. At a time when the country had a population coming of age with no memory of troubled times, Presley spoke to a yearning for disturbance.

It probably helped that Elvis's music made Mom and Dad climb the wall. 10 In any case, people who admired Elvis never talk about how relaxed and easy going he made them feel. They are more likely to tell you he introduced them to something new and exciting.

To explain each man in terms of changes in economic and political life 11 probably oversimplifies the matter. Something in the culture was also changing. Crosby's music, for example, paid great attention to the impor- tance of lyrics. The "message" of the song was as essential to the audience as the tune. The words were usually inane and witless, but Crosby—like Sinatra a little later—made them vital. People remembered them, sang them. Words still had meaning.

Although many of Presley's songs were highly lyrical, in most it wasn't 12 the words that moved audiences; it was the "sound." Rock 'n' roll, of which he was the great popularizer, was a "sound" event. Song stopped being song and turned into "sound," at least until the Beatles came along and solved the problem of making words sing to the new beat.

Thus a group like the Rolling Stones, whose lyrics are often elaborate, 13 seems to the Crosby-tuned ear to be shouting only gibberish, a sort of accompanying background noise in a "sound" experience. The Crosby generation has trouble hearing rock because it makes the mistake of trying to understand the words. The Presley generation has trouble with Crosby because it finds the sound unstimulating and cannot be touched by the inanity of the words. The mutual deafness may be a measure of how far we have come from really troubled times and of how deeply we have come to mistrust the value of words.

QUESTIONS ON MEANING AND CONTENT

1. In his opening paragraph, Baker says that Bing Crosby's popularity with one large group of Americans and Elvis Presley's popularity with another represented "a generational puzzle." Does Baker solve that puzzle in his essay? Do you leave the essay satisfied that you understand why the popular music tastes of two generations of Americans differed so drastically? How does Baker account for the fame of each entertainer?

2. Baker says that one generation needed Crosby's kind of music and another generation needed Presley's. So many people shared the same needs that each singer's music dominated popular music during its respective generation. What does the existence of so many different kinds of rock music along with strong competition from country-western, bluegrass, and a variety of others say about American culture right now? Can you form a generalization about what encourages such a great variety of current popular music? What needs are fulfilled by the music you prefer?

3. What is the fundamental role of popular singers in relation to their fans? Is it purely sexual? Baker says that Crosby was able to "caress millions" when he sang and that Elvis used the microphone as a symbolic woman and "made love to it unashamedly." Explain why it is that people are so interested in listening to popular music, but don't offer a vague answer like "for entertainment." This answer will require more than one reason. Begin with the most important one. Do you think your list would agree with lists made by your fellow students? Consider this question also: Is it possible that we really don't understand exactly why popular music is so appealing to so many?

QUESTIONS ABOUT RHETORICAL STRATEGIES

1. Notice how Baker organizes the essay. He first compares the two singers, showing similarities and tying these similarities together with the microphone that made it possible for two obscure people to become popular heroes. Then he devotes a section to contrasting the two singers while at the same time comparing and contrasting the *political* and *economic* conditions of the two generations. After this, Baker shifts again and contrasts not the singers but the songs, and at the same time he is also contrasting the *cultures* of the two generations. Where are these shifts made? Look carefully at Baker's language at each shift point and then explain how Baker makes these shifts without making the movement seem abrupt.

2. Since the essay stresses differences, the section on similarities is brief. Baker takes up similarities early in the essay (paragraphs 4, 5, 6). When differences are stressed in a piece of writing, the similarities play a minor role and receive less space. They, thus, sometimes pose the problem of where to place them in an essay. Placing them near the beginning is one option; placing them at the end is another. Sometimes they are taken up quickly in body paragraphs devoted to differences. Evaluate Baker's placement of similarities. Why are they incorporated into the essay structure early? How does this strengthen the essay? Is it helpful to the reader to have the similarities prior to the differences? Is it absolutely critical to have them there? What would be the impact on the essay if the similarities were moved to the end?

3. Examine the second paragraph very carefully, and then explain how this short paragraph is essential to the paragraph before it and to the ones following.

4. Write a paragraph explaining what Baker does for readers in paragraphs 1 and 2.

5. How often does the author contrast Bing and Elvis (or their songs) in the same paragraph? How many contrast paragraphs are devoted to just one?

QUESTIONS ON LANGUAGE AND DICTION

1. What does the term "mutual deafness" in the last sentence of the essay mean? How does this deafness create a generation gap?

2. What are the meanings of *inane, placid, surrogate?*

Computers and the Human Mind

LEWIS THOMAS

In this essay, scientist Lewis Thomas acknowledges that artificial intelligence is more efficient than natural intelligence but goes on to explain that some inefficiencies of the human mind may not be weakness after all.

I wrote a couple of essays a few years back on computers, in which I had a few things to say in opposition to the idea that machines could be made with what the computer people themselves call Artifical Intelligence; they always use capital letters for this technology, and refer to it in their technical papers as AI. I was not fond of the idea and said so, and proceeded to point out the necessity for error in the working of the human mind, which I thought made it different from the computer. In response, I received a great deal of mail, most of it gently remonstrative, but friendly, the worst kind of mail to get on days when things aren't going well anyway, pointing out to me in the simplest language how wrong indeed I was. Computers do proceed, of course, by the method of trial and error. The whole technology is based on this, can work in no other way. 1

One of the things I have always disliked about computers is that they are personally humiliating. They do resemble, despite my wish for it to be otherwise, the operations of the human mind. There are differences, but the Artificial Intelligence people, with their vast and clever computers, have come far enough along to make it clear that the machines behave like thinking machines. If they are right, the thing to worry about is not that they will ultimately be making electronic minds superior to ours but that already ours are so inferior to theirs, mine anyway. I have never heard of a computer, even a simple one, as dedicated to the deliberate process of forgetting information, losing it, restoring it out of context and in misleading forms, or generating such a condition of diffuse, inaccurate confusion as occurs every day in the average human brain. We are already so outclassed as to live in constant embarrassment. 2

I have been inputting, as they say, one bit of hard data after another into my brain all my life, some of it thruputting and outputting from the other ear, but a great deal held and stored somewhere, or so I am assured, but I possess no reliable device, anywhere in my circuitry, for retrieving it when needed. If I wish for the simplest of things, someone's name for example, I 3 cannot send in a straightforward demand with any sure hope of getting back the right name. I am often required to think about something else, something quite unrelated, and wait, hanging around in the mind's lobby, picking up books and laying them down, pacing around, and then, if it is a lucky day, out pops the name. No computer could be designed by any engineer to function, or malfunction, in this way.

I have learned, one time or another, all sorts of things that I remember learning, but now they are lost to me. I cannot place the Thirty Years War or the Hundred Years War in the right centuries, nor have I at hand the barest facts about the issues involved. I once knew Keats, lots of Keats, by heart; he is still there, I suppose, probably scattered across the lobes of my left hemisphere, or maybe translated into the wordless language of my right hemisphere and preserved there forever as a set of hunches, but irretrievable as language. I have lost most of the philosophers I studied long ago and liked; the only sure memory I retain of Heidegger, even when I reread him today, is bewilderment. I have forgotten how to do cube roots, and will never learn again. Slide rules. Solid geometry. Thomas Hardy. Chinese etymology, which I learned in great volumes just a few years ago. The Bible, most of all the Sunday-school Bible, long since gone, obliterated. 4

It occurs to me that the computer-brain analogy needs to take account of what must otherwise seem an unnatural degree of fallibility on the part of the brain. Maybe what we do, by compulsion, in order to make sure that our minds are always reasonably well prepared to get us through any new day, is something like what happens to a computer when you walk past it carrying a powerful magnet. Perhaps we are in possession of similar devices—maybe chemical messengers of some sort—that periodically sweep the mind clear of surplus information, leaving the chips and circuits open to the new needs of the day. I cannot remember Keats because he was expunged one day; if I want him back, which I don't very badly, I am obliged to learn him all over again; he is gone out of my temporal lobe, where I had him once lodged. 5

In a way, this could be a reassuring notion, especially for anyone getting on, as I am, in years. It would be nice to know that I have a mechanism, even if it is beyond my control, that sweeps through my brain periodically, editing away the accumulations of old and no longer usable information, clearing the desk so to speak, disposing of all the old magazines and partly read books, getting the rooms of the mind ready for new lodgers. Indeed, if there were not such a mechanism, the brain would sooner or later be stuffed, swollen, bulging with facts, and unable to take in anything new. Signs 6 would have to be displayed in all the lobes, reading OCCUPIED. Or NO ENTRY. Or worst of all, signs repainted, changed to read EXIT.

Come to think of it, you could not run a human brain in any other way,   7 and the clearing out of excess information must be going on, automatically, autonomically, all the time. Perhaps there are certain pieces of thought that must be classed as nonbiodegradable, like addition and one's family's names and how to read a taximeter, but a great deal of material is surely disposable. And the need for a quick and ready sanitation system is real: you cannot ever be sure, from minute to minute, when you will have to find a place to put something new. At the very least, you are required to have, and use, a mechanism for edging facts to one side, pushing them out of the way into something like a plastic kitchen bag. Otherwise you would run the risk of losing all good ideas. Have you noticed how often it happens that a really good idea—the kind of idea that looks, as it approaches, like the explanation for everything about everything—tends to hover near at hand when you are thinking hard about something quite different? On good days it happens all the time. There you are, halfway into a taxi, thinking hard about the condition of the cartilage in the right knee joint, and suddenly, with a whirring sound, in flies a new notion looking for a place to light. You'd better be sure you have a few bare spots, denuded of anything like thought, ready for its perching, or it will fly away into the dark. Computers cannot do this sort of thing. They can perform feats of mathematics beyond my comprehension, construct animated graphs at the touch of a finger, write with ease something like second-rate poetry, and they can even generate surprise for the operator, but I doubt very much that a computer, no matter how large and intricate, can itself *be* surprised, *feel* surprised; there isn't room enough for that.

Computers are good at seeing patterns, better than we are. They can   8 connect things that seem unrelated to each other, scanning the night sky or the stained blotches of 50,000 proteins on an electrophoretic gel or the numbers generated by all the world's stock markets, and find relationships that matter. We do something like this with our brains, but we do it differently; we get things wrong. We use information not so much for its own sake as for leading to thoughts that really are unrelated, unconnected, patternless, and sometimes therefore quite new. If the human brain had not possessed this special gift, we would still be sharpening bones, muttering to ourselves, unable to make a poem or even whistle.

These two gifts, the ability to lose information unpredictably and to get   9 relationships wrong, distinguish our brains from any computer I can imagine ever being manufactured. Artificial Intelligence is one thing, and I never spend a day without admiring it, but human intelligence is something else again. If I succeed in understanding the Shwartzman phenomenon, or in learning Homeric Greek, it will not be because the impulse to do so came in linear fashion from some prior stimulus. I will have blundered into it, thinking that something else led to it, when in fact the something else was heading in another direction, intent on other business.

This is not to say that I do not respect my mind, or anyone else's mind. I do, and I count it an added mark of respect to acknowledge that I do not understand it. My own mind, fallible, error-prone, forgetful, unpredictable, and ungovernable, is way over my head.   10

QUESTIONS ON MEANING AND CONTENT

1. Thomas says that artificial intelligence is superior to human intelligence. Do you think he believes that? Does he support this assertion in the essay?

2. In paragraph 7, he says that the computer can't be surprised but the human operator can be. Is this a strength of the computer and a weakness of the operator or vice versa? Or neither? What is the big difference being shown here? What is natural intelligence connected to that artificial intelligence is not? Is this the reason the computer writes the "second-rate poetry" mentioned in the same paragraph? Explain.

3. In paragraph 9, Thomas says that human minds "lose information unpredictably" and also "get relationships wrong." Yet he refers to each as an "ability" and a "gift." Why does he say this? Has he shown earlier in the essay that they really are gifts? Where? In what way are they abilities and gifts?

4. In the concluding paragraph, Thomas seems to be talking only about human minds, his own in particular. But is he really? Or is he still talking about computers and artificial intelligence? Explain.

QUESTIONS ABOUT RHETORICAL STRATEGIES

1. How much of the essay does Thomas devote to an introduction? The first paragraph? The first two paragraphs? In short, where does he stop preparing the reader for the essay and actually get into the body of the essay?

How can you tell? What is the nature of the background or overview he presents to get the essay going; that is, what kind of information does it supply?

2. How does Thomas use comparison and contrast? Is the emphasis on differences? Is he more interested in explaining how the mind thinks or how the computer thinks? Is his method to show how one works and then use the other as a point of contrast, or does he, more or less, compare them point by point? What similarities does he point out?

QUESTIONS ON LANGUAGE AND DICTION

1. Thomas relies heavily on metaphors of one kind or another in explaining the points he wants to make. He speaks of the mind several times as if it were a room that thoughts, like people, walk into and out of. He compares the process of forgetting to "clearing old magazines and partly read" books off of a desk, and there are many other metaphors. Did you notice these metaphors as you read through the essay or did they tend to blend invisibly into the flow of the essay? If they stood out for you, explain why. What called your attention to them? If they seemed to blend in and you took little notice of them, explain why. What is there about them or Thomas' writing that would cause them to blend in?

2. What other metaphors do you find in the essay? Do they help Thomas make his points more clearly and effectively? If so, how? If not, do any one of them weaken the essay or confuse you in any way? Is there anything about Thomas' subject that might create the need for metaphor?

3. Single out one of Thomas' metaphors and write several sentences or a paragraph making the same point but without using any metaphors—that is, without using comparisons that let us see one thing in terms of something else quite different. After you have done this, explain what you learned about metaphor in the process. What practical things can metaphor do for a writer?

Grant and Lee

BRUCE CATTON

*Civil War historian Bruce Catton recreates the moments at Appomattox
Courthouse, Virginia, when two famous generals came together to draw up
the papers ending the Civil War. Catton uses the occasion to talk about
changes taking place in America and to show how the commanders represented two different American societies.*

Until this Palm Sunday of 1865 the word Appomattox had no meaning. It   1
was a harsh name left over from Indian days, it belonged to a river and to a
country town, and it had no overtones. But after this day it would be one of
the haunted possessions of the American people, a great and unique word
that would echo in the national memory with infinite tragedy and infinite
promise, recalling a moment in which sunset and sunrise came together in a
streaked glow that was half twilight and half dawn.

The business might almost have been stage-managed for effect. No   2
detail had been overlooked. There was even the case of Wilmer McLean, the
Virginian who once owned a place by a stream named Bull Run and who
found his farm overrun by soldiers in the first battle of the war. He sold out
and moved to southern Virginia to get away from the war, and he bought a
modest house in Appomattox Court House; and the war caught up with him
finally, so that Lee and Grant chose his front parlor—of all the rooms in
America—as the place where they would sit down together and bring the
fighting to an end.

Lee had one staff officer with him, and in Mr. McLean's front yard a   3
Confederate orderly stood by while the war horse Traveler nibbled at the
spring grass. Grant came with half a dozen officers of his own, including the
famous Sheridan, and after he and Lee had shaken hands and taken their
seats these trooped into the room to look and to listen. Grant and Lee sat at
two separate tables, the central figures in one of the greatest tableaus of
American history.

It was a great tableau not merely because of what these two men did but   4
also because of what they were. No two Americans could have been in
greater contrast. (Again, the staging was perfect.) Lee was legend
incarnate—tall, gray, one of the handsomest and most imposing men who
ever lived, dressed today in his best uniform, with a sword belted at his
waist. Grant was—well, he was U.S. Grant, rather scrubby and undersized,

wearing his working clothes, with mud-spattered boots and trousers and a private's rumpled blue coat with his lieutenant general's stars tacked to the shoulders. He wore no sword. The men who were with them noticed the contrast and remembered it. Grant himself seems to have felt it; years afterward, when he wrote his memoirs, he mentioned it and went to some lengths to explain why he did not go to this meeting togged out in dress uniform. (In effect, his explanation was that he was just too busy.)

Yet the contrast went far beyond the matter of personal appearance.   5
Two separate versions of America met in this room, each perfectly embodied by its chosen representative.

There was an American aristocracy, and it had had a great day. It came   6
from the past and it looked to the past; it seemed almost deliberately archaic, with an air of knee breeches and buckled shoes and powdered wigs, with a leisured dignity and a rigid code in which privilege and duty were closely joined. It had brought the country to its birth and it had provided many of its beliefs; it had given courage and leadership, a sense of order and learning, and if there had been any way by which the eighteenth century could possibly have been carried forward into the future, this class would have provided the perfect vehicle. But from the day of its beginning America had been fated to be a land of unending change. The country in which this leisured class had its place was in powerful ferment, and the class itself had changed. It had been diluted. In the struggle for survival it had laid hands on the curious combination of modern machinery and slave labor, the old standards had been altered, dignity had begun to look like arrogance, and pride of purse had begun to elbow out pride of breeding. The single lifetime of Robert E. Lee had seen the change, although Lee himself had not been touched by it.

Yet the old values were real, and the effort to preserve them had nobility.   7
Of all the things that went to make up the war, none had more poignance than the desperate fight to preserve these disappearing values, eroded by change from within as much as by change from without. The fight had been made and it had been lost, and everything that had been dreamed and tried and fought for was personified in the gray man who sat at the little table in the parlor at Appomattox and waited for the other man to start writing out the terms of surrender.

The other man was wholly representative too. Behind him there was a   8
new society, not dreamed of by the founding fathers: a society with the lid taken off, western man standing up to assert that what lay back of a person mattered nothing in comparison to what lay ahead of him. It was the land of the mudsills, the temporarily dispossessed, the people who had nothing to lose but the future; behind it were hard times, humiliation and failure, and

ahead of it was all the world and a chance to lift oneself by one's bootstraps. It had few standards beyond a basic unformulated belief in the irrepressibility and ultimate value of the human spirit, and it could tramp with heavy boots down a ravaged Shenandoah Valley or through the embers of a burned Columbia without giving more than a casual thought to the things that were being destroyed. Yet it had its own nobility and its own standards; it had, in fact, the future of the race in its keeping, with all the immeasurable potential that might reside in a people who had decided that they would no longer be bound by the limitations of the past. It was rough and uncultivated and it came to important meetings wearing muddy boots and no sword, and it had to be listened to.

It could speak with a soft voice, and it could even be abashed by its own 9 moment of triumph, as if that moment were not a thing to be savored and enjoyed. Grant seems to have been almost embarrassed when he and Lee came together in this parlor, yet it was definitely not the embarrassment of an underling ill at ease in a superior's presence. Rather it was simply the diffidence of a sensitive man who had another man in his power and wished to hurt him as little as possible. So Grant made small talk and recalled the old days in the Mexican War, when Lee had been the polished staff officer in the commanding general's tents and Grant had been an acting regimental quartermaster, slouching about like the hired man who looked after the teams. Perhaps the oddest thing about this meeting at Appomattox was that it was Grant, the nobody from nowhere, who played the part of gracious host, trying to put the aristocrat at his ease and, as far as might be, to soften the weight of the blow that was about to come down. In the end it was Lee who, so to speak, had to call the meeting to order, remarking (and the remark must have wrenched him almost beyond endurance) that they both knew what they were there for and that perhaps they had better get down to business. So Grant opened his orderly book and got out his pencil. He confessed afterward that when he did so he had no idea what words he was going to write.

QUESTIONS ON MEANING AND CONTENT

1. Grant and Lee are presented as representatives of two distinctly different American societies. When the two met at Appomattox, they were dressed quite differently. How does the dress of each reflect the cultures they represented?

2. Grant excused his muddy boots and work uniform by explaining that he was too busy to dress formally for the occasion. Wouldn't Lee, as the commanding general of the other army, have been equally busy? Yet Lee found time to don his best uniform. This must say something about how the two—and the cultures each represented—valued appearances. Do the details in paragraph 6 and paragraph 8 suggest that the culture Lee represented would have expected him to be dressed spotlessly and the culture Grant represented wouldn't have been particularly concerned about his dress? Explain.

3. Catton refers to Lee as an "aristocrat." What word would you use to characterize Grant? Why do you suppose Catton doesn't use a general, descriptive term to describe Grant?

4. Paragraph 8, which talks about the society Grant represented, refers to common, ordinary people. Paragraph 6, which discusses Lee's society, does not talk about the common people at all. Yet we know that common, ordinary people made up most of Lee's society just as they did Grant's. How do you explain the absence of references to the people in paragraph 6? Is the absence of such references the key to what Catton is trying to say in this piece? Explain.

5. The essay shows that Lee was polished and gracious, and his bearing and his clothing reinforce this. Grant's appearance would suggest that he was not a particularly gracious man. What is the relationship between Grant's appearance and Grant as a person?

QUESTIONS ABOUT RHETORICAL STRATEGIES

1. This piece of writing is a good example of how one rhetorical mode can support another. Catton uses narrative (events placed in the movement of time) to enclose the comparison-contrast which forms the bulk of the essay. Identify the narrative sections. Where are the turning points from one to the other; that is, the point where narration leads into the comparison-contrast and the point where narration provides a means of concluding the comparison-contrast? Were you conscious of these swing points as you first read the essay?

2. Paragraphs 3 and 4 consider Grant and Lee side-by-side, a point about Lee, a point about Grant, and so forth. Yet the two cultures they represent are treated separately, one full paragraph to each (paragraphs 6 and 8). Is discussing the two generals side-by-side and the two cultures separately helpful to readers? How? Why might the two topics (two generals and two cultures) call for one method of development for one, another method for the other?

3. Paragraph 5 is very short. What does it contribute to the structure of the essay? Does paragraph 7, although longer, serve the same purpose?

4. In paragraph 6, Catton says that the people Grant represented "had nothing to lose but the future." What, then, did the people Lee represented have to lose?

QUESTIONS ON LANGUAGE AND DICTION

1. Catton speaks figuratively at many points in the essay, and it is important to understand the meaning of these figurative statements in order to comprehend the main idea. Interpret the following figurative statements:

  a. Paragraph 1 says that when Grant and Lee met, it was "a moment in which sunset and sunrise came together in a streaked glow that was half twilight and half dawn."

  b. In paragraph 6 the author says that a change had already begun to take place in Lee's society: "The old standards had been altered, dignity had begun to look like arrogance, and pride of purse had begun to elbow out pride of breeding."

  c. Paragraph 8 talks about the society Grant represented as if it were a single person: "It was rough and uncultivated and it came to important meetings wearing muddy boots and no sword, and it had to be listened to."

2. Check the meanings of any of the following words that are unfamiliar to you: *abashed, archaic, aristocracy, diffidence, dispossessed, incarnate, irrepressibility, poignance, tableau.*

Many Mansions

JOAN DIDION

Joan Didion evaluates two homes built for governors in two different ages. One, she finds, was built to accommodate a governor's family as well as governmental functions. As for the other, she seems puzzled by the purposes the designers had in mind.

The new official residence for governors of California, unlandscaped, 1 unfurnished, and unoccupied since the day construction stopped in 1975, stands on eleven acres of oaks and olives on a bluff overlooking the American River outside Sacramento. This is the twelve-thousand-square-foot house that Ronald and Nancy Reagan built. This is the sixteen-room house in which Jerry Brown declined to live. This is the vacant house which cost the State of California one-million-four, not including the property, which was purchased in 1969 and donated to the state by such friends of the Reagans as Leonard K. Firestone of Firestone Tire and Rubber and Taft Schreiber of the Music Corporation of America and Holmes Tuttle, the Los Angeles Ford dealer. All day at this empty house three maintenance men try to keep the bulletproof windows clean and the cobwebs swept and the wild grass green and the rattle-snakes down by the river and away from the thirty-five exterior wood and glass doors. All night at this empty house the lights stay on behind the eight-foot chainlink fence and the guard dogs lie at bay and the telephone, when it rings, startles by the fact that it works. "Governor's Residence," the guards answer, their voices laconic, matter-of-fact, quite as if there were some phantom governor to connect. Wild grass grows where the tennis court was to have been. Wild grass grows where the pool and sauna were to have been. The American is the river in which gold was discovered in 1848, and it once ran fast and full past here, but lately there have been upstream dams and dry years. Much of the bed is exposed. The far bank has been dredged and graded. That the river is running low is of no real account, however, since one of the many peculiarities of the new Governor's Residence is that it is so situated as to have no clear view of the river.

It is an altogether curious structure, this one-story one-million-four 2 dream house of Ronald and Nancy Reagan's. Were the house on the market (which it will probably not be, since, at the time it was costing a million-four, local real estate agents seemed to agree on $300,000 as the top price ever paid for a house in Sacramento County), the words used to describe it would be "open" and "contemporary," although technically it is neither. "Flow" is a word that crops up quite a bit when one is walking through the place, and so is "resemble." The walls "resemble" local adobe, but they are not: they are the same concrete blocks, plastered and painted a rather stale yellowed cream, used in so many supermarkets and housing projects and Coca-Cola bottling plants. The door frames and the exposed beams "resemble" native redwood, but they are not: they are construction-grade lumber of indeterminate quality, stained brown. If anyone ever moves in, the concrete floors will be carpeted, wall to wall. If anyone ever moves in, the thirty-five exterior wood and glass doors, possibly the single distinctive feature in the house, will be, according to plan, "draped." The bathrooms are small and standard. The family bedrooms open directly onto the nonexistent swimming pool, with all its potential for noise and distraction. To one side of the fireplace in the formal living room there is what is known in the trade as a "wet bar," a cabinet for bottles and glasses with a sink and a long vinyl-topped counter. (This vinyl "resembles" slate.) In the entire house there are only enough bookshelves for a set of the World Book and some Books of the Month, plus maybe three Royal Doulton figurines and a back file of *Connoisseur,* but there is $90,000 worth of other teak cabinetry, including the "refreshment center" in the "recreation room." There is that most ubiquitous of all "luxury features," a bidet in the master bedroom. There is one of those kitchens which seem designed exclusively for defrosting by microwave and compacting trash. It is a house built for a family of snackers.

And yet, appliances notwithstanding, it is hard to see where the million-four went. The place has been called, by Jerry Brown, a "Taj Mahal." It has been called a "white elephant," a "resort," a "monument to the colossal ego of our former governor." It is not exactly any of these things. It is simply and rather astonishingly an enlarged version of a very common kind of California tract house, a monument not to colossal ego but to a weird absence of ego, a case study in the architecture of limited possibilities, insistently and malevolently "democratic," flattened out, mediocre and "open" and as devoid of privacy or personal eccentricity as the lobby area in a Ramada Inn. It is the architecture of "background music," decorators, "good taste." I recall once interviewing Nancy Reagan, at a time when her husband was governor and the construction on this house had not yet begun. We drove down to the State Capitol Building that day, and Mrs. Reagan showed me how she had lightened and brightened offices there by replacing the old burnished leather on the walls with the kind of beige

3

burlap then favored in new office buildings. I mention this because it was on my mind as I walked through the empty house on the American River outside Sacramento.

From 1903 until Ronald Reagan, who lived in a rented house in Sacramento while he was governor ($1,200 a month, payable by the state to a group of Reagan's friends), the governors of California lived in a large white Victorian Gothic house at 16th and H Streets in Sacramento. This extremely individual house, three stories and a cupola and the face of Columbia the Gem of the Ocean worked into the molding over every door, was built in 1877 by a Sacramento hardware merchant named Albert Gallatin. The state paid $32,500 for it in 1903 and my father was born in a house a block away in 1908. This part of town has since run to seed and small business, the kind of place where both Squeaky Fromme and Patricia Hearst could and probably did go about their business unnoticed, but the Governor's Mansion, unoccupied and open to the public as State Historical Landmark Number 823, remains Sacramento's premier example of eccentric domestic architecture.

As it happens I used to go there once in a while, when Earl Warren was governor and his daughter Nina was a year head of me at C. K. McClatchy Senior High School. Nina was always called "Honey Bear" in the papers and in *Life* Magazine but she was called "Nina" at C. K. McClatchy Senior High School and she was called "Nina" (or sometimes "Warren") at weekly meetings of the Mañana Club, a local instutition to which we both belonged. I recall being initiated into the Mañana Club one night at the old Governor's Mansion, in a ceremony which involved being blindfolded and standing around Nina's bedroom in a state of high apprehension about secret rites which never materialized. It was the custom for the members to hurl mild insults at the initiates, and I remember being dumbfounded to hear Nina, by my fourteen-year-old lights the most glamorous and unapproachable fifteen-year-old in America, characterize me as "stuck on herself." There in the Governor's Mansion that night I learned for the first time that my face to the world was not necessarily the face in my mirror. "No smoking on the third floor," everyone kept saying. "Mrs. Warren *said*. No smoking on the third floor or *else*."

Firetrap or not, the old Governor's Mansion was at that time my favorite house in the world, and probably still is. The morning after I was shown the new "Residence" I visited the old "Mansion," took the public tour with a group of perhaps twenty people, none of whom seemed to find it as ideal as I did. "All those stairs," they murmured, as if stairs could no longer be tolerated by human physiology. "All those stairs," and "all that waste space." The old Governor's Mansion does have stairs and waste space, which is precisely why it remains the kind of house in which sixty adolescent girls might gather and never interrupt the real life of the household. The bedrooms are big and private and high-ceilinged and they do not open on the swimming pool and one can imagine reading in one of them, or writing a book, or closing the door and crying until dinner. The bathrooms are big and airy and they do not have bidets but they have room for hampers, and dressing tables, and chairs on which to sit and read a story to a child in the bathtub. There are hallways wide and narrow, stairs front and back, sewing rooms, ironing rooms, secret rooms. On the gilt mirror in the library there is worked a bust of Shakespeare, a pretty fancy for a hardware merchant in a California farm town in 1877. In the kitchen there is no trash compactor and there is no "island" with the appliances built in but there are two pantries, and a nice old table with a marble top for rolling out pastry and making divinity fudge and chocolate leaves. The morning I took the tour our guide asked if anyone could think why the old table had a marble top. There were a dozen or so other women in the group, each of an age to have cooked unnumbered meals, but not one of them could think of a single use for a slab of marble in the kitchen. It occurred to me that we had finally evolved a society in which knowledge of a pastry marble, like a taste for stairs and closed doors, could be construed as "elitist," and as I left the Governor's Mansion I felt very like the heroine of Mary McCarthy's *Birds of America*, the one who located America's moral decline in the disappearance of the first course.

A guard sleeps at night in the old mansion, which has been condemned   7
as a dwelling by the state fire marshal. It costs about $85,000 a year to keep guards at the new official residence. Meanwhile the current governor of California, Edmund G. Brown, Jr., sleeps on a mattress on the floor in the famous apartment for which he pays $275 a month out of his own $49,100 annual salary. This has considerable and potent symbolic value, as do the two empty houses themselves, most particularly the house the Reagans built on the river. It is a great point around the Capitol these days to have "never seen" the house on the river. The governor himself has "never seen" it. The governor's press secretary, Elisabeth Coleman, has "never seen" it. The governor's chief of staff, Gray Davis, admits to having seen it, but only once, when "Mary McGrory wanted to see it." This unseen house on the river is, Jerry Brown has said, "not my style."

As a matter of fact this is precisely the point about the house on the   8 river—the house is not Jerry Brown's style, but Mary McGrory's style, *not our style*—and it is a point which presents a certain problem, since the house so clearly *is* the style not only of Jerry Brown's predecessor but of millions of Jerry Brown's constituents. Words are chosen carefully. Reasonable objections are framed. One hears about how the house is too far from the Capitol, too far from the Legislature. One hears about the folly of running such a lavish establishment for an unmarried governor and one hears about the governor's temperamental austerity. One hears every possible reason for not living in the house except the one that counts: it is the kind of house that has a wet bar in the living room. It is the kind of house that has a refreshment center. It is the kind of house in which one does not live, but there is no way to say this without getting into touchy and evanescent and finally inadmissible questions of taste, and ultimately of class. I have seldom seen a house so evocative of the unspeakable.

1977

QUESTIONS ON MEANING AND CONTENT

1. Didion's attitude toward the two houses indicates that she likes what the old mansion represented but doesn't like what the new mansion represents. What, as Didion presents the two, did the old mansion and what does the new one represent?

2. What point is the author trying to convey in paragraph 2 by stressing how certain features of the new house "resemble" something else?

3. In paragraph 6, the author describes the marble topped pastry table in the kitchen of the old mansion and seems disappointed when the women present have no idea of its original use. How is Didion's reaction to this related to her adverse reactions to the new mansion? Do you think the women who are perplexed by the pastry table would object to the new mansion in the way that the author does? Why or why not?

4. What evidence do you find in the essay to suggest that Didion is not an admirer of Ronald and Nancy Reagan? What does she seem to see as their shortcomings?

5. Does the author's reactions to the two houses go beyond the buildings themselves? Is she also being critical of changes that have taken place in America? If so, what evidence in the essay suggests this?

QUESTIONS ABOUT RHETORICAL STRATEGIES

1. Didion writes the comparison-contrast using the block method; that is, she takes up the new residence and completes her description of it (paragraphs 1–3) and then goes on to the old residence and does the same (paragraphs 4–6). How well does this work? What would be the effect of devoting alternating paragraphs to each or comparing and contrasting each within single paragraphs? What would be gained or lost by using either of these other methods (or a combination of them)?

2. How necessary are the last two paragraphs of the essay? Are these a part of the comparison-contrast or do they serve a different purpose? If so, what purpose? Would omitting these paragraphs weaken or strenthen the essay, in your view? Explain.

3. What point do you think Didion is trying to make in paragraph 5 when she discusses her visits to the old mansion when she was a high school student? What does the paragraph have to do with the comparison-contrast? Does this paragraph tell us anything about her attitude toward both houses?

QUESTIONS ON LANGUAGE AND DICTION

1. In paragraph 1, Didion notes that the river, running past the new mansion has been low because of dams and drought. Then she says that this doesn't matter "since one of the many peculiarities of the new Governor's Residence is that it is so situated as to have no clear view of the river." How is she using the word *peculiarities*? In its usual sense? As understatement? Do her other criticisms of this house seem to suggest that she means something stronger than peculiarities? What other, stronger terms, can you suggest?

2. In the next-to-last sentence of the essay, the author says that government officials won't state the real reasons that the new mansion is unoccupied because doing so would involve "inadmissable questions of taste, and ultimately of class." Why are these questions "inadmissable"? Is the word *class* here used in the sense of social class or in the sense of style (having class)? Or are both meanings suggested? Explain.

3. Consider the language of the essay—how things are said. This use of language helps establish the tone of the essay or the author's attitude toward the two subjects. Describe the tone of the essay—or the tones if you believe

Didion shifts in tone as she moves from one house to the other. Does the way the author presents details convey a picture of the author? If so, what is the picture and how does the manner of presenting the details suggest the picture?

4. Paragraph 3 says that former governor Jerry Brown alluded to the new house as a "Taj Mahal." What does this allusion suggest about the new residence?

5. Paragraph 3 also states that the new house has been referred to as a "white elephant" and a "resort." Explain the view of the new mansion suggested by each of these.

6. Check the meanings of any of the following words that you do not already know: *evanescent, evocative, indeterminate, laconic, pantry, ubiquitous.*

WRITING SCENARIOS

1. The principal of your former high school has asked you to return and address this year's graduating class. For convenience, you plan to write your speech in essay form. You have decided to compare and contrast the "high school experience" with the "college experience." In what ways are they similar? How do they differ? Your purpose is to help younger students profit from your experience.

2. Your student government is preparing a booklet on popular entertainment spots located near your campus. You have been asked to write about one of your favorite hangouts for nighttime relaxation and recreation. This should be a place that you know primarily by night. It should also be an active place. For your project, however, you will want to visit this spot when it first opens for the day. Observe carefully and take notes. Then write an essay comparing and contrasting the place at two times: the early opening hours, and night hours when the activity is intense. Your audience is made up of two groups: interested students who are not familiar with the establishment, and students who are familiar with it but who know it mostly in one way—as it is during the quiet, daylight hours or as it is during the night, when it is intensely active.

3. The social/academic club of your major (for example, the English Club or the Biology Club) is sponsoring an orientation for new majors. The meeting will consist of presentations by club members, followed by a period for refreshments and discussions. Your club president has asked you to give a short presentation in which you compare and contrast two things or concepts related to your major. A finance major, for example, might show the difference between common and preferred stocks, an English major the distinction between a Shakespearean and an Italian sonnet; a biology major might explain how to tell very similar plants, trees, or animals apart. Your purpose is to teach novice majors to identify each of the subjects chosen for your comparison/contrast.

4. You are a senior, active in campus activities. Each year your college sponsors a Career Day, in which various students and professors make presentations to interested students about the job market and what to expect after graduation. The planning committee has asked you to make an introductory presentation in which you compare and contrast "college life" with "the real world." You will want to make your presentation informative as well as interesting. You will want to prewrite carefully in order to explore the differences, real or imagined, between these two worlds. Investigate methodically. First, do some brainstorming of your own to see what sort of list you can compile on how life at college differs from life in "the real world." Then see if you can separate the list into two lists, one of items that you think are fallacies about either the college world or the "real" world and one that contains what you think are valid characteristics. The lists will provide background information that should give you an intelligent starting point in your investigation. You may also want to gather information from people with a specific viewpoint on the two worlds, such as people who have recently graduated from college, or professors who practiced their area of expertise in "the real world" before making a change to college training.

5. You have been searching for a part-time job to help pay your way through school, but you don't want the typical job at a fast-food restaurant or grocery store; you want something interesting. Yesterday, you answered an advertisement for a college student to assist a technical writer at a computer-software manufacturing company. The position involves helping a professional writer prepare manuals that teach people how to use certain computers and computer software. In order to test your ability to perform the kinds of writing tasks you would have to do on the job, the employer has asked you to return home and write an essay. You have been asked to compare two items intended for the same general use, but to make sure that the items have design differences that account for specific variations in the general use. For example, you might compare an ice-racing skate and a hockey skate, or snowshoes designed to be used in brush and snowshoes designed for open country. Any such items will do, but choose ones that you know extremely well from your own experience. And, remember, you are not classifying the items but merely showing how each has a specific application. In order to mirror the kind of writing you would do on the job, you have been asked to assume (1) that you are an expert on the two items (that's why it's important to choose items that you know extremely well from your own experience) and (2) that you are explaining the similarities and differences to someone who just became interested in the general use of the two items.

6. In a contemporary sociology class studying the 1970s, you've learned that the "yuppies"—so much in the news in the mid-eighties—were the college students of the seventies. You've learned that yuppies are young men and women who have achieved financial and professional success, who believe strongly in enjoying the present moment, who live a "go for it" lifestyle, and who believe in sexual equality and independent-thinking, among other things. You've also learned that they've often been criticized for being self-indulgent and even selfish.

You've decided that your generation is very much like (or unlike) the yuppie stereotype, and you've decided to make part of your final sociology project a comparison and contrast of the behavior and characteristics of your generation of college students with those of yuppies. Your instructor—a yuppie generation person—has suggested that you put your ideas into an essay that will be the basis of a debate in the class.

You'll have to do two kinds of reserach for this essay. First, you'll need to get a good definition of yuppie. The periodical indexes would be a quick way to find articles on yuppies that appeared in the mid-eighties in major news magazines. Once you've identified characteristics of yuppies, you'll want to observe your own behavior and that of your classmates so that you can compare and contrast them in order to reach your conclusion.

7. Many college students are interested in religion and discovering what it can tell them about their lives. In fact, you've decided to meet with a campus religious group for a "retreat" where part of the schedule calls for discussing religious topics. You've been asked to discuss sexual morality, and you've decided to contrast and compare the sexual-ethical situation of your generation with that of your parents' generation as a way to deal with the tension many of your classmates feel exists between them and their parents. You don't necessarily have to draw any moral conclusions, although you certainly can. But you do want to pinpoint the differences and similarities between the two situations in an effort to open a discussion that will clarify the moral issue. To get your own thoughts together on this, you've decided to write an essay addressed to your fellow retreatants that will be the basis for your talk.

FIVE

DEFINING

The word **definition** probably makes you think immediately of dictionaries. Sometimes however, you yourself may be a better source of definitions than dictionaries. For example, in conversation you can give a listener or reader a more complete understanding of your subject by responding to questions and expanding on the subject's meaning. In writing, you can analyze beforehand what an audience may need to know in order to understand a term or to understand the sense in which you are using it. Also, dictionaries only provide a limited definition, only a general overview of the word itself. Frequently, terms and concepts are complex, and you need an indepth definition to explain them to your readers. In other words, often you must go beyond the mere dictionary definition of a word. Thus, you may be a better source for some definitions than dictionaries, because you can offer longer, more fully developed and illustrated definitions, especially since you do not face the same space constraints as dictionaries. Detailed, fully developed definitions are commonly called *extended definitions*.

All of us at one time or another ask people for definitions. The process can be formal or very casual—as it might be if your friend, Mary, said that she had parked her car overnight in front of the library and couldn't drive it away the next morning because Campus Security had *booted* it. If you did not understand exactly what the term *booted* meant, you would begin probing for a definition, asking "What do you mean by "booted"? If she answered, "Campus Security put a Denver boot on my car," you would not be helped much. However, since you form an active, face-to-face audience, you can hold Mary accountable for considering what her audience doesn't know. So you would probably ask, "But what's a Denver boot?" Your friend might respond with a definition roughly similar to what you might find in a dictionary: "A Denver boot is a big steel clamp that can be locked onto a wheel so you can't move your car."

Further probing could produce a more thorough definition. You could learn that the device clamps to the rim of the wheel and that it weighs about 20 or 25 pounds. You could learn that Mary could not just drive the car off to find someone to remove the boot because a large steel spike built into the device would damage the car when the wheel turned. She might also be able to explain that there are only two ways of removing the boot—one illegal and risky, the other legal but probably costly. One way is to have someone with an acetylene torch burn through the heavy steel clamp; this would be risky, since a wrong move of the torch could burn a hole through the tire—this in addition to the usual risks of violating a law. The other way is to have a Campus Security officer unlock the clamp, most likely after your friend had paid the appropriate fine for illegal parking. You could also walk over to the library to look at the boot to get a clearer idea of its design. Your friend or the Campus Security officer might tell you that the device is called a "Denver" boot because Denver was the first major city to use this clamp for parking violations.

The above is an example of an *extended definition*, the kind we are primarily concerned with in this chapter. This extended definition is relatively brief and roughly organized, as such definitions will frequently be when constructed from questions and answers during conversations. Nevertheless, it provides considerably more information than you would get from a dictionary. If you could find an entry for *Denver boot* in a dictionary—it's a term not widely used until recently—the definition might look something like this:

Denver boot: A heavy steel clamp which locks onto the wheel of a motor vehicle, preventing the vehicle from being moved.

Even though the extended definition drawn from your friend is brief, it provides many more details than the dictionary entry does. Extended definitions can be much longer and contain much more information than the Denver boot example.

An extended definition may appear as a paragraph or two in a piece of writing or by itself to form a separate piece of writing. When to use an extended definition and how long it will be depends on your assessment of what the reader needs to know about the term you are defining. Naturally, the length to which a definition may be extended varies from subject to subject. Length will depend on the complexity of the object, activity, idea, or quality the term stands for.

Extended definition is an important type of writing. Much of what readers most want to know comes in the form of extended definitions, and definitions are extended because simple definitions do not provide enough information for readers interested in the term. For example, the family of an alcoholic already understands the formal definition of alcoholism but might learn more about the problem by reading an extended definition of the disease. A forester addressing an audience of environmentalists knows that a brief formal definition of *clear-cutting* as a tree-harvesting method would not satisfy the audience. To be useful, the definition would have to show what clear-cutting is and is not. It would have to show the effects on the remaining forest, soil, watershed, wildlife, local communities, and so on.

Usually, you will want to write extended definitions to help readers understand difficult-to-define abstractions. Such definitions attempt to answer complex questions, such as "What is success?" "What is job satisfaction?" "What are the characteristics of an intelligently set goal?" "What is freedom?"

Often, writers begin definition essays (and many other kinds of writing) with a short, *formal definition*—the kind found in a dictionary. Formal definitions follow a set form or pattern. They first name the term to be defined (*Denver boot*), then place the term into a general class (*a heavy steel clamp*), and then go on to differentiate or distinguish the thing being defined from other members of the class, in this case other *heavy steel clamps*. The Denver boot definition distinguishes it from other heavy steel clamps by showing how this one is used: it *locks onto the wheel of a motor vehicle, preventing the vehicle from being moved.*

Sometimes writers *stipulate* a meaning for a term. This occurs when a word has several meanings and the writer or speaker is considering only one of them or is using the word in a new or unusual sense. Stipulative definitions normally follow the pattern of the formal definition. Someone, for example, might define *freedom* (term) as *a person's willingness to hold views based on reason and conscience* (general class), *even when the views conflict with those of friends and other support groups* (distinction from others in same general class).

While you can write an entire paper defining a certain term, you can also use definition within other types of papers. Often when writing, you will have to define terms in your paper that may be unfamiliar to your reader. This is usually done quickly and in an abbreviated way. For example, a writer might define *destroying angel* as *a poisonous mushroom,* using a short appositive phrase immediately following the term. Or someone writing about sailing mentioning *tacking* for the first time might—for the benefit of nonsailers in the audience—define it as *zig-zagging across the water in order to sail into the wind.* These are called *informal definitions.* An informal definition is a modified version of the formal definition abbreviated to omit the parts of the definition already clear to readers. Informal definitions usually follow the pattern of those found in a dictionary. This is true if a word has several meanings and you choose to write about only one of them or if you are defining a word in your own way.

In other words, in writing you will frequently need to define a term in order to increase your audience's understanding of the subject in some way. Both formal and abbreviated definitions do this by filling gaps between what you, as writer, know about a subject and what your readers may not know. Used well, abbreviated definitions prevent readers from becoming confused and losing touch with your topic. Brief formal definitions function in much the same way, although they tend to appear as guides before something is discussed or explained. For example, if you were going to compare and contrast two types of computer printers, dot matrix and letter quality, you might begin by defining both terms so that readers would be better prepared for the discussion that followed. Stipulative definitions are employed when a term will be used in a special sense or in one of its several meanings. By noting the stipulated sense, you provide directions for readers and keep them oriented to what otherwise might seem odd or confusing.

PREWRITING

If your instructor asks you to write an extended definition, choose a topic that you have an interest in and know something about. Perhaps it is best to begin your **prewriting** by trying to determine what readers need to know about your topic. If you are especially knowledgeable about the subject, and you know your readers are not, then you will need to define related terms along the way, and you should think about methods for tailoring your extended definition to your readers' unfamiliarity. For example, if auto mechanics is a hobby of yours, leading you to define a carburetor, then you will want to explain what the device does and provide illustrations that help your readers understand the subject. It stands to reason, however, that someone with expertise in carburetion would find such a definition neither enlightening nor very interesting and might read the essay only to see how accurately you presented the definition. In other words, have a clear concept of your audience before you begin to write.

On the other hand, you might have some knowledge about a topic but still want to check on certain information before you begin to write. This would be particularly true when a large part of the extended definition depends on examples of human behavior you have observed. For example, if you planned to define *male chauvinism,* you would want to make sure that you understood why the word *chauvinism* came to represent the examples of behavior you plan to use for illustrations.

Remember that you want to offer something to your readers. Your topic should at least be reasonably interesting to them and at the same time present them with new information or add something to what they might already know about your topic. You needn't choose a topic that is completely new to readers, especially if you work with a term whose meaning may differ somewhat from person to person—concepts such as *patriotism, justice,* or *discretion,* for example; such topics would permit you to stipulate the sense in which you are using the word. Terms like *laid back, ambience, atmosphere,* and *class* (as in "a person with class") are also concepts that people envision differently, and such topics can usually be treated freshly.

Understanding your readers' needs will help you establish a purpose for your paper. You should know whether you are defining a term that you understand much better than your readers, and you should have a sense of how complex the term is for those who are unacquainted with what it stands for. You should know whether or not you are establishing new boundaries or explaining a new way of looking at a familiar term. You should know whether your definition will primarily entertain or inform or whether you hope to achieve a measure of each.

Of course, most of these considerations depend on your precise audience. Obviously, you cannot be responsive to readers' needs until you have determined who your readers are. Are you addressing a formal meeting of the Philosophy Club during which you will provide an extended definition of *God?* Or are you writing a paper for the Young Historians Association in which you will define *freedom?* Or are you writing a humorous article for a computer magazine defining a *computer hacker?* It is difficult to make any important choices in a piece of writing before you know your exact audience.

Besides helping you determine your exact audience and purpose, your prewriting should provide you with the details needed to develop your definition. This would include any background reading that you have to do yourself, even if this amounts only to determining what traditional meanings exist for the term you are defining. Just checking the dictionary meanings for the term will sometimes suggest methods you might use to make your meaning clear. In fact, a good place to begin your prewriting is the *Oxford English Dictionary*. This very valuable book is shelved in the reference section of your university's library, and it provides a brief history of many words in the English language. Its definitions are much more comprehensive than those found in traditional dictionaries.

Definition requires the same careful brainstorming as other types of writing, but, to be productive, it should not begin until you can express in a sentence or two the general bounds you are placing on the meaning of your subject. For many topics, the formal definition may offer adequate direction or, if you plan to stipulate a definition, then this can be expressed in the pattern of a formal definition. You are telling readers what to expect in your essay and establishing bounds that will help you choose pertinent details to expand the meaning logically as you build your essay. You should know before you begin to write, and the reader should know at the outset of the essay, whether you are expanding on the traditional formal definition of the term, or whether you are stipulating a new or unusual meaning.

Once you know why you are writing—to inform, entertain, etc.—and know the boundaries you have set, you are ready to begin your brainstorming. How much of the extended meaning can be shown through illustrations or examples? Will a paragraph of comparison/contrast be helpful? It will be if you need to show what your subject *does not* mean. If you are defining *brassy behavior,* for example, you may want to show how this behavior is different from *impetuous behavior.* A paper on *tenacity* might require you to make a distinction between *tenacity* and *persistence.* Also, ask yourself how much description will be needed? How many process steps must be mentioned to show how a Denver boot (or any mechanical device) works?

After you have compiled a list of brainstorming details, it is perhaps best to put the list aside for a short time and then come back to it and brainstorm some more. Perhaps you will want to freewrite, and you can also use the definition heuristic that follows shortly to generate additional details. When you are satisfied with your list, then study it to identify the best possible details for developing the extended definition. Cross out details that are really only peripheral and those that crept in because they seemed accurate during brainstorming sessions but, after careful study, proved not to be. That is, you will want to consider your details carefully to be sure they do not illustrate something similar to but not the same as what you are defining. For example, an examination of your examples of brassy behavior may show that some details on your list really illustrate a desire to show off or to challenge people rather than brassiness.

Below is a heuristic to help you add details to your prewriting notes. Answer those questions that seem relevant to your subject.

Prewriting Questions for Definition

1. How much does my audience already know about the term I am defining?
2. Does my term refer to something that would seem complex to my audience, requiring me to restrict the definition to basic principles or applications?
3. Will my definition require me to show what my subject is not, as well as what it is?
4. Into what class does my subject fit?
5. What characteristics distinguish it from other things?
6. Will I have to compare and contrast to show the difference between my subject and another subject from the same general class?
7. What related terms will I have to define either formally or in an abbreviated form?
8. What other terms (synonyms) might be used to describe my subject?
9. What are some examples of my subject?
10. How does it work?
11. If my term names something physical, how much description will I need to show the subject clearly?
12. If it is something physical, are there certain parts that should be emphasized in the description?
13. What examples can I use to illustrate the meaning of my subject?
14. Am I defining the term in a special sense or using it in a new sense?
15. Am I emphasizing some special reason why the audience should know the term?

ORGANIZING

Your prewriting has given you the materials for **organizing** your extended definition. Now you can use these notes to the benefit of your reader by presenting your topic in an orderly and logical way. It may help to think of your subject as having layers of meaning. Your task is to unfold or reveal layer after layer until you have shown the dimensions of your subject.

You may wish to begin your essay by introducing the subject and explaining to the reader why it is important to know the term in the way you plan to present it. This can usually be done quickly when your term refers to a physical object. You can offer a brief formal definition of a Denver boot, for example, and go on to explain that drivers who park in restricted areas should know about this device, not only to understand the inconvenience and cost of ignoring regulations but also to know what to do and what not to do to free a "booted" car. Other terms, depending on your purpose, may require more explanation in order to orientate readers to your purpose. If you are defining a complex concept such as *cowardice,* for example, you would require a longer introduction. You would want to define the term without distorting the facts of human behavior.

Your introduction, if done thoughtfully, will help you to organize your paper. If you were extending the definition of the Denver boot to show that treating the device as a mechanical parking ticket would be both futile and damaging to the booted vehicle, then details that support this thesis should appear early in the paper. For example, you might first describe the device and then isolate and describe in more detail the features that make it nearly impossible to remove on your own and the features that would damage the car if you tried to drive off. Then you could turn your attention to other means of extending the definition, perhaps showing how the device evolved as part of an effort to control flagrant parking violators who collect tickets but never pay them. With a little library research added to your brainstorming, you could show how the boot has reduced the number of people who consistently ignore parking citations. You might devote a following segment to the advantages offered to police departments by the device: The violator must seek out a police officer; the violator must pay a fine before the car is released; and the boot usually eliminates the need to tow a violator's car. In your essay's conclusion you might reemphasize your purpose by indicating that the device was not designed for the average motorist but that any motorist might sometime be suddenly introduced to the boot and, therefore, should know something about it.

On the other hand, if your purpose is to emphasize that the Denver boot was developed as a way of dealing with parking scofflaws, then you would want to structure your extended definition to convey this emphasis.

Careful prewriting and careful study of the prewriting results should help you identify the purpose for your definition, and the purpose can then guide you in using your prewriting materials to organize your essay effectively. If you find that your prewriting was not as thorough as it should have been, you may want to correct that deficiency before beginning your first draft.

WRITING

Once you have sufficient details for your essay and an organizational strategy, you are ready to produce a first draft of your essay. Following your organizational scheme, write your first draft rapidly.

Remember, definition may use a variety of rhetorical modes for development. You can illustrate by using examples: An interview with a police officer might provide an example of actual damage caused by someone who tried to move a car with a Denver boot attached. Of course, many terms lend themselves to the use of examples since the terms themselves define behavior or activities. To define *bravado* as falsely brave behavior calls for examples in order to make clear what an abstract phrase like *falsely brave* means. Similarly, it would be hard to explain what a *pool hustler* is without illustrating the techniques of the hustler.

Your subject may call for comparison/contrast with words that refer to similar things in the same general class. Defining *value added tax* would almost require you to explain the differences between this tax and a sales tax. You will also need to use short definitions along the way to bridge the gap between what you know about the subject and what your audience might know. You may have to offer brief formal definitions of any term that is frequently confused with the term you are defining—the differences between *propaganda* and *slanting* or an *occupation tax* and a *wage tax*, for example.

As we mentioned in Chapter 1, it is a good idea to write your draft rapidly. If you have spent adequate time and effort prewriting and organizing your essay, the **writing** of a first draft should prove to be relatively easy. There is no need to spend time on small issues at this time; they can be taken care of while revising and proofreading. Of course, if you notice any surface errors while writing you can correct them now and thereby make your final proofreading that much easier. Your primary objective at this time, however, is to produce a complete first draft.

REVISING

Remember, **revising** is the key to effective writing. Before beginning to revise, you may wish to put your draft aside for a day or two if time permits. This will let you see your paper more objectively and clearly, something that is not possible for most writers immediately after completing a draft.

Perhaps it is best to begin by checking your organization. Do you have an introduction that tells the reader what you are going to define and also explains any special circumstances concerning your purpose or approach in expanding the definition? Do your body paragraphs contribute additional layers of meaning? Does your conclusion remind your reader of the essay's purpose and thesis?

A definition essay should supply a thorough, complete, and clear answer to a "what is" question: What is an oil field wildcatter? What is a floppy disk? What is the green corn ceremony of the Seminoles? Assume that your reader is curious and wants more than a brief definition of your subject. In light of this fact, examine your draft by asking yourself how well you have answered the "what is" question. You don't want your reader to say "I wonder about this" or "I wonder about that" after reading your essay. Instead, you will want to find these gaps during the revision process and eliminate them.

Also, it is a good idea to search for terms that may need defining for the convenience of your reader and to decide which ones can be handled with abbreviated definitions and which, if any, call for formal definitions. Now is the time to incorporate such information into your text if you overlooked them while writing your first draft.

You will want to check also to see that you have unfolded your meaning in a logical fashion. In what order have you presented your information? Will your arrangement of details make your definition easy to follow and understand? Why? Does each part of the definition logically follow the preceding part?

Look also at your sentences. Does each one express clearly what it is you want to say in that sentence? Try to step back from your paper when you do this and put yourself in the place of the reader. Assume that your reader is intelligent but is not familiar with your topic. Is any sentence clear to *you* (since you know what you are defining) but nonetheless confusing to your reader because you unconsciously left something out? Do any of your sentences need to carry additional information to be clear to a bright but uninformed reader? Do you need to add sentences in order to make an example or other detail clear or to show clearly its relationship to the evolving definition? In other words, do you need to do additional prewriting?

Keep in mind that you usually will want to spend more time revising than you spent in producing a first draft. Intelligent, careful revising is one of the key steps toward effective writing. So be demanding of yourself and revise until you have a product that satisfies you completely. Try to revise your draft more than once—revise until you are sincerely happy with your product.

PROOFREADING

After you have revised your definition essay thoroughly, remember to **proofread.** The proper attention to prewriting, organization, and revising will leave only the small details to be looked after in proofreading. You can spend less time here if you have done the earlier tasks well. Certainly, you don't want misspellings and other small faults to mar your paper and distract your readers. Remember to read through your revised draft at least three times: once for grammar, once for punctuation, and once for spelling.

After completing your essay, you may wish to check the list below to be sure you have not omitted important features of the definition.

Definition Checklist

1. Does your introduction show what it is you are defining plus any special emphasis you want to convey?
2. If you stressed in your introduction some important reason why your reader should know the subject you are defining, have you reminded the reader of this in the conclusion?
3. Have you presented the layers of meaning in a logical order?
4. Have you briefly defined all related terms?
5. Have you shown, if necessary, what your subject is *not*?
6. Have you shown how any closely related or likely-to-be-confused terms differ in meaning from the term you are defining?
7. Are your descriptions and examples clear enough for someone less familiar with the topic than you are?
8. Have you left meaning gaps anywhere because *you* know your subject so well?
9. Can you find places where an extra sentence or an added example would add to the reader's understanding?
10. Have you checked grammar, punctuation, and spelling?

Euphemism

NEIL POSTMAN

In this essay, Neil Postman discusses what happens when we choose between one kind of word and another, and he explains the dangers of either indiscriminately using words that "tell it like it is" or words that obscure "what it is."

A euphemism is commonly defined as an auspicious or exalted term (like "sanitation engineer") that is used in place of a more down-to-earth term (like "garbage man"). People who are partial to euphemisms stand accused of being "phony" or trying to hide what it is they are really talking about. And there is no doubt that in some situations the accusation is entirely proper. For example, one of the more detestable euphemisms I have come across in recent years is the term "Operation Sunshine," which is the name the U.S. Government gave to some experiments it conducted with the hydrogen bomb in the South Pacific. It is obvious that the government, in choosing this name, was trying to expunge the hideous imagery that the bomb evokes and in so doing committed, as I see it, an immoral act. This sort of process—giving pretty names to essentially ugly realities—is what has given euphemizing such a bad name. And people like George Orwell have done valuable work for all of us in calling attention to how the process works. But there is another side to euphemizing that is worth mentioning, and a few words here in its defense will not be amiss.

To begin with, we must keep in mind that things do not have "real" names, although many people believe that they do. A garbage man is not "really" a "garbage man," any more than he is really a "sanitation engineer." And a pig is not called a "pig" because it is so dirty, nor a shrimp a "shrimp" because it is so small. There are things, and then there are the names of things, and it is considered a fundamental error in all branches of semantics to assume that a name and a thing are one and the same. It is true, of course, that a name is usually so firmly associated with the thing it denotes that it is extremely difficult to separate one from the other. That is why, for example, advertising is so effective. Perfumes are not given names like "Bronx Odor," and an automobile will never be called "The Lumbering Elephant." Shakespeare was only half right in saying that a rose by any other name would smell as sweet. What we call things affects how we will perceive them. It is not only harder to sell someone a "horse mackerel" sandwich than a "tuna fish" sandwich, but even though they are the "same" thing, we are likely to enjoy the taste of tuna more than that of the horse mackerel. It would appear that human beings almost naturally come to *identify* names with things, which is one of our more fascinating illusions. But there is some substance to this illusion. For if you change the names of things, you change how people will regard them, and that is as good as changing the nature of the thing itself.

Now, all sorts of scoundrels know this perfectly well and can make us love almost anything by getting us to transfer the charm of a name to whatever worthless thing they are promoting. But at the same time and in the same vein, euphemizing is a perfectly intelligent method of generating new and useful ways of perceiving things. The man who wants us to call him a "sanitation engineer" instead of a "garbage man" is hoping we will treat him with more respect than we presently do. He wants us to see that he is of some importance to our society. His euphemism is laughable only if we think that he is not deserving of such notice or respect. The teacher who prefers us to use the term "culturally different children" instead of "slum children" is euphemizing, all right, but is doing it to encourage us to see aspects of a situation that might otherwise not be attended to. 3

The point I am making is that there is nothing in the process of euphemizing itself that is contemptible. Euphemizing is contemptible when a name makes us see something that is not true or diverts our attention from something that is. The hydrogen bomb kills. There is nothing else that it does. And when you experiment with it, you are trying to find out how widely and well it kills. Therefore, to call such an experiment "Operation Sunshine" is to suggest a purpose for the bomb that simply does not exist. But to call "slum children" "culturally different" is something else. It calls attention, for example, to legitimate reasons why such children might feel alienated from what goes on in school. 4

I grant that sometimes such euphemizing does not have the intended effect. It is possible for a teacher to use the term "culturally different" but still be controlled by the term "slum children" (which the teacher may believe is their "real" name). "Old people" may be called "senior citizens," and nothing might change. And "lunatic asylums" may still be filthy, primitive prisons though they are called "mental institutions." Nonetheless, euphemizing may be regarded as one of our more important intellectual resources for creating new perspectives on a subject. The *attempt* to rename "old people" "senior citizens" was obviously motivated by a desire to give them a political identity, which they not only warrant but which may yet have important consequences. In fact, the fate of euphemisms is very hard to predict. A new and seemingly silly name may replace an old one (let us say, 5 "chairperson" for "chairman") and for years no one will think or act any differently because of it. And then, gradually, as people begin to assume that "chairperson" is the "real" and proper name (or "senior citizen" or "tuna fish" or "sanitation engineer"), their attitudes begin to shift, and they will approach things in a slightly different frame of mind. There is a danger, of course, in supposing that a new name can change attitudes quickly or always. There must be some authentic tendency or drift in the culture to lend support to the change, or the name will remain incongruous and may even appear ridiculous. To call a teacher a "facilitator" would be such an example. To eliminate the distinction between "boys" and "girls" by calling them "childpersons" would be another.

But to suppose that such changes never "amount to anything" is to   6
underestimate the power of names. I have been astounded not only by how rapidly the name "blacks" has replaced "Negroes" (a kind of euphemizing in reverse) but also by how significantly perceptions and attitudes have shifted as an accompaniment to the change.

The key idea here is that euphemisms are a means through which a   7
culture may alter its imagery and by so doing subtly change its style, its priorities, and its values. I reject categorically the idea that people who use "earthy" language are speaking more directly or with more authenticity than people who employ euphemisms. Saying that someone is "dead" is not to speak more plainly or honestly than saying he has "passed away." It is, rather, to suggest a different conception of what the event means. To ask where the "shithouse" is, is no more to the point than to ask where the "restroom" is. But in the difference between the two words, there is expressed a vast difference in one's attitude toward privacy and propriety. What I am saying is that the process of euphemizing has no moral content. The moral dimensions are supplied by what the words in question express, what they want us to value and to see. A nation that calls experiments with bombs "Operation Sunshine" is very frightening. On the other hand, a people who call "garbage men" "sanitation engineers" can't be all bad.

QUESTIONS ON MEANING AND CONTENT

1. Were you familiar with the word *euphemism* before you read the essay? If not, how successful was Postman in defining the term for you? Could you now offer not only a quick definition for a friend but also answer followup questions to extend the definition?

2. List two things that you would consider the most important points Postman wants to make about euphemisms. Why are these points important?

3. In the last paragraph, Postman says that how people use euphemisms or fail to use them can tell us something about the people themselves. What does he mean by this? Can you make a descriptive statement about someone you know based on that person's habits in using or not using euphemisms? Has anyone ever tried to mislead you or someone you know through the use of euphemisms? Explain. What does your own use of euphemisms tell you about yourself?

4. Without borrowing from Postman, name one silly use of euphemism. Name one sensible use.

5. What makes a euphemism catch on and eventually replace an original term? What examples does Postman use to illustrate this? What reasons does he offer to suggest why some euphemisms fail to catch on?

QUESTIONS ABOUT RHETORICAL STRATEGIES

1. In the introduction to a definition essay we often find a formal definition of the term whose definition will be extended in the essay. Do you find a formal definition in Postman's introduction?

2. Would Postman's essay be of interest both to readers who already know something about euphemisms and to readers who had never heard the word before? If so, what evidence do you find to show that Postman has considered both audiences? Where does he provide information that would be needed by those who did not know the term? What might appeal to the other part of the audience?

3. One of the problems in any kind of writing is how to keep readers informed of what you are doing in a piece of writing, how to keep them aware of what you are telling them. Readers often aren't conscious of the words, phrases, and sentences that writers use to keep them informed of what is happening in a piece of writing, but readers would know that something was wrong if they weren't there. The writing would become harder to follow or, perhaps, would break down completely.

To find these readers' guides in a piece of writing, one place to look is at the opening and closing of paragraphs. Examine the following examples in Postman's essay and then explain how each provides a reference point for readers or aids them in some other way:

- The last sentence of paragraph 1.

- The first sentence of paragraph 3. (Look closely at the first ten or twelve words.)

- The opening words of the first sentence in paragraph 4.

- The first sentence of paragraph 6.

- The opening of the first sentence in paragraph 7.

QUESTIONS ON LANGUAGE AND DICTION

1. In paragraph 2, Postman notes that we don't name perfumes "Bronx Odor" or cars "The Lumbering Elephant." What kinds of names do we give to perfumes and cars? What principles are at work in these names? What sort of illusions are created by the names?

2. What are the meanings of *auspicious, incongruous, semantics*?

Are You a Man or a Wimp?

BRUCE FEIRSTEIN

Bruce Feirstein, with tongue in cheek, explains what American men used to be, and he laments the rapid disappearance of "real men" in America. The real test is whether or not a male eats quiche, Feirstein says, but his extended definition identifies a wide variety of other characteristics that must be present before a male can be stamped with the genuine "real man" label.

This was once a nation of *Real Men*—guys who could defoliate an entire 1
forest to make a breakfast fire, and then wipe out an endangered species for
lunch. Not anymore; we've become a nation of wimps. It's not enough that
we earn a living and protect women and children from plagues, famine and
encyclopedia salesmen. Now we're also supposed to be *supportive*. And
understanding. And *sincere*.

Where's it gotten us? We used to create things like the Panama Canal, 2
the '57 Chevy and the front line of the Green Bay Packers. It worries me that
ten million years from now we'll be remembered as the civilization that
created frozen yogurt, salad bars and restaurants that spin.

I ask you: When America was king, was Clark Gable ever worried about 3
giving his women "enough space"? Was Bogart ever lonely because he
couldn't have a "meaningful dialogue" with some dame? Would we have
won World War II if Ike thought Hitler was just going through a mid-life
crisis and should be allowed to "work it out"?

Real Men have always lived by one simple rule: never settle with words 4
what you can accomplish with a flame thrower.

But if you want to see what's happening to us now, look at today's 5
movies. Instead of having John Wayne fight Nazis and Commies for peace
and democracy, we've got Dustin Hoffman fighting Meryl Streep for a
six-year-old in *Kramer vs. Kramer*. It's no wonder things are so mixed up.
Thirty years ago the Duke would have slapped the broad around and
shipped the kid off to military school. Not anymore. I'm convinced things
were better in the past.

All a Real Man had to do was abuse women, steal land from Indians and 6
find some place to dump toxic waste. Now you're expected to be sympathetic, sensitive and to split the household chores.

Yet strength and bravery are still the hallmark of a Real Man. He has
found modern ways to show it.

Today's Real Men do not cower and shake in the face of double-digit
inflation. They do not worry about the diminishing ozone layer and are not
intimidated by microwave radiation. They don't have telephone-answering
machines, being secure enough to know that, if it's important, people will
call back. Real Men carry cash, never the American Express Card. They offer
to provide birth control.

Real Men do *not* put bunny stickers in the rear window; they don't have
flared fenders, moon roofs, air dams, fog lights, racing gloves, cruise control
or six-tone air horns that play "Here Comes the Bride." And they don't own
vans with murals of naked women or sunsets painted on the side.

What do Real Men drive? Massive, hulking, gas-guzzling Chryslers.
With four-barrel carburetors, automatic transmissions, and five million
cubic inches under the hood. After all, how are you ever going to lose a state
trooper in a Honda?

Basically, today's Real Man is unaffected by fads or fashion. Real Men
don't disco or eat brunch. They don't have their hair styled. They don't wear
bikini underwear or gold chains. They understand that satin go-go boots
don't make it with a blue suit and that it's best to avoid wearing Indian
headgear to the office, simply because the Indians lost the war, and you're
likely to be tagged as a loser by association. Nor do Real Men wear jump-
suits. They don't dress in Italian cyclist uniforms, camouflage gear, leather
pants or anything made of polyester.

What *do* Real Men wear? Wing tips, suits, and ties, button-down shirts.
And their jeans are designed by Levi Strauss.

Real Men eat beef, frozen peas and watermelon. French fries and apple
pie are their staples. As a general rule, Real Men won't eat anything that is
poached, sautéed, minced, blended, glazed, curried, flambéed, stir-fried or
en brochette. You will never find paté, bean curd, asparagus or creamed
spinach in their stomachs. Real Men don't know how to cook; they only
know how to thaw.

Unlike his predecessors, today's Real Man actually can feel things like
sorrow, pity, love, warmth and sincerity. He realizes that birds, flowers,
poetry and small children do not add to the quality of life in quite the same
manner as a Super Bowl, but he's learned to appreciate them anyway.
However, he'd never be so vulnerable as to admit this.

One criterion in particular sets Real Men apart from everything in
today's world that's phony, affected, limp or without merit: Real Men don't
eat quiche. Think about it. Could John Wayne, ever have taken Normandy,

Iwo Jima, Korea, the Gulf of Tonkin and the entire Wild West on a diet of quiche and salad?

Of course not.   16

QUESTIONS ON MEANING AND CONTENT

1. What is Feirstein's attitude toward his subject; that is, what is the tone of the essay?

2. Do you think this essay is attacking or satirizing any group in particular? If not, explain why you think it isn't. If you think it is, who is it attacking or satirizing? Men who don't fall into the real-man class? Men who *do* fall into the real-man class? Men who *want* to fall into the real man class? Women? Explain your answer.

3. Forget for the moment that the essay is humorous. The essay defines real men and, by implication, those who are not real men. Thus, men are placed in one of two categories. What is the problem in doing that? How does this placement affect the definition of real men?

4. Does Feirstein touch on matters that many people take seriously, males and females alike; that is, does a definition similar to Feirstein's, but perhaps less exaggerated, exist in the minds of many Americans? If so, where does Feirstein get close to that definition?

5. Feirstein begins by saying that, at one time, most men in America were real men. He names a few, but these men were from very recent history. Who were some earlier ones he might have named who were responsible for creating a real-man image? Who are some who are living today who might represent the kind of symbolic real man Feirstein is talking about?

6. The real men named by Feirstein—Clark Gable, Humphrey Bogart, John Wayne, and Dwight Eisenhower—were all movie stars, except one. Does that tell us something? What?

QUESTIONS ABOUT RHETORICAL STRATEGIES

1. Feirstein's essay does not offer a formal extended definition of the term *real man*. The definition here is an *operational definition*. Operational definitions tell us what to look for or what to do in order to learn what something is. The essay is full of concrete examples of what to observe in order to understand what a real man is. To find out how Feirstein went about organizing and grouping these many examples, we would have to identify the broad categories he uses. In the broadest of terms, we might say that he tells us what real men *do* and what they *don't do*. What are subcategories under these main groups?

2. Where in the essay does Feirstein use comparison/contrast in developing the extended definition?

3. Make a general statement about the audience this essay is most suited for and support your statement with specific references to what things the author says and the manner in which he says them.

QUESTIONS ON LANGUAGE AND DICTION

1. The essay begins with the exaggeration that American men once "could defoliate an entire forest to make a breakfast fire, and then wipe out an endangered species for lunch." What other exaggerations do you find in the essay? Do most of them suggest some sort of abuse that we, as a culture, have finally grown sensitive to—as the above exaggerations indicate a disregard for the natural environment and wildlife?

2. What do the following mean: *quiche, en brochette?*

"*Foreword*" to Elizabeth Kubler-Ross' *Death: The Final Stage of Growth*

JOSEPH L. BRAGA and LAURIE D. BRAGA

In this essay introducing readers to Elizabeth Kubler-Ross' Death: The Final Stage of Growth, the Bragas tell us that death is misdefined in the minds of most people. We must redefine it in terms of life, for neither of these two terms can be defined separately.

Death is a subject that is evaded, ignored, and denied by our youth-worshipping, progress-oriented society. It is almost as if we have taken on death as just another disease to be conquered. But the fact is that death is inevitable. We will all die; it is only a matter of time. Death is as much a part of human existence, of human growth and development, as being born. It is one of the few things in life we can count on, that we can be assured will occur. Death is not an enemy to be conquered or a prison to be escaped. It is an integral part of our lives that gives meaning to human existence. It sets a limit on our time in this life, urging us on to do something productive with that time as long as it is ours to use. 1

This, then, is the meaning of *Death: the Final Stage of Growth*: All that you are and all that you've done and been is culminated in your death. When you're dying, if you're fortunate enough to have some prior warning (other than that we all have all the time if we come to terms with our finiteness), you get your final chance to grow, to become more truly who you really are, to become more fully human. But you don't need to nor should you wait until death is at your doorstep before you start to really live. If you can begin to see death as an invisible, but friendly, companion on your life's journey—gently reminding you not to wait till tomorrow to do what you mean to do—then you can learn to *live* your life rather than simply passing through it. 2

Whether you die at a young age or when you are old is less important than whether you have fully lived the years you have had. One person may live more in eighteen years than another does in eighty. By living, we do not mean frantically accumulating a range and quantity of experience valued in fantasy by others. Rather, we mean living each day as if it is the only one 3 you have. We mean finding a sense of peace and strength to deal with life's disappointments and pain while always striving to discover vehicles to make more accessible, increase, and sustain the joys and delights of life. One such vehicle is learning to focus on some of the things you have learned to tune out—to notice and take joy in the budding of new leaves in the spring, to wonder at the beauty of the sun rising each morning and setting each night, to take comfort in the smile or touch of another person, to watch with amazement the growth of a child, and to share in children's wonderfully "uncomplexed," enthusiastic, and trusting approach to living. To live.

To rejoice at the opportunity of experience each new day is to prepare for   4
one's ultimate acceptance of death. For it is those who have not really lived—who have left issues unsettled, dreams unfulfilled, hopes shattered, and who have let the real things in life (loving and being loved by others, contributing in a positive way to other people's happiness and welfare, finding out what things are *really you*) pass them by—who are most reluctant to die. It is never too late to start living and growing. This is the message delivered each year in Dickens's "Christmas Carol"—even old Scrooge, who has spent years pursuing a life without love or meaning, is able through his willing it, to change the road he's on. Growing is the human way of living, and death is the final stage in the development of human beings. For life to be valued every day, not simply near to the time of anticipated death, one's own inevitable death must be faced and accepted. We must allow death to provide a context for our lives, for in it lies the meaning of life and the key to our growth.

Think about your own death. How much time and energy have you put   5
into examining your feelings, beliefs, hopes, and fears about the end of your life? What if you were told you had a limited time to live? Would it change the way you're presently conducting your life? Are there things you would feel an urgency to do before you died? Are you afraid of dying? Of death? Can you identify the sources of your fears? Consider the death of someone you love. What would you talk about to a loved one who was dying? How would you spend your time together? Are you prepared to cope with all the legal details of the death of a relative? Have you talked with your family about death and dying? Are there things, emotional and practical, that you would feel a need to work out with your parents, children, siblings before your own death or theirs? Whatever the things are that would make your life more personally meaningful before you die—do them now, because you *are* going to die; and you may not have the time or energy when you get your final notice.

QUESTIONS ON MEANING AND CONTENT

1. The authors say that within the meaning of death lies the meaning of life. Does this essay offer two definitions, one of life and one of death? Or does it say that death cannot be defined separately—that it is part of the definition of life?

2. What definition of *life* do the authors offer?

3. In your view, how accurate are the authors when they suggest that we can't really value life until we accept death as a part of it? If someone asked you what it meant to accept death as a part of life, how would you explain that?

4. How does the allusion to Scrooge support what the authors have to say here?

QUESTIONS ABOUT RHETORICAL STRATEGIES

1. The authors begin by discussing our traditional ways of defining *death*. Then they *stipulate* their own definition and go on to redefine death. This can be done with a great many other terms, especially abstract terms. The requirements are that you cover the common definitions for the reader and then present a *stipulated* definition that is reasonable and plausible. Biologists, for example, frequently maintain that we misdefine snakes by carrying in our heads faulty extended definitions of the word *snake*. We have the brief *formal* definition right but have many misconceptions about the extended definition.

2. Can you think of other terms, abstract or concrete, that could be the subject of an extended definition essay structured similarly to the Bragas' extended definition of death?

QUESTIONS ON LANGUAGE AND DICTION

1. In the last sentence of paragraph 2, how is the meaning of the word *live* changed by putting it into italics?

2. What are the meanings of *culminated,* and *finiteness*?

Trust

ANDY ROONEY

We want to trust each other, Andy Rooney says, and for the most part we do trust each other. That is why violations of trust, both large and small, upset us so much. Because trust is so important to us, it is better to be a patsy and lose once in a while, Rooney concludes at one point, than to mistrust everyone all the time. Something of value disappears from our lives when we behave in such a manner.

Last night I was driving from Harrisburg to Lewisburg, Pa., a distance of about eighty miles. It was late, I was late and if anyone asked me how fast I was driving, I'd have to plead the Fifth Amendment to avoid self-incrimination. Several times I got stuck behind a slow-moving truck on a narrow road with a solid white line on my left, and I was clinching my fists with impatience. 1

At one point along an open highway, I came to a crossroads with a traffic light. I was alone on the road by now, but as I approached the light, it turned red and I braked to a halt. I looked left, right and behind me. Nothing. Not a car, no suggestion of headlights, but there I sat, waiting for the light to change, the only human being for at least a mile in any direction. 2

I started wondering why I refused to run the light. I was not afraid of being arrested, because there was obviously no cop around, and there certainly would have been no danger in going through it. 3

Much later that night, after I'd met with a group in Lewisburg and had climbed into bed near midnight, the question of why I'd stopped for that light came back to me. I think I stopped because it's part of a contract we all have with each other. It's not only the law, but it's an agreement we have, and we trust each other to honor it: we don't go through red lights. Like most of us, I'm more apt to be restrained from doing something bad by the social convention that disapproves of it than by any law against it. 4

It's amazing that we ever trust each other to do the right thing, isn't it? And we do, too. Trust is our first inclination. We have to make a deliberate decision to mistrust someone or to be suspicious or skeptical. Those attitudes don't come naturally to us. 5

It's a damn good thing too, because the whole structure of our society depends on mutual trust, not distrust. This whole thing we have going for us would fall apart if we didn't trust each other most of the time. In Italy, they have an awful time getting any money for the government, because 6 many people just plain don't pay their income tax. Here the Internal Revenue Service makes some gestures toward enforcing the law, but mostly they just have to trust that we'll pay what we owe. There has often been talk of a tax revolt in this country, most recently among unemployed auto workers in Michigan, and our government pretty much admits if there was a widespread tax revolt here, they wouldn't be able to do anything about it.

We do what we say we'll do; we show up when we say we'll show up; 7 we deliver when we say we'll deliver; and we pay when we say we'll pay. We trust each other in these matters, and when we don't do what we've promised, it's a deviation from the normal. It happens often that we don't act in good faith and in a trustworthy manner, but we still consider it unusual, and we're angry or disappointed with the person or organization that violates the trust we have in them. (I'm looking for something good to say about mankind today.)

I hate to see a story about a bank swindler who has jiggered the books to 8 his own advantage, because I trust banks. I don't *like* them, but I trust them. I don't go in and demand that they show me my money all the time just to make sure they still have it.

It's the same buying a can of coffee or a quart of milk. You don't take the 9 coffee home and weigh it to make sure it's a pound. There isn't time in life to distrust every person you meet or every company you do business with. I hated the company that started selling beer in eleven-ounce bottles years ago. One of the million things we take on trust is that a beer bottle contains twelve ounces.

It's interesting to look around and at people and compare their faith or 10 lack of faith in other people with their success or lack of success in life. The patsies, the suckers, the people who always assume everyone else is as honest as they are, make out better in the long run than the people who distrust everyone—and they're a lot happier even if they get taken once in a while.

I was so proud of myself for stopping for that red light, and inasmuch as 11 no one would ever have known what a good person I was on the road from Harrisburg to Lewisburg, I had to tell someone.

QUESTIONS ON MEANING AND CONTENT

1. In the opening paragraph, Rooney admits he had exceeded the speed limit during his trip. Is this a violation of trust according to his own definition? According to yours?

2. What does Rooney mean in paragraph 4 when he says that most people are "more apt to be restrained from doing something bad by the social convention that disapproves of it than by any law against it"? After establishing what this means, offer your own opinion of the statement. Do you think Rooney is right? Does this account for why he had been speeding earlier in the evening yet wouldn't go through the red light? Are laws limiting speeds on highways no more than mere laws; that is, are they only legal rules without the force of social convention behind them, and, therefore, we don't feel we have violated a trust when we exceed speed limits? What other such "laws" come to mind?

3. In paragraph 5, Rooney suggests that "Trust is our first inclination." How do you react to this statement? Do the examples offered in the essay support this statement? If you agree with the statement, what other examples can you think of that would show the statement to be reasonably accurate? If you disagree, what evidence would you use to support your view?

4. "In the long run," Rooney says, patsies and suckers "make out better" and are "a lot happier" than those who "distrust everyone." He offers no support for this statement. Is the statement supportable? If so, how would you illustrate the point to convince someone that the statement is true? If you think the statement is not true, what argument would you use to show that?

5. Speculate about Rooney's reference to the company that reduced the amount of beer in a bottle from 12 ounces to 11. Only one ounce is involved. Isn't this trivial? Isn't this violation of trust too insignificant to be mentioned? Why or why not?

QUESTIONS ABOUT RHETORICAL STRATEGIES

1. Rooney does not offer a formal definition of trust. Instead, he talks about it as if we will know what it means. Would the essay benefit if he had offered a formal definition, or was he wise to handle the definition as he does?

2. This essay has a rather long introduction: an anecdote about stopping for a red light. How does the introduction contribute to the extended definition that develops?

3. Rooney's conclusion is a specific "type" of conclusion. It represents a concluding strategy that can be applied to many different kinds of writing, especially short pieces. What is that strategy?

QUESTIONS ON LANGUAGE AND DICTION

1. Define the term "social convention" used in paragraph 4. In a question above, you were asked about laws that lack the force of social convention. Can you think of social conventions that have nothing to do with laws, but which we obey? If so, what is at work here—trust? Something else?

Four-Letter Words Can Hurt You

BARBARA LAWRENCE

Barbara Lawrence examines the meanings and histories of words to show that the words we use may convey more than we think they do and have a greater effect on us than we would like to believe. Many words have a potential for harm, and using them casually without understanding their potential impact can affect our attitudes toward each other and make harmful attitudes almost impossible to change.

Why should any words be called obscene? Don't they all describe natural human functions? Am I trying to tell them, my students demand, that the "strong, earthy, gut-honest"—or, if they are fans of Norman Mailer, the "rich, liberating, existential"—language they use to describe sexual activity isn't preferable to "phony-sounding, middle-class words like 'intercourse' and 'copulate'?" "Cop You Late!" they say with fancy inflections and gagging grimaces. "Now, what is *that* supposed to mean?"   1

Well, what is it supposed to mean? And why indeed should one group of words describing human functions and human organs be aceptable in ordinary conversation and another, describing presumably the same organs and functions, be tabooed—so much so, in fact, that some of these words still cannot appear in print in many parts of the English-speaking world?   2

The argument that these taboos exist only because of "sexual hangups" (middle-class, middle-age, feminist), or even that they are a result of class oppression (the contempt of the Norman conquerors for the language of their Anglo-Saxon serfs), ignores a much more likely explanation, it seems to me, and that is the sources and functions of the words themselves.   3

The best known of the tabooed sexual verbs, for example, comes from the German *ficken*, meaning "to strike"; combined, according to Partridge's etymological dictionary *Origins*, with the Latin sexual verb *futuere*; associated in turn with the Latin *fustis*, "a staff or cudgel"; the Celtic *buc*, "a point, hence to pierce"; the Irish *bot*, "the male member"; the Latin *battuere*, "to beat"; the Gaelic *batair*, "a cudgeller"; the Early Irish *bualaim*, "I strike"; and so forth. It is one of what etymologists sometimes call "the sadistic group of words for the man's part in copulation."   4

The brutality of this word, then, and its equivalents ("screw," "bang," etc., is not an illusion of the middle class or a crotchet of Women's Libera-   5 tion. In their origins and imagery these words carry undeniably painful, if not sadistic, implications, the object of which is almost always female. Consider, for example, what a "screw" actually does to the wood it penetrates; what a painful, even mutilating, activity this kind of analogy suggests. "Screw" is particularly interesting in this context, since the noun, according to Partridge, comes from words meaning "groove," "nut," "ditch," "breeding sow," "scrofula" and "swelling," while the verb, besides its explicit imagery, has antecedent associations to "write on," "scratch," "scarify," and so forth—a revealing fusion of a mechanical or painful action with an obviously denigrated object.

Not all obscene words, of course, are as implicitly sadistic or denigrating   6
to women as these, but all that I know seem to serve a similar purpose: to reduce the human organism (especially the female organism) and human functions (especially sexual and procreative) to their least organic, most mechanical dimension; to substitute a trivializing or deforming resemblance for the complex human reality of what is being described.

Tabooed male descriptives, when they are not openly denigrating to   7
women, often serve to divorce a male organ or function from any significant interaction with the female. Take the word "testes," for example, suggesting "witnesses" (from the Latin *testis*) to the sexual and procreative strengths of the male organ; and the obscene counterpart of this word, which suggests little more than a mechanical shape. Or compare almost any of the "rich," "liberating" sexual verbs, so fashionable today among male writers, with that much-derided Latin word "copulate" ("to bind or join together") or even that Anglo-Saxon phrase (which seems to have had no trouble surviving the Norman Conquest) "make love."

How arrogantly self-involved the tabooed words seem in comparison to   8
either of the other terms, and how contemptuous of the female partner. Understandably so, of course, if she is only a "skirt," a "broad," a "chick," a "pussycat" or a "piece." If she is, in other words, no more than her skirt, or what her skirt conceals; no more than a breeder, or the broadest part of her; no more than a piece of a human being or a "piece of tail."

The most severely tabooed of all the female descriptives, incidentally,   9
are those like a "piece of tail," which suggest (either explicitly or through antecedents) that there is no significant difference between the female channel through which we are all conceived and born and the anal outlet common to both sexes—a distinction that pornographers have always enjoyed obscuring.

This effort to deny women their biological identity, their individuality,   10
their humanness, is such an important aspect of obscene language that one

can only marvel at how seldom, in an era preoccupied with definitions of obscenity, this fact is brought to our attention. One problem, of course, is that many of the people in the best position to do this (critics, teachers, writers) are so reluctant today to admit that they are angered or shocked by obscenity. Bored, maybe, unimpressed, aesthetically displeased, but—no matter how brutal or denigrating the material—never angered, never shocked.

And yet how eloquently angered, how piously shocked many of these   11
same people become if denigrating language is used about any minority group other than women; if the obscenities are racial or ethnic, that is, rather than sexual. Words like "coon," "kike," "spic," "wop," after all, deform identity, deny individuality and humanness in almost exactly the same way that sexual vulgarisms and obscenities do.

No one that I know, least of all my students, would fail to question the   12
values of a society whose literature and entertainment rested heavily on racial or ethnic pejoratives. Are the values of a society whose literature and entertainment rests as heavily as ours on sexual pejoratives any less questionable?

QUESTIONS ON MEANING AND CONTENT

1. Lawrence's essay was first published in 1973. In your view, have we changed much since then in our attitudes toward these words? In our use of these words? Is the student attitude described in paragraph 1 still the prevailing attitude among your peers?

2. If you have read Neil Postman's essay on euphemisms in this section, compare his conclusions about euphemisms with Lawrence's conclusions here. Do you think Postman would agree with Lawrence?

3. Speculate about how we might be different as a culture if we did restrict our references to male-female sexual relations to words carrying the meaning of *copulate* or *make love*—that is, words that emphasize the sharing together of an experience.

4. Aside from this essay, what efforts do you commonly encounter that are designed to address this specific problem? Have you seen this issue raised in newspapers or magazines, or on radio or television? What might be the result if this problem received the same attention as a campaign against cigarette smoking? Does the taboo nature of this subject prevent such campaigns? Or has our lack of interest prevented them?

5. Our attitudes toward these words and our use of them are injurious to women, Lawrence maintains. Are men also affected in some way? Are they injured?

QUESTIONS ABOUT RHETORICAL STRATEGIES

1. This essay illustrates the range that definition essays can have. Although Lawrence defines many words within the essay, the essay itself is offering an extended definition of *obscene* as that word applies to other words. This is a very complex undertaking in a short essay and imposes a relatively complex structure on the essay. The following questions are meant to help you analyze that structure:

  a. Let us, for practical purposes, consider the first three paragraphs to be the introduction to the essay. What does Lawrence establish in these three paragraphs? How is she preparing readers for the body of the paper? What statements does she use to guide readers into the next stage of the essay, into paragraphs 4, 5, and 6?

  b. Look carefully at paragraph 6, which sums up the point Lawrence makes in the first stage of the body of the essay. What in the paragraph tells you this? It is worth noticing the careful movement here since the structural principle at work can be applied to your own writing. Notice that paragraph 4 presents the information, paragraph 5 interprets that information, and paragraph 6 summarizes and states a conclusion about the information. In short, the first stage of the body of the essay is treated in much the same way as a whole essay might be.

  c. Notice how, for the second stage of the body, the same movement starts again. The first sentence of paragraph 7 guides readers into the second stage. The rest of paragraph 7 presents the information; then paragraph 8 interprets the information. Paragraph 8 also sets the reader up for the brief third stage of the body. How does it do this and what is the subject of the third stage?

  d. Consider, for practical purposes, the last three paragraphs to be the conclusion of the essay. What does Lawrence accomplish in the conclusion?

QUESTIONS ON LANGUAGE AND DICTION

1. Paragraphs 8 and 9 discuss contemptuous, sexually based names for females. Can you think of sexually based names for males? What is the nature of these names? Are they contemptuous of males or are they something else? What? What of the other names used over the years to refer to females—for example, *angel, doll, baby?* Are these also contemptuous names? Explain. Are there similar names for males?

2. What are the meanings of *aesthetically, antecedent, cudgel, denigrating, grimaces, pejorative?*

The Right Stuff

TOM WOLFE

The world of the risk-taker is exhilarating, and jet fighter pilots occupy one of the more exhilarating parts of this world where miscalculation or mechanical failure can mean sudden disaster. Among the many who train as fighter pilots, few ever last long enough to excel in this risky profession. Tom Wolfe explains why and defines the qualities shared by those who do last.

A young man might go into military flight training believing that he was   1
entering some sort of technical school in which he was simply going to acquire a certain set of skills. Instead, he found himself all at once enclosed in a fraternity. And in this fraternity, even though it was military, men were not rated by their outward rank as ensigns, lieutenants, commanders, or whatever. No, herein the world was divided into those who had it and those who did not. This quality, this *it*, was never named, however, nor was it talked about in any way.

As to just what this ineffable quality was . . . well, it obviously involved   2
bravery. But it was not bravery in the simple sense of being willing to risk your life. The idea seemed to be that any fool could do that, if that was all that was required, just as any fool could throw away his life in the process. No, the idea here (in the all-enclosing fraternity) seemed to be that a man should have the ability to go up in a hurtling piece of machinery and put his hide on the line and then have the moxie, the reflexes, the experience, the coolness, to pull it back in the last yawning moment—and then go up again *the next day*, and the next day, and every next day, even if the series should prove infinite—and, ultimately, in its best expression, do so in a cause that means something to thousands, to a people, a nation, to humanity, to God. Nor was there *a test* to show whether or not a pilot had this righteous quality. There was, instead, a seemingly infinite series of tests. A career in flying was like climbing one of those ancient Babylonian pyramids made up of a dizzy progression of steps and ledges, a ziggurat, a pyramid extraordinarily high and steep; and the idea was to prove at every foot of the way up that pyramid that you were one of the elected and anointed ones who had *the right stuff* and could move higher and higher and even—ultimately, God willing, one day—that you might be able to join that special few at the very top, that elite

who had the capacity to bring tears to men's eyes, the very Brotherhood of the Right Stuff itself.

None of this was to be mentioned, and yet it was acted out in a way that a young man could not fail to understand. When a new flight (i.e., a class) of trainees arrived at Pensacola, they were brought into an auditorium for a little lecture. An officer would tell them: "Take a look at the man on either side of you." Quite a few actually swiveled their heads this way and that, in the interest of appearing diligent. Then the officer would say: "One of the three of you is not going to make it!"—meaning, not get his wings. That was the opening theme, the *motif* of primary training. We already know that one-third of you do not have the right stuff—it only remains to find out who. 3

Furthermore, that was the way it turned out. At every level in one's progress up that staggeringly high pyramid, the world was once more divided into those men who had the right stuff to continue the climb and those who had to be *left behind* in the most obvious way. Some were eliminated in the course of the opening classroom work, as either not smart enough or not hardworking enough, and were left behind. Then came the basic flight instruction, in single-engine, propeller-driven trainers, and a few more—even though the military tried to make this stage easy—were washed out and left behind. Then came more demanding levels, one after the other, formation flying, instrument flying, jet training, all-weather flying, gunnery, and at each level more were washed out and left behind. By this point easily a third of the original candidates had been, indeed, eliminated . . . from the ranks of those who might prove to have the right stuff. 4

In the Navy, in addition to the stages that Air Force trainees went through, the neophyte always had waiting for him, out in the ocean, a certain grim gray slab; namely, the deck of an aircraft carrier; and with it perhaps the most difficult routine in military flying, carrier landings. He was shown films about it, he heard lectures about it, and he knew that carrier landings were hazardous. He first practiced touching down on the shape of a flight deck painted on an airfield. He was instructed to touch down and gun right off. This was safe enough—the shape didn't move, at least—but it could do terrible things to, let us say, the gyroscope of the soul. *That shape!—it's so damned small!* And more candidates were washed out and left behind. Then came the day, without warning, when those who remained were sent out over the ocean for the first of many days of reckoning with the slab. The first day was always a clear day with little wind and a calm sea. The carrier was so steady that it seemed, from up there in the air, to be resting on pilings, and the candidate usually made his first carrier landing successfully, with relief and even *élan*. Many young candidates looked like terrific aviators 5 up to that very point—and it was not until they were actually standing on the carrier deck that they first began to wonder if they had the proper stuff, after all. In the training film the flight deck was a grand piece of gray geometry, perilous, to be sure, but an amazing abstract shape as one looks down upon it on the screen. And yet once the newcomer's two feet were on it . . . *Geometry*—my God, man, this is a . . . skillet! It *heaved*, it moved up and down underneath his feet, it pitched up, it pitched down, it rolled to port (this great beast *rolled!*) and it rolled to starboard, as the ship moved into the wind and, therefore, into the waves, and the wind kept sweeping across, sixty feet up in the air in the open sea, and there were no railings whatsoever. This was a *skillet!*—a frying pan!—a short-order grill!—not gray but black, smeared with skid marks from one end to the other and glistening with pools of hydraulic fluid and the occasional jet-fuel slick, all of it still hot, sticky, greasy, runny, virulent from God knows what traumas—still ablaze!—consumed in detonations, explosions, flames, combustion, roars, shrieks, whines, blasts, horrible shudders, fracturing impacts, as little men in screaming red and yellow and purple and green shirts with black Mickey Mouse helmets over their ears skittered about on the surface as if for their very lives (you've said it now!), hooking fighter planes onto the catapult shuttles so that they can explode their afterburners and be slung off the deck in a red-mad fury with a *kaboom!* that pounds through the entire deck—a procedure that seems absolutely controlled, orderly, sublime, however, compared to what he is about to watch as aircraft return to the ship for what is known in the engineering stoicisms of the military as "recovery and arrest." To say that an F–4 was coming back onto this heaving barbecue from out of the sky at a speed of 135 knots . . . that might have been the truth in the training lecture, but it did not begin to get across the idea of what the newcomer saw from the deck itself, because it created the notion that perhaps the plane was gliding in. On the deck one knew differently! As the aircraft came closer and the carrier heaved on into the waves and the plane's speed did not diminish and the deck did not grow steady—indeed, it pitched up and down five or ten feet per greasy heave—one experienced a neural alarm that no lecture could have prepared him for: This is not an *airplane* coming toward me, it is a brick with some poor sonofabitch riding it (*someone much like myself!*), and it is not *gliding*, it is *falling*, a fifty-thousand-pound brick, headed not for a stripe on the deck but for *me*—and with a horrible *smash!* it hits the skillet, and with a blur of momentum as big as a freight train's it hurtles toward the far end of the deck—another blinding storm!—another roar as the pilot pushes the throttle up to full military power and another smear of rubber screams out over the skillet—and this is nominal!—quite okay!—for a wire stretched across the deck has grabbed the hook on the end of the plane as it hit the deck tail down, and the smash was the rest of the fifteen-ton brute slamming onto the deck, as it tripped up, so that it is now straining against the wire at full throttle, in case it hadn't held and the plane had "boltered" off the end of the deck and had to struggle up into the air again. And already the Mickey Mouse helmets are running toward the fiery monster . . .

And the candidate, looking on, begins to *feel* that great heaving sun-blazing deathboard of a deck wallowing in his own vestibular system—and suddenly he finds himself backed up against his own limits. He ends up going to the flight surgeon with so-called conversion symptoms. Overnight he develops blurred vision or numbness in his hands and feet or sinusitis so severe that he cannot tolerate changes in altitude. On one level the symptom is real. He really cannot see too well or use his fingers or stand the pain. But somewhere in his subconscious he knows it is a plea and a beg-off; he shows not the slightest concern (the flight surgeon notes) that the condition might be permanent and affect him in whatever life awaits him outside the arena of the right stuff.

Those who remained, those who qualified for carrier duty—and even more so those who later on qualified for *night* carrier duty—began to feel a bit like Gideon's warriors. *So many have been left behind!* The young warriors were now treated to a deathly sweet and quite unmentionable sight. They could gaze at length upon the crushed and wilted pariahs who had washed out. They could inspect those who did not have that righteous stuff.

The military did not have very merciful instincts. Rather than packing up these poor souls and sending them home, the Navy, like the Air Force and the Marines, would try to make use of them in some other role, such as flight controller. So the washout has to keep taking classes with the rest of his group, even though he can no longer touch an airplane. He sits there in the classes staring at sheets of paper with cataracts of sheer human mortification over his eyes while the rest steal looks at him . . . this man reduced to an ant, this untouchable, this poor sonofabitch. And in what test had he been found wanting? Why, it seemed to be nothing less than *manhood* itself. Naturally, this was never mentioned, either. Yet there it was. *Manliness, manhood, manly courage* . . . there was something ancient, primordial, irresistible about the challenge of this stuff, no matter what a sophisticated and rational age one might think he lived in.

Perhaps because it could not be talked about, the subject began to take on superstitious and even mystical outlines. A man either had it or he didn't. There was no such thing as having *most* of it. Moreover, it could blow at any seam. One day a man would be ascending the pyramid at a terrific clip, and the next—bingo!—he would reach his own limits in the most unexpected way. Conrad and Schirra met an Air Force pilot who had had a great pal at Tyndall Air Force Base in Florida. This man had been the budding ace of the training class; he had flown the hottest fighter-style trainer, the T–38, like a dream; and then he began the routine step of being checked out in the T–33. The T–33 was not nearly as hot an aircraft as the T–38; it was essentially the old P–80 jet fighter. It had an exceedingly small cockpit. The pilot could barely move his shoulders. It was the sort of airplane of which everybody said, "You don't get into it, you *wear it.*" Once inside a T–33 cockpit this man, this budding ace, developed claustrophobia of the most paralyzing sort. He tried everything to overcome it. He even went to a psychiatrist, which was a serious mistake for a military officer if his superiors learned of it. But nothing worked. He was shifted over to flying jet transports, such as the C–135. Very demanding and necessary aircraft they were, too, and he was still spoken of as an excellent pilot. But as everyone knew—and, again, it was never explained in so many words—only those who were assigned to fighter squadrons, the "fighter jocks," as they called each other with a self-satisfied irony, remained in the true fraternity. Those assigned to transports were not humiliated like washouts—*somebody* had to fly those planes—nevertheless, they, too, had been *left behind* for lack of the right stuff.

Or a man could go for a routine physical one fine day, feeling like a 10 million dollars, and be grounded for *fallen arches.* It happened!—just like that! (And try raising them.) Or for breaking his wrist and losing only *part* of its mobility. Or for a minor deterioration of eyesight, or for any of hundreds of reasons that would make no difference to a man in an ordinary occupation. As a result all fighter jocks began looking upon doctors as their natural enemies. Going to see a flight surgeon was a no-gain proposition; a pilot could only hold his own or lose in the doctor's office. To be grounded for a medical reason was no humiliation, looked at objectively. But it was a humiliation, nonetheless!—for it meant you no longer had that indefinable, unutterable, integral stuff. (It could blow at *any* seam.)

All the hot young fighter jocks began trying to test the limits themselves 11 in a superstitious way. They were like believing Presbyterians of a century before who used to probe their own experience to see if they were truly among *the elect.* When a fighter pilot was in training, whether in the Navy or the Air Force, his superiors were continually spelling out strict rules for him, about the use of the aircraft and conduct in the sky. They repeatedly forbade so-called hot-dog stunts, such as outside loops, buzzing, flat-hatting, hedgehopping and flying under bridges. But somehow one got the message that the man who truly *had* it could ignore those rules—not that he should make a point of it, but that he *could*—and that after all there was only one way to find out—and that in some strange unofficial way, peeking through his fingers, his instructor halfway expected him to challenge all the limits. They would give a lecture about how a pilot should never fly without a good solid breakfast—eggs, bacon, toast, and so forth—because if he tried to fly with his blood-sugar level too low, it could impair his alertness. Naturally, the next day every hot dog in the unit would get up and have a breakfast consisting of one cup of black coffee and take off and go up into a vertical climb until the weight of the ship exactly canceled out the upward pull of the engine and his air speed was zero, and he would hang there for one thick adrenal instant—and then fall like a rock, until one of three things happened: he keeled over nose first and regained his aerodynamics and all was well, he went into a spin and fought his way out of it, or he went into a spin and had to eject or crunch it, which was always supremely possible.

Likewise, "hassling"—mock dogfighting— was strictly forbidden, and so naturally young fighter jocks could hardly wait to go up in, say, a pair of F–100s and start the duel by making a pass at each other at 800 miles an hour, the winner being the pilot who could slip in behind the other one and get locked in on his tail ("wax his tail"), and it was not uncommon for some eager jock to try too tight an outside turn and have his engine flame out, whereupon, unable to restart it, he has to eject . . . and he shakes his fist at the victor as he floats down by parachute and his half-a-million-dollar aircraft goes *kaboom!* on the palmetto grass or the desert floor, and he starts thinking about how he can get together with the other guy back at the base in time for the two of them to get their stories straight before the investigation: "I don't know what happened sir. I was pulling up after a target run, and it just flamed out on me." Hassling was forbidden, and hassling that led to the destruction of an aircraft was a serious court-martial offense, and the man's superiors knew that the engine hadn't *just flamed out*, but every unofficial impulse on the base seemed to be saying: "Hell, we wouldn't give you a nickel for a pilot who hasn't done some crazy rat-racing like that. It's all part of the right stuff."

The other side of this impulse showed up in the reluctance of the young jocks to admit it when they had maneuvered themselves into a bad corner they couldn't get out of. There were two reasons why a fighter pilot hated to declare an emergency. First, it triggered a complex and very public chain of events at the field: all other incoming flights were held up, including many of one's comrades who were probably low on fuel; the fire trucks came trundling out to the runway like yellow toys (as seen from way up there), the better to illustrate one's hapless state; and the bureaucracy began to crank up the paper monster for the investigation that always followed. And second, to declare an emergency, one first had to reach that conclusion in his own mind, which to the young pilot was the same as saying: "A minute ago I still *had* it—now I need your help!" To have a bunch of young fighter pilots up in the air thinking this way used to drive flight controllers crazy. They would see a ship beginning to drift off the radar, and they couldn't rouse the pilot on the microphone for anything other than a few meaningless mumbles, and they would know he was probably out there with engine failure at a low altitude, trying to reignite by lowering his auxiliary generator rig, which had a little propeller that was supposed to spin in the slipstream like a child's pinwheel.

"Whiskey Kilo Two Eight, do you want to declare an emergency?"   14

This would rouse him!—to say: "Negative, negative, Whiskey Kilo Two   15
Eight is not declaring an emergency."

Kaboom. Believers in the right stuff would rather crash and burn.   16

QUESTIONS ON MEANING AND CONTENT

1. Do you think the definition of a fighter pilot that emerges in the essay represents what some people would consider to be a definition of the ideal American male? If so, who would the "some people" be? Also, what sort of men would have represented this "ideal male" definition before airplanes were invented? Can you think of any other modern occupations where having some sort of "right stuff" is necessary to success? Is this occupation similar in some way to piloting a jet fighter? Explain.

2. Paragraph 12 talks about "mock dogfighting," an activity frequently engaged in by young fighter pilots but officially forbidden by superiors. This official view, however, is offset by an unofficial view. What is this unofficial view, and how do you explain the existence of these two contradictory positions? What do you think would happen if the official view were strictly enforced? Would something be gained or something lost if the superiors decided to eliminate the official view and replace it with the unofficial view? Explain.

3. Wolfe is writing here about a category of American men. Are the traits that he identifies exclusively male traits? Does the definition that emerges suggest that females could not qualify as jet fighter pilots? Or, are certain elements in Wolfe's descriptions really male embellishments and not necessary ingredients for a fighter pilot? Suppose that a large number of females entered training to become fighter pilots. What do you think would happen—would this cause "the right stuff" to evolve and change or would it remain pretty much the same?

4. This question relates closely to the last two: Wolfe tries to account for what fighter pilots *are*. Is this what they *have* to be? Would the absence of any component of "the right stuff" make a more effective fighter pilot? Explain.

QUESTIONS ABOUT RHETORICAL STRATEGIES

1. Wolfe's extended definition is primarily an operational definition explaining what to look for in a pilot's behavior in order to determine whether the pilot does have "the right stuff." Can you take the parts of Wolfe's operational definition and offer a formal, nonoperational extended definition summarizing the many illustrations that Wolfe presents? What key character traits would you include in the summary?

2. Wolfe's definition points to an accumulation of qualities that constitute "the right stuff." Yet, any single weakness could stand for "the wrong stuff." Chart the steps on the hypothetical pyramid leading upward to where only those with "the right stuff" may stand. Determine what weakness at each step would represent "the wrong stuff." Then use this list of weaknesses to write a one- or two-paragraph extended definition of "the wrong stuff."

3. In paragraph 2, Wolfe says that having the right stuff "involved bravery. But it was not bravery in the simple sense of being willing to risk your life." In what sense is bravery involved? What definition of bravery does Wolfe present in order to show what he means?

QUESTIONS ON LANGUAGE AND DICTION

1. Wolfe proceeds through his definition in steps, beginning with flight school and proceeding according to the challenges confronting pilots from that point on. To show how these challenges represent a process of elimination, he uses the analogy of climbing the steps of a Babylonian pyramid. How does this analogy work to illustrate the elements making up "the right stuff"?

2. In paragraph 7, Wolfe says that fighter pilots eventually come to "feel a bit like Gideon's warriors." The analogy here is to the Israelite leader whose story is told in *Judges*, a book of the Old Testament. Read Chapters 6 and 7 in *Judges*, and then explain the specific ways in which this analogy adds meaning for anyone familiar with Gideon's story.

3. Near the middle of paragraph 5, Wolfe describes the shirts of the men on an aircraft carrier's flight deck as "screaming red and yellow and purple and green shirts." Isn't *screaming* an unusual adjective to use with colors? Is it a useful adjective, and, if so, in what way?

4. The same sentence that describes the shirts as "screaming" in color describes the men wearing them as "little men." Why?

5. Wolfe makes heavy use of metaphor to give readers a comparative way of understanding his descriptions and explanations. For example, in paragraph 5, he refers to an aircraft carrier as a "skillet," to an airplane trying to land on a carrier's deck as a "brick," and in paragraph 8 he refers to the trainee who has washed out but must sit in class "with cataracts of sheer mortification over his eyes." How do these metaphors make clearer or add to the meaning of what Wolfe is trying to describe? What other similar metaphors can you find?

6. Check the meaning of any of the following words that are unfamiliar to you: *elan, gyroscope, ineffable, motif, moxie, neophyte, pilings, primordial, stoicism, vestibular.*

Clutter

WILLIAM ZINSSER

A famous writer and writing teacher explains why writers must guard against clutter in the same way that a diligent gardener attacks weeds. Just as ignored weeds can suffocate what the gardener wants to produce, so can clutter weaken and obscure what a writer wants to say.

Fighting clutter is like fighting weeds—the writer is always slightly behind. New varieties sprout overnight, and by noon they are part of American speech. John Dean holds the record. In just one day of testimony on TV during the Watergate hearings he raised the clutter quotient by 400 percent. The next day everyone in America was saying "at this point in time" instead of "now." 1

Consider all the prepositions that are routinely draped onto verbs that don't need any help. Head up. Free up. Face up to. We no longer head committees. We head them up. We don't face problems anymore. We face up to them when we can free up a few minutes. A small detail, you may say—not worth bothering about. It *is* worth bothering about. The game is won or lost on hundreds of small details. Writing improves in direct ratio to the number of things we can keep out of it that shouldn't be there. "Up" in "free up" shouldn't be there. Can we picture anything being freed *up?* The writer of clean English must examine every word that he puts on paper. He will find a surprising number that don't serve any purpose. 2

Take the adjective "personal," as in "a personal friend of mine," "his personal feeling" or "her personal physician." It is typical of the words that can be eliminated nine times out of ten. The personal friend has come into the language to distinguish him from the business friend, thereby debasing not only language but friendship. Someone's feeling *is* his personal feeling—that's what "his" means. As for the personal physician, he is that man summoned to the dressing room of a stricken actress so that she won't have to be treated by the impersonal physican assigned to the theater. Someday I'd like to see him identified as "her doctor." Physicians are physicians, friends are friends, The rest is clutter. 3

Clutter is the laborious phrase which has pushed out the short word that means the same thing. These locutions are a drag on energy and momentum. Even before John Dean gave us "at this point in time," people had 4 stopped saying "now." They were saying "at the present time," or "currently," or "presently" (which means "soon"). Yet the idea can always be expressed by "now" to mean the immediate moment ("Now I can see him"), or by "today" to mean the historical present ("Today prices are high"), or simply by the verb "to be" ("It is raining"). There is no need to say, "At the present time we are experiencing precipitation."

Speaking of which, we are experiencing considerable difficulty getting *that* word out of the language now that it has lumbered in. Even your dentist will ask if you are experiencing any pain. If he were asking one of his own children he would say, "Does it hurt?" He would, in short, be himself. By using a more pompous phrase in his professional role he not only sounds more important; he blunts the painful edge of truth. It is the language of the airline stewardess demonstrating the oxygen mask that will drop down if the plane should somehow run out of air. "In the extremely unlikely possibility that the aircraft should experience such an eventuality," she begins—a phrase so oxygen-depriving in itself that we are prepared for any disaster, and even gasping death shall lose its sting. As for her request to "kindly extinguish all smoking materials," I often wonder what materials are smoking. Maybe she thinks my coat and tie are on fire.

Clutter is the ponderous euphemism that turns a slum into a depressed socioeconomic area, a salesman into a marketing representative and garbage collectors into waste disposal personnel. In New Canaan, Connecticut, the incinerator is now the "volume reduction unit." I think of Bill Mauldin's cartoon showing two hoboes riding a freight train. One of them says, "I started as a simple bum, but now I'm hard-core unemployed."

Clutter is the official language used by the American corporation—in its news release and its annual report—to hide its mistakes. When a big company recently announced that it was "decentralizing its organizational structure into major profit-centered businesses" and that "corporate staff services will be realigned under two senior vice-presidents" it meant that it had had a lousy year.

Clutter is the language of the interoffice memo ("The trend to mosaic communication is reducing the meaningfulness of concern about whether or not demographic segments differ in their tolerance of periodicity") and the language of computers ("Congruent command paradigms explicitly represent the semantic oppositions in the definitions of the commands to which they refer").

Clutter is the language of the Pentagon throwing dust in the eyes of the populace by calling an invasion a "reinforced protective reaction strike" and by justifying its vast budgets on the need for "credible second-strike capability" and "counterforce deterrence." How can we grasp such vaporous double-talk? As George Orwell pointed out in "Politics and the English Language," an essay written in 1946 but cited frequently during the Vietnam and Cambodia years of Johnson and Nixon, "In our time, political speech and writing are largely the defense of the indefensible. . . . Thus political language has to consist largely of euphemism, question-begging and sheer cloudy vagueness." Orwell's warning that clutter is not just a nuisance but a deadly tool came true in America in the 1960s.

In fact, the art of verbal camouflage reached new heights of invention   10
during General Alexander Haig's tenure as Secretary of State in the Reagan administration. Before Haig nobody had ever thought of saying "at this juncture of maturization" to mean "now." He told the American people that he saw "improved pluralization" in El Salvador, that terrorism could be fought with "meaningful sanctionary teeth" and that intermediate nuclear missiles were "at the vortex of cruciality." As for any worries that the public might have about such matters, his message—reduced to one-syllable words—was "leave it to Al." What he actually said was, "We must push this to a lower decibel of public fixation. I don't think there's much of a learning curve to be achieved in this area of content."

I could go on quoting examples from various fields—every profession   11
has its growing arsenal of jargon to fire at the layman and hurl him back from its walls. But the list would be depressing and the lesson tedious. The point of raising it now is to serve notice that clutter is the enemy, whatever form it takes. It slows the reader and robs the writer of his personality, making him seem pretentious.

Beware, then, of the long word that is no better than the short word: 12
"numerous" (many), "facilitate" (ease), "individual" (man or woman), "remainder" (rest), "initial" (first), "implement" (do), "sufficient" (enough), "attempt" (try), "referred to as" (called), and hundreds more. Beware, too, of all the slippery new fad words for which the language already has equivalents: overview and quantify, paradigm and parameter, infrastructure and interface, private sector and public sector, optimize and maximize, prioritize and potentialize. They are all weeds that will smother what you write.

Now are all the weeds so obvious. Just as insidious are the little growths   13
of perfectly ordinary words with which we explain how we propose to go about our explaining, or which inflate a simple preposition or conjunction into a whole windy phrase.

"I might add," "It should be pointed out," "It is interesting to note   14 that"—how many sentences begin with these dreary clauses announcing what the writer is going to do next? If you might add, add it. If it should be pointed out, point it out. If it is interesting to note, *make* it interesting. Being told that something is interesting is the surest way of tempting the reader to find it dull; are we not all stupefied by what follows when someone says, "This will interest you"? As for the inflated prepositions and conjunctions, they are the innumerable phrases like "with the possible exception of" (except), "due to the fact that" (because), "he totally lacked the ability to" (he couldn't), "until such time as" (until), "for the purpose of" (for).

Is there any way to recognize clutter at a glance? Here's a device I used at   15
Yale that students found helpful. I would put brackets around any component in a piece of writing that wasn't doing useful work. Often it was just one word that got bracketed: the unnecessary preposition appended to a verb ("order up"), or the adverb that carries the same meaning as the verb ("smile happily"), or the adjective that states a known fact ("tall skyscraper"). Often my brackets surrounded the little qualifiers that weaken any sentence they inhabit ("a bit," "sort of") or the announcements like "I'm tempted to say." Sometimes my brackets surrounded an entire sentence—the one that essentially repeats what the previous sentence said, or that tells the reader something he doesn't need to know or can figure out for himself. Most people's first drafts can be cut by 50 percent—they're swollen with words and phrases that do no new work whatever.

My reason for bracketing the extra words instead of crossing them out   16
was to avoid violating the sentence. I wanted to leave it intact for the student to analyze. I was saying, "I may be wrong, but I think this can be deleted and the meaning won't be affected at all. But *you* decide: read the sentence without the bracketed material and see if it works." In the early weeks of the term I gave back papers that were infested with brackets. Entire paragraphs were bracketed. But soon the students learned to put mental brackets around their own clutter, and by the end of the term their papers were almost clean. Today many of those students are professional writers and they tell me, "I still see your brackets—they're following me through life."

You can develop the same eye. Look for the clutter in your writing and   17
prune it ruthlessly. Be grateful for everything you can throw away. Reexamine each sentence that you put on paper. Is every word doing new work? Can any thought be expressed with more economy? Is anything pompous or pretentious or faddish? Are you hanging on to something useless just because you think it's beautiful?

Simplify, simplify.   18

QUESTIONS ON MEANING AND CONTENT

1. What reasons does Zinsser offer to account for clutter in writing? Can you think of others?

2. In paragraph 2, Zinsser maintains that "Writing improves in direct ratio to the number of things we can keep out of it that shouldn't be there." Can you explain this statement? In what way or ways would writing be improved by removing clutter?

3. Paragraph 4 suggests that good writing has "energy and momentum." Can you explain what that means? How would the examples mentioned in paragraph 4 act as "a drag on energy and momentum"? Have you read any essays in this book which stand out because they have energy and momentum? Have any impressed you as lacking in energy and momentum? If so, in either case, then test an energetic one for lack of clutter and a sluggish one to see if the "laborious phrase" or any other form of clutter accounts for the lack of energy and momentum.

4. In paragraph 11, the author says that clutter "robs the writer of his personality." How could this be so? What is there about clutter that would obscure a writer's personality? Can you remember anything you have read at one time or another that conveyed a strong sense of the writer's personality? If you can easily locate the piece, reread it and try to determine what makes the personality show through. Pay special attention to Zinsser's remarks about clutter.

QUESTIONS ABOUT RHETORICAL STRATEGIES

1. Each paragraph from 4 through 9—except number 5—begins with a formal definition of *clutter*. What is there about paragraph 5 that would account for this change? How does the author move logically from paragraph 4 to paragraph 5.

2. In what way is paragraph 11 a transitional paragraph? Does this paragraph work logically as a means of moving from preceding paragraphs and into the paragraphs that follow? Explain.

3. If you were going to divide this piece into an introduction, body, and conclusion, where would you make the separations? Why?

QUESTIONS ON LANGUAGE AND DICTION

1. In the opening paragraph, Zinsser compares clutter to weeds, noting that any new form of clutter seems to sprout as quickly as weeds. How does the author expand on this metaphorical comparison later in the essay?

2. Zinsser frequently uses metaphor to show how certain kinds of clutter affect writing. Study the following examples and be ready to explain how each suggests some weakening effect on writing:

Paragraph 2—"prepositions . . . draped onto verbs";
Paragraph 5—The clutter word *experiencing;"*
Paragraph 9—Words are "throwing dust in the eyes of the populace."

3. Explain the metaphor used to develop paragraph 11.

4. Do you find any examples of clutter in Zinsser's own language? Consider, for example, the use of the word *populace* instead of *people* in one of the metaphors mentioned above—"throwing dust in the eyes of the populace." Or do you think that Zinsser has consciously chosen *populace* for some reason? Look for other instances where you could argue that the author uses a longer or less common word when a shorter, more widely known one would do? Remember, however, to check your dictionary to see what other words were available and that a simpler word wouldn't change the intended meaning.

5. Check the meanings of any of the following words that are new to you: *faddish, locutions, pompous, ponderous, pretentious.*

WRITING SCENARIOS

1. Your campus newspaper is preparing its annual satirical issue, full of humorous articles about your college and about prominent students and faculty members. The editor has asked you to write a tongue-in-cheek piece that presents a stereotype of a college student. This stereotype should incorporate many of the unfavorable traits that are often ascribed to college students. Your audience is made up of students *and* faculty members. As a guide to tone, you might want to reread "Are You a Man or a Wimp?" in this chapter. This assignment will benefit from classroom discussion and brainstorming to produce a list of characteristics for each of the definitions.

2. Your uncle, an entertainment editor for *Reader's Digest* magazine, has decided to publish several short essays written from the perspective of college students. He has asked you to write an extended definition of something according to the way it is presented on American television. For example, you might write an extended definition of a rich, power broker as presented in television programs like "Dallas" or "Falcon Crest." Or you might offer an extended definition of the term "chase scene," based on the chase scenes in various police or private detective shows. Of course, while prewriting you may wish to refresh your memory by watching programs that illustrate your subject; you can use examples from these programs to support your assertions. (You may assume that your audience is familiar with your television references, but, with individual exceptions, your audience has not given much conscious thought to what you are defining. The audience should, therefore, recognize the accuracy of your description for the most part, and here and there audience members should see things in your writing that will be minor revelations; that is, some members of the audience will recognize that certain things in your definition are true even though they had not noticed them before.)

3. For the past two years you have been corresponding with a foreign student who is going to attend your college or university. This student has been watching American television shows, old and new, that depict family situations—shows like "Family Ties," "The Crosby Show," "The Jeffersons," and others. Your friend has been puzzled by the variety of these shows and has wondered how accurate they are in depicting American family life. What your friend wants from you is an extended definition answering the question, "What is the American family as you would define it on the basis of your own family and families similar to yours?" You will want to begin your definition with a reference point for your friend, showing what group or what kinds of Americans your family represents, so your friend will know that other ways exist of defining the American family. You may refer to any of the television shows, but remember, you are defining your family and similar families and not comparing either to a television "family."

4. In your spare time you work as a volunteer for an agency that assists adults who have just immigrated to the United States. Part of your job is to help these newcomers become familiar with the English language, and often you write short articles about language for the agency's newsletter. For one of your essays to be published in the newsletter, you have decided to write an extended definition of an idiomatic expression. Choose any one that interests you and that is complex enough to allow you first to offer a formal definition and then to extend the definition with one or two well-developed examples to illustrate the meaning of the expression. Although you may use one of the following, they are included here to get you thinking about possible topics:

Read between the lines	Make the feathers fly
Fight with no holds barred	Lay it on the line
Test the wind	Caught red-handed
Kill the goose who laid the golden egg	Take the law into your own hands
Jump from the frying pan into the fire	

Remember, you will want to design the paper for adults who speak English as a second language. Assume that this audience can read, write, and speak English fairly well but are encountering this expression for the first time.

5. You are very close to your grandparents, and you frequently correspond with them. Recently, your grandfather asked you to define a slang term used by your age group. You have decided to write an extended definition. Your purpose is to explain exactly what the expression means and why. Classroom discussions can help here in the selection of possible slang terms to be used as subjects. Before you start to write, it might also be helpful to conduct an informal survey of the older people you know, trying out slang terms on them to see which are more interesting or more amusing to them. (As an alternative, you may wish to interview one of your grandparents or someone else from the same age group, and ask this person about slang terms used when he or she was your age. Write an extended definition for an audience of your own age.)

6. You are a member of your campus Philosophy Club. At each club meeting, one member gives a presentation on an interesting topic, after which everyone discusses and debates the subject over refreshments. Since the members of your club enjoy intellectual challenge, you have decided to propose an extended definition of an abstract term such as *God, love, trust, freedom,* or *free will.* It is very difficult to offer an extended definition of an abstract term that everyone will agree on, so it is important to be as specific as possible. Remember, your audience enjoys intellectual challenge, so you may wish to be playful with your subject. You can decide to be serious or humorous.

7. As a business major with a strong sense of ethics, you were appalled to learn that large defense contractors had routinely defrauded the government of hundreds of millions of dollars. You were shocked by the disclosure that some of the nation's leading companies overcharged the Pentagon $400 for simple carpenter's hammers, $600 for toilet seats, $300 for coffee makers, and wrote off kennel expenses for pets and expensive gifts for generals' wives.

You've decided that this kind of corporate behavior is the most cynical kind of disloyalty and un-patriotism. And you've concluded that corporations in America have as strong a responsibility to be as patriotic as any individual citizen. In other words, businesses have to exercise patriotic virtues and act on behalf of the common good. Your thinking has led you to believe that any business behavior that systematically weakens the military, economic, social, or spiritual fabric of America is unpatriotic.

You want to address this issue in the prestigious business magazine that your department publishes. You have decided to submit an essay defining "Business Patriotism." In it you will define patriotism in terms of what a company can do by its products and services to make America a stronger and more stable society. Among other things, you might insist that patriotism means not only delivering good military products at a fair price, but it also means delivering products that make Americans healthier, more enlightened, more productive, and more satisfied citizens. In light of this idea, you define junk-foods, junk-entertainment, junk-products of all kinds as damaging to the social, personal, and inner fabric of Americans and hence unpatriotic. This essay requires some precise reasoning and specific details to make it a successful extended definition. Your audience is, first, fellow business majors, but also faculty members and other students as well.

SIX

CLASSIFYING
AND
DIVIDING

Both classification and division provide ways of understanding things in the world around you and enable you to explain these things more clearly to others. **Classification** is a system of sorting through a large number of related items, finding the items that share important similarities, and placing them into groups or classes. You can classify anything: people, animals, objects, ideas. Beginning with many things and then separating those things into similar groups is what distinguishes classification from division. **Division** is the process of taking one thing or unit and separating it into its parts, allowing readers to understand the single unit and how it functions. Both methods enable people to work and manage affairs sensibly and efficiently. They allow people to organize and better understand that which seems diverse and confusing or to see how parts work together to form a single unit.

Classification

Classification is the process of placing items into classes based on characteristics shared by those items. Systems of classification can vary considerably, depending on the purpose or needs of those doing the classifying. For example, a state might have one tax rate for beverages containing alcohol and another tax rate for alcohol-free beverages. If so, a two-class system for beverages, alcoholic and nonalcoholic, would serve the purposes of the state taxing agency. This two-class or two-part system would work because all the state needs to know is whether a beverage does or does not contain alcohol. The classification system is based on only one characteristic: the presence of alcohol in the beverage. Yet this characteristic is sufficient to separate all beverages into one class or the other. This simple, two-class system works in this case because the principle underlying the classification, the presence of alcohol, is reliable enough to separate all beverages into one class or the other, enabling the state to collect two different beverage taxes.

Classification systems that separate items into three or more classes are called *complex* systems. Complex classifying systems are more common because they are more informative and, therefore, more useful. Placing beverages into two groups, alcoholic and nonalcoholic, does not take into account the wide variety of drinks that would make up either group. Similarly, your college or university could not keep precise academic records or issue meaningful progress reports if it grouped undergraduate students into only two classes, say, full-time and part-time students. Instead, a college or university uses a complex classification system for undergraduate students. In most cases, this would produce the four familiar classes of Freshman, Sophomore, Junior, and Senior. The principle applied to place students would be the number of credit hours earned or accepted by transfer from another college or university.

Colleges, of course, classify students in many other ways—by major, by how well they are doing academically, by whether or not they receive financial aid, and so on. You could write a paper, for example, showing how experiencing college differs for students in three different classes: those who live in campus dormitories, those who live at home while attending college, and those who live in apartments off-campus.

Division

Division is a method of understanding or explaining something by breaking it into parts. When you look at a map of the United States, you expect to see the states themselves stand out on the map. With the states highlighted by colors or lines, or a combination of both, the map is easy to comprehend and to use efficiently. The division into states makes it easier to find Peoria or Dubuque or Salt Lake City.

Division applied to space imposes order, and this orderliness makes space more intelligible by providing us with reference points. This is why the weather reporter on television superimposes outlines of the states on satellite photographs. These outlines enable viewers to focus attention on the weather patterns directly affecting them. Similarly, you can find your way through cities because they have been divided into blocks. Because of division, you are better able to use and understand what were originally rather shapeless expanses of territory.

Using division to comprehend or work with space is quite common, but another common way of thinking about division is to begin with something that already has parts that fit together to form a whole. You could analyze a university to show its complete organizational structure, including financial, housekeeping, and other divisions providing support services, or you could limit yourself to a smaller organizational unit. Thus, you might analyze the university's academic division into schools or colleges or take one of these divisions and show how it is divided into administrative units and academic departments.

Division is a useful tool for analyzing and explaining organizations but is by no means limited to these subjects. Anything that can be separated into parts can be analyzed and explained using division. You could analyze a book according to its chapters or one of your own papers according to introduction, body, and conclusion. You could analyze an automobile by dividing it into its components, or you could analyze any unit of the automobile that has its own parts. For example, you could analyze the fuel system or the fuel pump, the entire drive train or just the transmission or the clutch.

PREWRITING

It is important to give careful consideration to selecting a topic for your classification or division paper. You will want to choose a subject that you already know well or one you know well enough so that a minimum of reading, research, or observation will fill any knowledge gaps you may have. Explaining the three ancient Greek architectural styles—Doric, Ionic, and Corinthian—would not be a wise choice unless you already have a strong understanding of them.

Most freshman English papers are relatively short, so it is advisable to limit your topic in a way that will allow you to explain the subject fully. You can do this by carefully selecting the principle that will control the classification or division. For example, if fishing were your hobby, you still would not want to attempt to classify all artificial lures used in sport fishing. This topic would require too many classes and subclasses and if properly treated would lead to a book-length study. On the other hand, you could adequately handle an essay that classified trout flies designed to imitate larva found in your favorite trout stream.

For division, you will want to follow the same practice: Choose a topic that you understand well yourself and that is limited enough to analyze and explain in an essay. This means that you would be wise to analyze the organizational structure of your campus sorority or fraternity chapter rather than the national organization, or Pickett's charge rather than the Battle of Gettysburg.

While selecting a topic, ask some questions about yourself and your audience. Exactly who are your readers? Other college students? High school students? Older adults? How well do you know your topic? Well enough to present it thoroughly without doing some last-minute research? Are you more familiar with your topic than your audience is likely to be? If so, you will want to devote a part of your brainstorming to the explanations or definitions that will be necessary for a reader who is intelligent but knows less about the topic than you do.

Once you have a topic, you will want to compile a list of details that will enable you to identify and discuss the classes or explain and describe the parts in relation to the whole. Here is where you must decide what purpose you have in classifying or dividing, since your purpose will determine what details you will need as well as suggest ways to organize your paper.

Remember, classifying and dividing can vary according to the needs or interests of the person doing the classifying or dividing. A boat builder would likely place sailboats into the traditional classes of catboats, sloops, yawls, and the like, based on size and the arrangement of masts and sails. However, an art instructor teaching beginners to draw sailboats might establish classes based on the level of skills needed to draw each type of boat. A forester, a landscaper, and a woodcarver would all have different reasons for classifying trees. Each would apply a different classifying principle and separate the trees into different classes. A civil engineer analyzing a new housing development might show how the division into lots, streets, and utility rights-of-way represents efficient use of space, while a realtor selling the homes might divide the development according to the view of a nearby lake offered by each section of the development.

Once you know the principle you wish to apply to do the classifying or dividing, you can use this principle as a guide to establishing classes or dividing into parts. Also, this principle will help guide you toward the details you will use to explain the classes or divisions. It is important, however, to be thorough as you brainstorm for details and to be sure the details fit only the purpose or principle that you are using to classify or divide. You would not want to mix details about the efficient use of space, for example, if you are analyzing the housing development according to each section's view of the lake.

If you are analyzing a physical object, it is a good idea to observe your subject visually while you are prewriting. While observing, you can take detailed notes so that you don't omit important characteristics.

The heuristic that follows is designed to help you prewrite for your classification and division essay. The first eight questions relate to classification; the remainder to division. You need answer only those questions appropriate to your essay. When jotting down the answers on your **prewriting** notes, feel free to take shortcuts. Your job here is to generate information and to develop a good idea of how to put your paper together.

Prewriting Questions for Classification and Division

1. What principle should I use to separate my subject into classes?
2. Is my principle reliable enough to account for all items or members of the group?
3. Can I separate my classes into subclasses?
4. If so, do I have a single, reliable principle to account for everything in each subclass?
5. How can I clearly introduce the reader to the principle I am using to separate my subject into classes?
6. How can I explain to my readers why my method of classifying has value for this subject?
7. What details will I need in order to explain and develop fully each class and subclass?
8. How much will the audience know about this subject, and in what ways will I have to tailor the essay to my audience?
9. Into what main parts can I divide my subject?
10. What principle should I use to make the division?
11. How can I clearly show the principle I am using to control the dividing into parts?
12. How can I show that my method of dividing this subject is a worthwhile one?

13. What will I need in my introduction to explain and describe the subject of my division? Will I have to define the subject?

14. In what order should I present my analysis of the parts? Why is this a logical order?

15. What details will I need to make my explanations and descriptions of the parts clear to my audience?

16. Will I need extra details, or will I have to provide definitions along the way?

17. If I expect my audience to be familiar with the topic, in what ways will this affect the details I will use?

ORGANIZING

Your prewriting should help you to **organize** your essay. Once you have identified the principle you are applying to the classification or division, you will be able to tell the reader this in your introduction. If you are classifying trees according to how they can enhance a yard or analyzing the parts of a racing car to show how it maintains stability at high speeds, then you will need to make this clear in the introduction.

Classification essays normally move from larger to smaller classes. For example, if you were classifying fly fishing lines, you could base the classes on whether the line has been designed to keep the fly on or near the surface or deep in the water. This would logically lead you to three major classes: floating, sinking, and combination floating and sinking lines. Thus, the principle applied to the original group separates the fly lines into three classes and accounts for all the original items (all fly lines).

Now you would be obliged to account for all members of each of these three groups by establishing smaller subclasses. You might discuss floating fly lines first, sinking fly lines second, and combination lines last. (It would be logical to delay introducing combination lines until the reader has an understanding of the other two.) In such a paper, you would present each class to the reader and explain the class completely, accounting for all members. For floating fly lines, you would discuss two subclasses: those which retain captured air on their own, and those which require a special dressing in order to retain air. Similarly, you would separate sinking lines into subclasses according to the design qualities that make them sink slowly or quickly.

You could, of course, classify fly lines according to another principle so long as the principle you choose accounts for all fly lines. The process, however, would remain the same. You would first separate the largest group and then proceed through the smaller groups, always accounting for all members of each group.

Usually, you will want to begin a division paper in the same fashion. That is, first explain to the reader what it is you are dividing into parts and why you are analyzing the whole in relation to its parts. Tell the reader that your analysis will show why a particular boat is slow but stable in the water or fast but unstable. Then move on to the parts, letting your reason for dividing the unit suggest which parts should be presented and in what order. Your objective is to explain how the parts go together to form a unit or fulfill a purpose.

The central question to answer before you begin is why you are making the division. Are you dividing a laboratory microscope just to show what sort of mechanism it is? If so, then the parts are more or less equal and you can proceed by any reasonable plan that will describe the mechanism in an orderly way—the base, which allows it to stand; the body, which holds the lens tube; the lens tube itself. But if your purpose is to show what a simple microscope can reveal about the unseen world, then the lens, the mirror, and the coarse and fine adjusting gears demand prominence in your essay because the relationship between these parts and your purpose is critical.

WRITING

After your prewriting and organizing activities have heightened your awareness of what your essay will require of you, then you are ready to begin **writing** your first draft. Try to write quickly, a practice we have been advising all along. There is no need to labor over each sentence or paragraph. Your purpose at this point is to produce a rough draft. If you can't think of the correct word in a sentence, draw a line and fill in the blank later. Your revising will take care of additions, deletions, and the fine-tuning of sentences.

As usual, follow your organizing plan, and use your brainstorming details to guide you through the first draft. While composing you will want to try to keep your audience in mind as you write so that you are generally on track according to what your prewriting activities have identified as audience concerns. However, work with as much speed as possible, saving your concern about details for the revision and proofreading processes. If you discover while writing that you are omitting important information, feel free to return to the prewriting or organizing processes.

REVISING

It is *essential* to remember that the key to effective writing is careful, thoughtful **revising.** The time you spend revising can transform your first draft into a finished essay that is sound in organization, content, and style.

A good first step is to read through your rough draft, giving careful attention to organization. Is your original organizing plan effective, or must you reorganize your paper? Does your introduction clearly identify or define what it is you are classifying or dividing? Have you set before the reader the principle used for classifying or analyzing the parts? Is the principle one that is reliable enough to show the relationship between the parts and the whole or to separate all the members of the group into classes? Remember, your principle has to be reliable; it has to account for each group member. You could not, for example, classify students academically by using a principle as unreliable as the postures they assume in class or the clothing they wear. Either an honor student or a student on academic probation might slouch in a classroom chair or dress in a bizarre fashion.

A good second step is to examine the paragraphs in the body of the paper. These paragraphs develop your topic, and this is where you must fulfill what you promised the reader in the introduction. If you are classifying, have you accounted for all the members of the group you are working with? Are the subclasses arranged according to some logical order? Is it immediately clear to your reader why you have arranged your subclasses as you have? What logic is at work in the order in which you present your classes? How does this particular order help the reader understand your subject?

If you are dividing, do your divisions always point back to the principle controlling the division? Are you letting the reader see how each part relates to this principle and the whole? If you are dividing space, are the divisions clearly connected to some focal point? For example, if you are explaining the layout of your hometown, you would need a focal point, perhaps a river or a central business district.

After working with the body of your paper, you may wish to study your conclusion. Do you end abruptly with your last class or division? Or have you taken the opportunity to tell your readers something about your general topic? Would reminding the reader about what was said in the introduction make an appropriate conclusion? Could you conclude by noting that there are other ways to classify or divide your subject but that understanding the subject from your guiding principle is a useful understanding to have? In short, does your conclusion do something for your reader?

Remember, it is best to study your introduction, body, and conclusion more than once, searching for places where you have left information gaps, where words or phrases need to be defined or extra sentences added in order to make something clear to an audience that may not know your topic as well as you know it. If time permits, you may wish to set the paper aside for awhile after each revision. This will give you distance from the paper and help you find trouble spots more easily.

After you are satisfied with your paper's organization and content, then you are ready to turn your attention to individual sentences, reading each carefully, looking for ways to improve any clumsy or ineffective ones. Are you certain that each sentence says exactly what you want it to say? Don't expect your reader to stop and puzzle out your meaning for you. Also, you will want to examine how each sentence and each paragraph leads to another. Have you included the transitional words and phrases that will make your writing move along smoothly and clearly? If you find places where you move abruptly from one point to another, then you can add what is necessary to make the movement seem expected, rather than unexpected, to the reader.

PROOFREADING

Your **proofreading** tasks are the same here as for any paper you must write. You have already taken care of the larger features of your essay. Now is the time to check your grammar, punctuation, and spelling.

As a final precaution, you may wish to check the classification or division checklist below to be sure you have not omitted elements essential to your essay.

Classification and Division Checklist

1. Does your introduction contain sufficient information about why you are classifying or dividing according to your chosen principle?
2. Does your introduction prepare readers for the body of your paper?
3. Have you considered your audience at every step of your essay?
4. Is your **organization** immediately clear to readers?
5. Have you been specific enough in explaining each class or division?
6. Have you oriented the reader specifically enough as each new class or division appears?

7. Are you sure your readers will see the relationship between the classes and the original large group or between the parts and the whole?

8. Have you provided adequate transitional words and phrases between elements in your paper?

9. Does your conclusion add strength to your essay?

10. Have you carefully examined each sentence to see that it is clear, grammatically correct, and free of misspellings and punctuation errors?

Critiquing Quack Ads

ROGER W. MILLER

The quack ads that appear in magazines and newspapers across America promise people what they want most: beautiful bodies, good health, instant riches. What the ads usually deliver, however, is disappointment. In this essay, Roger W. Miller discusses the variety of these ads and reflects on the people most likely to respond to them.

Freedom of speech doesn't give a person the right to shout "fire" in a crowded theater, Supreme Court Justice Oliver Wendell Holmes Jr. once noted. Nor should it give con artists the right to promote health frauds through ads in print or on the air. Yet, health fraud lives and even thrives, in no small part because of successful advertising.   1

To get an idea of the prevalence of advertising for possibly fraudulent health items, the Food and Drug Administration contracted with a clipping service to survey the nation's newspapers and magazines for one month. The clipping service came up with a total of 435 questionable ads in publications ranging from the smallest of weekly newspapers to multimillion-circulation magazines.   2

The 435 ads hardly indicate the true volume of dubious advertising during that period. With more than 10,000 daily and weekly newspapers and general-circulation magazines in the country, any clipping service asked to do a nationwide search is only going to be fractionally successful. However, the clippings give a good idea of what's being peddled to the gullible, the desperate, the people looking for something-too-good-to-be-true.   3

Weight-loss products such as body wraps are by far the most popular items being promoted by the fraud artists, according to the clipping survey. Of the 435 ads, 249 were for weight-loss products. Diet pills accounted for most of those, with 218 ads. That figure was ballooned somewhat by a number of ads for the so-called grapefruit pill ("No dieting—eat all you want; the pill does it all—$12 for a 14 day supply"). A total of 102 grapefruit pill ads were found in publications ranging from the 4,200-circulation weekly *Times* in Willard, Ohio, to the 358,265-circulation *Denver Post*. The ads appeared at a time when the U.S. Postal Service, acting in part on information supplied by FDA, was taking action against the pill's promoters, Citrus Industries. The Postal Service sought court permission to send all   4 of Citrus Industries' mail back to the senders, thus cutting off those $12 checks. A federal court in Los Angeles ordered the mail held until a Postal Service judicial officer decides on the value of the product. In the meantime, Citrus Industries has quit advertising the grapefruit pill.

Hair restoration schemes are next in popularity to diet hoaxes, the 5 clippings indicate. Eighty-nine ads for hair restorers were found, 42 of them for products and 47 for "clinics." FDA has counseled consumers that no product has ever been approved as safe and effective for preventing baldness or restoring hair. Wrinkle removers were also high on the quack ad hit parade.

The clippings indicate that California, our most populous state, is the 6 best place for a quack to advertise his bogus goods and services. Eighty-four of the ads were from publications in that state. Texas was second with 45 clippings; New York contributed 44.

There was no end to the imaginations of the promoters. One product 7 was guaranteed to take care of hemorrhoids, varicose veins and indigestion. One of the many hypnosis plans promised to handle the urge to smoke, hypertension and overeating. Although experts say exercise is necessary for most people who want to lose weight, dozens of hucksters, are promoting diet products that let you "lose while you snooze."

There were "rear end kits" for reshaping, pills for the "ultimate or- 8 gasm," and a $19.95 product that would "add 2 to 4 inches to your height in just 10 weeks." But all is not harmless fun and games in the health fraud business. Tragedy is written between the lines of much of the copy. Offers of cheap, quick ways to treat heart disease, arthritis, alcoholism, depression and high blood pressure are bound to be taken seriously by someone. And that someone is most apt to suffer even more as a result.

QUESTIONS ON MEANING AND CONTENT

1. Paragraph 3 suggests that the ads in question appeal "to the gullible, the desperate, the people looking for something-too-good-to-be-true." How do these three groups differ one from the other? What would make each group vulnerable to these ads?
2. Do the products being advertised appeal broadly to the three groups mentioned in paragraph 3 or would certain of the ads have more appeal to one of the groups than to another? Which ads might appeal more to the first group? The second? The third?

3. Can you place the various ads mentioned into categories based on human desires—for example, the desire to have a more beautiful body? What other categories can you suggest?
4. The author suggests that there is something humorous about many of these ads but also something very sad. Explain this. In what ways might our reactions differ when each of the following groups is "taken in" by the ads: "the gullible, the desperate, the people looking for something-too-good-to-be-true"?
5. What is a proper attitude toward the existence—and the success—of these ads? Do you think people should be protected from them by government regulations, or do you think people should look out for themselves? Explain.

QUESTIONS ABOUT RHETORICAL STRATEGIES

1. This essay calls attention to an existing situation or problem and provides enough information to give readers a good idea of the nature and dimensions of the problem. The purpose isn't to classify formally in a highly detailed way, using classes and subclasses. How do you see this purpose at work in the structure and content of the piece? What does this say about the intended audience?
2. How is paragraph 1 designed to prepare the reader for the body of the article? What writing strategies are at work here?
3. How do paragraphs 1 (introduction) and 8 (conclusion) relate to each other?

QUESTIONS ON LANGUAGE AND DICTION

1. From what you know about advertising language, do you think the label "rear end kits" was actually used in an ad? Do you think "ultimate orgasm" or "lose while you snooze" may have appeared? Explain.
2. Explain the meaning of the verb *was ballooned* as used in paragraph 4.
3. What do the terms "con artists," (paragraph 1), "bogus" (paragraph 6), and "hucksters" (paragraph 7) mean?

Everything You Ever Wanted to Know About the Kiss

CAROL TAVRIS AND LEONORE TIEFER

What are we doing when we kiss? Well, it depends on a number of things, but one thing kissing can do is send messages to others. In this essay, Carol Tavris and Leonore Tiefer tell us about these messages.

Throughout history, people have found occasion to kiss almost every 1
object that didn't fight back, and a few that did. We kiss icons, dice, the Bible
and lottery tickets for luck; we kiss the Blarney Stone for the gift of gab; we
kiss religious garments in reverence; we kiss to say hello, good-by, get well,
get lost.

There have been so many kinds of kisses that from time to time scholars 2
feel obliged to try to sort them into categories. The ancient rabbis divided
kisses into three kinds: greeting, farewell and respect. The Romans identified *oscula* (friendly kisses), *basia* (love kisses) and *suavia* (passionate
kisses)—it appears that they were somewhat bawdier than the ancient
rabbis. The German language had no fewer than 30 types of kisses at the
turn of the century, from *Abschiedkuss* (farewell kiss) to *Zuckerkuss* (sweet
kiss). They have since lost, unfortunately, *nachküssen,* which in 1901 meant
"making up for kisses that have been omitted."

However many types of kisses one makes up, though, they boil down 3
into only a few basic messages:

"I am your subordinate and I respect you." The kiss as a symbol of deference 4
and duty has a long tradition. In the Middle Ages the location of the kiss was
a precise clue to the status of the participants: one kissed the mouth or cheek
of an equal, the hand of a political or religious leader, the hem of the robe of a
truly great figure and—to express extreme respect—the foot or ground in
front of a king, saint or revered hero. The further away one was in status
from the kissee, the farther away from the face one kissed.

"I am your friend." To allow someone close enough to kiss you requires a 5
measure of trust; in its earliest form the kiss of greeting undoubtedly meant,
"It's safe. I will not bite your ear or stab your back." The kiss of reconciliation
preceded the handshake in many societies, and even today children—and
sometimes grownups—are encouraged to "kiss and make up."

"The bargain is sealed." Originally the kiss exchanged between bride and 6

groom was a business kiss—a pagan practice that meant the couple were officially assuming their legal and economic obligations. When all the guests kissed the new wife, they were publicly recognizing the legality of the union.

"I will take care of you and ward off evil." Mothers kiss their children's 7
scraped knees, feverish foreheads and bruised arms to "make the hurt go away," just as faith healers "kiss away" the ailments of grownup penitents. Belief in the magical powers of kisses has filtered into everyday superstition: When you kiss dice or a cross (or your crossed fingers) or any object "for luck," you are enlisting the aid of fortune, God or the fates.

"We are in and you are out." The "ins" may be family, neighborhood, 8
community or religious fellowship. When St. Paul instructed the faithful to "salute one another with an holy kiss," he established a ritual that came to reflect public adherence to the faith. St. Paul's kiss of peace, as it came to be known, was exchanged among Christians variously at services, baptism, confession, ordination and communion.

Because the kiss implies trust, solidarity and affection, deceptive kisses 9
are everywhere despised. Judas's betrayal of Christ in the garden of Gethsemane was, of course, the most famous Western example. The Judas kiss is practiced ritually even today. Among some Mafiosi, a man who has betrayed the organization will be kissed on the mouth by his assassin—a sign of loving farewell.

QUESTIONS ON MEANING AND CONTENT

1. Did any new information come to you through this classification of kisses or were you already familiar with them? How many of these types have you observed—or given or received yourself?

2. Can you think of any kisses that carry messages that aren't covered in this classification system? Don't some people tend to kiss more than others—Hollywood stars, for example? Often a male star will kiss a female star (and vice versa) as a greeting and after performances, even if the two scarcely know each other or aren't on particularly friendly terms. What messages are they sending? What is the message when Johnny Carson and a female kiss when the female first comes on stage? Is this merely a greeting or is there another message there? Do you know of families or ethnic groups that kiss more than others? If so, what seems to be the "message"?

QUESTIONS ABOUT RHETORICAL STRATEGIES

1. What do the classifications discussed in paragraph 2 tell you about classifying in general and about the purposes of those doing the classifying?

2. What is the basis of Tavris and Tiefer's classification system?

3. Explain how the conclusion of the paper relates back to the system used to classify kisses. Could an effective conclusion have referred to other purposes or systems of classifying kisses? Explain.

QUESTIONS ON LANGUAGE AND DICTION

1. How clear is the opening paragraph for you? If you didn't know the meaning of *icons* or *Blarney Stone,* was the paragraph still clear because of the other examples? What are icons? The Blarney Stone?

Notes on Class

PAUL FUSSELL

In the past, we tried to hide the facts of our sex lives more than anything else, but that has changed, according to Paul Fussell. Now, we try to hide the facts that would place us in one social class or another. This was easy to do when social classes were arranged according to income, a basis of classification that the author finds to be inadequate in telling us where we fit socially. Perception is the right base for sorting people into classes, Fussell insists, and anyone who knows the signs can see beyond our incomes and identify our social class. Perception can easily find us out because too many things in our lives give our social status away.

If the dirty little secret used to be sex, now it is the facts about social class. No subject today is more likely to offend. Over thirty years ago Dr. Kinsey generated considerable alarm by disclosing that despite appearances one-quarter of the male population had enjoyed at least one homosexual orgasm. A similar alarm can be occasioned today by asserting that despite the much-discussed mechanism of "social mobility" and the constant redistribution of income in this country, it is virtually impossible to break out of the social class in which one has been nurtured. Bad news for the ambitious as well as the bogus, but there it is. 1

Defining class is difficult, as sociologists and anthropologists have learned. The more data we feed into the machines, the less likely it is that significant formulations will emerge. What follows here is based not on interviews, questionnaires, or any kind of quantitative techniques but on perhaps a more trustworthy method—perception. Theory may inform us that there are three classes in America, high, middle, and low. Perception will tell us that there are at least nine, which I would designate and arrange like this: 2

Top Out-of-Sight
Upper
Upper Middle

—

Middle
High-Proletarian

Mid-Proletarian
Low-Proletarian

—

Destitute
Bottom Out-of-Sight

In addition, there is a floating class with no permanent location in this hierarchy. We can call it Class X. It consists of well-to-do hippies, "artists," "writers" (who write nothing), floating bohemians, politicians out of office, disgraced athletic coaches, residers abroad, rock stars, "celebrities," and the shrewder sort of spies.

The quasi-official division of the population into three economic classes called high-, middle-, and low-income groups rather misses the point, because as a class indicator the amount of money is not as important as the source. Important distinctions at both the top and bottom of the class scale arise less from degree of affluence than from the people or institutions to whom one is beholden for support. For example, the main thing distinguishing the top three classes from each other is the amount of money inherited in relation to the amount currently earned. The Top Out-of-Sight Class (Rockefellers, du Ponts, Mellons, Fords, Whitneys) lives on inherited capital entirely. Its money is like the hats of the Boston ladies who, asked where they got them, answer, "Oh, we *have* our hats." No one whose money, no matter how ample, comes from his own work, like film stars, can be a member of the Top Out-of-Sights, even if the size of his income and the extravagance of his expenditure permit him temporary social access to it. 3

Since we expect extremes to meet, we are not surprised to find the very lowest class, Bottom Out-of-Sight, similar to the highest in one crucial respect: it is given its money and kept sort of afloat not by its own efforts but by the welfare machinery or the prison system. Members of the Top Out-of-Sight Class sometimes earn some money, as directors or board members of philanthropic or even profitable enterprises, but the amount earned is laughable in relation to the amount already possessed. Membership in the Top Out-of-Sight Class depends on the ability to flourish without working at all, and it is this that suggests a curious brotherhood between those at the top and the bottom of the scale. 4

It is this also that distinguishes the Upper Class from its betters. It lives on both inherited money and a salary from attractive, if usually slight, work, without which, even if it could survive and even flourish, it would feel bored and a little ashamed. The next class down, the Upper Middle, may possess virtually as much as the two above it. The difference is that it has earned 5 most of it, in law, medicine, oil, real-estate, or even the more honorific forms of trade. The Upper Middles are afflicted with a bourgeois sense of shame, a conviction that to live on the earnings of others, even forebears, is not entirely nice.

The Out-of-Sight Classes at top and bottom have something else in common: they are literally all but invisible (hence their name). The façades of Top Out-of-Sight houses are never seen from the street, and such residences (like Rockefeller's upstate New York premises) are often hidden away deep in the hills, safe from envy and its ultimate attendants, confiscatory taxation and finally expropriation. The Bottom Out-of-Sight Class is equally invisible. When not hidden away in institutions or claustrated in monasteries, lamaseries, or communes, it is hiding from creditors, deceived bail-bondsmen, and merchants intent on repossessing cars and furniture. (This class is visible briefly in one place, in the spring on the streets of New York City, but after this ritual yearly show of itself it disappears again.) When you pass a house with a would-be impressive façade addressing the street, you know it is occupied by a mere member of the Upper or Upper Middle Class. The White House is an example. Its residents, even on those occasions when they are Kennedys, can never be classified as Top Out-of-Sight but only Upper Class. The house is simply too conspicuous, and temporary residence there usually constitutes a come-down for most of its occupants. It is a hopelessly Upper- or Upper-Middle-Class place. 6

Another feature of both Top and Bottom Out-of-Sight Classes is their anxiety to keep their names out of the papers, and this too suggests that socially the President is always rather vulgar. All the classes in between Top and Bottom Out-of-Sight slaver for personal publicity (monograms on shirts, inscribing one's name on lawn-mowers and power tools, etc.), and it is this lust to be known almost as much as income that distinguishes them from their Top and Bottom neighbors. The High- and Mid-Prole Classes can be recognized immediately by their pride in advertising their physical presence, a way of saying, "Look! We pay our bills and have a known place in the community, and you can find us there any time." Thus hypertrophied house-numbers on the front, or house numbers written "Two Hundred Five" ("Two Hundred and Five" is worse) instead of 205, or flamboyant house or family names blazoned on façades, like "The Willows" or "The Polnickis." 7

(If you go behind the façade into the house itself you will find a fairly trustworthy class indicator in the kind of wood visible there. The top three classes invariably go in for hardwoods for doors and panelling; the Middle and High-Prole Classes, pine, either plain or "knotty." The knotty-pine 8 "den" is an absolute stigma of the Middle Class, one never to be overcome or disguised by temporarily affected higher usages. Below knotty pine there is plywood.)

Façade study is a badly neglected anthropological field. As we work down from the (largely white-painted) bank-like façades of the Upper and Upper Middle Classes, we encounter such Middle and Prole conventions as these, which I rank in order of social status: 9

Middle
1. A potted tree on either side of the front door, and the more pointy and symmetrical the better.
2. A large rectangular picture-window in a split-level "ranch" house, displaying a table-lamp between two side curtains. The cellophane on the lampshade must be visibly inviolate.
3. Two chairs, usually metal with pipe arms, disposed on the front porch as a "conversation group," in stubborn defiance of the traffic thundering past.

High-Prole
4. Religious shrines in the garden, which if small and understated, are slightly higher class than

Mid-Prole
5. Plaster gnomes and flamingos, and blue or lavender shiny spheres supported by fluted cast-concrete pedestals.

Low-Prole
6. Defunct truck tires painted white and enclosing flower beds. (Auto tires are a grade higher.)
7. Flower-bed designs worked in dead light bulbs or the butts of disused beer bottles.

The Destitute have no façades to decorate, and of course the Bottom Out-of-Sights, being invisible, have none either, although both these classes can occasionally help others decorate theirs—painting tires white on an hourly basis, for example, or even watering and fertilizing the potted trees of the middle Class. Class X also does not decorate its façades, hoping to stay loose and unidentifiable, ready to re-locate and shape-change the moment it sees that its cover has been penetrated.

In this list of façade conventions an important principle emerges. Organic materials have higher status than metal or plastic. We should take warning from Sophie Portnoy's aluminum venetian blinds, which are also 10 lower than wood because the slats are curved, as if "improved," instead of classically flat. The same principle applies, as *The Preppy Handbook* has shown so effectively, to clothing fabrics, which must be cotton or wool, never Dacron or anything of that prole kind. In the same way, yachts with wood hulls, because they must be repaired or replaced (at high cost) more often, are classier than yachts with fiberglass hulls, no matter how shrewdly merchandised. Plastic hulls are cheaper and more practical, which is precisely why they lack class.

As we move down the scale, income of course decreases, but income 11
is less important to class than other seldom-involved measurements: for example, the degree to which one's work is supervised by an omnipresent immediate superior. The more free from supervision, the higher the class, which is why a dentist ranks higher than a mechanic working under a foreman in a large auto shop, even if he makes considerably more money than the dentist. The two trades may be thought equally dirty: it is the dentist's freedom from supervision that helps confer class upon him. Likewise, a high-school teacher obliged to file weekly "lesson plans" with a principal or "curriculum co-ordinator" thereby occupies a class position lower than a tenured professor, who reports to no one, even though the high-school teacher may be richer, smarter, and nicer. (Supervisors and Inspectors are titles that go with public schools, post offices, and police departments: the student of class will need to know no more.) It is largely because they must report that even the highest members of the naval and military services lack social status: they all have designated supervisors—even the Chairman of the Joint Chiefs of Staff has to report to the President.

Class is thus defined less by bare income than by constraints and in- 12
securities. It is defined also by habits and attitudes. Take television watching. The Top Out-of-Sight Class doesn't watch at all. It owns the companies and pays others to monitor the thing. It is also entirely devoid of intellectual or even emotional curiosity: it *has* its ideas the way it has its money. The Upper Class does look at television but it prefers Camp offerings, like the films of Jean Harlow or Jon Hall. The Upper Middle Class regards TV as vulgar except for the highminded emissions of National Educational Television, which it watches avidly, especially when, like the Shakespeare series, they are most incompetently directed and boring. Upper Middles make a point of forbidding children to watch more than an hour a day and worry a lot about violence in society and sugar in cereal. The Middle Class watches, preferring the more "beautiful" kinds of non-body-contact sports like tennis or gymnastics or figure-skating

(the music is a redeeming feature here). With High-, Mid-, and Low-Proles we find heavy viewing of the soaps in the daytime and rugged body-contact sports (football, hockey, boxing) in the evening. The lower one is located in the Prole classes the more likely one is to watch "Bowling for Dollars" and "Wonder Woman" and "The Hulk" and when choosing a game show to prefer "Joker's Wild" to "The Family Feud," whose jokes are sometimes incomprehensible. Destitutes and Bottom Out-of-Sights have in common a problem involving choice. Destitutes usually "own" about three color sets, and the problem is which three programs to run at once. Bottom Out-of-Sights exercise no choice at all, the decisions being made for them by correctional or institutional personnel.

The time when the evening meal is consumed defines class better 13 than, say, the presence or absence on the table of ketchup bottles and ashtrays shaped like little toilets enjoining the diners to "Put Your Butts Here." Destitutes and Bottom Out-of-Sights eat dinner at 5:30, for the Prole staff on which they depend must clean up and be out roller-skating or bowling early in the evening. Thus Proles eat at 6:00 or 6:30. The Middles eat at 7:00, the Upper Middles at 7:30 or, if very ambitious, at 8:00. The Uppers and Top Out-of-Sights dine at 8:30 or 9:00 or even later, after nightly protracted "cocktail" sessions lasting usually around two hours. Sometimes they forget to eat at all.

Similarly, the physical appearance of the various classes defines them 14 fairly accurately. Among the top four classes thin is good, and the bottom two classes appear to ape this usage, although down there thin is seldom a matter of choice. It is the three Prole classes that tend to fat, partly as a result of their use of convenience foods and plenty of beer. These are the classes too where anxiety about slipping down a rung causes nervous overeating, resulting in fat that can be rationalized as advertising the security of steady wages and the ability to "eat out" often. Even "Going Out for Breakfast" is not unthinkable for Proles, if we are to believe that they respond to the McDonald's TV ads as they're supposed to. A recent magazine ad for a diet book aimed at Proles stigmatizes a number of erroneous assumptions about body weight, proclaiming with some inelegance that "They're all a crock." Among such vulgar errors is the proposition that "All Social Classes Are Equally Overweight." This the ad rejects by noting quite accurately:

> Your weight is an advertisement of your social standing. A century ago, corpulence was a sign of success. But no more. Today it is the badge of the lower-middle-class, where obesity is *four times* more prevalent than it is among the upper-middle and middle classes.

It is not just four times more prevalent. It is at least four times more visible, as any observer can testify who has witnessed Prole women perambulating shopping malls in their bright, very tight jersey trousers. Not just obesity but the flaunting of obesity is the Prole sign, as if the object were to give maximum aesthetic offense to the higher classes and thus achieve a form of revenge.

Another physical feature with powerful class meaning is the wearing   15 of plaster casts on legs and ankles by members of the top three classes. These casts, a sort of white badge of honor, betoken stylish mishaps with frivolous but costly toys like horses, skis, snowmobiles, and mopeds. They signify a high level of conspicuous waste in a social world where questions of unpayable medical bills or missed working days do not apply. But in the matter of clothes, the Top Out-of-Sight is different from both Upper and Upper Middle Classes. It prefers to appear in new clothes, whereas the class just below it prefers old clothes. Likewise, all three Prole classes make much of new garments, with the highest possible polyester content. The question does not arise in the same form with Destitutes and Bottom Out-of-Sights. They wear used clothes, the thrift shop and prison supply room serving as their Bonwit's and Korvette's.

This American class system is very hard for foreigners to master,   16 partly because most foreigners imagine that since America was founded by the British it must retain something of British institutions. But our class system is more subtle than the British, more a matter of gradations than of blunt divisions, like the binary distinction between a gentleman and a cad. This seems to lack plausibility here. One seldom encounters in the United States the sort of absolute prohibitions which (half comically, to be sure) one is asked to believe define the gentleman in England. Like these:

A gentleman never wears brown shoes in the city, or
A gentleman never wears a green suit, or
A gentleman never has soup at lunch, or
A gentleman never uses a comb, or
A gentleman never smells of anything but tar, or
"No gentleman can fail to admire Bellini"—W.H. Auden.

In America it seems to matter much less the way you present yourself—green, brown, neat, sloppy, scented—than what your backing is—that is, where your money comes from. What the upper orders display here is no special uniform but the kind of psychological security they derive from knowing that others recognize their freedom from petty anxieties and trivial prohibitions.

"Language most shows a man," Ben Jonson used to say. "Speak, that 17 I may see thee." As all acute conservatives like Jonson know, dictional behavior is a powerful signal of a firm class line. Nancy Mitford so indicated in her hilarious essay of 1955, "The English Aristocracy," based in part on Professor Alan S. C. Ross's more sober study "Linguistic Class-Indicators in Present-Day English." Both Mitford and Ross were interested in only one class demarcation, the one dividing the English Upper Class ("U," in their shorthand) from all below it ("non-U"). Their main finding was that euphemism and genteelism are vulgar. People who are socially secure risk nothing by calling a spade a spade, and indicate their top-dog status by doing so as frequently as possible. Thus the U-word is *rich,* the non-U *wealthy.* What U-speakers call *false teeth* non-U's call *dentures.* The same with *wigs* and *hair-pieces, dying* and *passing away* (or *over*).

For Mitford, linguistic assaults from below are sometimes so shocking 18 that the only kind reaction to a U-person is silence. It is "the only possible U-response," she notes, "to many embarrassing modern situations: the ejaculation of 'cheers' before drinking, for example, or 'It was so nice seeing you' after saying goodbye. In silence, too, one must endure the use of the Christian name by comparative strangers. . . ." In America, although there are more classes distinguishable here, a linguistic polarity is as visible as in England. Here U-speech (or our equivalent of it) characterizes some Top Out-of-Sights, Uppers, Upper Middles, and Class X's. All below is a waste land of genteelism and jargon and pretentious mispronunciation, pathetic evidence of the upward social scramble and its hazards. Down below, the ear is bad and no one has been trained to listen. Culture words especially are the downfall of the aspiring. Sometimes it is diphthongs that invite disgrace, as in *be-yóu-ti-ful.* Sometimes the aspirant rushes full-face into disaster by flourishing those secret class indicators, the words *exquisite* and *despicable,* which, like another secret sign, *patina,* he (and of course she as often) stresses on the middle syllable instead of the first. High-class names from cultural history are a frequent cause of betrayal, especially if they are British, like Henry Purcell. In America non-U speakers are fond of usages like "Between he and I." Recalling vaguely that mentioning oneself last, as in "He and I were there," is thought gentlemanly, they apply that principle uniformly, to the entire destruction of the objective case. There's also no problem with *like.* They remember something about the dangers of illiteracy its use invites, and hope to stay out of trouble by always using *as* instead, finally saying things like "He looks as his father." These contortions are common among young (usually insurance or computer) trainees, raised on Leon Uris and *Playboy,* most of them Mid- or High-Proles pounding on the firmly shut doors of the Middle Class. They are the careful, dark-suited first-generation aspirants to American respectability and (hopefully, as they would put it) power. Together with their deployment of the anomalous nominative case on all occasions goes their preference for jargon (you can hear them going at it on airplanes) like *parameters* and *guidelines* and *bottom lines* and *funding, dialogue, interface,* and *lifestyles.* Their world of language is one containing little more than smokescreens and knowing innovations. "Do we gift the Johnsons, dear?" the corporate wife will ask the corporate husband at Christmas time.

Just below these people, down among the Mid- and Low-Proles, the 19
complex sentence gives trouble. It is here that we get sentences beginning with elaborate pseudo-genteel participles like "Being that it was a cold day, the furnace was on." All classes below those peopled by U-speakers find the gerund out of reach and are thus forced to multiply words and say, "The people in front of him at the theater got mad due to the fact that he talked so much" instead of "His talking at the theater annoyed the people in front." (But *people* is not really right: *individuals* is the preferred term with non-U speakers. Grander, somehow.) It is also in the domain of the Mid- and Low-Prole that the double negative comes into its own as well as the superstitious avoidance of *lying* because it may be taken to imply telling untruths. People are thus depicted as always *laying* on the beach, the bed, the grass, the sidewalk, and without the slightest suggestion of their performing sexual exhibitions. A similar unconscious inhibition determines that *set* replace *sit* on all occasions, lest low excremental implications be inferred. The ease with which *sit* can be interchanged with the impolite word is suggested in a Second World War anecdote told by General Matthew Ridgway. Coming upon an unidentifiable head and shoulders peeping out of a ditch near the German border, he shouted. "Put up your hands, you son of a bitch!", to be answered, so he reports, "Aaah, go sit in your hat."

All this is evidence of a sad fact. A deep class gulf opens between two 20
current generations: the older one that had some Latin at school or college and was taught rigorous skeptical "English," complete with the diagramming of sentences; and the younger one taught to read by the optimistic look-say method and encouraged to express itself—as the saying goes—so

that its sincerity and well of ideas suffer no violation. This new generation is unable to perceive the number of syllables in a word and cannot spell and is baffled by all questions of etymology (it thinks *chauvinism* has something to do with gender aggressions). It cannot write either, for it has never been subjected to tuition in the sort of English sentence structure which resembles the sonata in being not natural but artificial, not innate but mastered. Because of its misspent, victimized youth, this generation is already destined to fill permanently the middle-to-low slots in the corporate society without ever quite understanding what devilish mechanism has prevented it from ascending. The disappearance of Latin as an adjunct to the mastery of English can be measured by the rapid replacement of words like *continuing* by solecisms like *ongoing*. A serious moment in cultural history occurred a few years ago when gasoline trucks changed the warning word on the rear from *Inflammable* to *Flammable*. Public education had apparently produced a population which no longer knew *In-* as an intensifer. That this happened at about the moment when every city was rapidly running up a "Cultural Center" might make us laugh, if we don't cry first. In another few generations Latinate words will be found only in learned writing, and the spoken language will have returned to the state it was in before the revival of learning. Words like *intellect* and *curiosity* and *devotion* and *study* will have withered away together with the things they denote.

There's another linguistic class-line, dividing those who persist in 21 honoring the nineteenth-century convention that advertising, if not commerce itself, is reprehensible and not at all to be cooperated with, and those proud to think of themselves not as skeptics but as happy consumers, fulfilled when they can image themselves not as functioning members of a system by responding to advertisements. For U-persons a word's succeeding in an ad is a compelling reason never to use it. But possessing no other source of idiom and no extra-local means of criticizing it, the subordinate classes are pleased to appropriate the language of advertising for personal use, dropping brand names all the time and saying things like "They have some lovely fashions in that store." In the same way they embrace all sub-professional euphemisms gladly and employ them proudly, adverting without irony to hair stylists, sanitary engineers, and funeral directors in complicity with the consumer world which cynically casts them as its main victims. They see nothing funny in paying a high price for an article and then, after a solemn pause, receiving part of it back in the form of a "rebate." Trapped in a world wholly defined by the language of consumption and the hype, they harbor restively, defending themselves against actuality by calling habitual drunkards *people with alcohol problems,* madness *mental illness,* drug use *drug abuse,* building lots *homesites,* houses *homes* ("They live in a lovely $250,000 home"), and drinks *beverages.*

Those delighted to employ the vacuous commercial "Have a nice day" 22
and those who wouldn't think of saying it belong manifestly to different classes, no matter how we define them, and it is unthinkable that those classes will ever melt. Calvin Coolidge said that the business of America is business. Now apparently the business of America is having a nice day. Tragedy? Don't need it. Irony? Take it away. Have a nice day. Have a nice day. A visiting Englishman of my acquaintance, a U-speaker if there ever was one, has devised the perfect U-response to "Have a nice day": "Thank you, he says, "but I have other plans." The same ultimate divide separates the two classes who say respectively when introduced, "How do you do?" and "Pleased to meet you." There may be comity between those who think *prestigious* a classy word and those who don't, but it won't survive much strain, like relations between those who think *momentarily* means in a moment (airline captain over loudspeaker: "We'll be taking off momentarily, folks") and those who know it means for a moment. Members of these two classes can sit in adjoining seats on the plane and get along fine (although there's a further division between those who talk to their neighbors in planes and elevators and those who don't), but once the plane has emptied, they will proceed toward different destinations. It's the same with those who conceive that *type* is an adjective ("He's a very classy type person") and those who know it's only a noun or verb.

The pretense that either person can feel at ease in the presence of the 23
other is an essential element of the presiding American fiction. Despite the lowness of the metaphor, the idea of the melting pot is high-minded and noble enough, but empirically it will be found increasingly unconvincing. It is our different language habits as much as anything that make us, as the title of Richard Polenberg's book puts it, *One Nation Divisible.*

Some people invite constant class trouble because they believe the 24
official American publicity about these matters. The official theory, which experience is constantly disproving, is that one can earn one's way out of his original class. Richard Nixon's behavior indicates dramatically that this is not so. The sign of the Upper Class to which he aspired is total psychological security, expressed in loose carriage, saying what one likes, and imperviousness to what others think. Nixon's vast income from law and politics—his San Clemente property aped the style of the Upper but

not the Top Out-of-Sight Class, for everyone knew where it was, and he wanted them to know—could not alleviate his original awkwardness and meanness of soul or his nervousness about the impression he was making, an affliction allied to his instinct for cunning and duplicity. Hammacher Schlemmer might have had him specifically in mind as the consumer of their recently advertised "Champagne Recork": "This unusual stopper keeps 'bubbly' sprightly, sparkling after uncorking ceremony is over. Gold electro-plated." I suspect that it is some of these same characteristics that make Edward Kennedy often seem so inauthentic a member of the Upper Class. (He's not Top Out-of-Sight because he chooses to augment his inheritance by attractive work.)

What, then, marks the higher classes? Primarily a desire for privacy, 25 if not invisibility, and a powerful if eccentric desire for freedom. It is this instinct for freedom that may persuade us that inquiring into the American class system this way is an enterprise not entirely facetious. Perhaps after all the whole thing has something, just something, to do with ethics and aesthetics. Perhaps a term like *gentleman* still retains some meanings which are not just sartorial and mannerly. Freedom and grace and independence: it would be nice to believe those words still mean something, and it would be interesting if the reality of the class system—and everyone, after all, hopes to rise—should turn out to be a way we pay those notions a due if unwitting respect.

Exercise

To what class would you assign each of the following?

1. A fifty-five-year-old pilot for a feeder airline who cuts his own grass, watches wrestling on TV, and has a knotty-pine den?
2. A small-town podiatrist who says "Have a nice day" and whose wife is getting very fat?
3. A young woman trust officer in a large New York bank who loves to watch Channel 13, WNET, and likes to be taken out to restaurants said to serve "gourmet" food?
4. A periodontist in a rich suburb? Is his class higher than that of an exodontist in a large midwestern city who earns more?
5. A man in a rich Northeastern suburb who, invited to a dinner party on Tuesday night, appears in a quiet suit with a white shirt but at a similar, apparently more formal dinner party on Saturday night shows up in a bright green linen jacket, red trousers, no tie, and no socks?
6. Students of all kinds?

Answers

1. Pilots have roughly the same class as field-grade Army officers, that is, High Prole. Feeder airline pilots have less status than national airline pilots, and those who work for the longest established international airlines like Pan Am and TWA have the highest status of all. The Middle-Class den and the Mid-Prole TV wrestling addiction cancel each other out.
2. At the moment, High Prole. If his wife gets much fatter, he will sink to Mid-Prole.
3. Middle, with hopeless fantasies about being Upper-Middle.
4. The periodontist is Middle, because he is not a "professional specialist." The exodontist is slightly lower, regardless of where he lives or what he earns.
5. He is from the Upper Middle Class, but he'd like to be taken for a member of the Upper. The suit on Tuesday night is to give the impression that he's just returned from the city, where he "works." The weekend get-up validates his identity as a suburbanite, devoting his weekend to much-needed unbuttoning and frivolity. The difference between Tuesday and Saturday is supposed to be significant. But I don't trust this man. He pays too much attention to his clothes to be really Upper Class.
6. All students, regardless of age or institution attended, are Mid-Proles, as their large consumption of beer and convenience food suggests. Sometimes they affect the used clothing of the Destitute, but we should not be fooled.

QUESTIONS ON MEANING AND CONTENT

1. Fussell says that "a curious brotherhood" exists between the Top Out-of-Sight class and the Bottom Out-of-Sight class. Explain.

2. Why can't the President of the United States be placed in the Top Out-of-Sight class? Does Fussell adequately explain this point in paragraphs 6 and 7? Are there other reasons?

3. Examine the details of paragraph 10. Are Fussell's perceptions about organic and inorganic materials the same as your own? If not, how do your perceptions differ? If your perceptions match, offer other examples. Do you think Fussell is being serious in the last sentence of the paragraph?

4. Do you think Fussell likes or respects any one of the social classes over another? Or does he seem to be objective and without bias? If he seems to express biases, does he spread the biases more or less equally among the classes—does he seem to be insulting any class more than any other? Is he saying, "This is what we are," or is he saying, "Look how strange we are"? Explain.

5. In paragraph 12, Fussell says that "constraints and insecurities" are a better measure of class than income. What does he mean? Where in the essay does he list other similar criteria for sorting people into classes?

QUESTIONS ABOUT RHETORICAL STRATEGIES

1. In paragraph 2, Fussell says that "perception" is the method he uses to establish classes. Based on his other remarks and the classes he creates, what, exactly, does he mean by perception? He calls perception "a more trustworthy method" than the traditional way of identifying classes. Do you agree or disagree? Explain.

2. In paragraph 12, Fussell says that the Top Out-of-Sight class "is also entirely devoid of intellectual or even emotional curiosity." Doesn't this seem to be a bit of an exaggeration? What is the tone of this remark? Do you find other exaggerations? If so, are they expressed in a similar tone?

3. In the first paragraph, Fussell says of social class that "No subject today is more likely to offend." What is the tone of this remark? Is it tongue-in-cheek? What did the tone seem to be when you first read this statement? After you had read the entire essay? What is the tone of the essay as a whole?

4. Into what class would someone fall who had inherited wealth, had no job, lived in a mansion hidden by trees, sat on the boards of several philanthropic organizations, despised tennis, loved boxing, and watched anything on TV from "Bowling for Dollars" to "Masterpiece Theater"? Or couldn't such a person exist? After thinking about this question, what conclusions have you reached concerning Fussell's classifying system?

5. After reading the essay, which class system do you prefer—the traditional one based on income or Fussell's? Does Fussell's system make you more comfortable with your place in the system or less comfortable? Which classifying system do you think is more accurate?

6. What would be the ideal audience for this essay? Why?

QUESTIONS ON LANGUAGE AND DICTION

1. Paragraph 12 calls the films of Jean Harlow and Jon Hall "Camp offerings." What does that mean? Can you describe a Jean Harlow or Jon Hall film?

2. What are the meanings of the following words: *bohemians, honorific, bourgeois, lamaseries, hypertrophied, stigmatize, cad, pseudo, solecism, comity, sartorial?*

3. What does the vocabulary used in the essay suggest about the intended audience?

Censorship and Junk Food Journalism

CARL JENSEN

In this essay, Carl Jensen talks about the news, about how much of it we are subjected to each day and how little we seem to learn from it. News is like junk food, Jensen tells us. We can consume a great deal of it while gaining only a little nourishment.

Cathy is about twenty-seven years old and single. She has an occasional weight problem due to her addiction to sweets and other junk food. And, like many other Americans, she has another unrewarding habit.   1

One night, after having watched the late-night news, she thought about her TV news addiction.   2

"I watched the morning news, the noon news, the evening news and the late-night news. I saw the local news, the national news, and the world news. I watched 'News Briefs,' 'News Break,' 'News Update,' 'News Close-Up,' 'News Wrap-Up,' 'News Highlights,' 'News Analysis,' and 'News Review.' "   3

Then, in genuine frustration, Cathy confronts her television set and pleads: "Why don't I know what's going on?"   4

Cathy is not real. But her frustration is. She's the popular character created by cartoonist Cathy Guisewite for the Universal Press Syndicate. The strip referred to appeared in some 250 newspapers across the country. I asked the real Cathy what was behind that particular segment in the life and times of the fictional Cathy. She said it was based on her own concern about not feeling really well informed about what is happening in the world. "This is a case," she added, "where the strip literally depicted how I felt." The strip also generated mail from readers across the country who said they shared the same reactions to TV news.   5

News smorgasbord

The frustration of being inundated with news and still not knowing what's really going on is common to many Americans. Think for a moment about what you receive daily from the largest, most sophisticated, and most productive communications system in the world—an endlessly repetitive smorgasbord of people, places, and events that seem to come and go but never really have anything to do with what is happening in your life.   6

Have you ever wondered why, after you return from a vacation and pick   7
up a newspaper, it seems you didn't miss a thing? Year after year the news
seems to stay the same and only the names, dates, and locations appear to
change.

This journalistic phenomenon seems to draw on a forever churning   8
cauldron of what I call junk food journalism. The typical junk food news diet
consists of sensationalized, personalized, and homogenized inconse-
quential trivia that are slickly packaged, microwaved, and then spoon-fed
to us by the print and electronic news media at regular feeding hours. Junk
food journalism comes in the following varieties:

• Brand-Name News—The Claus Von Bulow Trial, the Jean Harris–   9
Herman Tarnower affair, the drug deaths of John Belushi and Elvis Presley,
Elizabeth Taylor's latest romantic involvement, Brooke Shields'
academic aspirations, and anything at all about Charles and Diana. Robert
Redford recently chastised the American Society of Newspaper Editors
when he said, "The press should be more concerned about pursuing the
nation's policymakers and government officials and less concerned about
what I eat for lunch."

• *Yo-Yo News*—The Stock Market is up or down, the employment rate is   10
up or down, the inflation rate is up or down, and gold, silver, and pork
bellies are up or down.

• *The You-Did-I-Didn't News*—Labor says management is responsible for   11
high prices and management says labor is responsible, the Democrats accuse the Republicans and vice versa, the Russians threaten the U.S. and the
U.S. rattles the saber in return, Reagan says he didn't say it and the media
say he did, the liberals accuse the Moral Majority of censorship and Jerry
Falwell accuses the liberals of censorship.

• *Crazed News*—The newest dance craze, fashion craze, food craze, diet   12
craze, computer craze, video game craze, drug craze, and, of course, the
latest crazed killer.

• *Play-It-Again News*—The fire across town, the freeway pile-up, the   13
hijacked airliner, the latest earthquake, the bank robbery downtown, and
another revolution in Latin America.

• *Bang-Bang News*—Television introduced us to this category in Vietnam   14
and since has served us exotic portions from Afghanistan, Iran-Iraq, Ireland,
El Salvador, Nicaragua, Guatemala, the Falklands, and Lebanon-Israel.

• *Seasonal News*—The drought in the Southwest, the floods in the   15
Northeast, the tornadoes in the Midwest, the fires in the West, and the ever
popular political news every two years when the politicians earnestly pledge
to solve all our problems. We are now entering the quadrennial news event

period, when warmed-over presidential hopefuls make headlines with their bold new plans to reduce taxes, lower prices, solve unemployment, defend us from foreign invaders, and balance the budget. And to give these political aspirants a news platform for their platitudes, we have devised what Senator Bob Packwood calls "psycho primaries" that lead to pseudo-events that generate the non-news that makes the headlines in tomorrow's newspapers.

A news explosion

In one way or another you pay for all that news, and you aren't getting   16
your money's worth even though you're getting more of it than ever before.

In recent years, there has been a virtual explosion in the quantity of news   17
available to the public. San Francisco area television nighttime news junkies now can plug into the tube at five P.M., when six separate channels start the nightlong news marathon. Some of the milestones include the traditional evening news, the ten o'clock news, the eleven o'clock news, the I.N.N. news, the Nightline News, the PBS Late Night News, and all the other kinds of news Cathy mentioned earlier.

Early birds daytime news junkies in the Bay Area can get the first fix of   18
the day at five A.M. when "CBS News Continues" is on two channels. The scramble for news time on the tube was so severe last year that even poor old Captain Kangaroo was shoved aside to make more room for news. Indeed, now news relief is never more than a channel away since Ted Turner introduced the Cable News Network.

Not all the changes have happened in television news. In 1982 *U.S.A.*   19
Today, touted as the nation's first national daily newspaper of general circulation, made its debut in Washington, D.C. They say it will be distributed in more than thirty-two states this year.

But like so much of the television news, it seems to add little to what can   20
be called responsible journalism. *U.S.A. Today* seems to be a case of putting television news out in the guise of a newspaper. As media critic Ben Bagdikian says, "It has no serious sense of priorities: stories are played up or down not because of their inherent importance but on the basis of their potential for jazzy graphics or offbeat features." Indeed, when it comes to junk food news, you could say that *U.S.A. Today* is the Big Mac of journalism.

Unfortunately, with all its flaws and lack of substance, *U.S.A. Today*   21
already has influenced the news industry. Newspapers are using substantially more color graphics in their pages. While it is interesting to see color borders, color charts, and color maps all used for the sake of color, I would appreciate it much more if the press would spend the additional money on journalists, preferably investigative journalists, rather than on color hype.

We seem to be suffering from news inflation; there is more of it, but it   22
isn't worth very much.

Edwin Diamond, head of the News Study Group at M.I.T., suggests   23
that the increase in TV news programming is not necessarily due to a sudden
desire to better inform the public. Instead, he says, "news has become a
money-maker in recent years, less expensive to produce than prime-time
television." Diamond charges that the news we are being given is "more
sizzle than steak . . . the ten-second newsbreak leads to a twenty-second
tease that leads to a ninety-five-second item . . . hype to hype to hype." All
of which, of course, leads to Cathy's frustration.

Archibald MacLeish once said, "We are the best informed people on   24
Earth. We are deluged with facts, but we have lost or are losing our human
ability to feel them." We may also be losing our interest in doing something
about changing the facts. In 1960, a record 62.8 percent of voting-age Americans went to the polls; twenty years later, in 1980, just 53.2 percent of the
people turned out to vote. While there has been a significant increase in the
amount of news disseminated since 1960, there has been a significant de-
crease in the voter turnout.

Part of the reason for this may be that we are on an editorial junk food   25
diet that leads to apathy, overweight, and intellectual constipation rather
than involvement and enlightenment.

QUESTIONS ON MEANING AND CONTENT

1. In paragraph 24, Jensen suggests that we scarcely react to the facts
presented to us in the news. He cites the drop in the number of people
voting as evidence of this. Do you think a real relationship exists between
the two? How much evidence does he offer to show that a relationship does
exist? Would it be possible to argue the opposite—that the drop in the
number of people voting might be the result of effective news reporting? If
so, what evidence would you use?

2. In paragraph 24, Jensen concludes that the news neither enlightens
us nor motivates us to become involved in affairs. In your view, could or
should the news lead us to become involved in causes or other activities?
Has a newspaper or television news show ever caused you or someone you
know to get involved in something?

3. Do you agree that even though we receive more news than ever, we
are poorly informed and apathetic toward what is happening in the world? If
so, why do people watch or read so much news?

4. Paragraph 23 seems to be suggesting that the desire to make a profit leads to television news that has more interest or entertainment value than information value. Do you see evidence of this in the news? Explain.

5. Paragraph 23 also mentions strategies used to get us to watch news shows. What main strategy is mentioned? What are other ways of making viewers want to watch the news? Are they similar to strategies used to entice us to watch other kinds of programs?

QUESTIONS ABOUT RHETORICAL STRATEGIES

1. After examining paragraph 8, explain the basis used to divide journalism into its various junk food components.

2. What purposes does the comic strip example serve in the introduction? How does it support the content of the essay? Does it also serve to interest and perhaps motivate readers to continue with the article?

3. Do the captions "News Smorgasbord" and "A news explosion" separate the essay logically into parts? Explain why each heading marks a strategic movement in the development of the essay.

QUESTIONS ON LANGUAGE AND DICTION

1. In paragraph 8, Jensen says that the news is "spoon-fed to us . . . at regular feeding hours," as if we were all children. What do the following terms from the same paragraph suggest about us or the news: *churning cauldron, homogenized, microwaved?*

2. In paragraph 15, what is meant by the " 'psycho primaries' that lead to pseudo-events that generate the non-news"?

3. Explain the analogy in paragraph 20 which calls *U.S.A. Today* "the Big Mac of journalism." Do the descriptions of *U.S.A. Today* in paragraphs 19–21 convince you that the analogy is an apt one? What, according to the author, are the characteristics that suggest the comparison? Examine a copy of *U.S.A. Today* to see if you agree or disagree with Jensen's conclusion. If this newspaper is "the Big Mac of journalism," then what is the filet mignon of journalism? The garbage of journalism?

Why I Want a Wife

JUDY SYFERS

In this essay, Judy Syfers reflects about her experience in being a wife and then uses that experience to explain what constitutes a wife. She concludes that a wife is such a convenient and cooperative support system that anybody would want one.

I belong to that classification of people known as wives. I am A Wife. And, not altogether incidentally, I am a mother.

Not too long ago a male friend of mine appeared on the scene fresh from a recent divorce. He had one child, who is, of course, with his ex-wife. He is looking for another wife. As I thought about him while I was ironing one evening, it suddenly occurred to me that I too, would like to have a wife. Why do I want a wife?

I would like to go back to school so that I can become economically independent, support myself, and, if need be, support those dependent upon me. I want a wife who will work and send me to school. And while I am going to school I want a wife to take care of my children. I want a wife to keep track of the children's doctor and dentist appointments. And to keep track of mine, too. I want a wife to make sure my children eat properly and are kept clean. I want a wife who will wash the children's clothes and keep them mended. I want a wife who is a good nurturant attendant to my children, who arranges for their schooling, makes sure that they have an adequate social life with their peers, takes them to the park, the zoo, etc. I want a wife who takes care of the children when they are sick, a wife who arranges to be around when the children need special care, because, of course, I cannot miss classes at school. My wife must arrange to lose time at work and not lose the job. It may mean a small cut in my wife's income from time to time, but I guess I can tolerate that. Needless to say, my wife will arrange and pay for the care of the children while my wife is working.

I want a wife who will take care of *my* physical needs. I want a wife who will keep my house clean. A wife who will pick up after my children, a wife who will pick up after me. I want a wife who will keep my clothes clean, ironed, mended, replaced when need be, and who will see to it that my personal things are kept in their proper place so that I can find what I need the minute I need it. I want a wife who cooks the meals, a wife who is a *good* cook. I want a wife who will plan the menus, do the necessary grocery shopping, prepare the meals, serve them pleasantly, and then do the cleaning up while I do my studying. I want a wife who will care for me when I am sick and sympathize with my pain and loss of time from school. I want a wife to go along when our family takes a vacation so that someone can continue to care for me and my children when I need a rest and change of scene.

I want a wife who will not bother me with rambling complaints about a   5
wife's duties. But I want a wife who will listen to me when I feel the need to explain a rather difficult point I have come across in my course of studies. And I want a wife who will type my papers for me when I have written them.

I want a wife who will take care of the details of my social life. When my   6
wife and I are invited out by my friends, I want a wife who will take care of the babysitting arrangements. When I meet people at school that I like and want to entertain, I want a wife who will have the house clean, will prepare a special meal, serve it to me and my friends, and not interrupt when I talk about things that interest me and my friends. I want a wife who will have arranged that the children are fed and ready for bed before my guests arrive so that the children do not bother us. I want a wife who takes care of the needs of my guests so that they feel comfortable, who makes sure that they have an ashtray, that they are passed the hors d'oeuvres, that they are offered a second helping of the food, that their wine glasses are replenished when necessary, that their coffee is served to them as they like it. And I want a wife who knows that sometimes I need a night out by myself.

I want a wife who is sensitive to my sexual needs, a wife who makes love   7
passionately and eagerly when I feel like it, a wife who makes sure that I am satisfied. And, of course, I want a wife who will not demand sexual attention when I am not in the mood for it. I want a wife who assumes the complete responsibility for birth control, because I do not want more children. I want a wife who will remain sexually faithful to me so that I do not have to clutter up my intellectual life with jealousies. And I want a wife who understands that *my* sexual needs may entail more than strict adherence to monogamy. I must, after all, be able to relate to people as fully as possible.

If, by chance, I find another person more suitable as a wife than the wife   8
I already have, I want the liberty to replace my present wife with another one. Naturally, I will expect a fresh, new life; my wife will take the children and be solely responsible for them so that I am left free.

When I am through with school and have a job, I want my wife to quit   9
working and remain at home so that my wife can more fully and completely take care of a wife's duties.

My God, who *wouldn't* want a wife?   10

QUESTIONS ON MEANING AND CONTENT

1. We think of a wife as the female partner in marriage. Yet, the conclusion to the essay suggests that analyzing the role of wife by division reveals the parts of a support system that anyone, not just the male partner in marriage, would find extremely handy if not indispensable. How would you answer the question posed at the end of the essay? If everyone would want a wife, then how must we redefine the word *wife?*

2. As a followup to question 1, what word or words could be used in the title to replace the word *wife?*

3. As a further followup to question 1, could you argue that the essay uses division to provide an extended definition of the word *wife?* If so, how would you explain this?

4. Would you expect this essay to cause two drastically different reactions, one for male readers, one for female readers? Is Syfers writing to both audiences?

5. The chances are that you, as a college student, have never been married. Yet, you have had the opportunity to observe marriages. This provides one base of experience for evaluating or reacting to the essay. Do you think people who are or have been married would evaluate or react to the essay differently from readers who have never been married? How and why?

6. In the opening paragraph, Syfers notes that she is also a mother. Does the essay imply that husbands look to wives in much the same way that children look to mothers? If the essay doesn't imply this, what do your own observations of husbands and children, including your own attitudes, tell you about the validity of such an implication?

QUESTIONS ABOUT RHETORICAL STRATEGIES

1. The expression "I want a wife who . . ." appears throughout the essay. To what divisions do these lead? Make a list of the division headings under which the various "I wants" could be placed.

2. The essay makes many assumptions about what husbands expect from a wife. Can you find assumptions that have exceptions? Which ones? Can you find any assumptions that have so many exceptions that they represent biases rather than reasonable assumptions? If you find any of these, how do you account for their presence? Do you think that an audience of males would find more of these than an audience of females? Which assumptions do you consider to be reasonable beyond question?

QUESTIONS ON LANGUAGE AND DICTION

1. In paragraph seven, the phrase "my sexual needs" occurs twice. In the second appearance, the word *my* appears in italics. Why? How do the italics affect the meaning of the phrase?

2. In the last sentence of the essay, the word *wouldn't* also appears in italics. Does this make a difference in some way? Do the italics suggest a change in meaning or merely offer an indication of how the word should be said if the sentence were read aloud? If so, would the spoken sentence change in meaning or simply represent a stylistic flourish? In short, why is it important to have the word appear in italics?

Pilgrimage to Nonviolence

MARTIN LUTHER KING, JR.

*The late civil rights leader and Nobel Peace Prize winner explains
nonviolence by examining the qualities found in the people with the courage
to practice it.*

Since the philosophy of nonviolence played such a positive role in the   1
Montgomery Movement, it may be wise to turn to a brief discussion of some
basic aspects of this philosophy.

First, it must be emphasized that nonviolent resistance is not a method   2
for cowards; it does resist. If one uses this method because he is afraid or
merely because he lacks the instruments of violence, he is not truly nonviolent. This is why Gandhi often said that if cowardice is the only alternative to
violence, it is better to fight. He made this statement conscious of the fact
that there is always another alternative: no individual or group need submit
to any wrong, nor need they use violence to right the wrong; there is the way
of nonviolence resistance. This is ultimately the way of the strong man. It is
not a method of stagnant passivity. The phrase "passive resistance" often
gives the false impression that this is a sort of "do-nothing method" in
which the resister quietly and passively accepts evil. But nothing is further
from the truth. For while the nonviolence resister is passive in the sense that
he is not physically aggressive toward his opponent, his mind and emotions
are always active, constantly seeking to persuade his opponent that he is
wrong. The method is passive physically, but strongly active spiritually. It is
not passive nonresistance to evil, it is active nonviolent resistance to evil.

A second basic fact that characterizes nonviolence is that it does not seek   3
to defeat or humiliate the opponent, but to win his friendship and understanding. The nonviolent resister must often express his protest through
noncoöperation or boycotts, but he realizes that these are not ends themselves; they are merely means to awaken a sense of moral shame in the
opponent. The end is redemption and reconciliation. The aftermath of
nonviolence is the creation of the beloved community, while the aftermath
of violence is tragic bitterness.

A third characteristic of this method is that the attack is directed against   4
forces of evil rather than against persons who happen to be doing the evil. It
is evil that the nonviolent resister seeks to defeat, not the persons victimized

by evil. If he is opposing racial injustice, the nonviolent resister has the vision of see that the basic tension is not between races. As I like to say to the people in Montgomery: "The tension in this city is not between white people and Negro people. The tension is, at bottom, between justice and injustice, between the forces of light and the forces of darkness. And if there is a victory, it will be a victory not merely for fifty thousand Negroes, but a victory for justice and the forces of light. We are out to defeat injustice and not white persons who may be unjust."

A fourth point that characterizes nonviolent resistance is a willingness to 5
accept suffering without retaliation, to accept blows from the opponent without striking back. "Rivers of blood may have to flow before we gain our freedom, but it must be our blood," Gandhi said to his countrymen. The nonviolent resister is willing to accept violence if necessary, but never to inflict it. He does not seek to dodge jail. If going to jail is necessary, he enters it "as a bridegroom enters the bride's chamber."

One may well ask: "What is the nonviolent resister's justification for this 6
ordeal to which he invites men, for this mass political application of the ancient doctrine of turning the other cheek?" The answer is found in the realization that unearned suffering is redemptive. Suffering, the nonviolent resister realizes, has tremendous educational and transforming possibilities. "Things of fundamental importance to people are not secured by reason alone, but have to be purchased with their suffering," said Gandhi. He continues: "Suffering is infinitely more powerful than the law of the jungle for converting the opponent and opening his ears which are otherwise shut to the voice of reason."

A fifth point concerning nonviolent resistance is that it avoids not only 7
external physical violence but also internal violence of spirit. The nonviolent resister not only refuses to shoot his opponent but he also refuses to hate him. At the center of nonviolence stands the principle of love. The non-violent resister would contend that in the struggle for human dignity, the oppressed people of the world must not succumb to the temptation of becoming bitter or indulging in hate campaigns. To retaliate in kind would do nothing but intensify the existence of hate in the universe. Along the way of life, someone must have sense enough and morality enough to cut off the chain of hate. This can only be done by projecting the ethic of love to the center of our lives.

In speaking of love at this point, we are not referring to some sentimental 8
or affectionate emotion. It would be nonsense to urge men to love their oppressors in an affectionate sense. Love in this connection means under-

standing, redemptive good will. Here the Greek language comes to our aid. There are three words for love in the Greek New Testament. First, there is *eros*. In Platonic philosophy *eros* meant the yearning of the soul for the realm of the divine. It has come now to mean a sort of aesthetic or romantic love. Second, there is *philia* which means intimate affection between personal friends. *Philia* denotes a sort of reciprocal love; the person loves because he is loved. When we speak of loving those who oppose us, we refer to neither *eros* nor *philia*; we speak of a love which is expressed in the Greek word *agape*. *Agape* means understanding, redeeming good will for all men. It is an overflowing love which is purely spontaneous, unmotivated, ground-less, and creative. It is not set in motion by any quality or function of its object. It is the love of God operating in the human heart.

Agape is disinterested love. It is a love in which the individual seeks not his own good, but the good of his neighbor (I Cor. 10:24). *Agape* does not begin by discriminating between worthy and unworthy people, or any qualities people possess. It begins by loving others *for their sakes*. It is an entirely "neighbor-regarding concern for others," which discovers the neighbor in every man it meets. Therefore, *agape* makes no distinction between friend and enemy; it is directed toward both. If one loves an individual merely on account of his friendliness, he loves him for the sake of the benefits to be gained from the friendship, rather than for the friend's own sake. Consequently, the best way to assure oneself that Love is disin-terested is to have love for the enemy-neighbor from whom you can expect no good in return, but only hostility and persecution. 9

Another basic point about *agape* is that it springs from the *need* of the other person—his need for belonging to the best in the human family. The Samaritan who helped the Jew on the Jericho Road was "good" because he responded to the human need that he was presented with. God's love is eternal and fails not because man needs his love. St. Paul assures us that the loving act of redemption was done "while we were yet sinners"—that is, at the point of our greatest need for love. Since the white man's personality is greatly distorted by segregation, and his soul is greatly scarred, he needs the love of the Negro. The Negro must love the white man, because the white man needs his love to remove his tensions, insecurities, and fears. 10

Agape is not a weak, passive love. It is love in action. *Agape* is love seeking to preserve and create community. It is insistence on community even when one seeks to break it. *Agape* is a willingness to sacrifice in the interest of mutuality. *Agape* is a willingness to go to any length to restore community. It doesn't stop at the first mile, but it goes the second mile to restore commun- 11 ity. It is a willingness to forgive, not seven times, but seventy times seven to restore community. The cross is the eternal expression of the length to which God will go in order to restore broken community. The resurrection is a symbol of God's triumph over all the forces that seek to block community. The Holy Spirit is the continuing community creating reality that moves through history. He who works against community is working against the whole of creation. Therefore, if I respond to hate with a reciprocal hate I do nothing but intensify the cleavage in broken community. I can only close the gap in broken community by meeting hate with love. If I meet hate with hate, I become depersonalized, because creation is so designed that my personality can only be fulfilled in the context of community. Booker T. Washington was right: "Let no man pull you so low as to make you hate him." When he pulls you that low he brings you to the point of working against community; he drags you to the point of defying creation, and thereby becoming depersonalized.

In the final analysis, *agape* means a recognition of the fact that all life is 12 interrelated. All humanity is involved in a single process, and all men are brothers. To the degree that I harm my brother, no matter what he is doing to me, to that extent I am harming myself. For example, white men often refuse federal aid to education in order to avoid giving the Negro his rights; but because all men are brothers they cannot deny Negro children without harming their own. They end, all efforts to the contrary, by hurting themselves. Why is this? Because men are brothers. If you harm me, you harm yourself.

Love, *agape*, is the ony cement that can hold this broken community 13 together. When I am commanded to love, I am commanded to restore community, to resist injustice, and to meet the needs of my brothers.

A sixth basic fact about nonviolent resistance is that it is based on the 14 conviction that the universe is on the side of justice. Consequently, the believer in nonviolence has deep faith in the future. This faith is another reason why the nonviolent resister can accept suffering without retaliation. For he knows that in his struggle for justice he has cosmic companionship. It is true that there are devout believers in nonviolence who find it difficult to believe in a personal God. But even these persons believe in the existence of some creative force that works for universal wholeness. Whether we call it an unconscious process, an impersonal Brahman, or a Personal Being of matchless power and infinite love, there is a creative force in this universe that works to bring the disconnected aspects of reality into a harmonious whole.

QUESTIONS ON MEANING AND CONTENT

1. In the essay, King refers repeatedly to Mahatma Gandhi. Who was Gandhi and why would King have been so strongly influenced by him?

2. What is the thinking behind the statement "If cowardice is the only alternative to violence, it is better to fight"? Do you agree with the reasoning underlying this conclusion? Why or why not?

3. What final result does nonviolence produce, according to King? What does violence produce? Can you think of examples from the past that would confirm or deny these predictions about the end products of either form of resistance?

4. Several times in the essay the author suggests that what seems passive is often really active. Find one or two instances where King points this out. Then develop an explanation to account for this seeming contradiction.

QUESTIONS ABOUT RHETORICAL STRATEGIES

1. Although King's purpose is to analyze nonviolence by dividing it into its components, he also spends a good deal of time analyzing love. How does this support his purpose of analyzing nonviolence? Why do you suppose King placed the discussions of love between the fifth and sixth components of nonviolence? Does its placement there logically fit the organization of the essay?

2. Parts of a whole are sometimes more difficult to see when the whole being divided is an abstraction. The parts are always less sharply defined than they are for something concrete. Thus, King focuses on the person who practices nonviolence to make his divisions. How clear are these divisions? In what ways do they focus on the person practicing nonviolence; that is, how much of the focus is on outward behavior and how much on something else?

3. If one of the named components of nonviolence were omitted by someone claiming to practice nonviolence, would nonviolence break down completely or would this be similar to a door with a rusty hinge or an automobile with a burned out headlight or a slow leak in a tire? Explain.

4. King's essay is really comprised of two separate instances of analyzing by dividing. In the second of these, he explains the components of *agape*. This is also an abstraction. How does King organize this analysis?

5. When the author analyzes the abstraction *love,* is he analyzing by classification or by division? Explain.

QUESTIONS ON LANGUAGE AND DICTION

1. In paragraph 9, *agape* is defined as "disinterested love." What does this mean, according to King? Would a significant difference in meaning occur if the phrase were changed to "uninterested love"? If the distinction puzzles you, resolve the question by checking the two words in a good dictionary.

2. In paragraph 10, King alludes to the good Samaritan. What information should this allusion call to our minds?

3. Who was Booker T. Washington?

4. Check the meanings of any of the following words that are unfamiliar to you: *aesthetic, infinite, succumb.*

Notes on Punctuation

LEWIS THOMAS

One can grow fond of certain punctuation marks, the author maintains, but many of these little symbols can never really be liked. Among the latter are those that confuse us or order us around.

There are no precise rules about punctuation (Fowler lays out some   1
general advice (as best he can under the complex circumstances of English
prose (he points out, for example, that we possess only four stops (the
comma, the semicolon, the colon and the period (the question mark and
exclamation point are not, strictly speaking, stops; they are indications of
tone (oddly enough, the Greeks employed the semicolon for their question
mark (it produces a strange sensation to read a Greek sentence which is a
straightfoward question: Why weepest thou; (instead of Why weepest thou?
(and, of course, there are parentheses (which are surely a kind of punctuation making this whole matter much more complicated by having to count
up the left-handed parentheses in order to be sure of closing with the right
number (but if the parentheses were left out, with nothing to work with but
the stops, we would have considerably more flexibility in the deploying of
layers of meaning than if we tried to separate all the clauses by physical
barriers (and in the latter case, while we might have more precision and
exactitude for our meaning, we would lose the essential flavor of language,
which is its wonderful ambiguity)))))))))))).

The commas are the most useful and usable of all the stops. It is highly   2
important to put them in place as you go along. If you try to come back after
doing a paragraph and stick them in the various spots that tempt you you
will discover that they tend to swarm like minnows into all sorts of crevices
whose existence you hadn't realized and before you know it the whole long
sentence becomes immobilized and lashed up squirming in commas. Better
to use them sparingly, and with affection, precisely when the need for each
one arises, nicely, by itself.

I have grown fond of semicolons in recent years. The semicolon tells you   3
that there is still some question about the preceding full sentence; something
needs to be added; it reminds you sometimes of the Greek usage. It is almost
always a greater pleasure to come across a semicolon than a period. The
period tells you that that is that; if you didn't get all the meaning you wanted

or expected, anyway you got all the writer intended to parcel out and now you have to move along. But with a semicolon there you get a pleasant little feeling of expectancy; there is more to come; read on; it will get clearer.

Colons are a lot less attractive, for several reasons: firstly, they give you the feeling of being rather ordered around, or at least having your nose pointed in a direction you might not be inclined to take if left to yourself, and, secondly, you suspect you're in for one of those sentences that will be labeling the points to be made: firstly, secondly and so forth, with the implication that you haven't sense enough to keep track of a sequence of notions without having them numbered. Also, many writers use this system loosely and incompletely, starting out with number one and number two as though counting off on their fingers but then going on and on without the succession of labels you've been led to expect, leaving you floundering about searching for the ninethly or seventeenthly that ought to be there but isn't.

Exclamation points are the most irritating of all. Look! they say, look at what I just said! How amazing is my thought! It is like being forced to watch someone else's small child jumping up and down crazily in the center of the living room shouting to attract attention. If a sentence really has something of importance to say, something quite remarkable, it doesn't need a mark to point it out. And if it is really, after all, a banal sentence needing more zing, the exclamation point simply emphasizes its banality!

Quotation marks should be used honestly and sparingly, when there is a genuine quotation at hand, and it is necessary to be very rigorous about the words enclosed by the marks. If something is to be quoted, the *exact* words must be used. If part of it must be left out because of space limitations, it is good manners to insert three dots to indicate the omission, but it is unethical to do this if it means connecting two thoughts which the original author did not intend to have tied together. Above all, quotation marks should not be used for ideas that you'd like to disown, things in the air so to speak. Nor should they be put in place around clichés; if you want to use a cliché you must take full responsibility for it yourself and not try to job it off on anon., or on society. The most objectionable misuse of quotation marks, but one which illustrates the dangers of misuse in ordinary prose, is seen in advertising, especially in advertisements for small restaurants, for example "just around the corner," or "a good place to eat." No single, identifiable, citable person ever really said, for the record, "just around the corner," much less "a good place to eat," least likely of all for restaurants of the type that use this type of prose.

The dash is a handy device, informal and essentially playful, telling you that you're about to take off on a different tack but still in some way connected with the present course—only you have to remember that the dash is there, and either put a second dash at the end of the notion to let the reader know that he's back on course, or else end the sentence, as here, with a period.

The greatest danger in punctuation is for poetry. Here it is necessary to   8
be as economical and parsimonious with commas and periods as with the words themselves, and any marks that seem to carry their own subtle meanings, like dashes and little rows of periods, even semicolons and question marks, should be left out altogether rather than inserted to clog up the thing with ambiguity. A single exclamation point in a poem, no matter what else the poem has to say, is enough to destroy the whole work.

The things I like best in T.S. Elliot's poetry, especially in the *Four*   9
Quartets, are the semicolons. You cannot hear them, but they are there, laying out the connections between the images and the ideas. Sometimes you get a glimpse of a semicolon coming, a few lines farther on, and it is like climbing a steep path through woods and seeing a wooden bench just at a bend in the road ahead, a place where you can expect to sit for a moment, catching your breath.

Commas can't do this sort of thing; they can only tell you how the   10
different parts of a complicated thought are to be fitted together, but you can't sit, not even take a breath, just because of a comma,

---

QUESTIONS ON MEANING AND CONTENT

1. How easy or how difficult is the first paragraph to read? If you find it difficult, what makes it so? Why do twelve right-hand parentheses appear at the end?

2. How many sentences are there in paragraph 1?

3. Thomas says that the Greeks used semicolons to indicate questions. Does this tell us something about punctuation? What?

4. Thomas also says that finding a semicolon after a question creates a "strange sensation" in him. Do you think you would mind if we changed our own system and substituted semicolons for questions marks? If you think you would mind, do you think your children or grandchildren would? What does that tell you about punctuation?

5. Thomas suggests that punctuation marks tell us something about the writers using them. If the commas in a piece of writing reminded you of a "swarm of minnows," what would that tell you about the writer? What can exclamation marks say about a writer? Quotation marks?

6. At the beginning of the essay, Thomas says "There are no precise rules about punctuation." What is the difference between rules and "precise" rules? If mathematics tells us that two plus two equals four, we always apply that. Yet, we often ignore or are confused by rules about commas. How do you account for that? If your answer is that mathematics represents a different kind of reality, what is the difference?

QUESTIONS ABOUT RHETORICAL STRATEGIES

1. Thomas' purpose seems to be to entertain us (or at least to express his own amusement) as much as it is to inform us. This is reflected in the structure of the essay and what it says about the various types of punctuation marks. If Thomas had written this as a chapter in a writing textbook, how might the structure differ?

2. Even though the author's purpose isn't strictly to inform, did you learn anything about punctuation from the essay that you might apply—or stop applying—in your own writing? Would you have learned more if the essay had been very serious in tone and formally structured with the punctuation marks broken down into classes and subclasses?

QUESTIONS ON LANGUAGE AND DICTION

1. What is the meaning of the term "citable person" found near the end of paragraph 6?

2. Thomas says that commas "can swarm like minnows." What other figurative comparisons does he use to illustrate his discussions? Do these help to make his points clear?

3. The word *ambiguity* appears several times in the essay. Why is this word likely to appear in a discussion of punctuation?

4. What are the meanings of *banal* and *parsimonious?*

WRITING SCENARIOS

1. While you are attending college, you work part-time as an assistant to a state legislator. This lawmaker asks you to run errands and occasionally to do some research. Presently, the legislator is preparing an antilitter bill and needs all the information she can get. She has asked you to conduct some informal research on the *types* of litter found around your city. She will use this information to help argue for passage of the bill. As usual, you will write a report to the legislator on your findings. If you can find a friend to do the driving, you might study a section of highway and takes notes on the litter you observe. It is important to select an area where litter is allowed to accumulate over a period of time. Don't use a sports stadium after a game, for example, since the litter there would be removed shortly after each stadium use. Don't classify the litter according to specific types like bottles, cans, paper cups, and so forth. Instead, use classes that represent our habits or living styles—we patronize fast-food restaurants; we consume large quantities of alcoholic beverages as well as soft drinks, etcetera. In short, you will want to pinpoint the sources of behavior that account for the types of litter. (Remember, however, that you are not accounting for the behavior that led someone to drop the litter in the first place.) You may also have to do some subclassifying. You may need to establish a class for miscellaneous items—items whose presence where you found them cannot be explained. Remember that you are not presenting an argument. You are arranging litter by classes.

2. Practically everyone is involved with some kind of sport or hobby, and many athletes and hobbyists develop the ability to judge or "read" conditions relative to some activity. For example, experienced surfers can look at the breakers and know whether the surfing conditions are anywhere from ideal to very poor. An experienced skier can do the same with ski slopes. If you have enough experience with an activity to have developed the ability to judge conditions, write an essay to novices who want to learn as much as they can about these conditions. Your essay will appear in a prominent magazine devoted exclusively to your hobby or activity. Thus, you will need to explain carefully and clearly the "condition signs" that allow you to classify them. Don't let your own knowledge cause you to overlook details that would be important to the novice.

3. The newspaper advertisement read "Wanted: college student to work part-time to help write copy for WHEN-TV's news and weather broadcasts." You immediately arranged an interview; this is just the type of opportunity you've always hoped for. In order to get a sense of your writing ability, the manager of the news room asked you to write a division paper in which you divide a television news show into its parts. To prepare yourself, watch the same news show for several nights. Observe carefully, taking notes as you watch. Choose either a local or a national show. The ideas presented in "Censorship and Junkfood Journalism" may be helpful to you as you begin to watch the news show of your choice. However, use these ideas only as guides to give you some idea of what to look for. Your divisions will come from what you learn from your own observations. Your readers will be those who work in the news room, and you can be certain that they will be interested in how an "outsider" views television news.

4. You have just been appointed entertainment editor of your campus newspaper. Your main task is to review records, films, and restaurants that students might be interested in. You have decided that in your first essay you will classify the *types* of restaurants in your community. This article may be serious or humorous, but you will want to make sure that you devise a classification system that will account for all eating establishments in the area, even though you won't, of course, be able to mention every one. You may want to make your classes amusingly descriptive: dives, greasy spoons, black-tie joints, and so on. Your audience is made up of students, administrators, and faculty members who read your school's newspaper.

5. Ever since your older brother went away to college, you have corresponded with him. Your brother attends a prestigious university in the east and is studying psychology and sociology. After reading Paul Fussell's essay in this text, you thought it would be fun to write an essay for your brother in which you place the students who live in your dormitory (or on your floor of the dormitory) into social classes based on your perceptions. You may want to make clear that a longer and more thorough study would be required to place every student into a class and that you have classified those with identifying characteristics strong enough to be classified without extended, formal study. You may wish to create humorous classes (jocks, book worms, jerks), or you may want to be serious in order to impress your brother.

6. You've been working for about two years in the financial aid office. Because of your experience there, your old high school counselor, who originally helped you get information about financial aid, has asked you to prepare a short booklet classifying types of financial aid available at your college through governmental and other agencies. As part of this, you will also want to classify types of eligibility requirements. This booklet will be used by students in your old high school. The research for this essay can be done at the financial aid office of your college and in the library. In addition to the material available for you to read, you might be able to arrange an interview with a financial aid officer.

SEVEN

ANALYZING A PROCESS

Process analysis is similar to analyzing by dividing. The chief difference is that the interest of the writer is not on how the parts fit and work together but on the steps by which something is done. Another difference is that analyzing by dividing most frequently explains something in order to increase the readers' understanding, whereas process analysis shows readers how to do something or how something takes place. Division, for example, would explain what a tent is by analyzing its parts; process analysis would explain how to set up the tent.

The situations calling for process analysis are countless, and appropriate applications come quickly to mind. For example: A recipe explains a process. So do the instructions that explain how to assemble the parts of a new bicycle or how to attach a flash unit to your camera. The owner's manual that comes with a new car explains many processes: how to start the car in cold weather, how to change a tire, and so on. Often a process paper explains how to behave or act in order to achieve a certain result: how to make friends, how to study, how to avoid being cheated, how to overcome a customer's sales resistance, how to offer a toast.

Some process analyses are meant to increase a reader's understanding rather than to show the steps to follow to accomplish a result, for example, how an elm tree dies from Dutch elm disease or how a caterpillar becomes a moth or butterfly. These essays help readers understand the world around them by explaining how things take place according to processes that can repeat themselves.

Process analysis is also similar to narration since steps in a process are based on the passage of time, just as narration presents events taking place in time. The purposes of narration and process analysis differ, however. A process analysis provides readers with instructions that they can repeat, or it enables them to understand something that may be repeated over and over in just about the same way—the reproductive cycle of the monarch butterfly, for example. Thus, a paper on how Clara Barton founded the American Red Cross could easily be a narrative describing her experience in accomplishing this great feat. The writer of a narrative would probably be interested in Barton's reaction to events and would place emphasis on what made the experience interesting or admirable rather than on the process she followed. However, narratives don't always supply the great amount of detail that process analysis papers usually do. A writer might have to read dozens of narratives about surviving in the desert, gleaning a little from each one before being able to write a manual explaining how to survive in the desert. In other words, while narration and process analysis share certain characteristics, they are still unique ways of approaching a subject.

When analyzing a process, you must have a precise concern for your audience. For example, many processes will omit small steps if the audience already understands the subject well. An engineer preparing a new-car repair manual for mechanics is addressing an audience of trained mechanics who already know most of the processes. But the writer who prepares the owner's manual for the average car owner cannot assume that readers will know the difference between a bumper jack and a scissors jack. And this writer cannot merely say, "First, remove the spare tire from the trunk," since many readers would need to know *how* to do this. Process writers who are experts in their field have to exercise great care in writing process papers for nonspecialists. Writers can too easily assume that the audience will understand when, in fact, the audience often will be confused by something as simple as a failure to define terms.

When analyzing a process, you will want to guard against information gaps in your prose; that is, don't confuse what you know about a topic with what readers may know. It is important to be particularly careful to define terms. When you are tempted to omit a small step, ask yourself why you are doing this: because you yourself would understand the process without this step? or because you are sure *readers* would not be misled by its absence?

PREWRITING

Before writing your process essay, it is a good idea to choose a topic that you know something about, unless you are willing to commit the time to reading about or researching the topic. You don't want to select a topic impulsively and then try to explain the process as you go along. For example, just because you are a student, do not select a topic like "How To Study Effectively" on the assumption that the topic is simple and the proper steps will automatically occur to you as you write. Such topics are not as simple as they appear, and treating them casually will produce an unconvincing paper. A good attitude to adopt is that *no process is simple except to the person who already understands it.* Even though this is a bit of an exaggeration, it is an attitude that will serve you well in explaining processes.

It is essential that you know what your paper will do for your readers. Is your purpose to *inform* the readers only, or are you going to *show* readers how to do something? Many process pieces are written because people are interested in knowing about them but would have no interest in trying the process themselves. For example, someone might want to know how certain high dives are performed before watching a high-dive competition. Many people would be interested in learning how archaeologists conduct digs or how treasure hunters locate sunken ships but would have no intention of trying to do any of these things themselves. Such essays must be clear and interesting, but both writer and reader should know from the start that the purpose is not to provide a step-by-step guide for repeating the process.

Of course, all of these concerns depend on your exact audience. *Who* are your readers and *why* are you writing to them? It is essential that you first answer these questions. Are you writing a humorous article for your campus newspaper about "How To Pass English 101"? Are you writing a serious essay to a computer magazine about "How To Write and Sell Video Games"? Or are you writing to high school students about "How To Prepare for College"? Certainly, your tone, style, word choice, and many other factors will vary depending upon your purpose and audience.

Process writing that intends only to familiarize the reader with the process may omit information that would otherwise be important. The treasure hunter explaining how artifacts are retrieved from the ocean floor may talk about a sand vacuum without explaining how it is held in the hands or maneuvered in order to make it work effectively. On the other hand, in explaining how to prepare a certain recipe, small matters become important because the reader may want to repeat the process. Thus, if certain ingredients must be mixed together beforehand and added later, then the reader must be told this. The difference between a tablespoon and a teaspoon becomes important, and to confuse a half cup of sugar with a teaspoon of salt would produce disastrous results.

Since processes are separated into steps, it is probably best to brainstorm for details after you have identified the necessary steps and determined your paper's purpose. This will give your brainstorming some direction and save time, since you won't have to sift through and reorganize a long list of details. Then, with the major steps in mind, try to think of every detail necessary to explain each step. What tools or materials will be needed? What precautions should readers take? What minor steps must not be omitted? If possible, try to do the process yourself and then spend some time free-writing immediately after you have performed the process. Afterwards, you can glean important details from your freewriting and add them to your prewriting notes.

Use the heuristic that follows to help you prewrite for your process essay. Answer those questions relevant to your subject and jot down the answers in your prewriting notes.

Prewriting Questions for Process

1. Can I first separate my process into major steps and then into smaller steps that support or complete each major step?
2. Exactly what are the major steps?
3. What minor steps are necessary to explain each major step? In what order should they be presented under the major step?
4. Which steps, major or minor, can be performed with relative ease and explained quickly?
5. Which steps are complex and will require careful explanation or specific details? What are those details?
6. Which steps require that the reader be alerted to some danger or some potential for failure if my directions are not followed precisely?
7. Will any steps be performed simultaneously with other steps?
8. Are there minor steps that I could easily reverse through carelessness?
9. What difficulties did I encounter when performing this process myself?
10. How can I help my readers to avoid these same difficulties?
11. Does my own experience tell me that there are minor steps that are really unnecessary and which may only confuse the reader if included?

12. What can I expect my readers to know about the process? What does this tell me about defining terms or making statements precise and clear?

13. What can I say in my introduction that will stress the simplicity of my process or show that it can be handled by most anyone if the steps are carefully followed?

14. If I am writing only to inform the reader about a process, what can I say in the introduction to generate interest?

15. Why am I, or people I know, interested in the subject?

16. Is it safe to assume that my audience would share my interest in the subject, or will I have to make a special effort to interest the audience?

17. What would I say to uninterested friends to convince them that the process really is interesting or valuable to know about?

18. If I am writing to inform only, what steps in the process can be omitted because they are not critical or are uninteresting to my reader?

19. What steps would confuse the reader if omitted?

20. Are there examples I can use to show how this process is similiar to other processes readers may already be familiar with?

ORGANIZING

If your process analysis shows readers how to do something, then your introduction should explain what the process will accomplish, how relatively simple or complex the process is, and how much time or how many steps are involved. If it is not self-evident, you will want to indicate the level of skills required to perform the process. This is sometimes necessary, especially when readers may falsely assume that a process is much harder to perform than it really is. Sometimes this simply means offering reassurances, stressing, for example, that anyone with ordinary skills can change a tire safely by following the proper steps. Of course, if a process requires special skills or past experience, then say so. Remember, too, that many processes are variations on a theme—a new recipe for a special kind of bread, a new project for a woodworker, and so on.

If your process merely provides information, then your introduction should concentrate on showing readers why the process is worth knowing about or interesting to learn about. Sometimes you will be appealing to natural curiosity: how does a creature with so small a brain as the Baltimore oriole build such a complicated nest; how did primitive peoples make rope or heat water without metal pots; or how does a magician "saw" someone in half? At other times, you will want to stress the importance of knowing. For example, most readers would consider it useful to know how advertisements appealing to the subconscious are designed. Many readers would consider it useful to know how microcomputers work, especially if they have considered purchasing one.

Obviously, you present the steps of the process in the body of your paper. If you are explaining how to do something, then you must exercise special care, since you want readers to be able to repeat the process successfully and with a minimum of frustration. For a process that informs, you may be telling the reader that "This is one of the especially interesting steps in the process"; whereas, when showing how to do something, you may have to warn the reader at certain steps: "Be sure to wear gloves when performing the following operation."

If you are showing how to do something, then it is important to explain how to prepare for the process before presenting the process itself. For example, you may need to devote a paragraph to preparation and to the tools, articles, or ingredients needed to perform the process.

The body of a process essay seems easy to organize because it moves from step-to-step chronologically. Nevertheless, a great deal of care is required. You will need to make sure that you do not omit steps that are small but important. Also, you will want to identify the small steps that must be completed separately, and separate them from the small steps that help to complete major steps. Be sure that all steps are presented in the correct order. It is important that you carefully identify any steps that must be performed simultaneously and devise a strategy for presenting them to the reader. If early preparation has to be made for a later step, then you'll need to alert the reader to this beforehand. This happens in recipes and many other processes where something has to be prepared at step 1 and then added at step 5 or 6.

After you have carefully compiled and arranged your steps, you are ready to decide which details from your prewriting notes are needed to make each step as clear as possible. If necessary, you may want to do some additional prewriting. Remember, your task is to show the reader what to look for or how to test something to see that critical steps have been completed successfully. You will need to point to what should be double-checked before proceeding to the next step. Also, explain what should *not* be done: "Do not go to the next step immediately. Allow ten minutes for the glue to dry," or "Do not attempt to remove the excess glue squeezed from the joints after clamping. This will leave smudge marks, and the dried glue can easily be removed later with a metal scraper." If you have had experience with the process, think back to your own early efforts and recall the steps that troubled you. Then you can prepare the reader to avoid these same problems.

In your conclusion, you will probably want to describe the finished product that should result from the process or the satisfaction it will bring. In short, the conclusion should relate back to the rest of the paper in some way. For example, you may tell readers that it is just as satisfying to watch the magician "saw" someone in half when they understand the deception. You may suggest that this will free them to concentrate on the details used to convince the audience that the person in the box is in real danger. In other words, use your conclusion to remind the reader of the purpose of your paper.

WRITING

Follow your organizing plan and the details produced during your prewriting sessions to produce a rough draft. As usual, **write** quickly and don't let small details bog you down; you can tinker with them while revising. Your task now is to produce a first version of your paper. Later you can revise the draft to produce a polished, finished product. Of course, if revising or proofreading concerns arise as you are writing your first draft, you have the option of addressing them as you write or of making a note in the margin and returning to them later in the writing process.

Before you begin your draft, you may wish to make a final check of your details and organizing scheme to be sure that you have not overlooked anything. It is extremely important that you have carefully worked out the stages in the process and generated the details necessary to explain fully each step, while alerting the reader to anything that will require special attention. If you need additional prewriting material, now is an excellent time to obtain it.

Your purpose in writing a process essay—to show the reader how to do something or to inform the reader about a process—can also affect the way you present the process. If you are explaining how to do something, then you are free to use the pronoun *you*: "*You* should mix the flour with water in a cup before adding it to the gravy. *You* must do this if *your* gravy is to be free of flour clumps." However, if you are providing information about a process, then perhaps you should write in the third person, since you will not be directly addressing the reader. Thus, you would not be saying "Here you must do this; there you must do that." Instead, you would say something on the order of "At least two divers are needed for the sand vacuuming, one to operate the device and one to observe. The sand and debris kicked up by the vacuum prevent the operator from seeing what has been uncovered."

Remember, you can come back to the rough draft and add and delete. On a separate sheet of paper, jot down any omissions that occur to you along the way. Even if you have prewritten carefully, you may have allowed an important detail to slip by. If any omissions occur to you as you write, merely jot them down, and then come back later and work them into the appropriate section of the paper.

During prewriting, you have carefully identified audience concerns. You will want to keep these concerns in mind as you write, but there is no need to stop to agonize over an audience-related detail. Just make a mark in your rough draft as a reminder to come back and work the problem out during revision.

REVISING

Remember, the success of your paper depends heavily on this trouble-shooting-and-repair stage of your writing. Therefore, be prepared to **revise** several times. You might begin by passing through the first draft and identifying specific terms that need further defining. Then you might look for statements that may not be clear enough for your readers. Tinker with them until you have them right, or add sentences to further develop or clarify the statements.

Next, perhaps you should examine each step in the process, looking for any explanations that you may have skimped on or any that you may have belabored. Can you make any of these steps clearer by simplifying your language or removing or revising sentences that obscure your point? Or can you make any step easier to understand by adding more details or sentences of explanation? You will want to test each step to see that you have included any necessary cautions. Examine how you have presented steps that must be done simultaneously or must be prepared for beforehand. Since each step will usually include a series of operations, it is important that you have included all of them and arranged them in the proper order. Presenting these steps clearly is the secret of effective process writing.

Next, you may want to make sure that you have provided guides for the reader in the form of transitions. Remember that you are explaining according to steps in time, and this requires terms like *first, second, next, now, then, before, after, finally,* or phrases such as *at the same time, as soon as,* and the like. However, it is possible to overuse transitions so that they get in the reader's way, and the distraction can make your writing hard to follow. Try to strike a balance, and while revising, use your best judgment to determine what that balance is. But also make this a proofreading concern later on. This will allow you to identify either overuse or underuse more accurately since some of the fog created by working with the paper intensely will have cleared by that time. You might also have a friend read your paper, giving attention to any revision concerns.

After you are satisfied with the body of your paper, you are ready to turn your attention to the introduction and conclusion. Does your introduction provide sufficient background for your reader and lead smoothly and logically into the body? Does your conclusion summarize, relate back to the introduction, or say something about the significance or results of the process?

As a final step in revising, you may wish to go over each sentence, tinkering where necessary, to see that each one says what you want it to say and says it in a way that is easy to follow. Again, a second reader can be helpful here. Check any doubtful sentences or those you haven't been able to revise to your satisfaction. Then ask a friend in whom you have confidence to read them and offer advice.

PROOFREADING

By this time, your hard work in revising may have caused you to tire of your own essay. Nevertheless, careful attention to the small matters of grammar, punctuation, and spelling can make quite a difference in your final draft. It is best to read through your paper at least once for each of these three concerns. Also, remember to devote one reading to transitions to see that each one assists the reader; guard against the overuse of transitions that can irritate a reader of a process paper.

After you have completed your process essay, you may wish to refer to the checklist that follows to make sure you have considered all the important aspects of your essay.

Process Checklist

1. Does your introduction contain sufficient background to prepare readers for the process that follows?
2. Does the introduction discuss the appropriate features of the process—its importance, its simplicity, or how readers will benefit from knowing about it?
3. Have you considered the audience at every step?
4. Have you included all the minor steps necessary to explain the major steps?
5. Can you make any of these steps clearer by simplifying your language or removing or revising sentences that obscure your point?
6. Or can you make any step easier to understand by adding more details or sentences of explanation?
7. Are you satisfied that you have been especially clear in explaining simultaneous steps or identifying potential trouble spots?
8. Are you satisfied that you have neither underused nor overused transitions?
9. Have you carefully examined each sentence for clarity and effective structure?
10. What does your conclusion add to your essay? Does it make your purpose clear?
11. Have you proofread carefully enough to have eliminated any mechanical errors?

How to Write with Style

KURT VONNEGUT

In this essay, a famous American novelist explains how writers can convey more in their writing than information alone. The trick to doing this, Vonnegut says, is to master writing techniques and then make yourself and your subject interesting.

Newspaper reporters and technical writers are trained to reveal almost   1
nothing about themselves in their writings. This makes them freaks in the world of writers, since almost all of the other ink-stained wretches in that world reveal a lot about themselves to readers. We call these revelations, accidental and intentional, elements of style.

These revelations tell us as readers what sort of person it is with whom   2
we are spending time. Does the writer sound ignorant or informed, stupid or bright, crooked or honest, humorless or playful—? And on and on.

Why should you examine your writing style with the idea of improving   3
it? Do so as a mark of respect for your readers, whatever you're writing. If you scribble your thoughts any which way, your readers will surely feel that you care nothing about them. They will mark you down as an egomaniac or a chowderhead—or worse, they will stop reading you.

The most damning revelation you can make about yourself is that you do   4
not know what is interesting and what is not. Don't you yourself like or dislike writers mainly for what they choose to show you or make you think about? Did you ever admire an empty-headed writer for his or her mastery of the language? No.

So your own winning style must begin with ideas in your head.   5

1. Find a subject you care about

Find a subject you care about and which you in your heart feel others   6
should care about. It is this genuine caring, and not your games with language, which will be the most compelling and seductive element in your style.

I am not urging you to write a novel, by the way—although I would not   7
be sorry if you wrote one, provided you genuinely cared about something. A petition to the mayor about a pothole in front of your house or a love letter to the girl next door will do.

2. Do not ramble, though

I won't ramble on about that.   8

3. Keep it simple

As for your use of language: Remember that two great masters of   9
language, William Shakespeare and James Joyce, wrote sentences which
were almost childlike when their subjects were most profound. "To be or not
to be?" asks Shakespeare's Hamlet. The longest word is three letters long.
Joyce, when he was frisky, could put together a sentence as intricate and as
glittering as a necklace for Cleopatra, but my favorite sentence in his short
story "Eveline" is this one: "She was tired." At that point in the story, no
other words could break the heart of a reader as those three words do.

Simplicity of language is not only reputable, but perhaps even sacred.   10
The *Bible* opens with a sentence well within the writing skills of a lively
fourteen-year-old: "In the beginning God created the heaven and the
earth."

4. Have the guts to cut

It may be that you, too, are capable of making necklaces for Cleopatra, so   11
to speak. But your eloquence should be the servant of the ideas in your head.
Your rule might be this: If a sentence, no matter how excellent, does not
illuminate your subject in some new and useful way, scratch it out.

5. Sound like yourself

The writing style which is most natural for you is bound to echo the   12
speech you heard when a child. English was the novelist Joseph Conrad's
third language, and much that seems piquant in his use of English was no
doubt colored by his first language, which was Polish. And lucky indeed is
the writer who has grown up in Ireland, for the English spoken there is so
amusing and musical. I myself grew up in Indianapolis, where common
speech sounds like a band saw cutting galvanized tin, and employs a
vocabulary as unornamental as a monkey wrench.

In some of the more remote hollows of Appalachia, children still grow   13
up hearing songs and locutions of Elizabethan times. Yes, and many Americans grow up hearing a language other than English, or an English dialect a
majority of Americans cannot understand.

All these varieties of speech are beautiful, just as the varieties of but-   14
terflies are beautiful. No matter what your first language, you should treasure it all your life. If it happens not to be standard English, and if it shows
itself when you write standard English, the result is usually delightful, like a
very pretty girl with one eye that is green and one that is blue.

I myself find that I trust my own writing most, and others seem to trust it   15
most, too, when I sound most like a person from Indianapolis, which is what

I am. What alternatives do I have? The one most vehemently recommended by teachers has no doubt been pressed on you, as well: to write like cultivated Englishmen of a century or more ago.

6. Say what you mean to say

I used to be exasperated by such teachers, but am no more. I understand   16
now that all those antique essays and stories with which I was to compare my own work were not magnificent for their datedness or foreignness, but for saying precisely what their authors meant them to say. My teachers wished me to write accurately, always selecting the most effective words, and relating the words to one another unambiguously, rigidly, like parts of a machine. The teachers did not want to turn me into an Englishman after all. They hoped that I would become understandable—and therefore understood. And there went my dream of doing with words what Pablo Picasso did with paint or what any number of jazz idols did with music. If I broke all the rules of punctuation, had words mean whatever I wanted them to mean, and strung them together higgledy-piggledy, I would simply not be understood. So you, too, had better avoid Picasso-style or jazz-style writing, if you have something worth saying and wish to be understood.

Readers want our pages to look very much like pages they have seen   17
before. Why? This is because they themselves have a tough job to do, and they need all the help they can get from us.

7. Pity the readers

They have to identify thousands of little marks on paper, and make   18
sense of them immediately. They have to *read*, an art so difficult that most people don't really master it even after having studied it all though grade school and high school—twelve long years.

So this discussion must finally acknowledge that our stylistic options as   19
writers are neither numerous nor glamorous, since our readers are bound to be such imperfect artists. Our audience requires us to be sympathetic and patient teachers, ever willing to simplify and clarify—whereas we would rather soar high above the crowd, singing like nightingales.

That is the bad news. The good news is that we Americans are governed   20
under a unique Constitution, which allows us to write whatever we please without fear of punishment. So the most meaningful aspect of our styles, which is what we choose to write about, is utterly unlimited.

8. For really detailed advice

For a discussion of literary style in a narrower sense, in a more technical   21
sense, I commend to your attention *The Elements of Style*, by William Strunk, Jr., and E.B. White (Macmillan, 1979). E.B. White is, of course, one of the most admirable literary stylists this country has so far produced.

You should realize, too, that no one would care how well or badly Mr.   22
White expressed himself, if he did not have perfectly enchanting things to
say.

QUESTIONS ON MEANING AND CONTENT

1. In this first paragraph, Vonnegut says that "Newspaper reporters
and technical writers are trained to reveal almost nothing about themselves
in their writing." Why would they be trained in this fashion?

2. In paragraph 4, Vonnegut says that writing should spring from good,
interesting ideas. Is he suggesting that ideas are more important than
effective style? Or equally important? What does the conclusion to the essay
tell you about the importance of having something interesting to say?

3. Summarize the point that Vonnegut makes in paragraphs 12–15. How
do you react to the last sentence in paragraph 15?

QUESTIONS ABOUT RHETORICAL STRATEGIES

1. Vonnegut numbers the points he makes. In what way is this numbering helpful to readers? Would the numbers be more helpful to someone
reading the advice for the first time or to someone who has read the essay but
wants to reread pieces of advice? Explain.

2. In what ways does the introduction (paragraphs 1–5) prepare readers
for the eight points; that is, do the points themselves benefit from what is
emphasized in the introduction?

3. What concerns does Vonnegut express about audience? Where do
you find these in the essay?

4. How does Vonnegut define "elements of style"?

QUESTIONS ON LANGUAGE AND DICTION

1. In paragraph 2, the author uses several terms to describe what writers
reveal about themselves as they write. What are other terms you can think of
to describe these revelations? What does Vonnegut reveal about himself?
What in the essay led you to this conclusion?

2. In paragraph 12, Vonnegut uses a simile (comparison using *like* or *as)* when he says that Indianapolis speech "sounds like a band saw cutting galvanized tin." What sort of comment is that on the "common speech" of Indianapolis? This is one of many similes used by the author. What are some of the others? Which ones do you find especially effective?

3. In paragraph 13, what does the word *hollows* mean? What readers would know this word? Which readers may not know it? Why?

4. Check the meanings of any of the following words that are new to you: *piquant, higgledy-piggledy, locutions.*

Parting the Formaldehyde Curtain

JESSICA MITFORD

With superb style and penetrating wit, Jessica Mitford examines the process of embalming and "restoring" a cadaver. In doing so, Mitford launched a now famous attack on the mortuary industry. This essay is fascinating reading, but you had better be prepared for some grisly details.

The drama begins to unfold with the arrival of the corpse at the mortuary.

Alas, poor Yorick! How surprised he would be to see how his counterpart of today is whisked off to a funeral parlor and is in short order sprayed, sliced, pierced, pickled, trussed, trimmed, creamed, waxed, painted, rouged and neatly dressed—transformed from a common corpse into a Beautiful Memory Picture. This process is known in the trade as embalming and restorative art, and is so universally employed in the United States and Canada that the funeral director does it routinely, without consulting corpse or kin. He regards as eccentric those few who are hardy enough to suggest that it might be dispensed with. Yet no law requires embalming, no religious doctine commends it, nor is it dictated by considerations of health, sanitation, or even of personal daintiness. In no part of the world but in North America is it widely used. The purpose of embalming is to make the corpse presentable for viewing in a suitably costly container; and here too the funeral director routinely, without first consulting the family, prepares the body for public display.

Is all this legal? The processes to which a dead body may be subjected are after all to some extent circumscribed by law. In most states, for instance, the signature of next of kin must be obtained before an autopsy may be performed, before the deceased may be cremated, before the body may be turned over to a medical school for research purposes; or such provision must be made in the decedent's will. In the case of embalming, no such permission is required nor is it ever sought. A textbook, *The Principles and Practices of Embalming*, comments on this: "There is some question regarding the legality of much that is done within the preparation room." The author points out that it would be most unusual for a responsible member of a bereaved family to instruct the mortician, in so many words, to *"embalm"* the body of a deceased relative. The very term "embalming" is so seldom used that the mortician must rely upon custom in the matter. The author concludes that unless the family specifies otherwise, the act of entrusting the body to the care of a funeral establishment carries with it an implied permission to go ahead and embalm.

Embalming is indeed a most extraordinary procedure, and one must   4
wonder at the docility of Americans who each year pay hundreds of millions of dollars for its perpetuation, blissfully ignorant of what it is all about, what is done, how it is done. Not one in ten thousand has any idea of what actually takes place. Books on the subject are extremely hard to come by. They are not to be found in most libraries or bookshops.

In an era when huge television audiences watch surgical operations in   5
the comfort of their living rooms, when, thanks to the animated cartoon, the geography of the digestive system has become familiar territory even to the nursery school set, in a land where the satisfaction of curiosity about almost all matters is a national pastime, the secrecy surrounding embalming can, surely, hardly be attributed to the inherent gruesomeness of the subject. Custom in this regard has within this century suffered a complete reversal. In the early days of American embalming, when it was performed in the home of the deceased, it was almost mandatory for some relative to stay by the embalmer's side and witness the procedure. Today, family members who might wish to be in attendance would certainly be dissuaded by the funeral director. All others, except apprentices, are excluded by law from the preparation room.

A close look at what does actually take place may explain in large   6
measure the undertaker's intractable reticence concerning a procedure that has become his major *raison d'être*. It is possible he fears that public information about embalming might lead patrons to wonder if they really want this service? If the funeral men are loath to discuss the subject outside the trade, the reader may, understandably, be equally loath to go on reading at this point. For those who have the stomach for it, let us part the formaldehyde curtain. . . .

The body is first laid out in the undertaker's morgue—or rather, Mr.   7
Jones is reposing in the preparation room—to be readied to bid the world farewell.

The preparation room in any of the better funeral establishments has the   8
tiled and sterile look of a surgery, and indeed the embalmer-restorative artist who does his chores there is beginning to adopt the term "dermasurgeon" (appropriately corrupted by some mortician-writers as "demi-surgeon") to describe his calling. His equipment, consisting of scalpels, scissors, augers, forceps, clamps, needles, pumps, tubes, bowls and basins, is crudely imita-

tive of the surgeon's, as is his technique, acquired in a nine-or twelve-month post-high-school course in an embalming school. He is supplied by an advanced chemical industry with a bewildering array of fluids, sprays, pastes, oils, powders, creams, to fix or soften tissue, shrink or distend it as needed, dry it here, restore the moisture there. There are cosmetics, waxes and paints to fill and cover features, even plaster of Paris to replace entire limbs. There are ingenious aids to prop and stabilize the cadaver; a Vari-Pose Head Rest, the Edwards Arm and Hand Positioner, the Repose Block (to support the shoulders during the embalming), and the Throop Foot Positioner, which resembles an old-fashioned stocks.

Mr. John H. Eckels, president of the Eckels College of Mortuary Science, thus describes the first part of the embalming procedure: "In the hands of a skilled practitioner, this work may be done in a comparatively short time and without mutliating the body other than by slight incision—so slight that it scarcely would cause serious inconvenience if made upon a living person. It is necessary to remove the blood, and doing this not only helps in the disinfecting, but removes the principal cause of disfigurements due to discoloration."   9

Another textbook discusses the all-important time element: "The earlier this is done, the better, for every hour that elapses between death and embalming will add to the problems and complications encountered. . . ." Just how soon should one get going on the embalming? The author tells us, "On the basis of such scanty information made available to this profession through its rudimentary and haphazard system of technical research, we must conclude that the best results are to be obtained if the subject is embalmed before life is completely extinct—that is, before cellular death has occurred. In the average case, this would mean within an hour after somatic death." For those who feel that there is something a little rudimentary, not to say haphazard, about this advice, a comforting thought is offered by another writer. Speaking of fears entertained in early days of premature burial, he points out, "One of the effects of embalming by chemical injection, however, has been to dispel fears of live burial." How true; once the blood is removed, chances of live burial are indeed remote.   10

To return to Mr. Jones, the blood is drained out through the veins and replaced by embalming fluid pumped in through the arteries. As noted in *The Principles and Practices of Embalming*, "every operator has a favorite injection and drainage point—a fact which becomes a handicap only if he fails or refuses to forsake his favorites when conditions demand it." Typical favorites are the carotid artery, femoral artery, jugular vein, subclavian vein. There are various choices of embalming fluid. If Flextone is used, it will   11 produce a "mild, flexible rigidity. The skin retains a velvety softness, the tissues are rubbery and pliable. Ideal for women and children." It may be blended with B. and G. Products Company's Lyf-Lyk tint, which is guaranteed to reproduce "nature's own skin texture . . . the velvety appearance of living tissues." Suntone comes in three separate tints: Suntan; Special Cosmetic Tint, a pink shade "especially indicated for young female subjects"; and Regular Cosmetic Tint, moderately pink.

About three to six gallons of a dyed and perfumed solution of formaldehyde, glycerin, borax, phenol, alcohol and water is soon circulating through Mr. Jones, whose mouth has been sewn together with a "needle directed upward between the upper lip and gum and brought out through the left nostril," with the corners raised slightly "for a more pleasant expression." If he should be bucktoothed, his teeth are cleaned with Bon Ami and coated with colorless nail polish. His eyes, meanwhile, are closed with flesh-tinted eye caps and eye cement.   12

The next step is to have at Mr. Jones with a thing called a trocar. This is a long, hollow needle attached to a tube. It is jabbed into the abdomen, poked around the entrails and chest cavity, the contents of which are pumped out and replaced with "cavity fluid." This done, and the hole in the abdomen sewn up, Mr. Jones's face is heavily creamed (to protect the skin from burns which may be caused by leakage of the chemicals), and he is covered with a sheet and left unmolested for a while. But not for long—there is much, much more, in store for him. He has been embalmed, but not yet restored, and the best time to start the restorative work is eight to ten hours after embalming, when the tissues have become firm and dry.   13

The object of all this attention to the corpse, it must be remembered, is to make it presentable for viewing in an attitude of healthy repose. "Our customs require the presentation of our dead in the semblance of normality . . . unmarred by the ravages of illness, disease or mutilation," says Mr. J. Sheridan Mayer in his *Restorative Art*. This is rather a large order since few people die in the full bloom of health, unravaged by illness and unmarked by some disfigurement. The funeral industry is equal to the challenge: "In some cases the gruesome appearance of a mutilated or disease-ridden subject may be quite discouraging. The task of restoration may seem impossible and shake the confidence of the embalmer. This is the time for intestinal fortitude and determination. Once the formative work is begun and affected tissues are cleaned or removed, all doubts of success vanish. It is surprising and gratifying to discover the results which may be obtained."   14

The embalmer, having allowed an appropriate interval to elapse, returns to the attack, but now he brings into play the skill and equipment of sculptor   15 and cosmetician. Is a hand missing? Casting one in plaster of Paris is a simple matter. "For replacement purposes, only a cast of the back of the hand is necessary; this is within the ability of the average operator and is quite adequate." If a lip or two, a nose or an ear should be missing, the embalmer has at hand a variety of restorative waxes with which to model replacements. Pores and skin texture are simulated by stippling with a little brush, and over this cosmetics are laid on. Head off? Decapitation cases are rather routinely handled. Ragged edges are trimmed, and head joined to torso with a series of splints, wires and sutures. It is a good idea to have a little something at the neck—a scarf or a high collar—when time for viewing comes. Swollen mouth? Cut out tissue as needed from inside the lips. If too much is removed, the surface contour can easily be restored by padding with cotton. Swollen necks and cheeks are reduced by removing tissue through vertical incisions made down each side of the neck. "When the deceased is casketed, the pillow will hide the suture incisions . . . as an extra precaution against leakage, the suture may be painted with liquid sealer."

The opposite condition is more likely to present itself—that of emacia-   16
tion. His hypodermic syringe now loaded with massage cream, the embalmer seeks out and fills the hollowed and sunken areas by injection. In this procedure the backs of the hands and fingers and the under-chin area should not be neglected.

Positioning the lips is a problem that recurrently challenges the in-   17
genuity of the embalmer. Closed too tightly, they tend to give a stern, even disapproving expression. Ideally, embalmers feel, the lips should give the impression of being ever so slightly parted, the upper lip protruding slightly for a more youthful appearance. This takes some engineering, however, as the lips tend to drift apart. Lip drift can sometimes be remedied by pushing one or two straight pins through the inner margin of the lower lip and then inserting them between the two front upper teeth. If Mr. Jones happens to have no teeth, the pins can just as easily be anchored in his Armstrong Face Former and Denture Replacer. Another method to maintain lip closure is to dislocate the lower jaw, which is then held in its new position by a wire run through holes which have been drilled through the upper and lower jaws at the midline. As the French are fond of saying, *it faut souffrir pour être belle.* [1]

If Mr. Jones has died of jaundice, the embalming fluid will very likely   18
turn him green. Does this deter the embalmer? Not if he has intestinal fortitude. Masking pastes and cosmetics are heavily laid on, burial garments

---

[1]You have to suffer to be beautiful.

and casket interiors are color-correlated with particular care, and Jones is displayed beneath rose-colored lights. Friends will say 'How *well* he looks." Death by carbon monoxide, on the other hand, can be rather a good thing from the embalmer's viewpoint: "One advantage is the fact that this type of discoloration is an exaggerated form of a natural pink coloration." This is nice because the healthy glow is already present and needs but little attention.

The patching and filling completed, Mr. Jones is now shaved, washed   19
and dressed. Cream-based cosmetic, available in pink, flesh, suntan, brunette and blond, is applied to his hands and face, his hair is shampooed and combed (and, in the case of Mrs. Jones, set), his hands manicured. For the horny-handed son of toil special care must be taken; cream should be applied to remove ingrained grime, and the nails cleaned. "If he were not in the habit of having them manicured in life, trimming and shaping is advised for better appearance—never questioned by kin."

Jones is now ready for casketing (this is the present participle of the verb   20
"to casket"). In this operation his right shoulder should be depressed slightly "to turn the body a bit to the right and soften the appearance of lying flat on the back." Positioning the hands is a matter of importance, and special rubber positioning blocks may be used. The hands should be cupped slightly for a more likelike, relaxed appearance. Proper placement of the body requires a delicate sense of balance. It should lie as high as possible in the casket, yet not so high that the lid, when lowered, will hit the nose. On the other hand, we are cautioned, placing the body too low "creates the impression that the body is in a box."

Jones is next wheeled into the appointed slumber room where a few last   21
touches may be added—his favorite pipe placed in his hand or, if he was a great reader, a book propped into position. (In the case of little Master Jones a Teddy bear may clutched.) Here he will hold open house for a few days, visiting hours 10 A.M. to 9 P.M.

All now being in readiness, the funeral director calls a staff conference to   22
make sure that each assistant knows his precise duties. Mr. Wilber Kriege writes: "This makes your staff feel that they are a part of the team, with a definite assignment that must be properly carried out if the whole plan is to succeed. You never heard of a football coach who failed to talk to his entire team before they go on the field. They have drilled on the plays they are to execute for hours and days, and yet the successful coach knows the importance of making even the bench-warming third-string substitute feel that he is important if the game is to be won." The winning of *this* game is predicated upon glass-smooth handling of the logistics. The funeral director has

notified the pallbearers whose names were furnished by the family, has arranged for the presence of clergyman, organist, soloist, has provided transportation for everybody, has organized and listed the flowers sent by friends. In *Psychology of Funeral Service* Mr. Edward A. Martin points out: "He may not always do as much as the family thinks he is doing, but it is his helpful guidance that they appreciate in knowing they are proceeding as they should. . . . The important thing is how well his services can be used to make the family believe they are giving unlimited expression to their own sentiment."

The religious service may be held in a church or in the chapel of the   23 funeral home; the funeral director vastly prefers the latter arrangement, for not only is it more convenient for him but it affords him the opportunity to show off his beautiful facilities to the gathered mourners. After the clergyman has had his say, the mourners queue up to file past the casket for a last look at the deceased. The family is *never* asked whether they want an open-casket ceremony; in the absence of their instruction to the contrary, this is taken for granted. Consequently well over 90 per cent of all American funerals feature the open casket—a custom unknown in other parts of the world. Foreigners are astonished by it. An English woman living in San Francisco described her reaction in a letter to the writer:

> I myself have attended only one funeral here—that of an elderly fellow worker of mine. After the service I could not understand why everyone was walking towards the coffin (sorry, I mean casket), but thought I had better follow the crowd. It shook me rigid to get there and find the casket open and poor old Oscar lying there in his brown tweed suit, wearing a suntan makeup and just the wrong shade of lipstick. If I had not been extremely fond of the old boy, I have a horrible feeling that I might have giggled. Then and there I decided that I could never face another American funeral—even dead.

The casket (which has been resting throughout the service on a Classic   24 Beauty Metal Casket Bier) is now transferred by a hydraulically operated device called Porto-Lift to a balloon-tired, Glide Easy casket carriage which will wheel it to yet another conveyance, the Cadillac Funeral Coach. This may be lavender, cream, light green—anything but black. Interiors, of course, are color-correlated, "for the man who cannot stop short of perfection."

At graveside, the casket is lowered into the earth. This office, once the   25 prerogative of friends of the deceased, is now performed by a patented mechanical lowering device. A "Lifetime Green" artificial grass mat is at the ready to conceal the sere earth, and overhead, to conceal the sky, is a portable Steril Chapel Tent ("resists the intense heat and humidity of summer and the terrific storms of winter . . . available in Silver Grey, Rose or Evergreen"). Now is the time for the ritual scattering of earth over the coffin, as the solemn words "earth to earth, ashes to ashes, dust to dust" are pronounced by the officiating cleric. This can today be accomplished "with a mere flick of the wrist with the Gordon Leak-Proof Earth Dispenser. No grasping of a handful of dirt, no soiled fingers. Simple, dignified, beautiful, reverent! The modern way!" The Gordon Earth Dispenser (at $5) is of nickel-plated brass construction. It is not only "attractive to the eye and long wearing"; it is also "one of the 'tools' for building better public relations" if presented as "an appropriate non-commercial gift" to the clergyman. It is shaped something like a saltshaker.

Untouched by human hand, the coffin and the earth are now united.   26

It is in the function of directing the participants through this maze of   27 gadgetry that the funeral director has assigned to himself his relatively new role of "grief therapist." He has relieved the family of every detail, he has revamped the corpse to look like a living doll, he has arranged for it to nap for a few days in a slumber room, he has put on a well-oiled performance in which the concept of *death* has played no part whatsoever—unless it was inconsiderately mentioned by the clergyman who conducted the religious service. He has done everything in his power to make the funeral a real pleasure for everybody concerned. He and his team have given their all to score an upset victory over death.

QUESTIONS ON MEANING AND CONTENT

1. Is Mitford's purpose merely to inform readers about the process of embalming, or does she have an additional purpose? What exactly is Mitford's *purpose?*

2. Mitford has a reputation for being a muckraker and a keen investigative reporter. Is she exposing any deceptions or misconduct in this essay? If so, what?

3. What is the *thesis* of this essay? How is this thesis related to Mitford's *purpose?*

4. How would you characterize Mitford's *attitude* toward morticians and the funeral industry? Can you cite specific examples from the text to support your characterization of her attitude?

5. On several occasions, Mitford quotes from various textbooks on embalming. Why does she do this? What do these quotations contribute to the meaning of the essay?

QUESTIONS ABOUT RHETORICAL STRATEGIES

1. What are the major stages in the process of embalming as presented by Mitford? How do these stages help support Mitford's thesis?

2. Notice that the first and second-to-last paragraphs are made up of one sentence each. Why does Mitford use these one-sentence paragraphs where she does? How do they contribute to the essay?

3. The final paragraph of the essay is quite caustic in tone. What makes this paragraph particularly effective? In what way does it bring the essay to an end?

QUESTIONS ON LANGUAGE AND DICTION

1. Is there any significance in the fact that Mitford names the cadaver *Mr. Jones?* What?

2. Mitford pays close attention to the *language* of embalming, especially to the euphemisms the industry uses. For example, the cadaver is said to be "reposing" in the "preparation room,' and then it is treated with products with names such as "Lyf-Lyk tint," before being exhibited in a "slumber room." Locate additional examples of such language. What is Mitford's attitude about this language? What point does she want to get across?

3. Frequently, Mitford's language is ironic and even sarcastic. For example, in her final sentence she comments that the mortician "and his team have given their all to score an upset victory over death." Locate other instances of ironic or sarcastic language in the essay. How do such instances help further her thesis?

Making Money

MIKE ROYKO

*In the following essay, Mike Royko makes us observers of police officers
on night duty in Chicago more than a decade ago. As he takes us from one
law enforcement situation to another, he shows us the processes used by
these law officers to add an extra dimension and an extra source of income to
their jobs.*

The desk sergeant was drunk. Not so drunk that he couldn't ramble   1
about the good old days, when he peeled down to the waist and fought the
toughest mug in the district toe to toe in the back room of the station, but
drunk enough so that he lolled in a chair and let a young patrolman handle
the phone calls and the people who came in off the street with problems. The
sergeant got drunk early every evening. But by midnight, when his shift
ended, he'd be coming out of it enough to drive the fifteen miles to his home
on the far South Side.

He'd complain about the long drive every night, and always working the   2
night trick, but when somebody asked him why he didn't get transferred to a
district near his home and rotate his shift, he'd say, "I got expenses. My
wife's health isn't good. And it took me years to get some of these taverns
lined up. I can't leave that now."

It was a practical explanation. Some taverns paid him to stay open   3
beyond the 2 A.M. closing hour. He was less expensive than a 4 A.M. license.
Others paid him to assure that if a bartender worked a customer over, the
customer would be charged with assault. He didn't keep it all: the detectives
on his shift got some, and the lieutenant in a little office in the back got more.
And his collection was small change compared to what the captain's bag
man picked up during the day.

The captain's bag man made the rounds of the bookies, the homosexual   4
bars, the hotels and lounges that were headquarters for prostitution rings.
That's where the real money was, but the captain didn't keep it all. He got
some, but most of it went to the ward committeeman. That's why the captain
was running the station: the ward committeeman had put him there because
he trusted him to collect the payoffs and give an honest accounting and a fair
split. If he didn't, the ward committeeman would call downtown to headquarters and have the captain transferred to a paper-shuffling job some-

where. Not that this was likely to happen: the captain knew what he was supposed to do, or the ward boss wouldn't have had him promoted through the ranks all the way to captain.

While the sergeant on the near North Side was nipping from his bottle and waiting for midnight, the sergeant at a South Side police station was ducking out the side door to get a beer in the tavern right across the street from the station. A hulking lesbian drew a glass for him, and at a table in the back one of a half-dozen black girls waved and said, "Hi, Sergeant." He laughed and winked. While he sipped his beer, a man came in, went to the back, talked to the big lesbian, then went out through the back door with one of the girls. Stairs led to rooms upstairs. He'd pay the girl twenty dollars, out of which the girl would keep about half. The lesbian would get the other half, and out of that she would eventually pay the captain's bag man a certain amount, and he would give it to the captain, and the captain would give some to the ward committeeman, and spread the rest down the ranks to the sergeant and others. The girls were a real force in the economy.

When the sergeant finished his beer, he returned to the station and got back behind the desk. Two vice detectives came out of the back and yelled to him, "We're gonna root around, Sarge," which meant they were going to look for a few drifting hookers, pimps, or junkies and shake them down. Not everybody was lined up by the captain's bag man.

A black man walked into the station and stood by the desk, mumbling and holding his hands over his stomach, which was bleeding. He had been in a fight and somebody cut him. The sergeant looked disgusted. He handed the man a newspaper. The man looked confused and held the newspaper as if to read it. "No, dummy," the sergeant said "go on over there by the wall and stand on it." He didn't want the man bleeding near the desk. The man did as he was told, the blood dripping on the paper. The sergeant told the patrolman to call downtown to the radio room. "See if you can get the wagon to take this guy to the county." About an hour and a couple of pints of blood later, the paddy wagon came and took the man to the county hospital. There were at least two private hospitals closer, but they did not welcome blacks in their emergency room.

Meanwhile, on the Outer Drive, two policemen in a squad car spotted a speeder. They flipped on their red light and one of them played the spotlight on the car's rear window. The motorist pulled onto the shoulder, stopped, took out his license, folded a ten-dollar bill around it, and handed it to one of the policemen. The policeman put the ten dollars in his pocket, cautioned the man against speeding, returned the license, and they parted. The motorist was the kind the policeman liked. If he had been shy, or dense, the

5

6

7

8

policeman would have had to stand there, hemming and hawing, trying to get the message across. That failing, he would have signed and written a ticket. There's no profit in tickets, but fortunately most Chicagoans weren't shy or dense.

On the Southwest Side, another policeman stopped a motorist and used 9 a different approach when the motorist didn't gift wrap his license. He carried wooden pencils in his pocket, and he would announce: "I have three kinds of pencils which I sell—a five-dollar pencil, a ten-dollar pencil, and a twenty-five dollar pencil. I think you need a ten-dollar pencil, don't you?" The pencils were seldom sold for more than twenty-five dollars, because that would have meant somebody had been run over, and fixing that required the cooperation of prosecutors and even judges and was not something that could be arranged on the scene.

While the policeman was selling pencils, a police captain in a $200 suit 10 and $25 shoes, purchased on a salary of $180 a week, was telling some friends in an expensive restaurant about the suspected burglar a couple of his men brought in. The suspect had been working a street of wealthy apartment-house dwellers. Burglaries in such apartments brought publicity and complaints from influential people, problems police captains tried to avoid. "They brought him into my office and I took out my .38 special and pointed it right between his eyes and cocked it. He opened his mouth to yell and I shoved it in, right to his tonsils, and I told him, 'You sonofabitch, I don't want you stealing in my district. You want to steal, you go steal in somebody else's district, but if I catch you here again, I'll blow your fucking head off!'" There was nothing more the captain could do, since the man hadn't been caught stealing.

Somewhere else, a suspected thief was shoved into a room in the back of 11 a station. The detectives followed him in, put him in a chair, and while two of them held his arms, a third picked up a phone book. Unlike a rubber hose or a wooden club, a phone book does not leave bruises, but after being hit in the head often enough a man feels like his spine has been compressed into a one-inch cube. The suspect would confess to almost every unsolved theft on the station's books, providing a fine clean-up record for the detectives.

In a hospital emergency room, a man awoke on a table. When they 12 brought him in, he was covered with blood and looked close to death. He had run his car into a light pole. As it turned out, he wasn't seriously hurt, just cut on his forehead, but he seemed without life because he had passed out drunk. In fact, his finger hurt him more than any of his cuts because it was raw. Somebody had pulled his gold wedding ring off his pudgy hand. It had been an honest mistake, though, the paddy wagon men believing he was dead or dying.

On Skid Row, somebody had died—an old pensioner in a flophouse.   13
The paddy wagon men hauled him into their van and drove as fast as they
could to a funeral home about two miles away. They went past a couple of
funeral homes along the way. The one they were going to paid the best
prices for stray bodies.

In an airplane flying toward Europe, Anthony J. Accardo, the "god-   14
father" in the Chicago Mafia, was beginning a vacation trip. His traveling
companion, an old friend, was on a one-month furlough from his lieutenant's job in the Police Department.

It was a typical night for the Chicago police in early 1960. They were out   15
making money. Some were making big money. Others took in smaller
sums, but it added up. If a two-man squad could stop just six or seven good
traffic violators in one night, that was an extra fifty dollars in the wallet when
midnight came. Some were so hungry they'd take anything. An old man
who worked in a poultry store was stopped for running a light. He was
broke, but when the policeman found that he worked in a poultry store, he
made the old man promise to return to the same spot the following night
with a chicken.

Not everybody was on the take. There were honest policemen. You   16
could find them working in the crime laboratory, the radio room, in desk
jobs in headquarters. There were college-educated policemen, and you
could find them working with juveniles. There were even rebelliously honest policemen, who might blow the whistle on the dishonest ones. You
could find them walking a patrol along the edge of a cemetery. The honest
policemen were distinguished by their rank, which was seldom above
patrolman. They were problems, square pegs in round holes. Nobody
wanted to work a traffic car with an honest partner. He was useless on a vice
detail because he might start arresting gamblers or hookers. So the honest
ones were isolated and did the nonprofitable jobs. It had to be so, because a
few good apples in the barrel could ruin the thousands of rotten ones.

QUESTIONS ON MEANING AND CONTENT

1. Do the situations presented by Royko shock you? Or are they about
what you would have expected for a big city police department? If you
expected such situations, explain why.

2. What would the effect be if Royko had omitted the discussion of
honest policemen in paragraph 16? Does the contrast strengthen the piece in
some way? If so, how? In answering, use the following as a guide: If this

section were omitted, do you think many readers would ask, "But aren't there any honest policemen in the city?" Speculate about how these readers would react upon hearing Royko's comments about honest policemen.

3. Which examples of conduct do you find most unsettling? If you were ranking each on a scale according to its offensiveness, which ones would be near the top, which near the bottom? How would you label those near the bottom? In your view, is any one more offensive than all the others?

QUESTIONS ABOUT RHETORICAL STRATEGIES

1. Royko begins with an example and continues to present examples. Not until paragraph 15 does he begin to show the purpose that ties the examples together. This is an *inductive* movement, a form of development that works from specifics toward a generalization that will show what these specific cases signify. Thus, paragraphs 15 and 16 tell us what we might ordinarily find in an introduction. Do you find Royko's method to be effective? Would the piece be more effective if the information in paragraphs 15 and 16 appeared at the beginning? Why or why not?

2. This piece of writing informs readers about several processes that fall under a single heading. Royko identifies the single heading in paragraph 15 when he says that the police "were out making money." You can see from the examples that the question of how the money is made cannot be answered by explaining only one process. The process of making money is really a series of processes governed by each money-making situation. Could any in the series be expanded into essay-length processes? If so, which ones? Could any process be rewritten with another purpose in mind—to show, in steps, how to perform the process? Which ones in particular?

3. Consider Royko's summary statement that the police "were out making money." Is this an example of *understatement?* Rephrase Royko's statement to make it more emotionally charged or harsher. Is your statement more specific than "out making money"? Do you like Royko's way of stating it? Does it fit his manner of expression throughout?

QUESTIONS ON LANGUAGE AND DICTION

1. In paragraph 12, Royko concludes the example of the paddy wagon officers stripping the wedding ring from an unconscious man by saying, "It had been an honest mistake, though, the paddy wagon men believing he was dead or dying." We might call this *understatement,* since Royko does not directly express indignation where we might expect him to. Instead, he makes a flat, unemotional statement. The technique of understatement is used throughout this piece. What are other examples? Do you think understatement is an effective technique for the author to be using here? Why or why not?

2. You probably found few, if any, words in this piece that you had to look up in order to determine their meanings. Do you think this is the case because Royko has tailored his writing for a broad audience or because of the nature of the subject matter? Both? Explain.

How Animals Weather Winter

SHARON BEGLEY with JOHN CAREY and MARY BRUNO

Sharon Begley, John Carey, and Mary Bruno explain how studying the processes by which animals regulate their temperatures can provide help for human beings suffering from a variety of ailments.

Easterners digging out of the recent blizzard must have envied the   1
ground hogs, bats and other hibernators who sleep out the winter and wake up to forsythia in bloom. During hibernation, an animal's body temperature drops with the mercury. Its heart rate, metabolism and blood pressure all plummet, yet even in this torpor some animals give birth and others awaken periodically and warm themselves. Lately scientists have begun to realize that hibernation offers hope to humans too. They are close to isolating the chemical trigger that causes it, and have discovered that the substance "contains factors that are ideal as antihypertensives, anesthetics, analgesics and antiobesity agents," says Robert D. Myers of the University of North Carolina.

Hibernation is only the most dramatic example of animals' internal   2
thermostats. If body temperature falls too low, there is a danger of death due to hypothermia. In humans this can strike at temperatures well above freezing, especially if the body is wet or the wind is blowing. Hypothermia begins with shivering, slurred speech and dulled mental acuity, followed by muscular rigidity, a falling pulse and, if the body is not warmed, death. Overheating can be fatal, too, for it makes life-sustaining enzymes denature into uselessness.

Huddle: Animals have evolved sophisticated tricks to regulate their   3
temperature. Many reptiles move black pigment cells to their top side, so that basking in the sun brings in more heat. Dogs route blood through their nose, which acts as a radiator and prevents blood from overheating the brain. Indeed, most animals know instinctively how to keep body temperature in the safe range. Emperor penguins, for instance, go into a huddle. After the female lays her egg on an ice floe in the dead of an antarctic winter, she trudges off to find food and leaves her mate to warm the egg—in temperatures that would freeze an unincubated egg solid in about a minute. Left alone, the male's body temperature would fall too low to warm the egg sufficiently. But he joins great circles of huddling penguins, a formation so

effective that it keeps his temperature around 97 degrees, warm enough to incubate his brood. Other birds can maintain their temperature by changing their posture or ruffling their feathers. Biologists have also reported that when sunlight hits their dark feathers directly, herring gulls absorb less heat than when the rays strike obliquely. Thus, to cool off, the bird can position itself to catch the rays straight on. If a honeybee becomes overheated on a pollen-gathering trip, it regurgitates some nectar onto its tongue, which it wags to speed evaporation and hence cooling.

Most of the time, thermoregulation operates automatically. When the   4
common horned lizard gets cold, its skin darkens so that it will absorb radiation more effectively. Nature has given polar bears hollow hairs that turn their fur into a forest of heating pipes: the hairs carry ultraviolet rays to the skin, presumably to warm it. Dragonflies are threatened more by heat than by cold, because their furiously flapping wing muscles overheat. To prevent the muscles from failing, the blood in some species is channeled through the abdomen which, like the dog's tongue, serves as a radiator to dissipate extra heat.

The thermostats of birds and mammals lie in the hypothalamus, a   5
structure in the brain sensitive to temperature. Homeowners are familiar with thermostats near a source of heat that react by keeping the rest of the house frigid. Similarly, biologists find that if they apply heat to the hypothalami of test animals, the creatures pant or sweat and cool off, even though their body temperature has not been elevated. Myers believes that the hypothalamus controls temperature by releasing neurochemicals, substances that carry messages in the brain. He finds that if neurons in the hypothalamus are cooled, they release serotonin, which orders other neurons to make muscles tremble so that the body is warmed by shivering. Heating neurons in the hypothalamus causes them to produce the chemicals norepinephrine and dopamine; they carry the "sweat" signal, telling other neurons to open pores.

Knockout: The most intriguing details of thermoregulation are emerg-   6
ing from studies of hibernation. Last year, researchers led by Peter R. Oeltgen of the Veterans Administration Medical Center in Lexington, Ky., reported that chemicals in the blood of hibernating woodchucks act like knockout drops. Injected into the brains of rhesus monkeys, they induced something like hibernation. The monkey's temperatures dropped as much as 10 degrees, their heart rates fell as much as 50 percent and they even yawned a lot. Scientists believe that the hibernation trigger resembles opiates. Alexander L. Beckman and colleagues at the Alfred I. duPont Institute in Delaware found that hibernating ground squirrels do not be-

come addicted to morphine. Nonhibernating squirrels do. The scientists suspect that the hibernation trigger occupies the same sites in the brain where opiates act.

The more biologists learn about the hibernation chemical, the more it resembles a wonder drug. In humans it might be used to lower body temperature during heart surgery, thus reducing metabolism and increasing the chance that heart cells will survive the operation despite the reduced blood flow. Oeltgen suggests that the chemical might also help preserve organs before transplant and, more prosaically, lower high blood pressure. The trick now is to break the chemical into components that perform only one of these functions. People trying to lower their blood pressure do not, in most cases, care to sleep for the winter.   7

QUESTIONS ON MEANING AND CONTENT

1. The purpose of the essay goes beyond the analysis of processes. What is that purpose ? Do the authors present the purpose in the introduction? Where?

2. If you were asked to group the various examples of strategies used by animals to maintain acceptable temperature levels, what categories would you use? How many categories would you have? What basis would you use for establishing categories?

QUESTIONS ABOUT RHETORICAL STRATEGIES

1. In paragraph 5, the authors present a simple definition of *hypothalamus* by calling it "a structure in the brain sensitive to temperature." This definition is not sufficiently detailed to be useful to a biologist or a chemist. How necessary is this definition for an audience of nonscientists? How comprehensible would the passage be without it? What other brief definition is offered in paragraph 5? How helpful or necessary is it? Were there other words in the essay that you thought should have been defined?

2. This is an interesting example of process writing since it sets out to acquaint readers with several different processes. Because of this complexity, each process explanation is brief. Is each one complete enough to give a good general understanding of the process involved? Are these processes all related in some way? What is the base that ties them together and allows them to be discussed in a single essay?

3. This essay tells us about processes rather than explains how to do something. Describe an audience that would be interested in reading an essay on this topic. Is the topic interesting to you?

4. Describe the conclusion to the essay. Does the conclusion strengthen the meaning and/or the organization of the essay? If so, how? How does the conclusion relate to the introduction?

QUESTIONS ON LANGUAGE AND DICTION

1. In paragraph 6, we are told "that chemicals in the blood of hibernating woodchucks act like knockout drops." This comparison enables us to see the point quickly because we have an idea of how knockout drops work. Without using the reference to knockout drops, how would you explain the effects of this chemical? What other comparisons to things we know about do you find in the essay?

2. What are the meanings of the following words from the essay: *acuity, denature, neurons, ultraviolet, woodchuck, metabolism?*

The Festivities

TRUMAN CAPOTE

The time is just after midnight on April 14, 1965, as Richard Hickock and Perry Smith are led separately into a warehouse at the Kansas State Penitentiary. Inside the warehouse, a scaffold, dubbed "Big Boy" by the inmates, awaits Hickock and Smith who are to die for the murder of a Kansas family. Watching the process along with the other witnesses is Al Dewey, who headed the murder probe for the Kansas Bureau of Investigation (KBI). The murders were real, and so is the account of the execution offered here by Truman Capote.

Dewey had watched them die, for he had been among the twenty-odd 1 witnesses invited to the ceremony. He had never attended an execution, and when on the midnight past he entered the cold warehouse, the scenery had surprised him: he had anticipated a setting of suitable dignity, not this bleakly lighted cavern cluttered with lumber and other debris. But the gallows itself, with its two pale nooses attached to a crossbeam, was imposing enough; and so, in an unexpected style, was the hangman, who cast a long shadow from his perch on the platform at the top of the wooden instrument's thirteen steps. The hangman, an anonymous, leathery gentleman who had been imported from Missouri for the event, for which he was paid six hundred dollars, was attired in an aged double-breasted pin-striped suit overly commodius for the narrow figure inside it—the coat came nearly to his knees; and on his head he wore a cowboy hat which, when first bought, had perhaps been bright green, but was now a weathered, sweat-stained oddity.

Also, Dewey found the self-consciously casual conversation of his fel- 2 low witnesses, as they stood awaiting the start of what one witness termed "the festivities," disconcerting.

"What I heard was, they was gonna let them draw straws to see who 3 dropped first. Or flip a coin. But Smith says why not do it alphabetically. Guess 'cause S comes after H. Ha!"

"Read in the paper, afternoon paper, what they ordered for their last 4 meal? Ordered the same menu. Shrimp. French fries. Garlic bread. Ice cream and strawberries and whipped cream. Understand Smith didn't touch his much."

"That Hickock's got a sense of humor. They was telling me how, about 5 an hour ago, one of the guards says to him, 'This must be the longest night of your life.' And Hickock, he laughs and says, 'No. The shortest.' "

"Did you hear about Hickock's eyes? He left them to an eye doctor. Soon 6 as they cut him down, this doctor's gonna yank out his eyes and stick them in somebody else's head. Can't say I'd want to be that somebody. I'd feel peculiar with them eyes in my head."

"Christ! Is that *rain?* All the windows down! My new Chevy. Christ!" 7

The sudden rain rapped the high warehouse roof. The sound, not unlike 8 the rat-a-tat-tat of parade drums, heralded Hickock's arrival. Accompanied by six guards and a prayer-murmuring chaplain, he entered the death place handcuffed and wearing an ugly harness of leather straps that bound his arms to his torso. At the foot of the gallows the warden read to him the official order of execution, a two-page document; and as the warden read, Hickock's eyes, enfeebled by half a decade of cell shadows, roamed the little audience until, not seeing what he sought, he asked the nearest guard, in a whisper, if any member of the Clutter family was present. When he was told no, the prisoner seemed disappointed, as though he thought the protocol surrounding this ritual of vengeance was not being properly observed.

As is customary, the warden, having finished his recitation, asked the 9 condemned man whether he had any last statement to make. Hickock nodded. "I just want to say I hold no hard feelings. You people are sending me to a better world than this ever was"; then, as if to emphasize the point, he shook hands with the four men mainly responsible for his capture and conviction, all of whom had requested permission to attend the executions: K.B.I. Agents Roy Church, Clarence Duntz, Harold Nye, and Dewey himself. "Nice to see you," Hickock said with his most charming smile; it was as if he were greeting guests at his own funeral.

The hangman coughed—impatiently lifted his cowboy hat and settled it 10 again, a gesture somehow reminiscent of a turkey buzzard huffing, then smoothing its neck feathers—and Hickock, nudged by an attendant, mounted the scaffold steps. "The Lord giveth, the Lord taketh away. Blessed is the name of the Lord," the chaplain intoned, as the rain sound accelerated, as the noose was fitted, and as a delicate black mask was tied around the prisoner's eyes. "May the Lord have mercy on your soul." The trap door opened, and Hickock hung for all to see a full twenty minutes before the prison doctor at last said, "I pronounce this man dead." A hearse, its blazing headlights beaded with rain, drove into the warehouse, and the body, placed on a litter and shrouded under a blanket, was carried to the hearse and out into the night.

Staring after it, Roy Church shook his head: "I never would have believed he had the guts. To take it like he did. I had him tagged a coward." 11

The man to whom he spoke, another detective said, "Aw, Roy. The guy was a punk. A mean bastard. He deserved it." 12

Church, with thoughtful eyes, continued to shake his head. 13

While waiting for the second execution, a reporter and a guard conversed. The reporter said, "This your first hanging?" 14

"I seen Lee Andrews." 15

"This here's my first." 16

"Yeah. How'd you like it?" 17

The reporter pursed his lips. "Nobody in our office wanted the assignment. Me either. But it wasn't as bad as I thought it would be. Just like jumping off a diving board. Only with a rope around your neck." 18

"They don't feel nothing. Drop, snap, and that's it. They don't feel nothing." 19

"Are you sure? I was standing right close. I could hear him gasping for breath." 20

"Uh-huh, but he don't feel nothing. Wouldn't be humane if he did." 21

"Well. And I suppose they feed them a lot of pills. Sedatives." 22

"Hell, no. Against the rules. Here comes Smith." 23

"Gosh, I didn't know he was a shrimp." 24

"Yeah, he's little. But so is a tarantula." 25

As he was brought into the warehouse, Smith recognized his old foe, Dewey; he stopped chewing a hunk of Doublemint gum he had in his mouth, and grinned and winked at Dewey, jaunty and mischievous. But after the warden asked if he had anything to say, his expression was sober. His sensitive eyes gazed gravely at the surrounding faces, swerved up to the shadowy hangman, then downward to his own manacled hands. He looked at his fingers, which were stained with ink and paint, for he'd spent his final three years on Death Row painting self-portraits and pictures of children, usually the children of inmates who supplied him with photographs of their seldom-seen progeny. "I think,' he said, "it's a helluva thing to take a life in this manner. I don't believe in capital punishment, morally or legally. Maybe I had something to contribute, something—" His assurance faltered; shy- 26 ness blurred his voice, lowered it to a just audible level. "It would be meaningless to apologize for what I did. Even inappropriate. But I do. I apologize."

Steps, noose, mask; but before the mask was adjusted, the prisoner spat   27
his chewing gum into the chaplain's outstretched palm. Dewey shut his eyes; he kept them shut until he heard the thud-snap that announces a rope-broken neck. Like the majority of American law-enforcement officials, Dewey is certain that capital punishment is a deterrent to violent crime, and he felt that if ever the penalty had been earned, the present instance was it. The preceding execution had not disturbed him, he had never had much use for Hickock, who seemed to him "a small-time chiseler who got out of his depth, empty and worthless." But Smith, though he was the true murderer, aroused another response, for Perry possessed a quality, the aura of an exiled animal, a creature walking wounded, that the detective could not disregard. He remembered his first meeting with Perry in the interrogation room at Police Headquarters in Las Vegas—the dwarfish boy-man seated in the metal chair, his small booted feet not quite brushing the floor. And when Dewey now opened his eyes, that is what he saw: the same childish feet, tilted, dangling.

QUESTIONS ON MEANING AND CONTENT

1. What do Dewey's reactions to the surroundings, the atmosphere and the executions themselves tell us about his character? Consider his reaction to the appropriateness of the warehouse as a place to die, his reaction to the small talk of the witnesses, and the differences in his own reactions to the first and second hangings.

2. What is the nature of the talk among the witnesses? What does the talk suggest about them? To what degree is the talk conditioned by the situation? Do you think they talk as they do because they are hardened and lacking in emotion, or do they talk in this way because they aren't hardened? Explain. Why is the conversation in paragraph 2 described as "self-consciously casual"?

3. Before he is executed, Smith tells the witnesses how "meaningless" and "inappropriate" it would be to apologize for what he had done. Yet he does apologize. In your view, was he right? That is, is an apology under the circumstances meaningless and inappropriate? Explain. Compare Smith's comments with those of Hickock. In what fundamental way do they differ?

How do they represent two ways of looking back at the crime and toward the punishment that is only moments away?

QUESTIONS ABOUT RHETORICAL STRATEGIES

1. This process analysis illustrates that processes can be written from a variety of points of view, based on how we have come to know the process. The process here is explained by an observer. How would this differ from the process guide that a prison warden would follow—a "how to" process? How would it be similar?

2. Does Capote give you some feeling of "being there" as you read this account? If so, how does he accomplish this?

3. Consider this as a followup to question 2: There is a subjective element in Capote's description of the hangings; that is, in addition to showing what took place, he also conveys some sense of the atmosphere in which the process unfolded. What details help create the atmosphere? How much do the conversations among witnesses contribute to the atmosphere?

4. How objectively is this process presented? Are there attempts to influence readers one way or another concerning capital punishment?

5. This process is meant to inform, but could you use the details in this piece to write a process essay showing, in a reasonably complete way, the steps to be followed in carrying out a hanging?

QUESTIONS ON LANGUAGE AND DICTION

1. Notice the large number of comparisons. For example, the hangman is "reminiscent of a turkey buzzard huffing, then smoothing its neck feathers," and one witness comments on Smith's size by comparing him to a tarantula. Do these add to the information in the essay or do they merely contribute to the feeling Capote is associating with the process taking place? What other similes or metaphors appear in the conversations?

2. In paragraph 2, Capote notes that one witness referred to the hangings as "the festivities." What kind of mental or verbal strategies lead to this sort of renaming or relabeling of an event? Why would Capote include this particular conversational detail?

The Maker's Eye: Revising Your Own Manuscripts

DONALD MURRAY

To produce good products, writers must submit themselves to an arduous, often frustrating process. They must write and rewrite and learn to read in a new way. The process is demanding and can be painful, and a good writer will never quite be satisfied with the finished product, according to Donald Murray. Even at the moment when the copy goes to the printer, the good writer is still thinking about one last revision.

When students complete a first draft, they consider the job of writing done—and their teachers too often agree. When professional writers complete a first draft, they usually feel that they are at the start of the writing process. When a draft is completed, the job of writing can begin. 1

That difference in attitude is the difference between amateur and professional, inexperience and experience, journeyman and craftsman. Peter F. Drucker, the prolific business writer, calls his first draft "the zero draft"—after that he can start counting. Most writers share the feeling that the first draft, and all of those which follow, are opportunities to discover what they have to say and how best they can say it. 2

To produce a progression of drafts, each of which says more and says it more clearly, the writer has to develop a special kind of reading skill. In school we are taught to decode what appears on the page as finished writing. Writers, however, face a different category of possibility and responsibility when they read their own drafts. To them the words on the page are never finished. Each can be changed and rearranged, can set off a chain reaction of confusion or clarified meaning. This is a different kind of reading which is possibly more difficult and certainly more exciting. 3

Writers must learn to be their own best enemy. They must accept the criticism of others and be suspicious of it; they must accept the praise of others and be even more suspicious of it. Writers cannot depend on others. They must detach themselves from their own pages so that they can apply both their caring and their craft to their own work. 4

Such detachment is not easy. Science fiction writer Ray Bradbury supposedly puts each manuscript away for a year to the day and then rereads it as a stranger. Not many writers have the discipline or the time to do this. We 5 must read when our judgment may be at its worst, when we are close to the euphoric moment of creation.

Then the writer, counsels novelist Nancy Hale, "should be critical of everything that seems to him most delightful in his style. He should excise what he most admires, because he wouldn't thus admire it if he weren't . . . in a sense protecting it from criticism." John Ciardi, the poet, adds, "The last act of the writing must be to become one's own reader. It is, I suppose, a schizophrenic process, to begin passionately and to end critically, to begin hot and to end cold; and, more important, to be passion-hot and critic-cold at the same time."   6

Most people think that the principal problem is that writers are too proud of what they have written. Actually, a greater problem for most professional writers is one shared by the majority of students. They are overly critical, think everything is dreadful, tear up page after page, never complete a draft, see the task as hopeless.   7

The writer must learn to read critically but constructively, to cut what is bad, to reveal what is good. Eleanor Estes, the children's book author, explains: "The writer must survey his work critically, cooly, as though he were a stranger to it. He must be willing to prune, expertly and hard-heartedly. At the end of each revision, a manuscript may look . . . worked over, torn apart, pinned together, added to, deleted from, words changed and words changed back. Yet the book must maintain its original freshness and spontaneity."   8

Most readers underestimate the amount of rewriting it usually takes to produce spontaneous reading. This is a great disadvantage to the student writer, who sees only a finished product and never watches the craftsman who takes the necessary step back, studies the work carefully, returns to the task, steps back, returns, steps back, again and again. Anthony Burgess, one of the most prolific writers in the English-speaking world, admits, "I might revise a page twenty times." Ronald Dahl, the popular children's writer, states, "By the time I'm nearing the end of a story, the first part will have been reread and altered and corrected at least 150 times. . . . Good writing is essentially rewriting. I am positive of this."   9

Rewriting isn't virtuous. It isn't something that ought to be done. It is simply something that most writers find they have to do to discover what they have to say and how to say it. It is a condition of the writer's life.   10

There are, however, a few writers who do little formal rewriting, primarily because they have the capacity and experience to create and review a large number of invisible drafts in their minds before they approach the   11 page. And some writers slowly produce finished pages, performing all the tasks of revision simultaneously, page by page, rather than draft by draft. But it is still possible to see the sequence followed by most writers most of the time in rereading their own work.

Most writers scan their drafts first, reading as quickly as possible to catch 12 the larger problems of subject and form, then move in closer and closer as they read and write, and reread and rewrite.

The first thing writers look for in their drafts is *information*. They know 13 that a good piece of writing is built from specific, accurate, and interesting information. The writer must have an abundance of information from which to construct a readable piece of writing.

Next writers look for *meaning* in the information. The specifics must 14 build to a pattern of significance. Each piece of specific information must carry the reader toward meaning.

Writers reading their own drafts are aware of *audience*. They put them- 15 selves in the reader's situation and make sure that they deliver information which a reader wants to know or needs to know in a manner which is easily digested. Writers try to be sure that they anticipate and answer the questions a critical reader will ask when reading the piece of writing.

Writers make sure that the *form* is appropriate to the subject and the 16 audience. Form, or genre, is the vehicle which carries meaning to the reader, but form cannot be selected until the writer has adequate information to discover its significance and an audience which needs or wants that meaning.

Once writers are sure the form is appropriate, they must then look at the 17 *structure,* the order of what they have written. Good writing is built on a solid framework of logic, argument, narrative, or motivation which runs through the entire piece of writing and holds it together. This is the time when many writers find it most effective to outline as a way of visualizing the hidden spine by which the piece of writing is supported.

The element on which writers may spend a majority of their time is 18 *development.* Each section of a piece of writing must be adequately developed. It must give readers enough information so that they are satisfied. How much information is enough? That's as difficult as asking how much garlic belongs in a salad. It must be done to taste, but most beginning writers underdevelop, underestimating the reader's hunger for information.

As writers solve development problems, they often have to consider 19 questions of *dimension*. There must be a pleasing and effective proportion among all the parts of the piece of writing. There is a continual process of subtracting and adding to keep the piece of writing in balance.

Finally, writers have to listen to their own voices. *Voice* is the force which 20
drives a piece of writing forward. It is an expression of the writer's authority
and concern. It is what is between the words on the page, what glues the
piece of writing together. A good piece of writing is always marked by a
consistent, individual voice.

As writers read and reread, write and rewrite, they move closer and 21
closer to the page until they are doing line-by-line editing. Writers read their
own pages with infinite care. Each sentence, each line, each clause, each
phrase, each word, each mark of punctuation, each section of white space
between the type has to contribute to the clarification of meaning.

Slowly the writer moves from word to word, looking through language 22
to see the subject. As a word is changed, cut, or added, as a construction is
rearranged, all the words used before that moment and all those that follow
that moment must be considered and reconsidered.

Writers often read aloud at this stage of the editing process, muttering or 23
whispering to themselves, calling on the ear's experience with language.
Does this sound right—or that? Writers edit, shifting back and forth from
eye to page to ear to page. I find I must do this careful editing in short runs,
no more than fifteen or twenty minutes at a stretch, or I become too kind
with myself. I begin to see what I hope is on the page, not what actually is on
the page.

This sounds tedious if you haven't done it, but actually it is fun. Making 24
something right is immensely satisfying, for writers begin to learn what they
are writing about by writing. Language leads them to meaning, and there is
the joy of discovery, of understanding, of making meaning clear as the
writer employs the technical skills of language.

Words have double meanings, even triple and quadruple meanings. 25
Each word has its own potential for connotation and denotation. And when
writers rub one word against the other, they are often rewarded with a
sudden insight, an unexpected clarification.

The maker's eye moves back and forth from word to phrase to sentence 26
to paragraph to sentence to phrase to word. The maker's eye sees the need
for variety and balance, for a firmer structure, for a more appropriate form. It
peers into the interior of the paragraph, looking for coherence, unity, and
emphasis, which make meaning clear.

I learned something about the process when my first bifocals were 27
prescribed. I had ordered a larger section of the reading portion of the glass
because of my work, but even so, I could not contain my eyes within this
new limit of vision. And I still find myself taking off my glasses and bending
my nose towards the page, for my eyes unconsciously flick back and forth

across the page, back to another page, forward to still another, as I try to see each evolving line in relation to every other line.

When does this process end? Most writers agree with the great Russian 28 writer Tolstoy, who said, "I scarcely ever reread my published writings, if by chance I came across a page, it always strikes me: all this must be rewritten; this is how I should have written it."

The maker's eye is never satisfied, for each word has the potential to 29 ignite new meaning. This article has been twice written all the way through the writing process, and it was published four years ago. Now it is to be republished in a book. The editors made a few small suggestions, and then I read it with my maker's eye. Now it has been re-edited, re-revised, re-read, re-re-edited, for each piece of writing to the writer is full of potential and alternatives.

A piece of writing is never finished. It is delivered to a deadline, torn out 30 of the typewriter on demand, sent off with a sense of accomplishment and shame and pride and frustration. If only there were a couple more days, time for just another run at it, perhaps then . . .

QUESTIONS ON MEANING AND CONTENT

1. Does the talk about the work required to write well make you apprehensive about future writing assignments? What comfort can be derived from knowing that even professional writers have to devote so much time, attention, and labor to writing well?

2. Here and there in the essay Murray asks direct questions, such as, "How much information is enough?" What are other questions he asks? Have you found yourself asking any of these while working on a writing assignment?

3. What specific things have you learned from the essay that you can apply in your own writing?

4. The author says in paragraph 18 that "most beginning writers underdevelop" their writing. He attributes this to "underestimating the reader's hunger for information." What does *hunger* imply about readers? Do you think this implication is always accurate? Would you suggest that another word be substituted for *hunger*? What?

5. In paragraph 3, Murray says that the reading we do in the ordinary course of events is not the kind of reading that writers must learn to do when reading their own writing. What does he mean by this? How does he go on to define the kind of reading required of writers?

QUESTIONS ABOUT RHETORICAL STRATEGIES

1. Murray begins the actual process analysis in paragraph 12. In what ways does the long introduction prepare readers for the process?

2. This essay was originally written for *The Writer,* a magazine read by both established and aspiring writers. Would the content of the essay be helpful to both groups? In what ways?

3. Murray quotes other writers to illustrate the points he makes. Do these quotations merely serve to make his points more legitimate and, therefore, more acceptable to readers? Or do they also offer something else to readers? Examine some of the quotations carefully and then draw conclusions concerning how these comments might have value for established writers, secure because of their successes, and aspiring writers, unsatisfied by their few successes or frustrated and insecure from a failure to publish at all.

4. In paragraphs 12 through 20, how much of the writing is devoted to identifying the steps in the process and how much to developing the steps by interpreting or explaining?

QUESTIONS ON LANGUAGE AND DICTION

1. Examine the sentence that forms paragraph 12. Notice the two transitions, *first* and *then,* which Murray uses to place process steps in chronological order. In paragraphs 13 through 20, what other transitions do you find that help guide readers through the steps. (Include longer transitions as well as single words, and don't confine your search to sentences that open paragraphs. Look at each sentence.) How many of these transitions do you find? How many are single words and how many are longer units? Did you find more or fewer transitions than you expected? Did you find any, especially among those of several words, that wouldn't have occurred to you as possibilities if you hadn't found them here? Which ones?

2. Is it fair to say that the essay does not contain many words that you would have to look up in a dictionary? If so, do you think this is because professional writers have not created specialized vocabularies to use in talking about their craft, words that someone only casually interested in writing might not recognize? Or do you think that such words exist but Murray chose not to use them? Explain. Remember, the essay was written for writers, so you can safely assume that the bulk of the audience would have understood the specialized terms.

3. What are some of the words whose meanings you did have to check? Paragraph 25 uses the words *connotation* and *denotation*. What do these words mean?

The Thrones

TOM WOLFE

What happens when rugged individualists accustomed to operating alone in dangerous situations find themselves in a passive role where others make the decisions, take the actions, and control their destiny? Tom Wolfe addresses this question in describing jet fighter pilots training to become astronauts.

In the eyes of the engineers assigned to Project Mercury the training of   1
the astronauts would be the easy task on the list. Naturally you needed a
man with the courage to ride on top of a rocket, and you were grateful that
such men existed. Nevertheless, their training was not a very complicated
business. The astronaut would have little to do in a Mercury flight except
stand the strain, and the engineers had devised what psychologists referred
to as "a graded series of exposures" to take care of that. No, the difficult, the
challenging, the dramatic, the pioneering part of space flight, as the engineers saw it, was the technology.

It was only thanks to a recent invention, the high-speed electronic   2
computer, that Project Mercury was feasible at all. There was an analogy
here with the great Admiral of the Uncharted Seas himself, Columbus. It
was only thanks to a recent invention of his day, the magnetic compass, that
Columbus had dared to sail across the Atlantic. Until then ships had stayed
close to the great land masses for even the longest voyages. Likewise,
putting a man into space the quick and dirty way without high-speed
computers was unthinkable. Such computers had not been in production
before 1951, and yet here it was, 1960, and engineers were already devising
systems for guiding rockets into space, through the use of computers built
into the engines and connected to accelerometers, for monitoring the temperature, pressure, oxygen supply, and other vital conditions of the Mercury capsule and for triggering safety procedures automatically—meaning
they were creating, with computers, systems in which machines could
communicate with one another, make decisions, take action, all with tremendous speed and accuracy . . .

Oh, genius-engineers!   3

Ah, yes, there was such a thing as self-esteem among engineers. It may   4
not have been as grandiose as that of fighter jocks . . . nevertheless, many

was the steaming encephalitic summertime Saturday night at Langley when some NASA engineer would start knocking back that good sweet Virginia A.B.C. store bourbon on the patio and letting his ego out for a little romp, like a growling red dog.

The glorification of the astronauts had really gotten out of control! In the   5 world of science—and Project Mercury was supposed to be a scientific enterprise—pure scientists ranked first and engineers ranked second and the test subjects of experiments ranked so low that one seldom thought about them. But here the test subjects . . . were national heroes! They created a zone of awe and reverence wherever they set foot! Everyone else, whether physicist, biologist, doctor, psychiatrist, or engineer, was a mere attendant.

At the outset it had been understood—it didn't even require   6 comment—that the astronauts would be just that: test subjects in an experiment. Mercury was an adaptation of the Air Force's Man in Space Soonest concept, in which you would attach biosensors to your human subject, seal him up in a capsule, propel him into space ballistically—i.e., like an artillery shell—and bring him back to earth with completely automatic guidance and see how he made out. In November 1959, six months after the seven astronauts were chosen, Randy Lovelace and Scott Crossfield presented a paper at an aerospace medical symposium in which they said that biomedical research was "the sole purpose of the ride," so far as having an astronaut on board was concerned. They added that an aerodynamic space vehicle, such as the proposed X–15B or X–20, would require "a much more highly trained pilot." Since he was involved in the X–15 project, Crossfield had his own ax to grind, but what he and Lovelace were saying was perfectly obvious to any engineer who knew the difference between ballistic and aerodynamic space vehicles. In short, the astronaut in Project Mercury would not be a pilot under any conventional definition.

Even as late as the summer of 1960, at an Armed Forces–National Re-   7 search Council conference at Woods Hole, Massachusetts, on "the training of astronauts," various engineers and scientists from outside NASA thought nothing of describing the Mercury rocket-capsule vehicle as a fully automated system in which "the astronaut does not need to turn a hand." They would say, "The astronaut has been added to a system as a redundant component." (A *redundant component!*) If the automatic system broke down, he might step in as a repairman or manual conductor. Above all, of course, he would be wired with biosensors and a microphone to see how a human being responded to the stress of the flight. That would be his main function. There were psychologists who advised against using pilots at all—and this was more than a year after the famous Mercury Seven had been chosen. The pilot's, particularly the hot pilot's, main psychological bulwark under stress was his knowledge that he controlled the ship and could always *do something* ("I've tried A! I've tried B! I've tried C!" . . .)This obsession with active control, it was argued, would only tend to cause problems on Mercury flights. What was required was a man whose main talent was for *doing nothing* under stress. Some suggested using a new breed of military flier, the radar man, the Air Force Strategic Air Command radar observer or the Navy radar intercept officer, a man who had experience riding in the rear in high-performance aircraft under combat conditions and doing nothing but reading the radar, come what may, abandoning all control of the craft (and protection of his own life) to someone else, the pilot ("I looked over at Robinson—and he was staring at the radar like a *zombie!*"). An experienced zombie would do fine. In fact, considerable attention had been given to a plan to anesthetize or tranquillize the astronauts, not to keep them from panicking, but just to make sure they would lie there peacefully with their sensors on and not *do something* that would ruin the flight.

The scientists and engineers took it for granted that the training of the   8
astronauts would be unlike anything ordinarily thought of as flight training. Flight training consisted of teaching a man how to take certain actions. He was taught how to control an unfamiliar craft or how to put a familiar craft through unfamiliar maneuvers, such as bombing runs or carrier landings. On the other hand, the only actions the astronauts would have to learn how to take would be to initiate the emergency procedures in the case of a bad rocket launch or a bad landing and to step in as a backup (redundant component) if the automatic control system failed to hold the heatshield in the correct position prior to re-entry through the earth's atmosphere. The astronaut would not be able to control the path or the speed of the capsule at all. A considerable part of his training would be what was known as de-conditioning, de-sensitizing, or adapting out fears. There was a principle in psychology that maintained that "bad habits, including overstrong emotionality, can be eliminated by a graded series of exposures to the anxiety-arousing stimulus." That was what much of astronaut training was to be. The rocket launch was regarded as a novel and possibly disorienting event, in part *because* the astronaut would have no control over it whatsoever. So they had devised "a graded series of exposures." They took the seven men to the Navy's human centrifuge facility in Johnsville, Pennsylvania. The centrifuge looked like a Wild Bolo ride; it had a fifty-foot arm with a cockpit, or gondola, on the end of it, and the arm could be whirled around at astonishing speeds, great enough to put up to 40 g's of pressure on the rider

inside the gondola, one g being equal to the force of gravity. The high g-forces generated by combat aircraft in dives and turns during the Second World War had sometimes caused blackouts, red-outs, gray-outs, or made it impossible for pilots to lift their hands to the controls; the giant centrifuge at Johnsville had been built to explore this new problem of high-speed flight. By 1959 the machine had been computerized and turned into a simulator capable of duplicating the g-forces and accelerations of any form of flight, even rocket flight. The astronaut was helped into his full pressure suit, with his biosensors attached and his rectal thermometer inserted, and then placed into the gondola, in a contoured seat molded for his body, where-upon all the wires, hoses, and microphones he would have in actual flight were hooked up, and the gondola was depressurized to five pounds per square inch, as it would be in space flight. The interior of the gondola had been converted into a replica of the Mercury capsule's interior, with all the switches and console displays. The taped noise of an actual Redstone rocket firing was played over the astronaut's headset, and the ride began. Using the computers, the engineers would put the man through an entire Mercury flight profile. The centrifuge built up the g-forces at precisely the same rate they would build up in flight, up to six or seven g's, whereupon the g-forces would suddenly drop off, as they would in flight as the capsule went over the top of its arc, and the astronaut experienced a tumbling sensation, as he would, presumably, in flight. All the while the astronaut would be required to push a few switches, as he would in actual flight, and to talk to a mock flight controller, forcing his words out into the microphone, no matter how great the pressure of the g-forces on his chest. The centrifuge could also duplicate the pressures of deceleration a man would experience during the return through the earth's atmosphere.

To get the seven men used to weightlessness, they took them on   9
parabolic rides in the cargo holds of C–131 transports and backseat in F–100Fs. When the jet came up over the top of the arc of the parabola, the subject would experience from fifteen to forty-five seconds of weightless-ness. This was the only flying scheduled for the astronauts' entire training program; and they were, of course, merely passengers on board, as they would be in the Mercury flights.

The only way the astronaut would be able to move the capsule in the   10
slightest would be to fire hydrogen-peroxide thrusters during the interval of weightlessness, tipping or swinging the capsule this way or that, in order to get a particular view out the portholes, for example. NASA built a machine, the ALFA trainer, to accustom each trainee to the sensation. He sat in a seat resting on air bearings and used a hand controller to make it pitch up and

down or yaw back and forth. On a screen in front of him, where the capsule's periscope screen would be, aerial photographs and films of the Cape, the Atlantic Ocean, Cuba, Grand Bahama Island, Abaco, all the landmarks, rolled by . . . and veered off as the astronaut pitched or yawed, just as they would in actual flight. The ALFA even made a whooshing sound like that of hydrogen-peroxide thrusters when the astronaut pushed the stick.

By mid-1960 the engineers had developed the "procedures trainer,"   11 which was in fact a simulator. There were identical procedures trainers at the Cape and at Langley. At the Cape the trainer was in Hangar S. It was there that the astronaut spent his long day's training. He climbed into a cubicle and sat in a seat that was aimed straight up at the roof. The back of the seat was flat on the floor of the cubicle, so that the astronaut rested on his back. He looked up at a replica of a console that would be used in the Mercury capsule. It was as if he were on top of the rocket, with his face aimed at the sky. The console was wired to a bank of computers. About twenty feet behind the astronaut, on the floor of Hangar S, sat a technician at another console, feeding simulated problems into the system.

The technician would start off saying, "Count is at T minus fifty seconds   12 and counting."

From inside the trainer, over his microphone, the astronaut would   13 answer: "Roger."

"Check your periscope—fully retracted?"   14

"Periscope retracted."   15

"Ready switch on?"   16

"Ready switch on."   17

"T minus ten seconds. Minus eight . . . seven . . . six . . . five . . .   18 four . . . three . . . two . . . one . . . Fire!"

Inside the trainer the dials in front of the astronaut would start indicating   19 that he was on his way, and he was supposed to start reading the gauges and reporting to the ground. He would say, "Clock is operating . . . okay, twenty seconds . . . one thousand feet [altitude] . . . one-point-five g's . . . Trajectory is good . . . Twelve thousand feet, one-point-nine g's . . . Inner cabin pressure is five p.s.i. . . . . Altitude forty-four thousand, g-level two-point-seven . . . one hundred thousand feet at two minutes and five seconds . . ." The instructor might pick this point to hit a button on his console marked "oxygen." A red warning light marked O_2EMERG would light up, and the astronaut would say: "Cabin pressure decreasing! . . . Oxygen is apparently leaking! . . . It's still leaking . . . Switching to emergency reserve . . ." The astronaut could throw a switch that brought more oxygen into the simulator system—i.e., into its computer calculations—but the instructor could hit his "oxygen" button again, and that meant that the leak was continuing, and the astronaut would say: "Still leaking . . . It's approaching zero-flow rate . . . Abort because of oxygen leak! Abort! Abort!" Then the astronaut would hit a button, and a button marked MAYDAY would light up red on the instructor's console. In actual flight the escape tower was supposed to fire at this point, pulling the capsule free of the rocket and bringing it down by parachute.

The astronauts spent so much time hitting the abort handle in the 20 procedures trainer that it got to the point where it seemed as if they were training for an abort rather than for a launch. There was very little action that an astronaut could take in a Mercury capsule, other than to abort the flight and save his own life. So he was not being trained to *fly* the capsule. He was being trained to ride in it. In a "graded series of exposures" he was being introduced to all sights, sounds, and sensations he might conceivably experience. Then he was reintroduced to them, day after day, until the Mercury capsule and all its hums, g-forces, window views, panel displays, lights, buttons, switches, and peroxide squirts became as familiar, as routine, as workaday as an office. All flight training had a certain amount of desensitizing built into it. When a Navy pilot practiced carrier landings on the outline of a flight deck painted on an airfield, it was hoped that the maneuver might also desensitize his normal fear of landing a hurtling machine in such a small space. Nevertheless, he was there chiefly in order to learn to land the machine. Not until Project Mercury had there been a flight training program so long and detailed, so sophisticated, and yet so heavily devoted to desensitizing the trainee, to adapting out man's ordinary fears, and enabling one to think and use his hands normally in a novel environment.

Oh, all of this had been well known at the outset! . . . so much so that 21 the original NASA selection committee had been afraid that the military test pilots they were interviewing would regard the job as boring or distasteful. Since they figured they needed six astronauts for Mercury, they had considered training twelve—on the assumption that half of them would resign once they fully understood how passive their role would be. And now, in 1960, they began to realize that they had been correct; or halfway, in any case. The boys were, indeed, finding the role of biomedical passenger in an automated pod, i.e., the role of human guinea pig, distasteful. That much had proved to be true. The boys' response, however, had not been resignation or anything close to it. No, the engineers now looked on, eyebrows arched, as the guinea pigs set about . . . *altering the experiment.*

QUESTIONS ON MEANING AND CONTENT

1. The author describes the process of the astronaut in training to show that the nature of the tasks required were the opposite of those required for fighter pilots. The question raised by this training was how people with character traits, mental set, and so forth, tailored to piloting jet fighters could adapt themselves to something requiring the opposite traits. What is the basic difference between the roles of fighter pilot and astronaut?

2. How was the process of "desensitizing" supposed to make this change of roles possible? What theory about human behavior lies behind desensitizing—what, supposedly makes it work?

3. Engineers and scientists who create the technology for the latest in jet aircraft might expect to generate less public esteem than the jet pilots who test and fly the planes. After all, the pilots face the dangers of high speed flight with no direct help from the ground. But with rockets and space capsules, the scientists and engineers on the ground control the flights. Yet the astronauts in their passive roles still receive public esteem while the scientists and engineers remain unknown to the public. Does Wolfe account for this or does he merely mention this odd circumstance? How would you account for this?

QUESTIONS ABOUT RHETORICAL STRATEGIES

1. Not only would most readers be unfamiliar with the processes explained by Wolfe but most also would be unfamiliar with the complex mechanisms used in the processes. How does Wolfe handle this problem and make the processes clear to the audience?

2. As a follow up to the previous question, examine paragraphs 11–20. What evidence do you find in the introduction to this process (paragraph 11) that the author is working very carefully to make things clear to a lay audience? In the process itself (paragraphs 12–19), what strategies does Wolfe use to keep readers aware of what the astronaut is doing in relation to the complex machinery? What information does the conclusion (paragraph 21) provide for the reader? Specifically, how does the conclusion add information that would help the reading audience to better understand the process?

3. Notice that the process described in paragraphs 8–10 is handled differently from the one you have just examined. What is that difference and how do you account for it?

QUESTIONS ON LANGUAGE AND DICTION

1. In paragraph 7, an astronaut is called "a redundant component" of the rocket and capsule. What does this phrase mean? What is its tone? What attitude toward the astronauts does it suggest?

2. How does Wolfe use the analogy to Columbus to explain why the first manned space flights became possible? What does this add to a reader's understanding of how the high-speed computer made space flight possible?

3. What is the tone of this piece of writing? Does Wolfe's language suggest that he stands in awe of the astronauts? If not, what does his attitude toward them seem to be? Explain.

4. Check the meanings of any of the following words that are unfamiliar to you: *bulwark, centrifuge, encephalitic, parabola, yaw.*

WRITING SCENARIOS

1. You are a member of a consumer group that monitors the merchants and advertisers in your community to make sure their practices are fair and honest. One of your tasks is to monitor television advertising and report on a new aspect at each meeting. Because your organization publishes the reports of members in its newsletter, you usually write your reports in essay form. For your next report, you have decided to write a process essay based roughly on the pattern that Royko uses to describe the various processes police officers employ to make extra money. (He describes several specific processes that are a part of the general process of making money on the job.) For your essay, explain several specific processes used by television advertisers for selling the same product. You could use fast foods as a topic or be more specific and talk about hamburgers or double burgers. You may use any other topic so long as different companies are involved and either variations on a theme are apparent in the ads or distinctly different approaches to the ads are used. You can treat your subject in a formal, serious manner, or you can treat the subject satirically. In the latter case, you would be writing for an audience who views either the products or the ads with amusement or light contempt, or perhaps even scorn. Remember, your audience is made up of interested citizens.

2. To help pay your way through college, you often write articles for a local magazine that publishes stories and news about your community. The publication specializes in stories about local citizens who are interesting or do interesting things. You have decided to write an essay to *inform* readers about a process performed by someone unusual like this. Every community, large or small (including college campuses), contains people who do unusual things. There are ice sculptors, wood carvers, bird watchers, people who keep bees on rooftops, people who restore furniture or old cars, people who collect odd things, people who dress up like Abe Lincoln every February, people who explore caves or climb mountains, people who keep track of the sightings of unidentified flying objects or big-footed creatures, and so on. There are also people with unusual occupations or businesses: auctioneers, iron workers, divers, scrap dealers, race-car drivers. Find out who some of these people are; arrange to talk with one; and after gathering information, write an essay that informs readers about how this person goes about pursuing the interest or occupation. Your paper should also include something about the "interest factors" that make the activity enjoyable. Although a wide range of readers subscribe to the magazine you write for, you will want to let your subject and your good judgment tell you something about your specific audience. Your topic could be one that only young people have much interest in; it could be of more interest to parents or older people; it might interest particularly those people who collect something or who have thought about doing so; or the topic could interest many people, no matter what their ages, special interests, or education.

3. The chamber of commerce in your hometown is preparing an informational booklet for newcomers to the region. The booklet will discuss where to go, what to see, and how to cope with problems specific to your geographic region. You have been asked to contribute a short essay explaining a process related to your local geography. If you live in an area of heavy snowfalls, for example, you might analyze the process of how to cope with heavy snowfalls, how to drive on icy roads, or how to be sure your car will start in the winter. Or you might explain what precautions to take when driving off-road on sandy soil or on a desert highway; or how to live through the black-fly period; or how to survive along with millions of mosquitoes; or how to control cockroaches; or how to deal with 100-degree-plus days. Look for a subject that people would not know much about unless they had experienced the same conditions that are common to you because of where you live. Look for something that might give outsiders trouble. You are presenting a guide detailing how to cope with something in your area;

therefore, your audience is anyone who might move to or visit your area for an extended period of time. Remember too, however, that you don't want to present your locality in an unattractive way.

4. You have been asked to explain a process that you have performed often enough to have developed a reasonable expertise in. That is, you are a specialist writing to a nonspecialist; you are a person experienced in this particular process and writing to someone with no experience but who wants, or is likely to want, to repeat the process. Be sure the process is the kind that a reader wouldn't attempt without help. Thus, even though you know the secrets of how to put the best possible shine on shoes, don't write about this or similar processes since any reader could shine shoes well enough without the aid of a written process. Beyond this, the particular process doesn't matter. What does matter is that you have some expertise in the process: The process could be anything from surfboard sailing, to tying a trout fly, to tuning up an automobile, with innumerable possibilities in between depending upon your own experiences. For this writing scenario, you will have to devise your own purpose and audience.

5. The student government and the counseling center at your school are sponsoring a "Study Skills Day," during which students and professors will give presentations about various issues related to improving study skills. There will be presentations on how to take effective notes, how to study for an exam, how to budget your time, and how to write essay exams. The president of the student government has asked you to make one of the presentations on a subject related to study skills. Your purpose is to explain how to perform the process you have chosen. Your audience is made up of your fellow students, the faculty, and the administration at your school.

6. Many students at your university live in off-campus housing and have to deal with less-than-ideal landlords. Because of your experience as one of these students, you have become very active in the local tenants' rights groups. In fact, you've become something of an expert in this area, and because of that the student government has asked you to prepare a basic booklet of student-tenants' rights, including how to use legal pressure to get your landlord to live up to his or her responsibilities. Your essay will become part of a student handbook on how to use all legal and political means available to obtain tenants' rights, from ways of getting landlords to make repairs to determining fair rents. To research this, you might check with your student government and local tenants' organizations and fellow students who have had problems.

7. You've been working as a lab assistant for two years in one of the computer labs around campus. For the thousandth time you've just explained how to perform a simple procedure involving one of the software programs used in the lab. To save yourself time, you've decided to prepare a brief user's manual that will demonstrate a simple procedure in either word processing, BASIC, Visicalc, or a graphics program that is most frequently asked about. For instance, you might want to instruct the user on how to boot up Visicalc and enter numerical and nonnumerical data and perform simple arithmetic operations. You will have to decide on how to limit the procedure so that it makes sense by itself and becomes a discrete unit of instruction. For this piece of process writing, you will, of course, have to be knowledgeable about some aspect of computers. Assuming that knowledge, this scenario takes for granted that you will use your imagination in deciding on the subject matter to write about. Your audience will be students who are in a beginners computer class.

EIGHT

ANALYZING
CAUSE AND EFFECT

People use **cause and effect analysis** to explain why things happen, often beginning with an event and then attempting to explain what caused it. After an airplane crash, experts examine the wreckage, listen to flight recordings, interview eye witnesses, and eventually issue a report explaining what caused the crash. Frequently, the experts are uncertain about the exact cause, or point to several possible causes. This is understandable because causes are frequently difficult to determine, and complex events rarely result from a single cause. Asking questions about causes is an important step to finding answers. If the crash investigators find evidence that an instrument failed to work properly, they ask additional questions to find related causes. Did the pilot mention the instrument in radio messages? When was it mentioned? What actions were taken to compensate for the faulty instrument? What compensating actions could have been taken? Was the pilot's judgment a cause? Were the work habits or judgments of technicians responsible for maintaining and checking the instrument a cause?

The answers to these questions would depend upon the circumstances of the particular crash. However, investigators would try to determine the *immediate cause* of the crash in addition to identifying remote or *contributing causes*. Assuming that the instrument had actually failed, would that inevitably lead to a plane crash? Answering that would require a comparison with similar situations. Had other pilots safely landed their planes when the same instrument failed under similar flight conditions? Did this pilot take measures to deal with the emergency? Were these measures the kind a skilled pilot would be expected to take? In short, what was the immediate cause of the crash? Instrument failure or the pilot's failure to take proper countermeasures?

Such questions are not easy to answer, given the scanty evidence available after plane crashes. But this example illustrates the care that has to be taken in analyzing **causes.** Airline crashes are not experiments that can be repeated in order to get a clearer view of causes, and many of the cause-and-effect relationships that you may be called on to analyze are similar. Most involve a number of remote or contributing causes, even if the immediate cause is apparent. For example, the wind chimes on a porch tinkle when the wind causes the pendants to bump against each other. It is easy enough to pinpoint the wind as the immediate cause of the tinkling. Yet, even such a simple event has many contributing causes. The pendants bump together because they are suspended on strings or something equally flexible. Once the pendants begin bumping one another, the bumping itself helps to keep the pendants in motion. Also, the special quality of the tinkling is caused by the pendant material: steel, brass, bamboo, ceramic, glass. Sticks wrapped in cloth wouldn't work, would not act as a cause of tinkling. Even the air itself, by providing a medium in which sound may travel, is a contributing cause.

In our daily lives, we deal with cause-and-effect situations frequently. Too often, however, we conduct our analysis in a superficial way. Even though we know that causes are complex and usually numerous, a strong tendency is to explain causes quickly and simply. "Why does he behave the way he does?" "Oh, he just wants attention." Or we sometimes prefer debating over causes rather than analyzing them. This produces Monday-morning quarterbacking after the weekend football games. Supporters of the winning team say their quarterback was at his best and the receivers ran perfect pass patterns. These were the causes. Fans of the loser say the pass coverage was poor; the players in the defensive secondary just were not up for the game. Their failure to play up to par was the cause. In the meantime, both coaches and both teams conduct a more thorough analysis by carefully studying game films.

In writing, cause-and-effect must be treated much more carefully than the casual treatment people sometimes give it in day-to-day affairs. You must search out the causes or effects and not be satisfied with discussing only the obvious or immediate ones. If you observed a fisherman land a trout, you might want to identify the lure used and switch to the same one yourself, but it would be foolish to assume offhand that the particular lure was the immediate cause of the catch. You might be better advised to study the successful fisherman's casting techniques or his knowledge of where the fish might be located in certain water conditions.

Also, you will want to reject as causes those events that are merely coincidental. Just because one event happens after another event doesn't mean that the first event caused the second. This is known as the *post hoc, ergo proper hoc* fallacy ("After this, therefore because of this"). For example, robins do not bring spring to northern states just because spring comes shortly after they arrive. As you know, their arrival is an effect of the approach of spring. To say that lightning causes thunder is to overlook the fact that both are effects of other causes. Many times, however, such supposed causes are neither causes nor effects, or they cannot reasonably be shown to be such. This is obvious when people attribute a rainstorm to the fact that they have just washed a car. Conclusions are less certain but highly questionable when a politician attributes defeat at the polls to a critical newspaper article published just before the election. This may or may not have been the cause of the defeat. You would have to gather much evidence before concluding that this was the immediate cause.

Although we have been emphasizing causes in this discussion, it is sometimes equally valuable to concentrate attention on **effects.** This is especially so when the causes are well known or a cause is modified in some controlled way. For example, a company specializing in bringing down old structures with explosives might experiment with special placements of the explosives in order to study the effects. Engineers use wind tunnels to study the effects of air resistance on new body configurations of cars and airplanes. Legislators might pass a new bill on the condition that the effects of the legislation be studied over a period of time. Thus, a cause-and-effect essay could devote major attention to effects stemming from already known causes. Effects are sometimes as difficult to analyze as causes, and people often take actions with little knowledge of what the effects might be. Thus, like an analysis of causes, an analysis of effects can increase a reader's understanding of events.

PREWRITING

It is advisable to begin your **prewriting** by selecting a topic with care. If possible, select several topics, and eventually choose the one you are most knowledgeable about while making certain that the topic is narrow enough to develop thoroughly in a brief essay. A good place to begin your search for a topic is with events from your own experience or events that you were able to observe carefully. Also, consider events that you have learned about from reading or from your education.

We are using the word *event* in a broad sense. An event could be a thought that came to you while you were walking to class so long as the thought occurred because of past happenings or caused you to do something later. An event could be a decision you made, or it could be an automobile accident, a drought, or a flood. It could be something you did where you were the actor, as in quitting a job, or it could be something done to you, as in being fired from a job. Events could be all of these and many other things, too. You can write about events that took place in history or speculate intelligently about future events—for example, the effects that acid rain will have on North America by the year 2000 if no corrective measures are taken. You can write about the causes or effects of an act of violence or of an idea that changed the way people live.

After you have several possible topics, you will want to test them to learn something about their nature. Assuming that each represents an event of some sort, ask "Why did this happen?" or "What resulted because this happened?" Your relationship to the event or your knowledge of it should suggest which question is more important for your purposes. At this stage, you want to determine whether to emphasize causes or effects in your paper. Which question reveals more, the "Why" question or the "What resulted" question? What point do you want to make in writing the paper? Does the point relate primarily to the causes or primarily to the effects? The answer will give you a cause or effect focus for your paper.

Once you have selected a topic, it is best to narrow it as much as you can. If your hometown had been flooded at some time in the past, and you decide to write about the effects of the flood on the lives of the people, then think about limiting your analysis to the effects of the people living on your block, or in your neighborhood, or perhaps on your own family—or, better yet, on *one* member of your family.

Of course, to do a good job in any essay you must understand whom you are writing to and why. Are you writing an article for your school newspaper, examining the effects of excessive drinking on students' study habits? Are you writing a letter to your father explaining what caused the auto accident you just survived? Understanding your exact purpose and audience will help you make many decisions about the style and content of your essay.

After you have narrowed your topic and analyzed your purpose and audience, you are ready to list causes and effects in your prewriting notes. Naturally, you will devote more time to the one which you will emphasize in your essay. Nevertheless, neither causes nor effects exist in isolation, and you cannot analyze one without referring to the other. If your essay explains the effects someone has had on your life, then that person has to be presented to the reader and the connection between the effects and the manner in which they came about will have to be shown.

Try listing causes and effects in more than one fashion to see more clearly what each listing tells you. For example, list them in sequential order, allowing for the fact that two or more causes or effects can sometimes occur simultaneously. Then list causes according to immediate causes, less immediate, and remote. List effects according to their importance, or the degree of impact they had on you or other people or things. Finally, place all the remote or indirect causes on a list and all the minor and seemingly insignificant effects on a separate list.

Seeing causes and effects in these ways can suggest possibilities for development that you may otherwise have overlooked. For example, in analyzing the effects of a serious automobile accident you may discover that a significant effect the accident had on your life came not from the accident itself but from an offhand remark made by a police officer or someone else at the scene. In short, looking at causes and effects from more than one perspective can often provide you with another type of focus—a purpose or thesis for your essay. Your lists may tell you that a sequential approach is the best way to show what you learned from the causes or effects of an event, or isolating the remote causes and minor effects can remind you that small acts often cause horrible events and that small events can have strong effects.

While brainstorming, you can make lists of the important details that will help develop or make clear the various causes and effects to be discussed in the paper. You will want to think of examples that might be used to illustrate important points. Also, you'll want to consider what the audience can be expected to know or not know about the subject, and identify what will have to be defined or explained clearly in consideration of your audience.

Remember, too, that you are not a scientist conducting a carefully controlled experiment. There is no need to analyze all causes or all effects. You may choose to omit some remote causes or insignificant effects depending upon your purpose in writing. At the same time, however, you do not want to oversimplify or merely state causes or effects without showing their relationships carefully. You will want to develop and explain them so that readers can see that they are, in fact, causes and effects that clearly support the purpose of your essay.

The following is a brief heuristic to help you prewrite for your cause-and-effect paper. You may wish to consider these questions and jot down answers to the relevant questions on your notes. Be as specific as possible, but feel free to abbreviate and take shortcuts. These questions are to help you generate specific information to add to your prewriting notes.

Prewriting Questions for Cause and Effect

1. What are the causes and effects making up my topic?
2. Which causes are immediate and which are remote?
3. Which effects are major and which minor?
4. Are any remote causes more important to my topic than their remoteness indicates?
5. Will any minor effects be highly significant to my essay?
6. Which causes or effects will be most significant in developing my essay?
7. Which is the most significant of all causes? All effects?
8. What is my purpose in writing this essay?
9. Will my major emphasis be on causes or effects?
10. How does this emphasis relate to my purpose?
11. What does my purpose tell me about how to organize the body of my paper?
12. How much background will I have to offer in my introduction to prepare readers for the cause-and-effect analysis in the body of the paper?
13. Are there causes or effects that I can omit without distorting events and without weakening the development of my essay?
14. Have I confused any causes with events that are merely coincidental?
15. Have I compiled enough details and examples to make each of my points clearly and effectively?
16. How much can I expect my audience to know about my topic?
17. Do I know what terms or concepts will have to be defined for my audience and what details will require careful explanations to be clear to my audience?
18. How can I make my conclusion add something important to the content and structure of my paper?

ORGANIZING

After you have prewritten thoroughly, you are ready to think of an **organizing** plan for your essay. Your prewriting activities may have suggested a sequential approach to either causes or effects. Or you might want to take up the more immediate causes first and then go on to remote ones. Your purpose in writing should lead you to the proper organizing scheme. For example, if your purpose is to explain why you jump when you hear a siren or get cold chills when you hear metal being cut or pried on, then you could build your paper around the immediate cause: the accident five years ago when you were huddling inside an overturned car, not knowing how badly injured you were, listening to sirens screaming and then to the rescuers cutting and prying the metal to get you out.

Situations similar to the one above are powerful enough in themselves to demand attention wherever they are placed in a paper, but good sense dictates that you wouldn't introduce such a dramatic event abruptly but would lead into it, perhaps sequentially. You would also refer back to the even in some way while discussing effects. Such situations allow you to highlight causes that, on the surface, seem minor—the hour you spent convincing your mother that John was a safe driver because of his racing experience or how just two beers had blurred your judgment enough so that you accepted an invitation to a joy ride that you would ordinarily have turned down. These can be used to cast forward to the accident or look backward to it; that is, they can be placed before or after it in the body of your paper.

Either arrangement offers advantages, and each could suggest a thesis. Placed early in the paper, these minor causes could show that something that seems exciting, something that you are eager to do, can bring about a tragic effect: They can lead to an event whose bad effects will never leave you. Placed after the accident, the minor cause could support a variation of this thesis—that lying on your back in a hospital and thinking about the effects of a major disaster led you to understand for the first time that one's involvement in disasters can develop from remote, seemingly insignificant causes.

In other words, your purpose in writing should guide your organization. Listing causes and effects under more than one heading should help generate a purpose for your essay. The purpose then should determine how you present them in your paper. If you are showing what you learned from causes or effects, then you can identify the ones of most significance to that lesson and arrange them accordingly, no matter whether they are immediate or remote, major or minor.

The nature of your event and your purpose should help you construct an introduction. One topic may require more background information than another. You may have to offer a description of your town in relation to a river to enable readers to better understand the causes and effects of the flood. You will also want to establish your thesis in the introduction, explaining, for example, that drought may merely inconvenience a city dweller but may ruin a farmer, or that some people have to experience tragic events before taking seriously the small events that set the stage for them.

By this time in the semester you have had much experience with both introductions and conclusions. You know that the introduction prepares the reader for the information presented in the body of the paper. Thus, an introduction includes necessary background details and explains your thesis or purpose in writing—unless a strong reason exists for holding this from the reader until a later point. A conclusion offers the opportunity to strengthen your paper by summarizing important points, stressing your thesis, or reminding readers of why or how the information presented will be useful to them.

If you yourself know and can explain what you have tried to do in your introduction and conclusion as well as why you have organized the body as you have, then your paper will probably be sound in structure. Knowing what you did at each stage and why are signs of thoughtful organization. By the time you finish your prewriting and organizing activities, you should be able to explain each of these why's.

WRITING

Begin to **write** only after you have compiled sufficient details and have devised an organizing plan. You can use your details and plan as guides so that you are able to write quickly and without interruption. Of course, you can address any revision or proofreading concerns while you are writing the first draft, but there is no need to labor over fine points at this time; you can save them for the revising stage.

If you discover that you somehow overlooked an important detail in prewriting, it is a good idea to make a check or a brief note to remind yourself to come back and work out the oversight while revising. Try not to let anything get in the way of producing a first draft with reasonable speed.

Also, try to monitor the amount of detail you are using as you write. If you made good notes during prewriting, this concern should take care of itself. Try also to keep the audience in mind and take care of as many of the audience concerns identified during prewriting as you can, but don't let this interrupt the flow of your writing.

REVISING

As a first step in **revising,** it is a good idea to read through your essay carefully and determine whether your organizing plan is an effective one. Do you need to go back and devise a new organizing plan? Is there a clear thesis or purpose statement in your introduction that the body of your essay clearly develops? Now that you have a rough draft constructed from your prewriting plans, does your first reading indicate that your organizing plan was a sound one. If not, you will want to rearrange paragraphs or make the additions or deletions that will correct the weaknesses.

Similarly, you will want to work carefully with your introduction until you are entirely satisfied that it contains enough background or a clear enough overview to prepare your readers for the body of the paper. Is your purpose clearly expressed in the introduction?

Spend as much time as necessary on the conclusion. Your readers should leave the paper with a feeling of satisfaction about your writing. This feeling arises especially when the conclusion says something that relates to the content and purpose of the essay. Both introductions and conclusions benefit from extra care in revising. A poorly written introduction can ruin your paper since without the good orientation of a careful introduction, readers are uncertain about what to expect in the body and may have difficulties in following your point. A weak conclusion can cause the reader to leave the paper with a feeling of having been let down. Introductions and conclusions are short units, but they must receive generous amounts of your attention. Revise both until you are absolutely satisfied that each is doing the job it has to do.

Also, you will want to make sure that your body paragraphs are well developed and clear. Read them over carefully, correcting weak spots and adding extra details, sentences, or examples to make your points clear. Does each paragraph contribute something important to the purpose of your paper?

You may want to reserve at least one reading in order to search for any terms that you should have defined for your audience but overlooked while writing. At the same time, search for explanations or statements that may be clear to you but may be unclear to your audience based on your prewriting assessment of audience needs.

After you are satisfied with the introduction, body, and conclusion, then you are ready to turn from paragraph- to sentence-level concerns; you'll want to examine each sentence carefully to assure yourself that each says what it is supposed to say and is also sound in structure. Do your sentences contain enough information? Do you need to do additional prewriting? You should read through your latest revision at least once, identifying sentences or paragraphs that would be easier to read or understand if transitions were added. Some of the transitions common to cause-and-effect writing are those that occur in all writing that proceeds chronologically or by sequence: *first, second, next, before, after, as soon as, at the same time,* and so forth. Others are more common to discussing cause-and-effect: *since, because, as a result, consequently,* and so on.

PROOFREADING

In **proofreading,** follow the same advice we have been giving in each chapter: Locate all errors of grammar, punctuation, and spelling. Try not to proofread hastily, even if you are, at this stage, weary of working with your paper. Certainly, you don't want to spoil the hard work done during pre-writing, organizing, writing, and revising by overlooking mechanical errors.

After you have completed your cause-and-effect essay, you may wish to refer to the checklist below to make sure you have not omitted important aspects of your essay.

Cause-and-Effect Checklist

1. Does your essay have a purpose or thesis statement that can be easily identified by readers?
2. Will readers clearly understand this purpose by the time they have finished reading your introduction?
3. Does your introduction provide enough background information to prepare readers for the body of the paper?
4. Have you organized the body so that each paragraph helps convey your purpose to readers?
5. What makes your conclusion a good one for this paper?
6. What do you accomplish in the conclusion?

7. If asked, could you explain convincingly why you have organized your paper as you have?

8. Can you point to each place in your paper where you have taken special care because of your concern for audience?

9. Does each of your sentences say what you want it to say?

10. Are you satisfied with the way you have put each sentence together?

11. Do your sentences move smoothly from one to another? Do your paragraphs? Can you explain what you did to avoid abruptness in moving from point to point?

12. Have you proofread to catch misspellings and other errors?

The Secret Attraction of Kissing

MAURY M. BREECHER

In this essay, Maury M. Breecher describes an experiment showing that the female's sense of smell and chemical scents given off by the male have more to do with kissing and sex appeal than we had previously thought.

What's the attraction behind kissing? A New Mexico State University   1
psychologist believes the secret attraction—at least for women—is that it
allows them to get a deep, intoxicating whiff of pheromones, those chemical scents that play an important role in sexual attraction.

Dr. Victor Johnson, an associate professor of psychology, says the nose   2
"knows," that is, it recognizes the pheromone scent of "love," even though
women are consciously unaware of the odorous lure.

While the role pheromones play in the sexual attraction of animals and   3
insects has been known and documented for years, the role of these chemical substances in human courtship has been suspected, but never proven.
Now, however, Dr. Johnston has, for the first time, documented that humans are affected by pheromones. Dr. Johnston documented the real attraction of pheromones by tracking their effect on brain waves.

He devised an experiment in which reactions of volunteers could be   4
measured while they were unaware of the presence of the pheromone. Six
male and six female volunteers were shown a series of photos of attractive
males and females. Electrodes were attached to measure their brain waves.
A plastic tube was run under the nose of each volunteer. They were told the
tube was to measure their breathing, but actually it carried the odor of
alcohol or, masked by the alcohol, very low concentrations of the
pheromone Androstenol, a musky-smelling steroid which is secreted by
glands under the roots of hair.

The subjects were asked to look at the photos. As they looked at the   5
photos of the attractive men and women, Johnston measured the subjects'
brain-wave activity while they were under the influence of the pheromone
and while not under its influence. He looked at a particular brain wave—the
P3 brain wave—which in earlier experiments had been found to reveal how
much an individual liked or disliked a particular stimulus, such as a photo or
a scene from a movie.

Without the added Androstenol, men had much larger P3 responses   6 when they looked at photos of women—their P3 responses indicated they clearly preferred to look at photos of women rather than men. Women reacted about the same to photos of both sexes, but when the pheromone was added, the situation changed.

"My results startled me," Johnston said. "The responses of both males and females changed markedly under the influence of the pheromone. While males actually were less responsive when Androstenol was released, females became more selective. Females not exposed at all to Androstenol gave P3 brain waves the same size when they looked at both males and females. However, when the 'love scent' was released, they clearly preferred pictures of males.   7

"The P3 brain wave of men, on the other hand, dropped when they were under the influence of the pheromone. When they weren't under the influence of the pheromone, they showed increased P3 levels when they saw photos of attractive females. However, their P3 brain wave levels dropped when under the influence of Androstenol. This drop occurred when they looked at both male and female slides. However, they still reacted stronger to the female than to the male."   8

Johnston's findings that people respond sexually to odors—even if they aren't conscious of their response—suggest to him that body hair, particularly facial hair, has a previously unsuspected biological function.   9

For years, scientists have wondered why modern man still has zones of body hair. Dr. Johnston believes the answer is obvious—that hair "carries" Androstenol. As further support for the belief that hair has a biological function, he points out that the pheromone is produced at puberty, the same time coarse hair appears on the body.   10

Dr. Johnson believes that the act of kissing brings the female lovers' nose into close contact with her male lover's mustache and beard, allowing her nose to more easily whiff the pheromone. (The hair at the top of the head doesn't carry the pheromone. It has a totally different function—to keep the head cool and protect it from the sun.)   11

"I think we now have a better understanding of the biological function of hair and the reason why lovers kiss," Johnston said. "When a female kisses and is kissed, she is brought closer to the man's mustache and beard. The act of kissing seals her mouth and requires her to breathe through her nose. Her nose detects the hair's pheromone. Since the act of kissing closes off the mouth, she has to breathe in through the nose, thus increasing the 'intoxicating' effects of the pheromone."   12

Why are we unaware of the pheromone's scent?   13

Dr. Johnston points out that the information picked up by the nose   14 doesn't get transmitted directly to the cortex, the part of the brain that makes logical decisions, but instead is fed into the limbic or "old brain"—the part of the brain which makes emotional decisions.

"The nose appears to be the meeting place between the chemistries of   15 the sexes," Dr. Johnston says. "Silent chemical messages pass between us, expressing our inner desire and our readiness to respond."

Another expert, Dr. John Labows (Ph.D. in organic chemistry), a re-   16 search scientist at the Monell Chemical Senses Research Center in Philadelphia—a non-profit research institute set up to investigate the senses of smell and taste—points out that it has long been known that pheromones act as sexual attractors in insects and some lower animals, and it's long been suspected that they played some role in human sexual interactions. Speaking of Dr. Johnston's research, he said, "The research was innovative and imaginative. His research provides a tool to measure the effectiveness of these odors. He is using an objective measure of the effect of the odor rather than a subjective one. His research adds to the evidence that pheromones have a role in human sexual attraction."

"Sociobiologically speaking, this research is significant," said Dr.   17 Robert A. Wallace, an adjunct professor of biology at the University of Florida and author of the books *The Genesis Factor* (William Morrow, 1979) and *How They Do It,* a book on how animals mate (William Morrow, 1980). "From a biological standpoint, research of this kind is becoming increasingly significant. There is a controversial area called sociobiology that states that a broad array of human social patterns are firmly grounded in biological principles. This is one more line of evidence that supports this position."

"When people are in love they often speak of an 'irresistible attraction'   18 or desire to kiss, hug and touch the loved person," Dr. Wallace said. "Dr. Johnston's research provides evidence that the attraction is a chemical signal designed by nature to attract women to certain men. Other pheromones, so far unidentified, probably also serve as sexual attractants."

QUESTIONS ON MEANING AND CONTENT

1. What information in the essay about pheromones and sexual attraction can we accept as having an extremely high probability of being true? Why? What information is more speculative? Why is it more speculative?

2. Theoretically, how does the female pick up the pheromone scent?

3. The conclusion suggests that other still unknown pheromones "probably also serve as sexual attractants." What evidence presented in the essay would suggest such a conclusion? Would the speculation about how the female picks up the pheromone scent leave room for this conclusion? If so, how? Would differences in males from culture to culture also suggest additional pheromones? Explain.

4. Are there any stereotypes about males that Johnston's theory, if proved, would confirm? Or does sex appeal have so many variables that pheromones would seem to be only one small factor among a great many?

QUESTIONS ABOUT RHETORICAL STRATEGIES

1. Paragraph 10 notes that the body begins to produce Androstenol at puberty, which is "the same time coarse hair appears on the body." This is cited as "further support for the belief that hair" gives off the pheromone Androstenol. In such an argument we have to be very careful in identifying causes and effects. Explain the danger in drawing conclusions here. What logical fallacy must we be alert to?

2. What are the causes and effects established in the experiment described in paragraphs 4 through 8? What are further causes or effects suggested by the experiment and mentioned elsewhere in the essay?

3. Where does the introduction to the essay end and the body begin? How does the information contained in the introduction prepare the reader for the body of the essay? How effective, in your view, is the opening sentence of paragraph 1? Are there indications in paragraph 1 that the author is trying to create interest and draw the reader into the essay? If so, how do you recognize this?

4. The essay has four movements in its development: The introduction, the description of the experiment, speculation by Dr. Johnston about his experiment, and comments on the subject by other authorities. Examine these movements. How does the author make the transition from one to another?

5. Do the comments by other authorities in paragraphs 16 through 18 add something significant to the essay? If so, do they serve to keep readers interested? Do they add information that makes the earlier information clearer or more complete? Or do they simply make Dr. Johnston's conclusions seem more valid because these authorities find Johnston's research to be important?

6. How does the essay define *sociobiology*? Is it important to the essay that this field of study be mentioned and defined? Why or why not?

QUESTIONS ON LANGUAGE AND DICTION

1. In paragraph 1, notice how the author has defined *pheromones* for us by using an *appositive*—a noun or noun phrase that renames the original noun that it follows. Notice also that the original noun could be dropped, and the sentence, although less clear, would still make sense: ". . . it allows them to get a deep, intoxicating whiff of those chemical scents that play an important role in sexual attraction." The sentence is less clear because we now have a brief definition but lack the term being defined. The two working together provide readers with more information. Where else does the author define terms with appositives? Check each to see if the original term can be dropped while retaining the sense of the sentence?

2. The author uses dashes frequently as punctuation marks. Two different uses of the dash occur—dashes which enclose something (a dash at each end) and those which separate something near the end of the sentence from the rest of the sentence (one dash). In this essay, does the type of information differ when the dashes *enclose* and when the dash *separates*? Point out any differences. Do you think the author has overused dashes? Would commas do in some instances? Where? What dashes would you preserve? Why?

Where Has Childhood Gone?

PATRICIA O'BRIEN

The hard plastic sophistication of the Barbie doll and Barbie's un-quenchable appetite for new fashions made old-fashioned dolls all but obsolete and obscured the boundaries enclosing the childhood years. Barbie started all this back in the 1950s, and, according to the author, we still haven't found our way out of the restlessness of the dramatic changes she created.

I still remember the first time I saw a Barbie doll. It was on a summer 1 evening in the late '50s, in the Los Angeles living room of a friend. A salesman from the Mattel Toy Co. was present, and he regaled us with tales of an unusual new doll that he said was about to revolutionize his industry.

Noting my skeptical face, he handed me a small, miniaturized female 2 form. "Here," he said proudly. "Look at this. I guarantee you, childhood will never be the same."

I couldn't believe what I was holding. This was no doll: This was a tiny 3 plastic woman, complete with breasts and hips, molded with sly sophistication. The facial features were saucily non-virginal, the limbs were pleasingly curved. It was angular and hard, not soft and cuddly. It was different.

"What little girl would ever want this?" I burst out. 4

I soon learned. 5

A few years later, my own children were clamoring for Barbie. She wore 6 such pretty clothes, they said; it would be so much fun to dress her up.

Like most parents, I resisted at first, then gave in. Barbie had taken over, 7 and soon it was commonplace to watch a cluster of 10-year-olds busily tucking and snapping tiny creations of silk and lace (often made by doting grandmothers) onto the plastic woman with the somber face.

Children didn't exactly play with Barbie; she was much too sophisticated 8 for that. Instead they took her through the motions of consuming, and in the process, sharpened their own lists of wants.

Barbie brought a new and revolutionary message to the world of 9 childhood, and it was this: Hurry up, children! Don't waste time cuddling teddy bears or playing "let's pretend." Here is grown-up glamour, and it's more fun. Make your mommies buy as many new outfits for Barbie as you can. This is what growing up is all about.

Parents resigned themselves to ever-increasing quantities of Barbie   10
paraphernalia. Grandmothers sewed busily.

But Barbie was never satisfied. It was not in her nature to be satisfied,   11
and you could see the reflection of her discontent on the faces of children
eyeing the wardrobes of their friends' dolls. Somehow, other Barbies always
had it "better." Their Barbies needed "more."

It all seems like a long time ago, and my daughters long ago discarded   12
Barbie and moved on with their lives. But the Barbie phenomenon was a
prelude to a significant development that has only recently come into our
consciousness.

Childhood is not what it used to be. It is a period of life that is shrinking   13
rapidly.

This disturbing process did not, of course, begin only because of a   14
hard-bodied doll. Television, family breakdowns, the sexual revolution of
the 1960s and the rapid increase in working mothers all have contributed to
pushing children into premature adulthood.

It was only in recent years, as the evidence came in, that we could see   15
how children are changing. The statistics tell the story:

Close to four million children between the ages of seven and 13 spend at   16
least part of every weekday at home without adult supervision. Half of all
girls between the ages of 15 and 19 have had sexual intercourse (and the
greatest increase is at the lower end of that age scale). Teenage pregnancies
are epidemic. Suicides among children are up and alcoholism among teenagers is common.

Where has childhood gone?   17

"There's no question that something major is happening," says Dr.   18
Peter B. Neubauer, director of New York's Child Development Center.
"There are enormous pressures on children and young adolescents now,
and we are running behind in our understanding of what's going on."

We know a few things. We know that once upon a time, children could   19
afford to remain innocent through a slow maturation period. They were
left some time to believe in certitude, to remain comfortable in their knowledge of what was "good" and what was "bad."

The rules of life were clear and simple. It was possible for them to believe   20
that all policemen were kindly protectors, that all teachers were dedicated,
that all parents stayed married, and that all adults shared a kind of wisdom
that came with age.

When children, who were much too smart to stay in the dark about the   21
changes of the 1970s, ceased to believe all those things, they quickly "grew
up." They became cynical and disillusioned, and they walked away from
childhood.

Waiting in the wings, primed to capitalize on what is happening, are 22
today's commercial advertisers, the direct descendants of the toy salesman
who showed me the future in one tiny doll.

They know what to do: Sell sex. Sell excitement. 23

And so we have Brooke Shields, a 16-year-old model, posing for televi- 24
sion commercials with her legs sprawled provocatively, cooing, "If my jeans
could talk, I'd be in trouble." And we have Remco, a children's toy manufacturer, launching a trade advertising campaign for a line of children's cosmetics with an ad showing the made-up face of a little girl. "She's your
market," trumpets the ad. "She's between the ages of four and nine."

In the movies, Tatum O'Neal and Kristy McNichol have a contest to see 25
which nubile teenybopper can lose her virginity first. On the radio, Rod
Stewart sings about sexual desire ("We'd be a fool to stop this time, spread
your wings and let me come inside"). Eleven- and 12-year-olds laugh and
listen and learn.

I am most concerned by the impact of all those high-pressure messages 26
on ordinary children. Yet a special sadness surrounds those children co-
opted by the advertisers to sell the illusions.

I look at them and think of Barbie. But they're not plastic, they're real. 27

Not long ago, I appeared on a television show with a group of young 28
fashion models to discuss the pros and cons of the growing sophistication of
children. One girl I remember well.

She sat bored on a sofa, a child-woman whose smoky, languorous 29
beauty was accentuated by heavy makeup and high-style clothes. She tried
to explain how detached she felt from her beauty and her job.

"It's packaging, you know," she told me earnestly. "I sell an image. 30
Thank goodness everything for my body is tax-deductible." She giggled, the
high-pitched giggle of a 14 year old, which was natural, because she is 14.

But she had learned to be an illusion. 31

I am quite sure she is the envy of her friends, but how strange and sad to 32
have one's body be tax-deductible at the age of 14.

Like any parent, I have watched with apprehension as my children 33
made their way through the labyrinth of childhood. The rules have changed
so drastically and the stakes are so high.

I look at other parents just beginning the struggle and I see how meager 34
their resources are. Those who try to impart moral values find themselves
talking to children deafened by the siren songs of the sexual revolution.
Those who try to prepare their children against disaster by providing practical information and prescriptions for the pill worry that they aren't doing
enough. Everybody tiptoes over eggshells.

Many parents choose silence. They don't know what to say. 35

And yet I hear from children conflicting cries for freedom and direction.   36
That's when something important seems lost, or at least left behind, like a
mitten or a hat.

A friend once told me about a mother whose 15-year-old daughter asked   37
whether she should have sex with her boyfriend. The mother launched into
a modern talk, the kind she felt was required of her, about the "ifs" and the
"whens." When she was finished, the girl asked, "Can I tell him you won't
let me?"

I am convinced that children would give anything to be allowed to stay   38
children just a while longer. When I watched them curl up in their Calvin
Klein jeans, their eyes glazed over from listening to records, I sometimes can
detect a crack in their sophisticated armor.

They want something they do not have: They want boundaries.   39

In a way, the saga of Barbie has come full circle. Children who learned to   40
want too many things, to crave things that were bigger, better and faster,
have found themselves unsure and anxious. They hurried too much and
only some will learn to slow down.

Sometimes I wonder what happened to that toy salesman I met so long   41
ago. I wonder if he ever had children of his own. If he did, he probably spent
some years with a plastic doll who couldn't be cuddled or nurtured. He must
have seen the quickening pace of childhood, then the headlong dash
towards sophistication.

If he saw all that, I wonder how long he stuck with selling toys.   42

QUESTIONS ON MEANING AND CONTENT

1. The author speculates about effects caused by the Barbie doll. Does
she make clear the causes leading to the doll's creation?

2. How accurate do you think the author is in the connections she makes
between Barbie dolls and the changes in the lifestyles of teenagers? She
acknowledges that Barbie dolls are only one cause of these changes. What
does she identify as other causes? Do these other causes seem reasonable to
you? How well does she support these with illustrations and evidence?

3. What, essentially, is the difference between a Barbie doll and the
old-fashioned baby doll; that is, what cultural values is a child addressing
and practicing while dressing and fantasizing with the "baby" doll? How
and where does the attention (and the values) shift when a child dresses and
fantasizes with a Barbie doll?

4. O'Brien's essay was published in 1981. Assume for the moment that the author was accurate in her conclusion that teenage values changed dramatically after the introduction of Barbie dolls and that the period of childhood shrank. Is the condition described in the essay still with us or is the essay dated? How popular are Barbie dolls at this time? Do you think the recent popularity of a radically different doll, the Cabbage Patch doll, signals another change? What cultural values would a child be practicing and reinforcing while playing with a Cabbage Patch doll?

5. What does the author mean in paragraph 31 when she says that the 14-year-old fashion model "had learned to be an illusion"?

6. Is the essay really about the folly of pursuing illusions? If so, what is the illusion O'Brien describes? Is this illusion really made clear in the essay? Isn't there also an illusion associated with the type of childhood she refers to in paragraphs 19 and 20? What? Did that illusion prove to be harmful? Was it also a contributing cause of the shrinking of childhood?

7. Paragraphs 19 and 20 seem to suggest that there are healthy illusions or that illusions can help to maintain stability—in this case preserve or extend childhood. Can you name illusions that we foster in ourselves that have some value to us? Why and how do they have value?

8. Paragraph 20 says that children who grew up under the illusion that policemen, teachers, and so forth, were all "good," became cynical once they became "disillusioned." What is the message here? That even workable illusions must eventually disappear? That changing one illusion for another may be changing a lesser for a greater evil? What?

9. What do the descriptions of Tatum O'Neal and Kristy McNichol in paragraph 25 suggest is a "fact" and not an illusion about teenagers? Does O'Brien seem to be looking for some way to control the behavior stemming from this fact? Does the call for "boundaries" in paragraph 39 offer a workable illusion to control the teenage facts so visibly displayed by Tatum O'Neal and Kristy McNichol? Or would boundaries be anything more than an illusion? Why would a culture want to—or have to—extend childhood?

QUESTIONS ABOUT RHETORICAL STRATEGIES

1. O'Brien begins the essay with a narrative recounting her childhood experience with the Barbie doll just at the time it was being introduced. What advantages does beginning with this narrative offer to the author? What does the narrative do for the essay? What effect does the author achieve by quoting the toy salesman in paragraph 2?

2. Look at the short, one- or two-sentence paragraphs, beginning with paragraph 13. How do most of them work to block off sections of the organization and development of the essay? Select one of these short paragraphs and explain how it functions in relation to the paragraphs immediately preceding or following it.

3. Describe the audience that this essay seems to be directed to. What is there about the essay that suggests this audience?

QUESTIONS ON LANGUAGE AND DICTION

1. This essay contains many short sentences; for example, the opening sentences of paragraphs 19 and 20 and the two sentences making up paragraph 35. Some of these sentences could be combined. Paragraph 35 could easily be turned into a single sentence by connecting the two sentences with *because.* The first two sentences of paragraph 20 could be connected by *and.* Why aren't they connected? Do they convey some effect because of their shortness? If so, what effect? Examine some of the other short sentences and explain whether you think their shortness enhances the writing in some way or whether they are just characteristics of the author's writing style.

2. What are the meanings of *siren song, languorous, nubile?*

Who Speaks for Earth?

CARL SAGAN

When it comes to nuclear affairs, Carl Sagan says, the dark side of our natures will destroy us if we don't watch out. Governments and military establishments speak to this dark side, while our efforts in space exploration speak to the inquisitive, caring side of our natures, the side that wants to preserve ourselves and the planet. Sagan suggests that we must speak from and to this inquisitive, caring side of our beings if we are to survive, if we are to speak for the planet Earth.

The Cosmos was discovered only yesterday. For a million years it was 1
clear to everyone that there were no other places than the Earth. Then in the
last tenth of a percent of the lifetime of our species, in the instant between
Aristarchus and ourselves, we reluctantly noticed that we were not the
center and purpose of the Universe, but rather lived on a tiny and fragile
world lost in immensity and eternity, drifting in a great cosmic ocean dotted
here and there with a hundred billion galaxies and a billion trillion stars. We
have bravely tested the waters and have found the ocean to our liking,
resonant with our nature. Something in us recognizes the Cosmos as home.
We are made of stellar ash. Our origin and evolution have been tied to
distant cosmic events. The exploration of the Cosmos is a voyage of self-
discovery.

As the ancient mythmakers knew, we are the children equally of the sky 2
and the Earth. In our tenure on this planet we have accumulated dangerous
evolutionary baggage, hereditary propensities for aggression and ritual,
submission to leaders and hostility to outsiders, which place our survival in
some question. But we have also acquired compassion for others, love for
our children and our children's children, a desire to learn from history, and a
great soaring passionate intelligence—the clear tools for our continued
survival and prosperity. Which aspects of our nature will prevail is uncertain, particularly when our vision and understanding and prospects are
bound exclusively to the Earth—or, worse, to one small part of it. But up
there in the immensity of the Cosmos, an inescapable perspective awaits us.
There are not yet any obvious signs of extraterrestrial intelligence and this
makes us wonder whether civilizations like ours always rush implacably,
headlong, toward self-destruction. National boundaries are not evident

when we view the Earth from space. Fanatical ethnic or religious or national chauvinisms are a little difficult to maintain when we see our planet as a fragile blue crescent fading to become an inconspicuous point of light against the bastion and citadel of the stars. Travel is broadening.

There are worlds on which life has never arisen. There are worlds that 3 have been charred and ruined by cosmic catastrophes. We are fortunate: we are alive; we are powerful; the welfare of our civilization and our species is in our hands. If we do not speak for Earth, who will? If we are not committed to our own survival, who will be?

The human species is now undertaking a great venture that if successful 4 will be as important as the colonization of the land or the descent from the trees. We are haltingly, tentatively breaking the shackles of Earth—metaphorically, in confronting and taming the admonitions of those more primitive brains within us; physically, in voyaging to the planets and listening for the messages from the stars. These two enterprises are linked indissolubly. Each, I believe, is a necessary condition for the other. But our energies are directed far more toward war. Hypnotized by mutual mistrust, almost never concerned for the species or the planet, the nations prepare for death. And because what we are doing is so horrifying, we tend not to think of it much. But what we do not consider we are unlikely to put right.

Every thinking person fears nuclear war, and every technological state 5 plans for it. Everyone knows it is madness, and every nation has an excuse. There is a dreary chain of causality: The Germans were working on the bomb at the beginning of World War II; so the Americans had to make one first. If the Americans had one, the Soviets had to have one, and then the British, the French, the Chinese, the Indians, the Pakistanis. . . . By the end of the twentieth century many nations had collected nuclear weapons. They were easy to devise. Fissionable material could be stolen from nuclear reactors. Nuclear weapons became almost a home handicraft industry.

The conventional bombs of World War II were called blockbusters. Filled 6 with twenty tons of TNT, they could destroy a city block. All the bombs dropped on all the cities in World War II amounted to some two million tons, two megatons, of TNT—Coventry and Rotterdam, Dresden and Tokyo, all the death that rained from the skies between 1939 and 1945: a hundred thousand blockbusters, two megatons. By the late twentieth century, two megatons was the energy released in the explosion of a single more or less humdrum thermonuclear bomb: one bomb with the destructive force of the Second World War. But there are tens of thousands of nuclear weapons. By the ninth decade of the twentieth century the strategic missile and bomber forces of the Soviet Union and the United States were aiming warheads at over 15,000 designated targets. No place on the planet was safe. The energy contained in these weapons, genies of death patiently awaiting the rubbing of the lamps, was far more than 10,000 megatons—but with the destruction concentrated efficiently, not over six years but over a few hours, a blockbuster for every family on the planet, a World War II every second for the length of a lazy afternoon.

The immediate causes of death from nuclear attack are the blast wave, which can flatten heavily reinforced buildings many kilometers away, the firestorm, the gamma rays and the neutrons, which effectively fry the insides of passersby. A school girl who survived the American nuclear attack on Hiroshima, the event that ended the Second World War, wrote this first-hand account: 7

> Through a darkness like the bottom of hell, I could hear the voices of the other students calling for their mothers. And at the base of the bridge, inside a big cistern that had been dug out there, was a mother weeping, holding above her head a naked baby that was burned bright red all over its body. And another mother was crying and sobbing as she gave her burned breast to her baby. In the cistern the students stood with only their heads above the water, and their two hands, which they clasped as they imploringly cried and screamed, calling for their parents. But every single person who passed was wounded, all of them, and there was no one, there was no one to turn to for help. And the singed hair on the heads of the people was frizzled and whitish and covered with dust. They did not appear to be human, not creatures of this world.

The Hiroshima explosion, unlike the subsequent Nagasaki explosion, was an air burst high above the surface, so the fallout was insignificant. But on March 1, 1954, a thermonuclear weapons test at Bikini in the Marshall Islands detonated at higher yield than expected. A great radioactive cloud was deposited on the tiny atoll of Rongalap, 150 kilometers away, where the inhabitants likened the explosion to the Sun rising in the West. A few hours later, radioactive ash fell on Rongalap like snow. The average dose received was only about 175 rads, a little less than half the dose needed to kill an average person. Being far from the explosion, not many people died. Of course, the radioactive strontium they ate was concentrated in their bones, and the radioactive iodine was concentrated in their thyroids. Two-thirds of the children and one-third of the adults later developed thyroid abnormalities, growth retardation or malignant tumors. In compensation, the Marshall Islanders received expert medical care.   8

The yield of the Hiroshima bomb was only thirteen kilotons, the equivalent of thirteen thousand tons of TNT. The Bikini test yield was fifteen megatons. In a full nuclear exchange, in the paroxysm of thermonuclear war, the equivalent of a million Hiroshima bombs would be dropped all over   9 the world. At the Hiroshima death rate of some hundred thousand people killed per equivalent thirteen-kiloton weapon, this would be enough to kill a hundred billion people. But there were less than five billion people on the planet in the late twentieth century. Of course, in such an exchange, not everyone would be killed by the blast and the firestorm, the radiation and the fallout—although fallout does last for a longish time: 90 percent of the strontium 90 will decay in *96 years;* 90 percent of the cesium 137, in *100 years;* 90 percent of the iodine 131 in *only a month.*

The survivors would witness more subtle consequences of the war. A full nuclear exchange would burn the nitrogen in the upper air, coverting it to oxides of nitrogen, which would in turn destroy a significant amount of the ozone in the high atmosphere, admitting an intense dose of solar ultraviolet radiation.[1] The increased ultraviolet flux would last for years. It would produce skin cancer preferentially in light-skinned people. Much more important, it would affect the ecology of our planet in an unknown way. Ultraviolet light destroys crops. Many microorganisms would be killed; we do not know which ones or how many, or what the consequences might be. The organisms killed might, for all we know, be at the base of a vast ecological pyramid at the top of which totter we.   10

The dust put into the air in a full nuclear exchange would reflect sunlight and cool the Earth a little. Even a little cooling can have disastrous agricultural consequences. Birds are more easily killed by radiation than insects. Plagues of insects and consequent further agricultural disorders are a likely consequence of nuclear war. There is also another kind of plague to worry about: the [bubonic] plague bacillus is endemic all over the Earth. In the late twentieth century humans did not much die of plague—not because it was absent, but because resistance was high. However, the radiation produced in a nuclear war, among its many other effects, debilitates the body's immunological system, causing a deterioration of our ability to resist disease. In the longer term, there are mutations, new varieties of microbes and insects, that might cause still further problems for any human survivors of a nuclear holocaust; and perhaps after a while, when there has been enough time for the recessive mutations to recombine and be expressed, new and horrifying varieties of humans. Most of these mutations, when expressed, would be lethal. A few would not. And then there would be other agonies: the loss of loved ones; the legions of the burned, the blind and the mutilated; disease, plague, long-lived radioactive posions in the air and water; the   11

---

[1]The process is similar to, but much more dangerous than, the destruction of the ozone layer by the fluorcarbon propellants in aerosol spray cans, which have accordingly been banned by a number of nations; and to that invoked in the explanation of the extinction of the dinosaurs by a supernova explosion a few dozen light-years away.

threat of tumors and stillbirths and malformed children; the absence of medical care; the hopeless sense of a civilization destroyed for nothing: the knowledge that we could have prevented it and did not. . . .

The global balance of terror, pioneered by the United States and the 12 Soviet Union, holds hostage the citizens of the Earth. Each side draws limits on the permissible behavior of the other. The potential enemy is assured that if the limit is transgressed, nuclear war will follow. However, the definition of the limit changes from time to time. Each side must be quite confident that the other understands the new limits. Each side is tempted to increase its military advantage, but not in so striking a way as seriously to alarm the other. Each side continually explores the limits of the other's tolerance, as in flights of nuclear bombers over the Arctic wastes; the Cuban missile crisis; the testing of anti-satellite weapons; the Vietnam and Afghanistan wars—a few entries from a long and dolorous list. The global balance of terror is a very delicate balance. It depends on things not going wrong, on mistakes not being made, on the reptilian passions not being seriously aroused. . . .

[T]he development of nuclear weapons and their delivery systems will, 13 sooner or later, lead to global disaster. Many of the Americans and European émigré scientists who developed the first nuclear weapons were profoundly distressed about the demon they had let loose on the world. They pleaded for the global abolition of nuclear weapons. But their pleas went unheeded; the prospect of a national strategic advantage galvanized both the U.S.S.R. and the United States, and the nuclear arms race began.

In the same period, there was a burgeoning international trade in the 14 devastating non-nuclear weapons coyly called "conventional." In the past twenty-five years, in dollars corrected for inflation, the annual international arms trade has gone from $300 million to much more than $20 billion. In the years between 1950 and 1968, for which good statistics seem to be available, there were, on the average, worldwide several accidents involving nuclear weapons per year, although perhaps no more than one or two accidental nuclear explosions. The weapons establishments in the Soviet Union, the United States and other nations are large and powerful. In the United States they include major corporations famous for their homey domestic manufactures. According to one estimate, the corporate profits in military weapons procurement are 30 to 50 percent higher than in an equally technological but competitive civilian market. Cost overruns in military weapons systems are permitted on a scale that would be considered unacceptable in the civilian sphere. In the Soviet Union the resources, quality, attention and care given to military production is in striking contrast to the little left for consumer goods. According to some estimates, almost half the scientists and high technologists on Earth are employed full- or part-time on military matters.

Those engaged in the development and manufacture of weapons of mass destruction are given salaries, perquisites of power and, where possible, public honors at the highest levels available in their respective societies. The secrecy of weapons development, carried to especially extravagant lengths in the Soviet Union, implies that individuals so employed need almost never accept responsibility for their actions. They are protected and anonymous. Military secrecy makes the military the most difficult sector of any society for the citizens to monitor. If we do not know what they do, it is very hard for us to stop them. And with the rewards so substantial, with the hostile military establishments beholden to each other in some ghastly mutual embrace, the world discovers itself drifting toward the ultimate undoing of the human enterprise.

Every major power has some widely publicized justification for its pro-   15
curement and stockpiling of weapons of mass destruction, often including a reptilian reminder of the presumed character and cultural defects of poten- tial enemies (as opposed to us stout fellows), or of the intentions of others, but never ourselves, to conquer the world. Every nation seems to have its set of forbidden possibilities, which its citizenry and adherents must not at any cost be permitted to think seriously about. In the Soviet Union these include capitalism, God, and the surrender of national sovereignty; in the United States, socialism, atheism, and the surrender of national sovereignty. It is the same all over the world.

How would we explain the global arms race to a dispassionate extrater-   16
restrial observer? How would we justify the most recent destabilizing de- velopments of killer-satellites, particle beam weapons, lasers, neutron bombs, cruise missiles, and the proposed conversion of areas the size of modest countries to the enterprise of hiding each intercontinental ballistic missle among hundreds of decoys? Would we argue that ten thousand targeted nuclear warheads are likely to enhance the prospects for our survi- val? What account would we give of our stewardship of the planet Earth? We have heard the rationales offered by the nuclear superpowers. We know who speaks for the nations. But who speaks for the human species? Who speaks for Earth?

QUESTIONS ON MEANING AND CONTENT

1. What does Sagan call "The clear tools for our continued survival and prosperity"? What are the human traits he refers to as "dangerous evolu- tionary baggage"? Why does he say that we have inherited the dangerous qualities but "acquired" the helpful traits? How logical is this separation of our selves into two parts? Is anything significant overlooked in the middle?

2. Among the behavioral traits of our darker side, Sagan lists an inclination toward or a desire for ritual. What rituals do you think he has in mind? Could he also have listed ritual as an item common to the other side of our nature? Can you think of some danger in ritual that he is trying to point out?

3. Are the two questions which end the essay meant to be answered or are they rhetorical questions—questions that have obvious answers? Is Sagan saying, in effect, that no one speaks for the human species and no one speaks for Earth? Who should speak for Earth? If our leaders are not speaking for their people and the planet, who and what are they speaking for, according to Sagan?

4. In paragraph 4, Sagan mentions "a great venture" that human beings are undertaking by exploring and gathering information from outer space. He suggests that this exploration can unshackle us from the primitive side of our nature. Can you explain what he means? How would this liberation come about? Is this also what he is talking about in paragraph 1 when he says, "The exploration of the Cosmos is a voyage of self-discovery"? How is this "a voyage of self-discovery"?

5. Why do movies and television programs set in outer space still pit "good forces" against "evil forces," the same sides of our own natures that Sagan points out as an earthly phenomenon? What kind of outer-space movie script do you think Sagan would write? Would we want to watch the movie? Explain.

6. "Sooner or later," Sagan says in paragraph 13, "nuclear weapons and their delivery systems" will produce a "global disaster." Does he convince you of this in the essay? Why or why not? In Sagan's view, what is it that can prevent such a disaster?

QUESTIONS ABOUT RHETORICAL STRATEGIES

1. In paragraph 5, Sagan lists the "dreary chain of causality" leading to the present state of nuclear affairs. Has he omitted any immediate or remote causes from the list or is it relatively complete? He begins with Germany and World War II. Can the causes be extended back through time from that point? Explain. The fact that the Germans were working on a nuclear bomb must have been an effect caused by something else. What? Would this, too, if carefully examined, produce a long, historical list of causes?

2. In paragraph 13, Sagan predicts that continued concern with developing nuclear weapons and delivery systems will eventually produce a disastrous effect, a "global disaster." What are the causes that he thinks will make the predicted effect inevitable? Do these causes seem to you to be *capable* of producing this effect? Do they seem *highly likely* to produce the effect? Do they seem *certain* to produce the effect? Explain your answer.

3. In paragraph 14, Sagan talks about the unusually high profits made by American corporations supplying military weapons to the government. To what point in the essay in this directed? Does it relate to other points made in the same paragraph; that is, is this information necessary because it is leading to a point made later on in the paragraph? Or is it a digression?

QUESTIONS ON LANGUAGE AND DICTION

1. Here and there in the essay Sagan uses adjectives that have to be interpreted by the reader. In paragraph 2 he says that we have "a great soaring passionate intelligence." What do *soaring* and *passionate* mean in this instance? In what way is *passionate* a curious word to associate with intelligence? In paragraph 12, he speaks of "reptilian passions." Isn't this also a curious combination? Why? How do you interpret this phrase? Do Sagan's earlier comments prepare us for the use of this combination? Explain.

2. Paragraph 16 refers to a "dispassionate extraterrestrial observer." What does *dispassionate* mean? What assumptions would lead Sagan to use this adjective here? What is Sagan's point?

3. Examine the last sentence of paragraph 8 in which Sagan mentions the compensation for nuclear fallout given to the Marshall Islanders. Notice how the sentence understates the situation. Sagan could have made an emotional statement here, perhaps even an overstatement by noting how inadequate, irresponsible, conscienceless, appalling, and so forth this settlement was. Is his understatement more powerful than an emotionally charged statement might have been? Explain.

4. Notice Sagan's description in paragraph 7 of gamma rays and neutrons on Hiroshima victims. Their effect was to "fry the insides of passersby." Comment on the use of the word *fry*. What other word choices did Sagan have? Why does Sagan *emphasize* here and *understate* in the Marshall Islander's example? That is, what does he achieve by emphasizing horror in paragraph 7 and deemphasizing horror in paragraph 8? Explain your answer.

5. Following the same line of thought, comment on the use of *longish* in the statement in paragraph 9 that says "fallout does last for a longish time."

6. What are the meanings of the following words from the essay: *admonition, bastion, kilotons, megatons, dolorous, propensities?*

The New (and Still Hidden) Persuaders

VANCE PACKARD

In 1957, Vance Packard wrote a best-selling book called The Hidden Persuaders. *In it he described the techniques used by advertisers to make us willing customers. In this essay, Packard explains what he discovered by taking a second look at advertisers 20 years later. They are working just as hard to sway us, he found. Their current techniques aren't quite as "wacky" as they once were, he says, but they are "more weird."*

People keep asking me what the hidden persuaders are up to nowadays. 1
So, for a few months, I revisited the persuasion specialists. The demographers and motivational researchers, I found, are still very much with us, but admen today are also listening to other kinds of behavior specialists. It's a less wacky world than 20 years ago perhaps, but more weird.

Admen seek trustworthy predictions on how we the consumers are 2
going to react to their efforts. Years ago they learned that we may lie politely when discussing ads or products, so increasingly, the advertising world has turned to our bodies for clues to our real feelings.

Take our eyes. There is one computerized machine that tracks their 3
movement as they examine a printed ad. This spots the elements in the ad that have the most "stopping power." For overall reactions to an ad or commercial, some admen have been trying the pupillometer, a machine that measures the pupil under stimulation.

The pupil expands when there is arousal of interest, although this can 4
lead to mistaken conclusions. A marketer of frozen french fries was pleased by reports of significant dilation during its TV ad. But further analysis indicated that it was the sizzling steak in the ad, not the french fries, that was causing the dilation. What's more, the pupillometer cannot tell whether a viewer likes or dislikes an ad. (We are also aroused by ads that annoy us.) This caused some of its users to become disgruntled, but others stick with it as at least helpful. Arousal is *something*. Without it the admen are inevitably wasting money.

There are also machines that offer voice-pitch analysis. First, our normal 5
voices are taped and then our voices while commenting on an ad or product. A computer reports whether we are offering lip service, a polite lie or a firm opinion.

In the testing of two commercials with children in them, other kids' 6
comments seemed about equally approving. The mechanical detective,
however, reported that one of the commercials simply interested the kids,
whereas the other packed an emotional wallop that they found hard to
articulate.

Viewing rooms are used to try out commercials and programs on off- 7
the-street people. Viewers push buttons to indicate how interested or bored
they are.

One technique for gauging ad impact is to measure brain waves with 8
electrodes. If a person is really interested in something, his brain emits fast
beta waves. If he is in a passive, relaxed state, his brain emits the much
slower alpha waves. An airline has used brain-wave testing to choose its
commercial spokesman. Networks have used the test to check out actors and
specific scenes in pilot films that need a sponsor.

Admen also seek to sharpen their word power to move us to action. 9
Some have turned to psycholinguistics—the deep-down meaning of
words—and to a specialty called psychographic segmentation.

A few years ago Colgate-Palmolive was eager to launch a new soap. 10
Now, for most people, the promise of cleanliness ranks low as a compelling
reason for buying soap. It's assumed. So soap makers promise not only
cleanliness but one of two gut appeals—physical attractiveness (a tuning up
of complexion) or a deodorant (a pleasant smell).

Colgate-Palmolive turned to psychographic segmentation to find a posi- 11
tion within the "deodorant" end of the soap field. The segmenters found a
psychological type they called Independents—the ambitious, forceful, self-
assured types with a positive outlook on life, mainly men, who like to take
cold showers.

Their big need, over and above cleanliness, was a sense of refreshment. 12
What kind of imagery could offer refreshment? Colgate researchers thought
of spring and of greenery and that led them to think of Ireland, which has a
nationally advertised image epitomizing cool, misty, outdoor greenery.

So, the Colgate people hired a rugged, self-assured male with a bit of a 13
brogue as spokesman and concocted a soap with green and white striations.
The bar was packaged in a manly green-against-black wrapper (the black
had come out of psychological research, and they hailed it as Irish Spring
—now a big success in the soap field.

Advertising people have long fretted about not being able to say much in 14
a 15- or 30-second commercial. So they experimented with faster talking.
Typically, when you run a recorded message at speeds significantly faster
than normal you get Donald Duck quackery. But psychologists working

with electronic specialists came up with a computerized time-compression device that creates a normal-sounding voice even when the recording is speeded up by 40 percent. Research has also indicated that listeners actually preferred messages at faster-than-normal speed and remembered them better.

Meanwhile, at one of the world's largest advertising agencies, J. Walter   15
Thompson, technicians forecast that by 1990 many TV messages will be coming at us in three-second bursts, combining words, symbols and other imagery. The messages will be almost subliminal.

The subliminal approach is to get messages to us beneath our level of   16
awareness. It can be a voice too low for us to hear consciously. It can be a message flashed on a screen too rapidly for us to notice, or a filmed message shown continuously but dimly. It can even be a word such as SEX embedded in the pictures of printed ads.

Subliminal seduction has been banned by most broadcasters, but noth-   17
ing prevents its use in stores, movies and salesrooms. Several dozen department stores use it to reduce shoplifting. Such messages as "I am honest, I will not steal" are mixed with background music and continually repeated. One East Coast retail chain reported a one-third drop in theft in a nine-month period.

The sale of imagery and symbols continues to fascinate admen. In one   18
experiment, 200 women were questioned, ostensibly about color schemes in furniture design. For their co-operation the women were given a supply of cold cream. They were to take home and try out two samples. When they came back for their next advice-giving session, they would be given an ample supply of the cold cream of their choice.

Both sample jars were labeled "high-quality cold cream." The cap of one   19
jar had a design with two triangles on it. The cap of the other jar had two circles. The cold cream inside the jars was identical, yet 80 percent of the women asked for the one with the circle design on the cap. They liked the consistency of that cream better. They found it easier to apply and definitely of finer quality. All because, it seems, women prefer circles to triangles.

The use of sexuality in the media has become standard. Interestingly, a   20
research report stated that women now are more aroused by nudity in ads than men. This may account for one twist recently employed by admen. In 1980, a highly successful campaign for men's Jockey-brand underwear was aimed at women, based on the finding that women often buy clothing for their mates.

For this campaign the star was the handsome pitcher of the Baltimore   21
Orioles, Jim Palmer. In the ads he was nude except for the snug-fitting Jockey briefs. Sales soared—as did Palmer's female fan mail.

Today, as when I first reported on persuasion techniques in advertising,   22
our hidden needs are still very much on admen's minds. One need that has
grown greatly in two decades—perhaps because of all the moving and
breaking up of families—is warm human contact.

The American Telephone and Telegraph Company used this need to   23
generate more long-distance calls. Historically, such calls were associated
with accidents, death in the family and other stressful situations. AT&T
wanted long-distance calling to become casual spur-of-the-moment fun.
Hence the jingle, "Reach out, reach out and touch someone," played against
various scenes filled with good friendship.

Then there was a manufacturer of hay balers who sought more farmers   24
to buy his machine. Psychologist Ernest Dichter, an old master at persuasion, came up with a technique based on the theory that instant reward is
better in creating a sense of achievement than long-delayed reward—in this
case a check for the hay two months later.

Dichter recommended attaching a rear-view mirror and a bell to the   25
baler. Every time a bundle of hay was assembled as the machine moved
across a hayfield, the farmer could see it in the mirror. And when the bale
dropped onto the field the bell rang. Thus the reward was not only instant
but visual and audible. Farmers loved it. And so did the manufacturer, who
started ringing up the hay-baler sales.

QUESTIONS ON MEANING AND CONTENT

1. Does the information contained in the essay suggest that a game is
constantly taking place in which advertisers are trying to score against us (as
measured by sales) or to strike us out or checkmate us (overcome our
resistance)? If so, how aware are we that a game is taking place? If not, how
would you characterize what is taking place?

2. Does the discussion of subliminal advertising in paragraphs 16-19
suggest to you that advertisers can go beyond reasonable means of persuasion? Why would broadcasters (paragraph 18), who rely on advertising
revenues, ban subliminal ads? Can you think of current TV ads that are
subliminal or close to being subliminal?

3. What is the significance of the "cold cream case" described in paragraphs 18 and 19? What does this tell us about the difficulty of distinguishing
between illusion and reality?

4. How many "hidden needs" of people have been identified in the essay? What are they? Can you think of hidden needs not mentioned here that advertisers do appeal to in selling products?

QUESTIONS ABOUT RHETORICAL STRATEGIES

1. This essay examines many individual cases of cause-and-effect, with advertisers working to isolate causes that will produce a desired result or effect. How many individual cases are discussed altogether? Does each one help support the thesis expressed in paragraph 2, which says that "Admen seek trustworthy predictions on how we the consumers are going to react to their efforts"?

2. How are the individual cause-and-effect cases organized within the essay? Can you divide them into groups and label each group, perhaps beginning with "visual effects" or "visual appeals" or "appeals to the eye," the first group Packard examines?

3. Is there any logic in the way Packard presents the experiments by groups? Could the groups be arranged in another logical way? How does the author move from group to group or from case to case within groups? What transitions or language signals does he incorporate to tell readers that a movement is taking place? Do you find the movement to be abrupt at any point? If so, what is missing that makes the movement abrupt? If not, how has Packard achieved smoothness?

QUESTIONS ON LANGUAGE AND DICTION

1. In paragraph 1, Packard calls the world "less wacky than 20 years ago . . . but more weird." How is he using the words, *wacky* and *weird*? Does the essay show the distinction he is making? Or would you have to know Packard's earlier writing to determine the differences?

2. What technique does the author use in each case to define the following terms for the audience: *pupillometer* (para. 3), *alpha* and *beta waves* (para. 8), *psycholinguistics* (para. 9), *independents* (para. 11), and *subliminal* (para. 16)?

3. What are the meanings of the following words from the essay: *striations, ostensibly, epitomizing.*

Memoirs of a Non-Prom Queen

ELLEN WILLIS

Ellen Willis challenges the view that students who are popular in high school have already reached the apex of their lives and that the unpopular students go into the world determined to be successful and thereby make up for being nobodies in high school.

There's a book out called *Is There Life after High School?* It's a fairly silly 1
book, maybe because the subject matter is the kind that only hurts when you
think. Its thesis—that most people never get over the social triumphs or
humiliations of high school—is not novel. Still, I read it with the respectful
attention a serious hypochondriac accords the lowliest "dear doctor" column. I don't know about most people, but for me, forgiving my parents for
real and imagined derelictions has been easy compared to forgiving myself
for being a teenage reject.

Victims of high school trauma—which seems to have afflicted a dispro- 2
portionate number of writers, including Ralph Keyes, the author of this
book—tend to embrace the ugly duckling myth of adolescent social relations: the "innies" (Keyes's term) are good-looking, athletic mediocrities
who will never amount to much, while the "outies" are intelligent, sensitive, creative individuals who will do great things in an effort to make up for
their early defeats. Keyes is partial to this myth. He has fun with celebrity
anecdotes: Kurt Vonnegut receiving a body-building course as a "gag prize"
at a dance; Frank Zappa yelling "fuck you" at a cheerleader; Mike Nichols, as
a nightclub comedian, insulting a fan—an erstwhile overbearing classmate
turned used-car salesman. In contrast, the ex-prom queens and kings he
interviews slink through life, hiding their pasts lest someone call them
"dumb jock" or "cheerleader type," perpetually wondering what to do for
an encore.

If only it were that simple. There may really be high schools where life 3
approximates an Archie comic, but even in the Fifties, my large (5000
students), semisuburban (Queens, New York), heterogeneous high school
was not one of them. The students' social life was fragmented along ethnic
and class lines; there was no universally recognized, schoolwide social
hierarchy. Being an athlete or a cheerleader or a student officer didn't mean
much. Belonging to an illegal sorority or fraternity meant more, at least in

some circles, but many socially active students chose not to join. The most popular kids were not necessarily the best looking or the best dressed or the most snobbish or the least studious. In retrospect, it seems to me that they were popular for much more honorable reasons. They were attuned to other people, aware of subtle social nuances. They projected an inviting sexual warmth. Far from being slavish followers of fashion, they were self-confident enough to set fashions. They suggested, initiated, led. Above all—this was their main appeal for me—they knew how to have a good time.

True, it was not particularly sophisticated enjoyment—dancing, pizza eating, hand holding in the lunchroom, the usual. I had friends—precocious intellectuals and bohemians—who were consciously alienated from what they saw as all that teenage crap. Part of me identified with them, yet I badly wanted what they rejected. Their seriousness engaged my mind, but my romantic and sexual fantasies, and my emotions generally, were obsessively fixed on the parties and dances I wasn't invited to, the boys I never dated. I suppose what says it best is that my "serious" friends hated rock & roll; I loved it.

If I can't rationalize my social ineptitude as intellectual rebellion, neither can I blame it on political consciousness. Feminism has inspired a variation of the ugly duckling myth in which high school wallflower becomes feminist heroine, suffering because she has too much integrity to suck up to boys by playing a phony feminine role. There is a tempting grain of truth in this idea. Certainly the self-absorption, anxiety and physical and social awkwardness that made me a difficult teenager were not unrelated to my ambivalent awareness of women's oppression. I couldn't charm boys because I feared and resented them and their power over my life; I couldn't be sexy because I saw sex as a mine field of conflicting, confusing rules that gave them every advantage. I had no sense of what might make me attractive, a lack I'm sure involved unconscious resistance to the game girls were supposed to play (particularly all the rigmarole surrounding clothes, hair and cosmetics); I was a clumsy dancer because I could never follow the boy's lead.

Yet ultimately this rationale misses the point. As I've learned from comparing notes with lots of women, the popular girls were in fact much more in touch with the reality of the female condition than I was. They knew exactly what they had to do for the rewards they wanted, while I did a lot of what feminist organizers call denying the awful truth. I was a bit schizy. Desperate to win the game but unwilling to learn it or even face my feelings about it, I couldn't really play, except in fantasy; paradoxically, I was consumed by it much more thoroughly than the girls who played and played well. Knowing what they wanted and how to get it, they preserved their sense of self, however compromised, while I lost mine. Which is why they were not simply better game players but genuinely more likable than I.

The ugly duckling myth is sentimental. It may soothe the memory of social rejection, but it falsifies the experience, evades its cruelty and uselessness. High school permanently damaged my self-esteem. I learned what it meant to be impotent; what it meant to be invisible. None of this improved my character, spurred my ambition, or gave me a deeper understanding of life. I know people who were popular in high school who later became serious intellectuals, radicals, artists, even journalists. I regret not being one of those people. To see my failure as morally or politically superior to their success would be to indulge in a version of the Laingian fallacy—that because a destructive society drives people crazy, there is something dishonorable about managing to stay sane.

7

QUESTIONS ON MEANING AND CONTENT

1. In the second paragraph, Willis discusses the "effects" of high school as described by Ralph Keyes in his book. The effects he describes are much different from those identified by Willis. She also challenges Keyes' view that those who are popular in high school are shallow people destined to be unpopular later. How does Willis evaluate the effects of high school and why does she reject Keyes' conclusions?

2. In paragraph seven, Willis says that "High school permanently damaged my self-esteem." On what or whom does she blame this?

3. How does Willis account for the popularity of certain people in high school? What were these people like, according to Willis? How does this differ from Keyes' view?

4. What effect do you think the size of Willis' high school (5000 students) had on her experience there?

5. From your own experience, do high schools tend to be made up of "innies" and "outies"? Is there a middle group? If so, how would you characterize its members? Would the middle group, in fact, be made up of several groups?

6. Willis seems to accuse Keyes indirectly of making excuses for being unpopular and of dabbling in illusion. Is she doing the same? Why should her self-esteem have been damaged "permanently" in high school? Why not just temporarily?

7. What point is Willis making in the last sentence of the essay? (Here she refers to the thinking of R. D. Laing, a Scottish psychiatrist who maintained that the complex experiences of the modern world are bound to split our personalities.)

QUESTIONS ABOUT RHETORICAL STRATEGIES

1. What caused the damage to Willis' self-esteem? What, specifically in the high school experience, were causes? What in Willis' own nature were causes? Can you pinpoint an immediate cause or one or two significant causes? What were contributing or remote causes?

2. Does paragraph 2, which discusses Keyes' book, mention any causes beyond what would fall under the general heading of "high school"? If so, identify the causes.

3. What age group do you think would be most interested in this essay? Explain your reasoning. In your view, would this essay have strong appeal to an audience of current high school students or recent high school graduates? Explain.

QUESTIONS ON LANGUAGE AND DICTION

1. What does Willis mean in paragraph 6 when she says, "I was a bit schizy." After you have determined what this means, explain whether her descriptions of herself in high school show that she was or was not "a bit schizy."

2. What is "the ugly duckling myth" (paragraph 7)? Willis calls the myth "sentimental." What does she mean by that?

3. Interpret the phrase "precocious intellectuals and bohemians" in paragraph 4.

4. What are the meanings of the following words: *derelictions, nuances, ineptitude, ambivalent?*

5. Identify Kurt Vonnegut, Frank Zappa, and Mike Nichols.

Dr. Brand

NORMAN COUSINS

Norman Cousins explains how a dedicated physician's careful studies of cause and effect relationships led to dramatic progress in the treatment of leprosy.

If an account is ever written about the attempts of the medical profession to understand pain, the name of Paul Brand may have an honored place. Dr. Brand has worked with lepers for most of his medical career. He is an English orthopedic surgeon, recognized throughout world medical circles for his work in restoring crippled or paralyzed hands to productive use. His principal work at Medical College at Vellore, India, was as director of orthopedic surgery.   1

Paul Brand went to Vellore as a young man in 1947. His wife, also a surgeon, joined him at Vellore a year later. Together, they constituted one of the most remarkable husband-and-wife medical teams in the world. Paul Brand restored to thousands of lepers the use of their hands and arms. Margaret Brand saved thousands of lepers from blindness. Both of them taught at the medical college, undertook important research, and worked at the hospital and in field clinics.   2

Paul Brand's main purpose in coming to the Christian Medical College and Hospital at Vellore was to see whether he might be able to apply his highly developed skills in reconstructive surgery to the special problems of lepers. Commonly, lepers' fingers tend to "claw" or partially close up because of the paralysis of vital nerves controlling the muscles of the hand. Brand wanted to try to reactivate the fingers by connecting them to healthy nerve impulses in the leper's forearm. This would require, of course, reeducating the patient so that his brain could transmit orders to the lower forearm instead of the hand for activating the fingers.   3

He wasn't at Vellore very long, however, before he realized he couldn't confine himself to problems caused by the clawish hands of lepers. He would have to deal with the total problem of leprosy—what it was, how it took hold in the human body, how it might be combated. He immersed himself in research. The more he learned, the greater was his awareness that most of the attitudes toward leprosy he had carried with him to Vellore were   4 outmoded to the point of being medieval. He became determined to pit the scientific method against the old mysteries of leprosy.

He was to discover that the prevailing ideas about "leprous tissue" were   5 mistaken. Wrong, too, was the notion that missing toes or fingers or atrophy of the nose were direct products or manifestations of the disease. Most significant of all perhaps was his awareness that leprosy was a disease of painlessness.

As head of the research section, Paul Brand first needed to find out as   6 much as he could about tissue from the affected parts of lepers. Medicine had long known that leprosy was produced by a bacillus somewhat similar to the organism that causes tuberculosis. This discovery had been made by Gerhard Henrik Hansen almost a century and a half ago; the term "Hansen's disease" became synonymous with leprosy. As in the case of tuberculosis, the *bacillus leprae* produced tubercles. The leprosy tubercles varied in size from a small pea to a large olive. They appeared on the face, ears, and bodily extremities. It was commonly thought that the bacillus was responsible in some way for the sloughing-off of fingers and toes, and even of hands and feet. Yet very little had been done in actual tissue research. Was there anything in the flesh of finger stumps or toes that differentiated this tissue from healthy cells? Was the *bacillus leprae* an active agent in the atrophy? Dr. Brand put the pathologists to work. Through research, they came up with the startling finding that there was no difference between healthy tissue and the tissue of a leper's fingers or toes.

One point, however, was scientifically certain: the *bacillus leprae* killed   7 nerve endings. This meant that the delicate sense of touch was missing or seriously injured. But the flesh itself, Dr. Brand ascertained, was otherwise indistinguishable from normal tissue.

As is often the case in medical research, some of Paul Brand's most   8 important discoveries about leprosy came about not as the result of systematic pursuit but through accident. Soon after arriving in Vellore he observed the prodigious strength in lepers' hands. Even a casual handshake with a leper was like putting one's fingers in a vise. Was this because something in the disease released manual strength not known to healthy people?

The answer came one day when Paul Brand was unable to turn a key in a   9 large rusty lock. A leprous boy of twelve observed Dr. Brand's difficulty and asked to help. Dr. Brand was astonished at the ease with which the youngster turned the key. He examined the boy's thumb and forefinger of the right hand. The key had cut the flesh to the bone. The boy had been completely unaware of what was happening to his fingers while turning the key.

Dr. Brand had his answer at once. The desensitized nerve endings had   10
made it possible for the child to keep turning the key along past the point
where a healthy person would have found it painful to continue. Healthy
people possess strength they never use precisely because resistant pressure
causes pain. A leper's hands are not more powerful, he reasoned; they just
lack the mechanism of pain to tell them when to stop applying pressure. In
this way serious damage could be done to flesh and bone.

Was it possible, Dr. Brand asked himself, that the reason lepers lost   11
fingers and toes was not because of leprosy itself but because they were
insensitive to injury? In short, could a person be unaware that, in the
ordinary course of a day's activity, he might be subjecting his body to serious
physical damage? Paul Brand analyzed all the things he himself did in the
course of a day—turning faucets and doorknobs, operating levers, dislodg-
ing or pulling or pushing things, using utensils of all kinds. In most of these
actions, pressure was required. And the amount of pressure was determined both by the resistance of the object and the ability of his fingers
and hands to tolerate stress. Lacking the sensitivity, he knew, he would
continue to exert pressure even though damage to his hands might be
incurred in the process.

He observed lepers as they went about their daily tasks and was con-   12
vinced he was correct. He began to educate lepers in stress tolerance; he
designed special gloves to protect their hands; and he set up daily examina-
tions so that injuries would not lead to ulceration and to disfigurement, as
had previously occurred. Almost miraculously, the incidence of new injuries was sharply reduced. Lepers became more productive. Paul Brand
began to feel he was making basic progress.

Some mysteries, however, persisted. How to account for the continuing   13
disappearance of fingers, in part or whole? Why was it that parts of fingers
would vanish from one day to the next. Were they knocked off? There was
nothing to indicate that bones of lepers were any more brittle than the bones
of normal people. If a leper cut off a finger while using a saw, or if a finger
were somehow broken off, it should be possible to produce the missing
digit. But no one ever found a finger after it had been lost. Why?

Paul Brand thought about the problem. Then, suddenly, the answer   14
flashed through his mind. It had to be rats. And it would happen at night,
while the lepers were asleep. Since the hands of lepers were desensitized,
they wouldn't know they were being attacked and so would put up no
resistance.

Paul Brand set up observation posts at night in the huts and wards. It   15 was just as he had thought. The rats climbed the beds of lepers, sniffed carefully, and, when they encountered no resistance, went to work on fingers and toes. The fingers hadn't been dropping off; they were being eaten. This didn't mean that all "lost" fingers had disappeared in this way. They could be knocked off through accidents and then carried away by rats or other animals before the loss would be observed. But a major cause of the disappearance had now been identified.

Paul Brand and his staff went to work, mounting a double-pronged   16
attack against the invaders. The program for rodent control was stepped up many times. Barriers were built around the legs of beds. The beds themselves were raised. The results were immediately apparent. There was a sharp drop in the disappearance of fingers and toes.

All this time, Paul Brand kept up his main work—reconstructing hands,   17
rerouting muscles, straightening out fingers. Where fingers were shortened or absent, the remaining digits had to be made fully operative. Thousands of lepers were restored to manual productivity.

One of the grim but familiar marks of many lepers is the apparent decay   18
of their noses. What caused the shrinkage? It was highly unlikely that the nose suffered from the kind of persistent injury that frequently affected the desensitized hands and feet. What about rats? This, too, seemed unlikely. Enough sensitivity existed in a leper's face, especially around the mouth, to argue strongly against the notion of rodent assault.

As Paul Brand pursued the riddle, he became convinced that neither   19
injuries nor rats were involved. Finally, he found his answer in his research on the effect of *bacillus leprae* on the delicate membranes inside the nose. These membranes would contract severely in lepers. This meant that the connecting cartilage would be yanked inward. What was happening, therefore, was not decay or loss of nasal structure through injury. The nose was being drawn into the head.

It was a startling discovery, running counter to medical ideas that had   20
lasted for centuries. Could Brand prove it? The best way of proceeding, he felt, was by surgery that would push the nose back into the face. He therefore reconstructed the nose from the inside. It was a revolutionary approach.

He knew that the operation couldn't work in all cases. Where the leprosy   21
was so far advanced that membrane shrinkage left little to work with, it was doubtful that the operation would be successful. But there was a good chance that, in those cases where the disease could be arrested and where the shrinkage was not extreme, noses could be pushed back into place.

The theory worked. As a result, the nose restorative operation de- 22
veloped at Vellore has been used for the benefit of large numbers of lepers at
hospitals throughout the world.

Next, blindness. Of all the afflictions of leprosy, perhaps none is more 23
serious or characteristic than blindness. Here, too, it had been assumed for
many centuries that loss of sight was a specific manifestation of advanced
leprosy. At Vellore, this assumption was severely questioned. Intensive
study of the disease convinced Paul Brand and his fellow researchers that
blindness was not a direct product of leprosy but a by-product. A serious
vitamin A deficiency, for example, could be a major contributing cause of
cataracts and consequent blindness. Where cataracts were already formed, it
was possible to remove them by surgery.

It was in this field that Dr. Margaret Brand became especially active and 24
effective. On some days she would perform as many as a hundred cataract
operations. This number would seem high to the point of absurdity to many
European and American eye surgeons for whom twelve such operations in a
single day would be considered formidable. But the eye surgeons at Vellore
have to contend with literally thousands of people waiting in line to be saved
from blindness. They often work fourteen to sixteen hours a day, using
techniques that facilitate rapid surgery.

Dr. Margaret Brand was part of a medical and surgical field team that 25
would make regular rounds among villages far removed from the hospital.
Surgical tents would be set up. Electricity would be supplied by power
take-off devices from the jeep motors.

Cataracts, however, were not the whole story in blindness among lep- 26
ers. Many lepers at Vellore didn't suffer from cataracts, yet were losing their
sight from eye ulcerations. Did the *bacillus leprae* produce the infection and
the resultant ulcerations and blindness? Or, as in the case of fingers and
toes, was the loss of function a by-product in which other causes had to be
identified and eliminated.

The latter line of reasoning proved to be fruitful. Human eyes are 27
constantly exposed to all sorts of irritations from dust and dirt in the air. The
eyes deal with these invasions almost without a person being aware of the
process. Thousands of times a day the eyelids close and open, washing the
surface of the eye with soothing saline fluid released by the tear ducts.

Paul Brand and his colleagues believed this washing process didn't take 28
place in lepers because there was a loss of sensation on the eye surface
caused by the atrophy of nerve endings. This hypothesis was easily and
readily confirmed. They observed the eyes of lepers when subjected to

ordinary irritations. There was, as they had suspected, no batting of the eyelids; therefore, there could be no washing process. The big problem, then, was to get the eyelids working again.

Why not educate lepers to make a conscious effort to bat their eyes? 29
There being no impairment of a leper's ability to close his eyes at will, it ought to be possible to train lepers to be diligent in this respect. But experiments quickly demonstrated the disadvantages of this approach. Unless a leper concentrated on the matter constantly, it wouldn't work. And if he did concentrate, he could think of almost nothing else. No; what was needed was a way of causing eyelid action that would clean the eyes automatically.

In the case of fingers or toes, it was possible to educate lepers in stress 30
tolerances and to give them protective gloves or shoes. How to keep dirt and foreign objects from getting into the eye? Eye goggles might be one answer but they were not airtight, were cumbersome, would fog up because of the high humidity, and were too easily lost. Something more basic would have to be found.

The answer, again, was found in reconstructive surgery. Paul Brand and 31
his team devised a way of hooking up the muscles of the jaw to the eyelid. Every time a leper opened his mouth the new facial muscles would pull the eyelids and cause them to close, thus washing the eyball. In this way, a leper could literally talk and eat his way out of oncoming blindness. Countless numbers of lepers have their sight today because of this ingenious use of surgery in facilitating the use of nature's mechanism to get rid of dirt and dust in the eyes.

* * *

Gradually, as the result of research at Vellore and other leper centers 32
throughout the world, the terrible black superstition about leprosy is receding. Contrary to popular impressions, it is not highly contagious. In fact, it is virtually impossible to transmit leprosy to a healthy person. As with tuberculosis, of course, persons in weakened conditions are vulnerable in varying degrees. The disease is not hereditary; again, however, as with other diseases, increased susceptibility can be passed along from parent to child.

Basically, leprosy is the product of filth, poverty, and malnutrition. It is 33
not, as is generally supposed, a disease of the tropics and subtropics. It can exist wherever unsanitary conditions, hunger, or poorly balanced diet exist. It has existed in countries as far north as Iceland. Scarcely a country in the world has been untouched by it. But the important thing is that it is eradica-

ble, and its victims can be cured or appreciably helped and rehabilitated. And it can once and for all be rescued from the general ignorance and associated superstitions assigned to it over the ages.

Medical researchers have given high recognition to Dr. Brand and his colleagues for their new insights into the nature of leprosy, but even greater accolades within the profession have come his way because of his work in rehabilitative surgery. He has been able to transform hands, long clawed and rigid because of nerve atrophy brought on by leprosy or other causes, into functioning mechanisms. Almost legendary in India is the case of a lawyer on whom he operated. For many years, the lawyer had been at a disadvantage in court. His gestures, so essential a part of the dramatic courtroom manner, were actually a liability; judge and jury were distracted by the hideously deformed and frozen hand. Then one day the lawyer raised his hand to emphasize a point. The hand was supple; the fingers moved, the gesture was appropriate. Paul Brand had operated on the hand, hooking up muscle and nerve connections to the forearm, then educating the patient to retrain his command impulses. 34

Paul Brand and his staff have performed thousands of similar operations on patients at Vellore. But they have also gone far beyond surgery into what they consider an even more vital phase of the total treatment. This is psychological rehabilitation. A man who, as a leper, has been a beggar for twenty years is not considered to be fully treated at Vellore until he is mentally and physically prepared to be a useful and proud citizen in his society. At Vellore, handicapped patients are given the kind of training that will enable them to be as self-supporting as possible. They gain a respect for the limitless potentialities and adaptabilities of the human organism. They learn that even as little as a 10 percent mobility can be made to yield a high return in terms of effective productivity. And, in the Emersonian sense, self-reliance creates self-respect. 35

It is not necessary, of course, to provide any precise assessment of the relative importance of the three main phases of Paul Brand's work—taking the black curse and superstition out of leprosy, reconstructive surgery, and personal and psychological rehabilitation. All are important; all are interrelated. But one aspect of his work may perhaps be more evocative and compelling than any of the others. He is a doctor who, if he could, would move heaven and earth just to return the gift of pain to people who do not have it. For pain is both the warning system and the protective mechanism that enables an individual to defend the integrity of his body. Its signals may not always be readily intelligible but at least they are there. And the individual can mobilize his response. 36

QUESTIONS ON MEANING AND CONTENT

1. We sometimes forget that pain is a protective mechanism and to be without it would expose us to greater physical problems than pain itself. Cite examples from the essay that illustrate this point.

2. Paul Brand's work not only demonstrates that he was a keen observer but also shows that he was capable of using imagination to solve problems. How does the essay show each of these powers at work?

3. Among the problems initially faced by Paul Brand were some old, inaccurate ideas about leprosy. What were some of these, and how did he go about disproving them?

QUESTIONS ABOUT RHETORICAL STRATEGIES

1. The first five paragraphs of the essay serve as the introduction. What does each of these do to prepare readers for the body of the essay? In what sort of logical order are these paragraphs arranged?

2. Although this is a cause and effect essay, much of the development comes through short narratives showing Brand in the act of solving problems. Thus, readers see Brand observing people and pondering over possible causes and experimenting with solutions in order to confirm his analysis. When appropriate to purpose and audience, cause and effect analyses sift out this human element and focus only on the analysis. What is the author's purpose here? Describe the audience that he seems to be writing to. What sort of audience might demand a different purpose and a different structure?

3. Paragraph 34 discusses Paul Brand's achievements in restoring hands malformed by nerve atrophy. In what way does the lawyer-patient illustration strengthen the paragraph?

4. Moving smoothly and logically from paragraph to paragraph is a sign of coherence in writing. Can you pinpoint and describe any of Cousins' techniques in connecting one paragraph to another. For example, what is the technique used in each of the following cases: moving between paragraphs 7 and 8, 8 and 9, 9 and 10, 10 and 11. Do you find any of these to be particularly effective? Why or why not?

QUESTIONS ON LANGUAGE AND DICTION

1. Writing that examines effects in order to identify causes has to place heavy emphasis on questions: Why did this happen? What caused it? In this essay, Paul Brand is examining effects to determine causes. How often does the author, in recounting Brand's experiences, use the technique of raising questions as a means of moving the cause-effect analysis forward?

2. Examine paragraphs 13 through 16, giving attention to sentence length. What seems to be the author's method in using sentences of different lengths? In this stretch, which is fairly characteristic of the essay as a whole, Cousin uses many short sentences. How does he balance these with longer sentences? Do the shorter sentences ever seem to make the writing move abruptly? Or is this offset by longer sentences? Do you find instances in which the placement of longer sentences make the shorter sentences more dramatic or just generally more effective?

3. Check the meanings of any of the following words that are unfamiliar to you: *accolades, atrophy, cumbersome, eradicable, orthopedic, prodigious.*

Political Dogs

DICK GREGORY

Dick Gregory, the well-known comedian, writer, and civil rights advo-cate, tells us some of the things politicians know about getting elected and, of course, re-elected. Dogs, Gregory says, can have an effect on the outcome of elections. In this essay, he explains the cause and effect relationship existing between dogs and political campaigns.

When it comes to persuading the electorate, there is currently nothing   1
more important to a candidate than a wife, kids, and the right kind of animals. Dogs are great assets to candidates, and the feeling seems to be engendered that if a dog loves the candidate, he can't be all that bad.

If it can be said that Richard Nixon's road to the White House began with   2
his first election to the Vice President's office, then it can be asserted that a dog saved his political life. In 1952 young Richard Nixon was the Republican Vice Presidential nominee. Early in the fall the candidate was questioned about an $18,235 trust fund he maintained. The opposition accused him of taking money under the table and questioned such conduct on the part of a Senator, especially a Senator representing the national party ticket.

Nixon appeared on national radio and television to defend himself—   3
indeed, to fight for his political life. The broadcast was aired from Los Angeles, September 23, 1952. Affecting his best folksy manner, he explained that he was not a wealthy man. That already established common ground with most of his listeners. He said he had accepted money from supporters for the necessary expenses his office entailed. He said he had never granted any special favors as a result, nor had the money been used secretly.

Nixon gave a breakdown of his personal assets. He said he had $10,000 in   4
government bonds when he left the service; he received $1,600 from estates in his law practice; he inherited about $4,500; his family lived modestly in one mortgaged house in Washington, D.C., and another one in California; he had no stocks or bonds; he had life insurance on himself but not on his wife, Pat, or the children; and they owned a 1950 Oldsmobile. Nixon listed his debts: a $20,000 mortgage on the Washington house and a $10,000 mortgage on the California home; $4,500 to a bank in Washington; $3,500 to parents; and $500 on a loan from his life insurance.

The Vice Presidential nominee said that some Senators put their wives   5 on the payroll, but he could never do that. "My wife's sitting over here," Nixon said proudly. "She's a wonderful stenographer. She used to teach stenography and she used to teach shorthand in high school. That was when I met her. I can tell you folks that she's worked many hours at night and many hours on Saturdays and Sundays in my office and she's done a fine job. And I'm proud to say tonight that in the six years I've been in the House and Senate of the United States, Pat Nixon has never been on the government payroll."

Of course, Pat had to pay a price for her husband's honesty. Said Nixon,   6
"Pat doesn't have a mink coat. But she does have a respectable Republican cloth coat. And I always tell her that she'd look good in anything."

Then in one brilliant, sentimental stroke, Candidate Nixon got the *wife*,   7
the *kids*, and a *dog* into the story all at the same time. Just to show he wasn't hiding a thing, not one little thing, from the public, Nixon told a little story about his personal life.

"One other thing I probably should tell you, because if I don't they'll   8
probably be saying this about me too. We did get something—a gift—after the election." (Suspense.) "A man down in Texas heard *Pat* on the radio mention the fact that our *two youngsters* would like to have a dog. And, believe it or not, the day before we left on this campaign trip we got a message from the Union Station in Baltimore saying they had a package for us. We went down to get it. You know what it was?

"It was a *little cocker spaniel dog* in a crate that he sent all the way from   9
Texas. Black-and-white spotted. And our little girl Tricia—the six-year-old—named it Checkers. And you know, the kids love the dog, and I just want to say this right now, that, regardless of what they say about it, we're gonna keep it."

Nixon kept Checkers and the Vice Presidential nomination. The black-   10
and-white-spotted cocker spaniel removed whatever spots had blotted the Nixon image.

Another President who used a dog to garner public support and sym-   11
pathy was Franklin Delano Roosevelt. His dog Fala became as popular a White House figure as Dr. Henry Kissinger is today. And probably a plot to kidnap Fala would have produced more public outrage than the alleged plot to abduct Kissinger. During the 1944 Presidential campaign, when Roosevelt was going after his fourth term in the White House, the candidate spoke before the Teamsters' Union and issued a devastating attack upon the Republicans, answering their libels against "my little dog Fala."

So it's nice to have a dog around the house when you are seeking public   12
office. Dogs not only breed affection, but they can breed and be promiscu-

ous in other ways without danger of producing a public scandal. Dogs are a rare political asset: close friends, liked by almost everybody, unassailable in the public eye, and never able to get the candidate caught in a compromising situation. However, the candidate can bring disgrace upon himself by abusing the dog, as Lyndon B. Johnson found out when he picked up his beagles by the ears in full view of newspaper reporters. Johnson claimed the dogs liked it, but the public was not convinced.

QUESTIONS ON MEANING AND CONTENT

1. Paragraph 10 says that Nixon's dog Checkers "removed whatever spots had blotted the Nixon image." Gregory merely tells us this, and not until later does he explain why a dog could bring about this effect. What is the cause and effect relationship between the dog Checkers and the removal of the blots on Nixon's image?

2. This essay tells us what politicians know about creating effects favorable to themselves. In doing so, it also indirectly says something about the nature of the people who do the voting. What?

3. Can you think of something other than dogs that political candidates commonly use to create effects favorable to themselves? If so, what is the cause and effect relationship that makes each of these work to the candidate's advantage?

4. Dogs can also create an effect that could harm a politician. But the harmful effect must also have its own causes. What possible actions by a politician could cause a dog to have an ill effect on a politician's popularity? What example does Gregory use to illustrate this?

QUESTIONS ABOUT RHETORICAL STRATEGIES

1. Except for the Nixon example, Gregory does not offer much background information on the other dogs mentioned in the essay—those of Franklin Roosevelt and Lyndon Johnson. He seems to assume that readers will already have that background information. How does this help identify the audience to whom Gregory is writing?

2. Paragraphs 3–6 contain many cause and effect possibilities in addition to those associated with dogs. In these paragraphs, a political candidate, Richard Nixon, is trying to say things that will have a positive effect on his audience. Only near the end of his talk does he turn his attention to the dog Checkers. Examine the details of these paragraphs, isolating causes that could lead to the desired effect—having people believe the candidate and creating a desire in listeners to vote for the candidate.

QUESTIONS ON LANGUAGE AND DICTION

1. Paragraph 3 refers to Richard Nixon's "best folksy manner." What is a folksy manner? Why was he using a folksy manner? What is the cause and effect relationship between his use of the folksy manner and the reaction he wants from his audience? Among the Nixon quotations in the essay, are there any you would classify as "folksy"?

2. What is the tone of the essay—Gregory's attitude toward the subject? Point to particular uses of language or examples used by the author which help establish this tone?

3. What does Gregory's language suggest about his attitude toward Richard Nixon? Explain.

4. What are the meanings of the following words: *promiscuous, unassailable?*

What Killed George Washington?

ANNABEL HECHT

The youngest of the three physicians attending George Washington during his final illness suggested an operation that was daring and innovative for the times though common enough today. It would likely have worked, according to modern medical authorities. But the two older doctors rejected the procedure and chose more common treatments: bran and honey poultices to soothe the throat, beetles to create blisters on the legs, and incisions to draw blood from the body.

1   It is of no consequence now to the principals. They are long gone. But the question remains something of a medical conundrum—just what caused George Washington's death?

2   There is no question that Washington suffered a sore throat. It started Dec. 13, 1799, the day after he had made a tour of his Mount Vernon, Va., estate in a freezing rain. But he took nothing for it, since, according to his secretary Tobias Lear, the general was always averse to nursing himself for minor complaints.

3   Early the following day Washington's throat worsened. Breathing became difficult and swallowing was painful. At daybreak, the estate overseer was summoned to bleed Washington. Bleeding was a common medical practice of the day, performed by lay persons as well as physicians.

4   Washington was given a mixture of molasses, vinegar and butter, but he could not swallow it. Applications of poultices and soaking the feet were of no help. In the course of the day, three physicians were summoned to Mount Vernon. Their initial diagnosis was "inflammatory quinsy," and their only treatment was bleeding.

5   The youngest of the medical trio proposed performing an immediate tracheostomy—cutting an opening in the throat to provide an emergency airway. It was a daring suggestion for that time. One of the other physicians seemed convinced but was persuaded by the third that the operation would be fatal. The only thing they could agree on was to bleed the patient for the third and fourth time.

6   Despite his loss of blood, Washington insisted on sitting up. "Blisters" (beetles used to raise blisters) were applied to his legs, a "bran" (a poultice of bran and honey) to his throat. He almost choked to death leaning his head back to swallow medicine.

At about 10 p.m., Washington's breathing seemed to improve and his   7
restlessness subsided. But suddenly, less than two hours later, the president
died. His final illness had lasted 21 hours.

Because of Washington's stature and fear of criticism, the three physi-   8
cians published a statement in the *Alexandria* (Va.) *Times,* Dec. 19, 1799. In
this report they changed their diagnosis to an inflammatory affliction of the
upper part of the windpipe, called "Cynanche trachealis." They reported
that their treatment consisted of bleeding during which one quart of blood
was withdrawn. (The average man has five or six quarts of blood.)

Predictably, the physicians were attacked by laymen and other physi-   9
cians alike. One colleage was sure Washington's problem had been "croup"
and that he could have cured him in four hours. One claimed too much
blood was taken, while another said the main mistake was in not taking
enough blood the first time.

Twentieth century writers have speculated that Washington died of   10
diphtheria or strep throat. It has also been suggested that Washington's
demise was due to acute epiglottitis, a severe, rapidly progressing infection
of the epiglottis (the small flap of tissue that covers the windpipe when food
is being swallowed), usually caused by an influenza virus.

One of those supporting this diagnosis is Dr. Heinz H.E. Scheide-   11
mandel. Writing in the *Archives of Otolaryngology* (September 1976) he notes
that epiglottitis is consistent with the signs and symptoms described by
those attending Washington: the rapid onset of the disease, difficulty in
swallowing, sore throat, an unintelligibly muffled voice, increased airway
obstruction when leaning backward, a desire to sit up despite weakness,
persistent restlessness, and, finally, a short period of seeming improvement
just before death.

When infected, the epiglottis may enlarge to 10 times its normal size.   12
This creates a ball-valve effect that tends to block air from being drawn into
the lungs. The patient tries to relieve this obstruction by sitting up and
leaning forward. Tilting the head backward to swallow closes the airway and
obstructs breathing.

Washington's voice was muffled and unintelligible because of the   13
enlargement of the epiglottis. He was not hoarse, however, because the
vocal chords were not involved.

The inability to draw fresh air into the lungs causes hypoxemia—a lack of   14
oxygen in the blood. As hypoxemia develops, the patient becomes restless
and then euphoric, conditions that were noted in Washington's case.

Epiglottitis is not a disease relegated to the history books. Even today it is   15
one of the most destructive and dramatic diseases of childhood. Interestingly, Scheidemandel writes, "in spite of all the advances of modern

medicine in the last 200 years, this otolaryngologic emergency would have been treated the same way then as now [that is, with a tracheostomy]. Only the rapid establishment of an airway guarantees survival in acute epiglottitis, while a 'quinsy' may have drained itself and 'croup' would never have led to death in a patient 67 years of age."

The young physician at Washington's bedside had been right in sug- 16 gesting a tracheostomy after all.

QUESTIONS ON MEANING AND CONTENT

1. Why would someone in the late twentieth century be interested in what caused a death in 1799? Is this because Washington was such a famous American? Or can you suggest other reasons?

2. Paragraph 9 tells how people reacted to Washington's death. What principle of human nature is at work in these reactions? Can you name modern situations where you see this same principle operating?

3. What were some of the specific treatments used by the attending physicians? Why was the one treatment that might have worked finally rejected—was this merely because one physician argued more persuasively than the others? What factors may have led the physicians to be cautious and to stay with the standard treatments of the day?

4. What cause and effect evidence supports the conclusion that Washington died of acute epiglottitis?

QUESTIONS ABOUT RHETORICAL STRATEGIES

1. Paragraphs 2–9 form a narrative which describes the events in Washington's illness, his death, and the reaction afterward. Do all these details serve as cause and effect evidence for Dr. Scheidemandel? Which details may be there to create reader interest?

2. What purpose does paragraph 9 serve in the overall structure of the essay? As a conclusion to the narrative portion? As a way of leading into the cause-effect analysis? Both? Explain.

QUESTIONS ON LANGUAGE AND DICTION

1. The essay contains many terms that have to be explained or defined for readers. What are some of these and how are they handled by the writer?

2. Check the meanings of any of the following words that are new to you: *conundrum, croup, demise, euphoric, poultices, quinsy, relegated.*

WRITING SCENARIOS

1. Like many people, you keep a journal in which you analyze and discuss your thoughts and feelings about various subjects of importance to you. You have decided to write an entry in essay form about an instance in your life in which you underwent some important change or recognized some truth about yourself. Analyze the causes leading to the growth or change. Although you are your own audience in this case, you are particularly interested in a thorough, honest analysis of the causes of your growth. Perhaps, during prewriting, you will want to act as if you were analyzing someone else; this role playing may help you analyze causes a bit more objectively.

2. Presume that you are 25 years older than you actually are. You are writing to your daughter who has just entered college as a freshman. You know that she will have to make many decisions on her own now that she is away from home, so you have decided to explain how you have made important decisions in the past. Choose an important decision you have made and analyze what caused you to make it. What led you to the decision? What possible future effects did you consider during the decision-making process? What have been the results of having made the decision? Remember, you aren't constructing an argument in an effort to persuade someone to make the same decision; you are showing the anatomy of a decision.

3. You are an investigative reporter for your campus newspaper, and the news editor has asked you to analyze through cause-and-effect some feature of the enrollment patterns at your college or university. Have enrollments been rising? Why? Have enrollments been tapering off or remaining steady? What are the causes? Are more older adults now enrolling?

Are full-time enrollments down and part-time enrollments up? What are the causes? What are the effects on your school? You might want to narrow your analysis to your own major. Is your major more or less popular among students now than in the past? Why? You will want to interview officials at your school—perhaps your instructor, the Chair of your major department, and the Director of Admissions—in order to gather information and to learn what written sources you can consult for additional information. Your readers are all readers of the student newspaper: students, faculty members, and administrators. If you write about your own major, then your primary audience would include fellow majors and the faculty and administrators responsible for your major program, in addition to past and future majors; your secondary audience would be all other readers of the paper.

4. The history and journalism departments of your college are sponsoring a public conference on the role of college students in modern politics. At the conference, several students and professors will discuss various aspects of the subject. The conference was organized because recent surveys have shown that people below the age of 30 tend not to read newspapers as much as older people and are less likely to vote in elections when eligible. You have been asked to select either one of these activities and write a paper in which you emphasize causes and explain why this particular age group cares less about the news or less about voting than do older people. Remember, you aren't arguing that this age group should or should not vote or read newspapers more often. You are merely analyzing causes of this behavior. Since both students and faculty members will be in the audience, you will want to direct your writing to both groups of readers.

5. Most communities at one time or another have experienced some kind of natural disaster or intense weather-related phenomenon. Your community is no exception, and a local publisher is preparing a souvenir booklet, complete with color photographs, of the event that had such an impact on your city. The publisher has paid you $50.00 to write an essay showing the effects just after the natural disaster that you have experienced. This could be a flood, hurricane, tornado, ice storm, heavy snow storm, earthquake, or any other natural disaster. Although the emphasis is on effects, you will have to give some attention to causes, especially those that account for one part of an area having been more affected than another or the failure of a community to take proper precautions. In fact, if you know of a situation in which a failure to take preventive measures led to special damages, then the emphasis in your paper can be on causes. This essay will require some description and may even be organized as a narrative if your particular disaster lends itself to that treatment. Your primary audience is comprised of those who also experienced the disaster. You are, in a sense, recalling the event for your fellow citizens. However, a secondary audience includes anyone who has experienced a natural disaster and who would, therefore, understand in a personal way the powerful forces at work. Beyond this secondary audience is a third audience comprised of those whose curiosity would make your essay interesting reading. Such people may, in fact, make up a large part of your audience. Remember that your second and third audiences will not be familiar with the area you are writing about.

6. You're applying for a summer job as a counselor at a junior high school summer camp near Lake Placid. The students there will have a full program including some orientation to college level subjects. The counselors will consist of majors from a number of college disciplines, and each counselor will have to present some informal classes in a subject in their major. One of the screening tests you will have to pass to get the job is to compose an essay written for junior high school students in which you explain a major concept in your area of study. You've decided to show how a cause and effect relation exists between two important phenomena in your discipline. For instance, if it's biology, you may want to explain the relation between sunlight and the products of photosyntheis. If it's economics, you may want to explain the cause and effect relationship between supply and demand. Because your audience is junior high school students, you'll have to keep technical terminology to a minimum and everything will have to be extra clear—no small job!

NINE

ARGUING YOUR CASE
AND PERSUADING
YOUR AUDIENCE

Argument is the process of convincing someone that your idea, proposal, or theory is correct. **Persuasion** is the process of convincing someone to take (or not take) a certain action. In reality, the two are often mixed; the purpose is usually the same—to persuade your readers to believe or agree with something or to motivate them to take some action.

Everyone has experience with argument and persuasion. Each day you encounter speech and writing that tries to convince you of something or to motivate you to do something. You receive letters urging you to buy some gadget, support some cause, or subscribe to something. Radio and television attempt to persuade you in one way or another. Newspapers and magazines contain editorials and advertisements that attempt to convince you that a certain political view or product is the best. Your friends try to convince you that the football coach should be fired or that the local schools are not really educating students. Of course, while all this goes on, you probably make similar efforts, attempting to convince others to share your views on some matter or to do something you recommend.

Although the energy directed toward argument and persuasion seems inexhaustible, people pay little attention, for the most part, to the methods used in these attempts. Yet, if you think about the subject carefully, you could piece together some of the features common to argument and persuasion. You know, for example, that when someone wants to convince or motivate you, the person must first identify what it is you are being asked to believe or do.

These identifying statements are called *assertions*. An assertion is a statement that affirms something positively. An assertion often makes a claim: "Our school system is as effective as any in the state," or "The War Hawks have the best defensive team in the league." Frequently, an assertion will propose action: "I suggest we form a Neighborhood Watch," or "The city should erect a stop sign at Fourth and Grant Streets." An argumentative paper begins with an assertion and sets out to prove or at least defend the validity of the assertion. Your objective in such writing is to supply enough reasons for your readers to agree with you. You may make several assertions in an essay, but the main assertion around which the entire essay revolves is called a *thesis*.

Certainly, an important aspect of an effective argumentative or persuasive essay is sound logical reasoning. In examining arguments, look for logical *fallacies*, or lapses in logical thinking. Conclusions must be logically sound or must logically follow sufficient evidence. A flock of robins in Ohio in February does not mean that spring has arrived. Seeing police officers on every other corner does not support the conclusion that crime is rampant in the city. These are overgeneralizations and show a naive willingness to jump to conclusions at the first sign of evidence.

Look also for statements that shift attention from the argument onto something else. Mentioning the names of famous or beloved people or renowned experts often does this. Statements like "Abraham Lincoln was really a Democrat at heart because he cared about people," may sound pleasant if you are a Democrat, but how does the statement relate to the issue at hand? And must anyone who cares about people therefore be a member of the Democratic party? And how did Lincoln stand on other principles of the Democratic party?

It is acceptable, however, to mention famous people so long as what you mention clearly relates to the point at hand. If not, then the reader can assume that the name has been mentioned for emotional appeal. Similarly, it can be beneficial to cite expert opinion. An expert's opinion on whether or not a part on an airplane should have failed could be of extreme value in a law suit asking for crash damages. But an expert's opinion must be to the point and must be on the subject of his or her expertise. In contrast, you will want to avoid using your own opinions or those of friends or someone you have merely heard of unless you can show that any one of these persons is an expert on the topic at issue. Ask yourself, "Would a judge permit this person to testify in court as an expert on the question before me"? If not, you don't want to use the opinion in your argument.

Another way of distracting attention from the question and injecting emotion at the same time is to attack people who hold an opposite view: "The man who suggested we establish zoning laws does have some experience with the law. He was arrested for drunkenness in Detroit last month." This may be true, but what does this have to do with zoning laws? In fact, what does this have to do with the arguments in the man's proposal that zoning laws be established? Effective argumentative papers avoid attacking the opponents and concentrate instead on the relevant issues.

False comparisons are another logical fallacy:"Allowing your children into video game centers is about the same as lowering the legal drinking age to ten. Either one will destroy a child's character." Such a statement is not valid because it is a comparison of two completely different things—like comparing apples with oranges. A related fallacy is two-valued logic, which assumes that only two possibilities exist: "Either stop criticizing the food or stop eating in the dining halls." Aren't there other alternatives?

There are other logical fallacies besides the ones illustrated here. Fallacies are often more subtle and more difficult to identify in arguments. Nevertheless, search them out. Try to adopt the questioning attitude of the clever, fictional detectives who do not rush in and assume that the butler did it. These smart investigators make everyone a possible suspect, guard against being distracted by false evidence, and test their own conclusions to be sure they are not being led away from rather than toward the real culprit.

An essay that presents an argument may contain a variety of rhetorical methods. For example, city council members proposing a rapid transit system for their city might use comparison and contrast to show the differences in traffic congestion between their city and cities that employ rapid transit systems. Cause and effect is also quite common, since arguments often propose the elimination of something that has an undesirable effect—a call for the closing of a waste dump, for instance. Arguments that ask that something be created will likely discuss the resulting effects. You can also use narration, description, definition, and other rhetorical modes to develop parts of your argument.

PREWRITING

When preparing to write an argumentative or persuasive paper, it is best to choose a topic that interests you and that you know something about. Having an active interest can motivate you to work hard in supporting your main assertion. In addition, you will want to have a clear conception of your purpose and audience. Are you addressing the members of your fraternity or sorority to convince them to adopt a controversial new policy? Are you making a formal appeal to your campus student government? Are you writing a persuasive "letter to the editor" of your community newspaper, arguing that a certain law should or should not be passed? Your writing tasks become much easier once you have clearly formulated your purpose and audience.

Also, be aware that an issue with great personal importance can create blind spots in your reasoning and may cause you to make statements simply because you want them to be true and not because they logically follow the evidence. You may also have unconsciously accepted logical fallacies from other supports of your position. When you have already embraced a position, it is easy to overlook the validity of your opponent's views and weaknesses in your own.

Your topic must be arguable. In short, some noticeable controversy has to exist. Scientists do not argue that dinosaurs actually lived. Everyone already accepts that. They may, however, argue about what caused dinosaurs to disappear. If your topic is arguable, an audience of any size should have members who share your view, members who disagree with it, and members who are undecided.

Once you formulate an assertion, check to see that it raises only one question. To argue that your family should sell its second car and invest the money in the stock market is to argue two questions. Your parents would likely suggest that one question be settled before going on to the second: "First, why should we sell the car?" Even if your parents discussed your assertions with you, one issue would get in the way of the other and confuse the discussion. The same thing happens in writing. Be sure you have only one main assertion, and follow the same practice throughout your essay by never arguing more than one point at a time.

Before you gather evidence to support your argument, you may want to spend some time analyzing what it is you are asserting. What exactly is your argument? Are you going to identify a problem and argue for a certain solution? Are you going to identify a condition and propose that the condition be changed? Are you going to urge readers to do something for some reason or urge them not to do something? Such assertions suggest taking action or not taking action. Here are some examples:

- Cities should (or should not) be forced to provide shelter for street people.

- The university's mandatory attendance policy should (or should not) be abolished.

- Smoking should (or should not) be banned on all commercial aircraft.

- Toy advertisements should (or should not) be banned from television.

- People who enjoy driving should own a sports car at some time in their lives.

If your argument does not call for action (or ask people not to act), then it will make a claim that something exists or something is true. Detailed discussions of such arguments would divide them into more specific categories, but the following will give you an idea of their range:

- The two-way traffic on Grant Street causes the congestion in Celebrity Square.

- Conditions at Riverside Park are unsanitary.

- Mayor Jones is a public relations artist.

- Breakdancing is a dangerous activity.

When you have formulated an assertion and can place it in the action or claim category, then you are ready to generate evidence. If your assertion falls into the action group, then perhaps you should do two things before brainstorming for evidence. First, write down your assertion and put a *because* after it: "The mandatory attendance policy should be abolished because . . ." Then think of the most important general reason that summarizes why you hold this view. The reason should be significant enough so that someone would likely respond to it by asking "Why do you think that?" rather than "What are your other reasons?" If someone asks the latter question, you have probably listed a minor or supporting point, or perhaps your reason is insignificant. For example, if you said the policy should be abolished because mandatory attendance inconveniences students, you have an insignificant reason because it does not take into account the complexities of the subject.

A workable summarizing statement would sound something like this ". . . because mandatory attendance creates a restrictive atmosphere that weakens the learning process." This is not insignificant, and it does summarize. It allows you to gather evidence to support your point. The statement can become the conclusion you are working toward in your paper. Also, you will want to avoid simple, highly judgmental statements like "abolishing the policy is the right thing to do." Such a statement does not convince readers of anything.

Once your prewriting produces a sound summarizing statement, it is a good practice to reverse your assertion and say that the policy should *not* be abolished. This places you on the other side of the argument. Now, think of the strongest summarizing reason you can to oppose your original one. Remember, it must answer the summarizing reason you already have, not a different one. That is, don't say the policy should be kept because it forces students to acquire self-discipline or that students should learn that life's circumstances will always limit their freedom. Instead, say that the mandatory policy permits a *good* learning atmosphere.

This role reversal gives you the opposing thesis, and you can begin to list the points for both views side by side on your prewriting notes. List your own first, and next to each one list the opposing view. You are outlining both arguments in order to understand your own argument more precisely and to learn what points you will have to address and what evidence you will need.

Think about why some people disagree with the view you are presenting. You should know why they disagree because this information can give you an idea of how to approach your argument and present evidence, and it gives you a chance to test statements held by those who oppose your view. Begin with points of theirs that you consider weak. Then try to determine whether they are weak or whether your own biases have led you to think so. In short, what weaknesses do you find in another view? What does another viewpoint tell you about weaknesses in your own argument?

Examining another position can also make you more sensitive to how easily your own feelings can lead you to argue unsoundly. You can more easily find flaws in another's argument because you want to find them— particularly if you oppose the argument. At the same time, it is difficult to locate the faults in your own because you may not really want to find them. Try to adopt the opposite attitude. Search as aggressively for flaws in your own argument as you do when examining one that opposes your views. You may even wish to freewrite—once for each side of the argument.

By examining another view, you can also learn the points which do agree with yours, and you can acknowledge them. Remember, the point of honest argument is not to flatten people with a verbal steamroller or to show that you are absolutely right or that something is absolutely true. You want to show that your views can be accepted as having a high probability of being true.

As you work on the two lists, modify your assertion as necessary. You are not obligated to keep your original summarizing statement. Feel free to fine-tune it. For example, after examining your prewriting notes you may realize that you really do not want to abolish the attendance system but to modify it by allowing a certain number of absences. Remember, you have the flexibility, especially early in the writing process, to alter your original point.

If instead of using an action assertion you claim that something exists or is so, then you will have to demonstrate that there is a high degree of probability that the claim is true. For example, if you assert that the two-way traffic on Grant Street causes congestion in Celebrity Square, you have to establish that congestion does exist there. Then you have to show that the congestion was the effect of the two-way traffic on Grant. This would mean showing Grant Street as the significant cause while eliminating the other streets leading to the square as significant causes. In a topic like this you have to know the facts well, and you might want to modify the assertion to say that Grant Street is the most significant cause of the congestion. You could also change the argument into one of action and propose that Grant Street be made a one-way street.

Different claims will have different requirements. Asserting that break-dancing is a dangerous activity will require you to define and describe breakdancing before going on to demonstrate the dangers. Similarly, if you argue that Riverside Park is unsanitary, you must define exactly what *unsanitary* means. And in what sense do you mean that Mayor Jones is a public relations artist? What is a public relations artist? You will want to resolve such matters for readers early in your paper in order to prevent misunderstanding. Even common words in the assertion must often be defined. You would not want to assert that the most important characteristic for a nurse is patience or kindness and assume that readers would define those terms exactly as you do.

As usual, it is best to gather all the facts you need before you begin to write. You will want to look for causes and effects and for similar situations that you can compare and contrast and use as illustrations. Although such illustrations may not "prove" anything, they can add clarity. What do the experts say on the issue you are arguing? What do the police officers who direct traffic on Celebrity Square say about the congestion? What will readers already know about the subject? What explanations will you need in order to show that each bit of evidence supports the assertion? At times, you may have to explain something to readers that opponents would know well. You may have to say, for example, that a certain point has always been considered the central one by those who oppose your view.

The following is a brief heuristic to help you prewrite for your argumentative paper. Answer only those questions relevant to your topic and add this new information to your prewriting notes.

Prewriting Questions for Argument and Persuasion

1. What exactly is my main assertion (thesis)?
2. Am I going to identify a problem and argue for a certain solution?
3. Or am I going to identify a condition and propose that the condition be changed?
4. Or am I going to urge readers to do (or not do) something for some reason?
5. Does my assertion raise only one question for argument?
6. If my assertion proposes change or action, can I derive a general statement from it that summarizes the point of my argument?
7. Am I sure this summarizing statement is the one I wish to argue? What alternative summarizing statements could I generate?
8. If my assertion makes a claim, do I know precisely what kind of claim it makes?
9. What kind of evidence will I need to show the reader that what I am claiming does exist or is true?
10. What would my opponents' counterargument be on each point I make?
11. Will my readers be familiar with the issue or must I provide extra background to prepare them for the argument?
12. How familiar will my audience be with the opposing view?
13. What must I do in order not to alienate those who oppose my view?
14. What terms or concepts must I define?
15. Will I need to use cause and effect, comparison and contrast, or definition in the essay?
16. Will I need to describe something or use examples or a narrative to illustrate any point or subpoint in the essay?
17. Do I need more information to develop my argument? If so, where can I get it? How much have I already read on the topic?
18. What have experts in the field said about my issue?
19. Have I prepared a list of logical fallacies to check from time to time as I gather evidence?

ORGANIZING

For action arguments, we recommend that you place a *because* after your assertion and experiment until you had stated the significant conclusion to be drawn by your essay. For instance, the example of mandatory attendance led to the assertion that the policy "creates a restrictive atmosphere that weakens the learning process." This statement serves as a conclusion for the argument, and everything in the essay should support that conclusion: it should show it to be a reasonable one. This conclusion offers a guide to follow throughout the paper—a guide for **organizing** and presenting evidence in an effective way.

If yours is an argument of action, you now have a good start toward an organizing plan. You have an assertion and a conclusion. During prewriting, you have outlined the points of your own argument and those of a hypothetical opponent, and you have brainstormed for supporting evidence. Thus, you know where you are going to start—with your assertion—and where you are going to end—with your conclusion. In between, you must present the evidence in a way that will convince your readers to accept your conclusion or at least acknowledge that the conclusion is reasonable, that it follows the evidence.

Remember, however, that your conclusion means nothing at this point. No reason yet exists for anyone to accept it. It is like a roof of a building balanced on only a few supports. Your job is to build strong walls beneath it. For example, the hypothetical mandatory attendance argument rests on the assumption that anything that weakens the learning process should be avoided. Most everyone would accept this belief. The argument maintains that the mandatory system weakens learning. If this can be shown, then it is reasonable to suggest that the system be abolished.

The problem facing the argument is in the middle. You have only *asserted* that the system weakens learning. Anyone can assert anything, but your task is to prove your assertion to the reasonable satisfaction of the audience. This is what you must construct under the suspended roof. What points in the argument will best show that the present system weakens learning? How would a counterargument square with these points? What is the best arrangement of these points? What evidence supports them? Do you have enough evidence to make each one convincing or do you need to do additional prewriting? You should not allow any statements along the way to hang in the air without support; you need solid building materials to support your argument.

For arguments that make claims, you can begin organizing in much the same way. Determine what it is that you must show the reader. Ask "What am I claiming?" That something exists? That one thing is causing another? That something is unfair to the elderly or some other group? That something is badly wrong with something? That some person, group, or thing can be defined as something else beyond its assumed titles or functions—"Mayor Jones is a public relations artist"?

Once you know the nature of your claim, it is time to begin to organize, using the claim as a guide. Sometimes you can work with a *because* after your assertion and find the summarizing conclusion. For example, "the policy prohibiting smoking is unfair *because* . . ." The conclusion becomes the suspended roof. At other times the assertion will guide you. If you claim that Grant Street is the principal cause of congestion in Celebrity Square, then you must eliminate other streets as primary causes and establish Grant Street as the most significant cause. If you say that Mayor Jones is a public relations artist, then what are the examples of his behavior that show this? What has he done to make you say this in the first place? Have public relations firms said they would like to hire him? If so, were they speaking tongue-in-cheek? If you did not find this information while prewriting, perhaps you should make some telephone calls and find out. How many illustrating examples do you have? How would people who disagree express their views? Are you similar to an art expert examining a painting and finding sufficient evidence for your claim that it is an original, or after examining your evidence must you honestly conclude that your assertion is no more than an offhand remark that the evidence won't support?

Tinker with the points you will make in the argument until you have them arranged in an effective order, an order that will lead the reader to accept your claim. This may be from your least important reason to the most important, or it may be a series of equally important points with subpoints underneath each. In all cases, the points and subpoints must be more than empty statements that anyone could make. The evidence must make the statements acceptable to the reader. How would opponents of your view react to each statement? What weaknesses in the use of evidence would they find? The points must logically follow the evidence. One or two public relations extravaganzas do not make Mayor Jones a public relations artist any more than a flock of robins in Ohio means that spring has arrived in February.

WRITING

Usually it is best to write quickly to produce a rough draft. Your first draft may be "rougher" than you would prefer, since argument is a more demanding form of writing than the other types you have done. Nevertheless, you can make any adjustment at all later during revising, including the modification of your main assertion. Argument is a form to learn from, and the process can sometimes lead writers to modify their own views. So, it is not necessary to stick with something your rough draft shows to be a weakness. Your purpose is not to cling to what you had thought previously. Your purpose is to proceed honestly to show that your view is a sound one. Honesty demands that you make changes whenever your evidence says you should.

In addition, it is important not to alienate your audience. The amount of care you take varies according to the degree of controversy involved. You should assess this and be sensitive to possible audience reactions. You don't want to lose your argument by alienating readers. In fact, it sometimes helps to show that you understand the opposing point of view, merely to show that you are not ignorant of it. You can also point out—if it is true—that you agree on certain points. Such concessions help increase your credibility because they help you appear "reasonable." Finally, remember to control your language. A sarcastic or condescending tone shows itself in writing as well as in speech and is likely to offend your audience.

If you discover that you have incomplete information on one or more of your main points, feel free to go back and do some additional prewriting. It is especially important with argumentative and persuasive papers that you have sufficient information to convince your readers.

REVISING

As usual, you will want to direct your **revising** to the organizing structure first. Now that you have your argument in a roughly completed form, does reading through it suggest any rearrangements in the order of the argument? Should you delete something or add something? If you discover that your original organizing plan is inappropriate, now is the time to make adjustments. Don't be afraid to reorder entire paragraphs.

You will want to work out problems with the larger units of your paper first, and then test every general statement you have made. Are any hanging in air with no support? If so, provide the explanation or evidence that will make the point clear to the audience and fortify it against the pointing finger of an opponent. If you cannot provide sufficient support, then try some additional prewriting or modify or eliminate the statement.

It is important that you test all of your supporting evidence. Is each bit of it sound? Have you taken advantage of the reader anywhere? Have you compared something in your argument to something else in a way that seems impressive on the surface but which really doesn't relate to what you are arguing? Have you fallen into the cause and effect trap of assuming that one thing caused another just because it happened first? Have you kept strictly to your primary issue at every point in the essay? Or have you resorted to personal attacks similar to one suggesting that some professors prefer mandatory attendance because it's the only way they can get students to attend their boring classes? Such personal attacks are logical fallacies that defy proof and divert attention. Even if you suspected it to be true, you would not say that Mayor Jones creates problems and then rushes in and solves them just to gain credit with voters. If true, that would suggest that Mayor Jones is a charlatan, not a public relations artist. If not true, it would suggest that the writer is a charlatan interested in manipulating the audience.

After you are satisfied with the arrangement of parts, the soundness of your logic, the sufficiency and quality of your evidence, and the thoroughness of development for each point, then examine and test each sentence for clarity and good structure. Finally, check to see that your sentences and paragraphs flow smoothly one to another.

Remember, it is best to revise your paper as often as it takes to produce a version you are proud to put your name on.

PROOFREADING

Proofread as you would for any other paper. You don't want to allow the energy devoted to producing a carefully constructed argument to be wasted. Proofread carefully to eliminate the small, surface errors that can distract readers from the quality of your argument. Be alert while proofreading to catch any weakness in the paper that might have escaped your notice while you were revising.

After you have completed your paper, you may wish to refer to the checklist below to make sure you have not overlooked anything important.

Argument and Persuasion Checklist

1. Does your essay clearly argue one question?
2. Does your introduction contain sufficient background to prepare your readers for the argument?
3. If you have written an action argument, does all your evidence work to support your *because* conclusion?
4. If your argument makes a claim, are you satisfied that you have shown

that what you say exists really does exist or what you claim is so really is so?

5. Have you examined the paper at least twice for logical fallacies?

6. Have you provided enough evidence to support every part of your argument?

7. Are you certain your paper is free of statements that are in need of explanation or supporting evidence?

8. What parts of your paper do you think those with opposing views would look at most closely? Have you given these parts enough attention?

9. Have you given enough attention to each sentence to make all of them clear and sound in structure?

10. Have you proofread carefully for misspellings and other errors?

Second Strike

HENRY KENDALL

In this essay, MIT professor Henry Kendall argues that America and the Soviet Union already have sufficient nuclear strength to deter each other from attacking first. Neither can strike first without being destroyed by the return strike. The important goal, according to Kendall, is not nuclear superiority but keeping both sides aware of the certainty of mutual destruction.

The United States faces a grave national security crisis because we have fallen behind in the nuclear arms race. Soviet nuclear weapons arsenals have expanded to the point where a surprise Soviet nuclear attack can lay waste the U.S. arsenals, destroy our vastly inferior military capability, and leave practically unscathed the USSR as an unrivalled world power. The dominant nuclear strength of the Soviet Union will give them long-sought political leverage which they can ruthlessly exploit free from any meaningful U.S. military challenge. Our European allies—indeed most countries—will be at their mercy. World trade in food and critical raw materials will be set on their terms, the hapless United States reduced to a cowering servant state manipulated for Soviet purposes.   1

This chilling scenario of an emerging Soviet "nuclear superiority" and its consequences is now being used by military hardliners in a national campaign aimed at expanding the already enormous U.S. nuclear weapons arsenal. It's a scenario that is remote from reality, however.   2

No Soviet attack on the United States could preclude a devastating counterattack on the Soviet Union. This is because it only takes a small number of nuclear weapons to inflict awesome damage on any attacker. And the United States has *thousands* of nuclear warheads that can be delivered by a diverse array of vehicles. There is no technical possibility of an attack so successful as to deprive the United States of the number of warheads needed for a second strike of unprecedented devastation. Such a response aimed at the highly concentrated Soviet industrial base would destroy the USSR as a modern industrial state. There is no way Russian leaders could ever hope to "win" a nuclear war, and they know it.   3

The public and our national decision-makers should come to under-stand the second-strike nuclear capability of the United States and the   4 damage it could do to the Soviet Union. The campaign for new weapons systems and rejection of the imminent SALT treaty is in full swing; and it is a campaign that is relying heavily on public acceptance of the erroneous, simple-minded notion of a threatening "Russian build-up" that could result in their "nuclear superiority."

Just how damaging the U.S. response would be in the event the Soviets 5 struck their most powerful first nuclear blow is not widely appreciated. It would be destructive beyond precedence. No known countermeasures or civil defense efforts could blunt or frustrate it to the extent of making the damage "acceptable" in any practical sense of that word. Soviet leaders are rational enough to understand that the Soviet Union would be unable to function as an industrial state following retaliation by the United States. Many, perhaps most, other nations would be cruelly affected by nuclear war between the United States and the Soviet Union.

Of course the United States might not wish to launch an all-out retalia- 6 tory attack. Since the mid-1960s the United States has had a wide variety of "flexible options" in its targeting plans: missiles and bombers can be re-targeted with relative ease and small salvos or even individual weapons can be delivered. It is, however, a full destructive response that is the principal concern here, because most thoughtful Department of Defense officials and many other experts believe a small nuclear exchange would, with high probability, escalate to a full exchange.

This article re-examines the expected consequences of first and second 7 strikes to determine whether the Soviet Union *can* achieve nuclear superior-ity in the sense of a war-winning capacity in the foreseeable future (or, for that matter, the United States). In other words, how real is the portrait presented in the above scenario about the Soviets' military potential?

The First Strike

The U.S. strategic nuclear forces constitute a triad: the intercontinental 8 ballistic missiles (now all in hardened silos, dispersed mostly in the western plains states); the nuclear-powered missile submarines (60 percent of which are permanently "on-station," hidden securely in the oceans); interconti-nental bombers (30 percent of which are on constant runway alert). Together these forces carry almost 3,000 megatons (3,000 million tons of TNT equiva-lent) of nuclear explosive power. There are thousands of other bombers and shorter range missiles in the tactical forces of which about 6,000 can be targeted against some parts of the Soviet Union.

It is worth recalling what modern nuclear weapons can do. A single 9 one-megaton airburst has a fireball more than 1½ miles in diameter, and will flatten almost everything over about 50 square miles. The intense heat from the fireball will set fires over an area approaching 100 square miles and cause second-degree burns over 250 square miles. A ground burst's damage area is somewhat smaller but the radioactive fallout is greater; the burst forms a crater 950 feet across and 200 feet deep.

Large exposures to radiation kill by direct interference with body functions: death comes slowly after a few hours to a few weeks. Lower exposures can also cause leukemia, cancers of the lung, thyroid, breast, bone and the intestine, genetic damage, birth defects in offspring, constitutional and degenerative diseases, and mental retardation. Following a one-megaton ground burst, typically some 600 to 1,000 square miles would receive fallout lethal to unprotected persons, and over an area of about 2,000 square miles there would be a substantial risk of death or incapacitation. An additional 2,000 square miles would be contaminated beyond safe use. Much of Hiroshima was devastated and over 100,000 people killed by a 15 kiloton weapon, doing damage to only about 6 percent of the territory that would be destroyed by a modern one-megaton weapon. The allies employed, in aggregate, about 1.2 megatons of conventional high explosive in World War II.

Suppose the Soviets attempted to launch a first strike against the U.S. nuclear forces: an attack on the ICBMs, on the bomber force, and on submarines in their ports.

The ICBMs. Modern U.S. ICBMs are encased in silos that are hardened to resist 2,000 pounds per square inch of blast overpressure. (By comparison, most buildings collapse at 5 pounds per square inch.) To destroy these silos, missile warheads must have impressive accuracies. Neither the Soviets nor the Americans now have the accuracy necessary to destroy more than a militarily insignificant fraction of the other side's ICBM silos. However it has been estimated that sometime in the 1980s the Soviets might be able to destroy all but a few of all American ICBMs *if* they used their modified SS-18 missiles, each with eight warheads, each warhead releasing the equivalent of 1.5 megatons of TNT, or the smaller six-warhead SS-19 improved accuracy missile, and *if* each warhead had an even chance of landing within 600 feet of its intended target. An optimal attack would be two warheads fired at each ICBM (to ensure killing the missile), one an airburst, the other a ground burst. But there are good reasons for believing that this one-two punch cannot work owing to the first explosion's neutron burst, gravel sucked into the mushroom cloud, and winds of over 1,000 mph, all interfering with the detonation or targeting of the second missile. This difficulty is called "fratricide."

10

11

12

What could the Soviet Union reasonably expect to achieve in this attack?   13
This is to say, what fraction of the ICBMs, submarines, and bombers would
be destroyed? Given projected Soviet missile accuracies for the next decade,
at least 5 to 15 percent of U.S. ICBMs will remain usable.

The United States, with just these ICBM remnants, could demolish the   14
22 largest Soviet cities, holding a combined population of 32 million, and
most of the country's advanced industrial installations. And this is a highly
optimistic scenario from the Soviet point of view; the damage would probably be far worse.

The bomber force. One cannot ignore the bombers on alert. They carry   15
about half of U.S. megatonnage. Without any prior notice (that is, in the
highly unlikely event of a bolt-from-the-blue surprise attack), the first
bomber can get off the airfield within 7 minutes. All 124 bombers on alert (30
percent of the force) can get off the ground within 15 minutes' warning.

Assuming that the Soviets destroy *all* U.S. bombers not on runway   16
alert—leaving 124 aloft—and even assuming a greater than expected attrition of our bombers enroute to targets, the United States could still deliver,
with the surviving bomber force alone, about 700 megatons.

This, too, unrealistically understates the potential U.S. response. If the   17
Soviets were ever to launch a first strike, it would almost certainly be the
culmination of escalating international tensions. The attack would probably
be preemptive in nature. So some of the bombers would be on airborne alert,
and others dispersed throughout the country at emergency civilian and
military airfields. With only two days' notice the bomber force could deliver
almost 1,800 megatons.

The submarine fleet. The Soviet attack would also include strikes against   18
the U.S. nuclear missile-bearing submarine fleet. Twenty-five boats (60
percent of this fleet) are on station at all times and, hidden in the depths of
the sea, are unreachable and invulnerable. So only those 16 in port would be
destroyed.

Each of the submarines at sea carries 16 missiles, and in about ¾ of the   19
submarines each missile bears 10 warheads. Each of these multiple
warheads has an explosive power of 50 kilotons, the equivalent blast power
of over two Hiroshima weapons. Even if 20 percent of all these were to fail, in
launch or in re-entry, there would still be over 2,200 warheads in the
submarine fleet alone that would survive the first strike and that could reach
the Soviet Union.

It has been argued that a Soviet first strike could be a "surgical" opera-   20
tion that would disarm the United States, yet leave the civilian sector largely
untouched, and that this would, as a consequence, sap the political will of

the United States to respond with a second strike. But even if the Soviets scrupulously sought to avoid the killing of civilians, millions of Americans would die. Damage to the civilian sector would be vast, in part a consequence of radioactive fallout across major portions of the country and in part from global effects. Each megaton of ground burst leads to levels of contamination lethal to unprotected persons over about 1,000 square miles. A strike against the ICBM silos would probably be about 50 percent ground bursts, so that something approaching one million square miles of American territory would be rendered heavily contaminated by this supposedly "surgical" strike. The lethal levels of radioactive fallout would hit people hundreds of miles downwind from the actual detonations. Most of the farmland in Kansas, Nebraska and Iowa would be contaminated with very high levels of radioactivity, especially strontium-90. Huge quantities of this deadly material would extend for more than 1,000 miles from each detonation, and would contaminate the bulk of the U.S. milk production.

According to a 1975 study conducted by a panel of the Office of Technology Assessment 12 to 18 million people would be killed from the collateral (or unintended) damage resulting from a Soviet attack intended merely to wipe out America's land-based missile force.   21

If the Soviets tried to destroy the non-alert bombers on various airfields, and the submarines in port—which any military planner going for an effective first strike would surely want to do—fatalities could easily reach totals as high as 20 million or over. As many people would die in such an attack as would be the case if the Russians deliberately killed one-quarter of the people in this nation's 25 largest metropolitan areas.   22

In other words, a "limited" counterforce attack against American strategic nuclear weapons would hardly be a "clean, surgical strike" and neither the President nor the American people would consider the attack as being limited. Hence the likelihood of massive American retaliation to this "limited" attack is high.   23

The Second Strike: Retaliation

The U.S. forces that would survive the first strike would constitute a deadly threat to the Soviet Union. These surviving forces are listed in the table for day-to-day alert. If the U.S. forces were put on alert by a heightening of tensions before the Soviet strike or from intelligence of Soviet intentions the numbers of surviving warheads and bombs would jump by over half and the total megatonnage nearly double.   24

What damage would ensue if this force, or the bulk of it, were used in a retaliatory strike? There are a variety of ways it could be employed, and thus   25 there are a variety of possible consequences. It is the policy of the United States not to target Soviet Union population per se but rather to direct attacks at military and industrial targets. Because so many of these targets are in or near major urban areas population centers would nevertheless be subject to the bulk of the damage.

In fact, it would require only about 1,350 Poseidon warheads, less than 26 half of the warheads on the submarines that are always at sea, to level just about everything in every one of the 220 Soviet cities with population exceeding 100,000. Critical components of the highway, rail and electricity, petroleum- and gas-transportation systems would be targeted with air and ground bursts along with important industrial facilities, ports, airports, and industrial complexes outside of urban areas including mines, oil fields, and refineries. One can reasonably conclude that in excess of 60 percent of the Soviets' industrial capacity would be destroyed by the effects of blast alone, disregarding damage from initial radiation, fallout, and subsequent fires.

But this is not the whole story. The functioning of a modern industrial 27 state like the Soviet Union depends on sophisticated coordination of continuing supply of energy, industrial components, and a usable transportation system. With the bulk of energy sources gone and transportation destroyed, the nation would be deprived of the ability to restore a functioning industrial system for a very long period of time.

U.S. strikes against the industrial base of the Soviet economy would also 28 be disastrously effective. Soviet industry is highly concentrated and centralized. Sixty percent of all steel output comes from only 25 plants. There are only 34 major petroleum, and eight copper, refineries. Chemicals are largely produced in only 25 cities. All cars are manufactured in 12 large cities. There are only eight major shipbuilding works, 16 heavy machine and 15 agricultural machine production plants. Nine tractor plants make 80 percent of the entire Soviet output; 47 percent is produced in five of the 20 largest cities, 20 percent in the huge Kama Truck Plant alone. The entire Central and Volga regions, with a population of almost 60 million, get most of their electricity from three hydroelectric and two nuclear power plants, all located in large cities.

Some industrial facilities are quite fragile. Thus a large petroleum refin- 29 ery would be damaged so badly by a one-megaton blast *eleven miles distant* as to require a quarter of a million man days to repair. Many of the most crucial industries *cannot* be protected by hardening, including oil refineries, electric generating plants, steel works, truck and tractor plants, and others.

As in the United States, radioactive fallout would be extensive with 30 hundreds of thousands of square miles affected. Fallout shelters would lead to a reduction in the number of prompt human fatalities from the fallout but little could be done to protect livestock and crops, as well as other plants and animals, from its effects. Large masses of decaying bodies—human and animal—would create an extremely toxic environment and spread disease unless heroic clean-up measures were successfully carried out.

Long-Term Consequences

In addition to the immediate consequences of a large nuclear exchange   31 there can be long-term global consequences, physical and biological as well as social, political, and economic. Some of these stem from the likelihood of climatic alterations brought on by the exchange as well as from dispersed radioactivity. The extent, duration, and impact of the effects are not very well known at present. Yet what is known or reasonably expected constitutes a grim picture.

The ionizing radiation and high temperatures in nuclear fireballs pro-   32 duce large quantities of nitrogen oxides (component of what is known as smog). These oxides rise and are dispersed in the atmosphere, some fraction reaching the stratosphere. There they react with and destroy ozone in the important layer that normally absorbs, and hence protects us from, most of the ultraviolet rays in the sun's radiation. The reduction of ozone might reach 30 to 70 percent in the northern hemisphere and be less, but significant, in the southern hemisphere. The amount of harmful ultraviolet rays reaching the ground could then rise by a factor between six and one hundred. Recovery of the prewar ozone levels might require 3 to 5 years, or even longer. In the meantime, ultraviolet rays reaching the Earth's surface could cause incapacitating sunburn in as little as 10 minutes, and induce severe burns (snow blindness) of the eye. Fatal sunburn would be the consequence of long exposure. The incidence of skin cancer would rise markedly.

During this period persons outdoors in daytime would need to be   33 swathed and goggled. Because the ultraviolet rays inhibit photosynthesis there would probably be stunted plant growth. Sensitive crops, such as tomatoes and peas, would be scorched and killed. Ultraviolet penetrates water to a depth of a few feet so that damage to aquatic species is possible. The rays would injure not only humans but also bacteria, fungi, higher plants, insects, and animals. Crops would be at risk and work would be hazardous, difficult, and inefficient for all persons engaged in agriculture and outdoor activities.

Both the high levels of ultraviolet radiation and the globally dispersed   34 radioactivity would cause genetic damage and mutations. Mutation of some pathogens would possibly lead to novel virulent strains that could cause disease epidemics both of crops and animals on a global scale. Moreover, in the target countries and those nearby where fallout radiation would be most intense, widespread destruction of plant and animal life could lead to major ecological imbalance, some species being far more radiosensitive than others. The changes would very likely be unfavorable to agriculture and animal husbandry. These imbalances could persist for one or more decades.

Ground-burst nuclear explosions throw great quantities of gravel and   35
debris into the atmosphere. In a large nuclear exchange this would involve several cubic miles of material, more than from the world's largest natural explosion, the volcano Krakatoa in 1883. Some of the material is so fine it would remain in the atmosphere for years. Additional smoke and dust would come from huge fires, which in some periods of the year could encompass hundreds of thousands of square miles. Because these dusts reflect or absorb small amounts of sunlight which would otherwise warm the Earth's surface they can lead to global cooling and to changes in the distribution and amount of rainfall.

The effects of the suspended particulates as well as consequences of   36
ozone depletion might lead to global cooling with an average temperature drop as great as several degrees centigrade although it might be smaller or even negligible. As a result the possibility of climatic changes of a very dramatic nature can by no means be ruled out. And only one degree of cooling would, according to a National Academy of Sciences report, eliminate wheat growing in Canada. The normal ranges of crops could everywhere be altered and normally consistent weather patterns upset. For example, the monsoon in the Indian subcontinent could be altered, affecting half a billion people. Climatic alteration would directly affect the growing of food in virtually every nation on earth. With the halting of U.S. and Canadian grain exports two-thirds of the international commerce in these critical foods would disappear, causing widespread famine in both the developing and industrial countries.

The Soviet Union has had perennial problems with food production and   37
its current agricultural conditions are far from the ideal. One-fourth of the labor force is devoted to agriculture, as compared with 5 percent in the United States and yet the country is a net importer of food. Its own seasonal carryover stocks of food are generally inadequate.

Grains, primarily wheat, and potatoes provide about 50 percent of the   38
Soviet diet. Accordingly, the nation is highly vulnerable to damage in this crucial sector. Grain planting and harvesting are almost entirely mechanized and are, therefore, highly sensitive to shortages of spare parts, absence of

fuel, and replacement of machines. The major grain growing areas are at the same latitude as the prairie provinces of Canada. Thus the possible climatic cooling could be more than sufficient to wipe out their yield. More southerly regions are deficient in water and in the aftermath of nuclear war could not be converted easily to new crops.

At present 30 percent of the value of Soviet crops is lost to pests, insects, rodents, plant pathogens, weeds, and the like. The immensely difficult problems of conducting survival agriculture and extensive radioactive contamination coupled with the effects of ecological imbalances would further aggravate the losses. If the Soviets were, very improbably, to save a large fraction of their population by an effective evacuation and shelter program, there would be major prospect of widespread, perhaps near-total, famine.   39

Soviet survivors of a U.S. second strike, many of them dealt lingering and ultimately fatal afflictions, would face a devastated environment, with urban areas and the bulk of their industrial capacity destroyed, and much of the land and the urban wreckage intensely radioactive and inaccessible for months. They would be without fuels, a transportation system, or the tools, industry and resources necessary to restore an industrial base. The injured, with most hospitals destroyed, would largely have to fend for themselves, for the uninjured would have grave survival problems themselves.   40

The scale of destruction and the dim prospect for recovery—with no hope of outside assistance—would so numb and psychologically shock the survivors that no effective action toward reconstruction could be begun for a long time. There is a real possibility that the survivors would turn on the remaining Soviet leadership, rejecting reimposition of direction from those seen as responsible for their plight.   41

Modern industrial nations depend for their functioning on interweaving and coordinating numerous technical, social, political, and economic activities. It is the integration of these activities that constitutes the national structure and makes it greater than the sum of its parts. As with a complex machine, some portion of a nation's parts must *all* work at least at some minimum level of efficiency, or the socioeconomic system ceases to function. A large nation is especially vulnerable to assaults that threaten its organized functioning. It should be abundantly clear that a major nuclear strike poses such a peril.   42

In our judgment there is little doubt that the Soviet Union, in the aftermath of a U.S. second strike, would no longer have national coherence, that it would be unhinged and dismembered to such an extent that even the remnants that did not suffer direct damage could no longer function as a   43 modern industrial society. And the Soviet Union has the capacity to inflict the same level of damage on the United States. Whether this damage could be remedied in a foreseeable period, or would persist indefinitely, is beyond confident prediction. Yet so real is this possibility that neither the Soviet military authorities nor the central government could fail to consider it most carefully. And so awesome is the cost, so beyond the price that any nation would be willing to pay for any conceivable political objective that only madmen could choose such a course. Whatever characteristics the Soviet leadership has revealed over the years it has never displayed that sort of reckless, lunatic inclination.

The immense megatonnage of nuclear weaponry in the superpowers' 44 arsenals, the huge number of relatively invulnerable delivery systems, and the likelihood that a large nuclear exchange would obliterate the target nations, along with inducing disastrous global effects, tell us that further search for "nuclear superiority" by either side is futile. It only leads to the construction and deployment of new and more accurate weapons of destruction that make the nuclear standoff increasingly fragile. By raising fears of "first strike" it could create a hair trigger situation in serious crises and thus gravely weaken deterrence.

Notwithstanding there is continuing pressure from the military and 45 civilian hardliners in the United States and from their Soviet counterparts to enhance and expand their respective nuclear capabilities. These pressures are based on obsolete *military* views surviving from the age of purely conventional weapons, when having the more powerful armed force was regarded as essential to command the field. But this is not the way that citizens or their political leaders in *any* country see the situation today. This is because they understand that a retaliatory nuclear force far smaller than the one we have today is sufficient to ensure deterrence. As McGeorge Bundy, National Security Advisor to President Kennedy stated:

> There is an enormous gulf between what political leaders really think about nuclear weapons and what is assumed in complex calculations of relative "advantage" in simulated strategic warfare. Think-tank analysts can set levels of "acceptable" damage well up in the tens of millions of lives. They can assume that the loss of dozens of great cities is somehow a real choice for sane men. They are in an unreal world. In the real world of real political leaders—whether here or in the Soviet Union—a decision that would bring even one hydrogen bomb on one city of one's own country would be recognized in advance as a catastrophic blunder; ten bombs on ten cities would be a disaster beyond history; and a hundred bombs on a hundred

cities are unthinkable. Yet this unthinkable level of human incineration is the least that could be expected by either side in response to any first strike in the next ten years, *no matter what happens to weapons systems in the meantime.**

The central fact of the nuclear age is that nuclear arms are too powerful   46 and numerous to be used to gain a nation's political or military objectives. Hence we and the Soviet Union must continue to recognize mutual deterrence as the essential, indispensable foundation of a stable military relationship between the two countries and to forego the futile and risky contest for nuclear superiority.

QUESTIONS ON MEANING AND CONTENT

1. Does this essay reassure you or make you apprehensive about the possibilities of nuclear disaster? Is the author suggesting that we are relatively safe because both U.S. and Soviet leaders know how destructive and self-defeating any kind of nuclear war would be? If so, is that something substantial to cling to or does that represent a delicate balance that could be upset easily? Explain.

2. Kendall believes that a nuclear first-attack probably wouldn't be a surprise attack. Worsening events would alert us to it. What are his reasons for thinking this? How does this point relate to his main argument?

3. In paragraph 45, the author quotes at length from McGeorge Bundy, who distinguishes between the "real world of political leaders" and the theoretical world where leaders examine choices relating to nuclear strikes. Does Bundy assume that the decisions governing nuclear strikes will always be "real world" decisions? Is this argument simply Kendall's argument in miniature form? Does the argument soothe you or unsettle you? What is Bundy saying when he refers in his last sentence to "the next ten years"? What of the years after ten?

4. Is there any way that proponents of continued nuclear buildup could use Kendall's argument to press their own views? Are there elements in Kendall's argument that would lend themselves to such use?

---

*Reprinted by permission of *Foreign Affairs,* October 1969. Copyright © 1969 by the Council on Foreign Relations, Inc.

QUESTIONS ABOUT RHETORICAL STRATEGIES

1. What does the author gain by presenting the gloomy scenario about preparedness at the beginning of his essay?

2. In paragraph 4, the author calls the fear that the Russians will gain an edge by outstripping us in weaponry as an "erroneous, simple-minded notion." How would opponents of the author's view react to this? What assumptions must the author have made about the possibilities of changing the minds of people who support this "notion"? Who, then, is the author directing the argument to?

3. What is Kendall arguing for? What is his main assertion (thesis)? Where do you find the assertion expressed in the essay? Does the assertion logically lead to the remarks made in the final paragraph of the essay?

4. In the course of the argument, Kendall makes various claims. One of these is that, no matter what, the Soviets could not prevent the United States from answering a nuclear attack with a counterattack. How convincingly does he support this claim? What evidence does he use to support it? What are other claims made in the essay? In what ways and how convincingly does the author support these claims?

5. What purpose is served by dividing the essay into sections with headings? In what way is this helpful to readers? How would this system be especially helpful to someone who wanted to go back and reread parts of the essay? What purpose do the italicized subheadings have? Do you think the essay would be more effective or easier to read if it were printed as continuous text, without divisions marked by headings or subheadings?

QUESTIONS ON LANGUAGE AND DICTION

1. The author uses parentheses frequently in the essay. Could you group the sets of parentheses according to the kinds of information they contain; that is, the author defining, clarifying, emphasizing, and so forth? How do you account for such heavy use of parentheses? The subject matter? Are these devices helpful to readers or a distraction? Explain.

2. What are the meanings of the words *triad, fratricide, attrition, culmination, preemptive, per se, pathogens, virulent?*

Battering Back

SUSAN JACOBY

Susan Jacoby points to the outcome of a Michigan murder trial to argue against using unwritten laws as a means of giving women the right to control their own lives.

A new feminist heroine has arisen in the person of Francine Hughes, a   1
thirty-year-old woman who put an end to her husband's brutal beatings by
pouring gasoline around his bed and setting him aflame while he slept. A
jury of ten women and two men in Lansing, Michigan, found Mrs. Hughes
not guilty of murder by reason of temporary insanity.

What disturbs me is not the acquittal itself—who could want further   2
punishment for a woman who had endured a man's punishing assaults for
thirteen years—but the fact that the case has become a feminist *cause
célèbre.* Feminists who rallied to the support of Mrs. Hughes saw the issue as
one of a woman's right to self-defense and the acquittal as a warning to
millions of men who beat up their wives and children each year.

The brother of the slain man, interestingly, drew much the same conclu-   3
sion from the jury's decision as the feminists did; the only difference was
that he viewed the implications with dismay rather than enthusiasm. In a
television interview he said, "I think this decision will give a lot of violent
women an excuse to go out and commit violent acts . . . to take their
revenge." I was watching the news with a friend who observed that "if
revenge is what it takes for a woman to be in control of a situation like that,
then I'm for it."

How, I asked my friend, can one possibly use the word "control" to   4
describe the act of a woman so desperate, so driven, in such a state of psychic
bondage that she could free herself from a brutal man only by killing him
while he slept. It seems to me that the attitude of many feminists toward the
Hughes case violates the basic feminist belief that women can and should
take control of their own lives.

Those who maintain that Mrs. Hughes had a moral (as opposed to a   5
legal) right to do what she did are suggesting that a woman who would not
be victimized must turn murderous. As anyone who has studied the history
of master-slave relations knows, the master's fear of violent retaliation has

always coexisted with his assumption of the slave's passivity. But women are not slaves—or they do not have to be slaves.

Mrs. Hughes, like most women who endure long-term physical abuse 6 from men, had assumed a number of psychological characteristics more commonly associated with slaves than with free human beings. The details of the case, most of which were omitted from national news accounts of the trial, are enlightening.

Newspaper articles generally referred to the dead man as Mrs. Hughes's 7 husband. He was, in fact, her former husband; she had divorced him in 1971 after seven years of marriage and four children. But it is perfectly reasonable to use the term "husband," because Mrs. Hughes continued to relate to him as a wife after the divorce. It was clear from her testimony that she remained bound to him emotionally, on many occasions sexually, and always as a victim and target for abuse.

But Mrs. Hughes did not play the role of the total victim. She was taking 8 courses at a local business college because she wanted to support her children and get off welfare. On the day of his death, Mr. Hughes not only had beaten his wife several times but had forced her to burn her business-school textbooks in the back yard.

Francine Hughes was living in the same house with her former husband 9 because she had agreed to nurse him back to health after a serious automobile accident. He had, of course, made a good enough recovery from his injuries to beat her up many times in gratitude for her care. This situation offers a classic and extreme example of the psychological victimization that characterizes battered wives. It is impossible to imagine a man returning with concern to the bedside of a wife who had systematically subjected him to physical torture.

The drama of the Hughes case arouses extraordinary interest in Lansing, 10 which is my hometown. I discussed the case with several women friends there and found their reactions fell into two distinct categories. Some maintained that Francine Hughes was driven mad by years of humiliation and simply did not know what she was doing. Others said they were sure she *did* know what she was doing and that she "finally gave the creep what he deserved."

I do not think either of these reactions bodes well for the cause of 11 women's rights. If we say Mrs. Hughes was crazy, we are equating self-assertion with insane violence. If we say she was sane and did the right thing, we are ruling out the rational means of self-defense that lie between victimization and murder.

There are other choices. A battered wife can leave her husband. She can 12 testify against him in court. She can become economically and emotionally self-sufficient and never go near the bum again. Or, in some cases, she can force the man to get the kind of help that might make it possible for him to change. (It does happen from time to time.)

These are not easy choices. Many areas of the country have no shelters to   13
provide wives with temporary protection while they figure out how to cope with a brutal husband. Many policemen and law-enforcement agencies are unsympathetic. In a recent ABC-TV movie on battered wives, an indifferent policeman says, "A good punchin' around is what some of these women need to turn 'em on."

But the attitudes that have long enabled men to get away with wife   14
beating are changing: The Hughes case is evidence of that. If a jury is willing to acquit a wife who set fire to a sleeping man, it would surely have listened with sympathy to the testimony of a woman who wanted to protect herself from the assaults of a living husband.

Battered wives today are in much the same situation as rape victims were   15
ten years ago. The possibility for change exists, but it cannot become a reality unless women are willing to appear in court, to put their bruised bodies and minds on the line for essential changes in the law and in social services.

My reservations about the Hughes case are similar to the ones I held   16
when Inez Garcia was tried in 1974 for the shooting of a man twenty minutes after an alleged rape. Mrs. Garcia's lawyer insisted at the trial that an "unwritten law" allows a woman "to take the law into her own hands to protect her integrity."

Unwritten laws used to allow men to kill their wives if they found them   17
in bed with a lover. Unwritten laws required rape victims to defend their past sexual conduct. Unwritten laws intimidated wives into silence when their husbands beat them.

Feminists who advocate a woman's right to "self-defense" against a   18
sleeping man—however brutal the man may have been—are really talking about the substitution of one unwritten law for another. What Francine Hughes and all of us need is a written law to protect us and the guts to use it.

QUESTIONS ON MEANING AND CONTENT

1. Why does Susan Jacoby object to unwritten laws as a means of protecting people who are vulnerable to abuse? How do unwritten laws fail to address the underlying problem affecting the lives of people like Francine Hughes and Inez Garcia?

2. What examples does the author use to illustrate the evils of unwritten laws?

3. In the last paragraph, Jacoby says that what women "need is a written law and the guts to use it." Which of these, based on what the essay has to say, do you think would be easier to achieve—the law or the guts? Specifically, what written law is the author asking for? What does paragraph 15 say about the kind of guts that will be needed?

4. In your view, how accurate is Jacoby when she says in paragraph 8 that Francine Hughes was not a "total victim"?

5. The jury that exonerated Francine Hughes was comprised of ten women and two men. Do you think a jury of ten men and two women would have arrived at the same decision? Explain.

QUESTIONS ABOUT RHETORICAL STRATEGIES

1. Jacoby says in paragraph 11 that it doesn't help women's rights to claim that Francine Hughes was sane (and just delivering a deserved punishment to her husband) or insane (and acting without an awareness of what she was doing)—the two views that Jacoby's friends used to justify the killing. What reasoning does Jacoby use to support this conclusion?

2. In paragraph 9, Jacoby says that she can't imagine any man behaving as Francine Hughes did during the time she lived with her husband. How is this pertinent to the argument Jacoby is making in the essay? Is she suggesting that women should behave more like men? Or is she suggesting that battered wives behave in this way for some as yet unexplained reason? Or is she suggesting something else entirely? How do paragraphs 12 and 13 relate to this point? Paragraphs 5 and 6?

3. How much influence do you think the changing attitudes described in paragraph 14 may have had on Jacoby in forming the views she presents in the essay? How critical to her argument is this paragraph? Is it more critical to readers who would sympathize with the Francine Hughes decision or to those who would have been dismayed by the decision? Explain.

4. In the last sentence of paragraph 4, Jacoby notes that "many feminists" thought that Francine Hughes was justified in her actions because this was the only way she could "control" her situation. Jacoby rejects that view and says that this attitude "violates the basic feminist belief that women can and should take control of their own lives." What line of reasoning and what evidence does Jacoby use in arguing this point?

QUESTIONS ON LANGUAGE AND DICTION

1. Define "psychological victimization" as it is used in paragraph 9. What examples of psychological victimization, as opposed to physical abuse, are mentioned in the essay? Is the book burning an example? Explain.
2. What are the meanings of the terms *cause célèbre, passivity, bondage, bodes?*

The Scientists' Responsibility

ISAAC ASIMOV

In this essay, science fiction writer Isaac Asimov suggests that a wise and powerful world government is needed if human beings are to survive much longer on this planet. He offers a rationale for such a government and identifies the group from which the leaders should be chosen.

I think it may be reasonably maintained that neither the United States   1
nor any other nation can, by itself, solve the important problems that plague
the world today. The problems that count today—the steady population
increase, the diminishing of our resources, the multiplication of our wastes,
the damage to the environment, the decay of the cities, the declining quality
of life—are all interdependent and are all global in nature.

No nation, be it as wealthy as the United States, as large as the Soviet   2
Union, or as populous as China, can correct these problems without reference to the rest of the world. Though the United States, for instance,
brought its population to a firm plateau, cleaned its soil, purified its water,
filtered its air, swept up its waste, and cycled its resources, all would avail it
nothing as long as the rest of the world did none of these things.

These problems, left unsolved, will weigh us down under a steady   3
acceleration of increasing misery with each passing year; yet to solve them
requires us to think above the level of nationalism. No amount of local pride
anywhere in the world; no amount of patriotic ardor on a less-than-all-
mankind scale; no amount of flag waving; no prejudice in favor of some
specific regional culture and tradition; no conviction of personal or ethnic
superiority, can prevail against the cold equations. The nations of the world
must co-operate to seek the possibility of mutual life, or remain separately
hostile to face the certainty of mutual death.

Nor can the co-operation be the peevish agreement of haughty equals: 4
each quick to resent slurs, eager to snuff out injustice to itself; and ready to
profit at the expense of others. So little time is left and so high have become
the stakes, that there no longer remains any profitable way of haggling over
details, maneuvering for position, or threatening at every moment to pick
up our local marbles and go home.

The international co-operation must take the form of a world govern-   5
ment sufficiently effective to make and enforce the necessary decisions, and
against which the individual nations would have neither the right nor the
power to take up arms.

Tyranny? Yes, of course. Just about the tyranny of Washington over   6
Albany; Albany over New York City; and New York City over me. Though
we are each of us personally harried by the financial demands and plagued
by the endless orders of the officialdom of three different levels of government, we accept it all, more or less storically, under the firm conviction that
life would be worse otherwise. To accept a fourth level would be a cheap
price to pay for keeping our planet viable.

But who on Earth best realizes the serious nature of the problems that   7
beset us? As a class, the scientists, I should think. They can weigh, most
accurately and most judiciously, the drain on the world's resources, the
effect of global pollution, the dangers to a fragmenting ecology.

And who on Earth might most realistically bear a considerable share of   8
responsibility for the problems that beset us? As a class, the scientists, I
should think. Since they gladly accept the credit for lowering the death rate
and for industrializing the world, they might with some grace accept a good
share of the responsibility for the less desirable side effects that have accompanied those victories.

And who on Earth might be expected to lead the way in finding solutions   9
to the problems that beset us? As a class, the scientists, I should think. On
whom else can we depend for the elaboration of humane systems for
limiting population, effective ways of preventing or reversing pollution,
elegant methods of cycling resources? All this will clearly depend on steadily
increasing scientific knowledge and on steadily increasing the wisdom with
which this knowledge is applied.

And who on Earth is most likely to rise above the limitations of national   10
and ethnic prejudice and speak in the name of mankind as a whole? As a
class, the scientists, I should think. The nations of the world are divided in
culture: in language, in religion, in tastes, in philosophy, in heritage—but
wherever science exists at all, it is the same science; and scientists from
anywhere and everywhere speak the same language, professionally, and
accept the same mode of thought.

Is it not, then, as a class, to the scientists that we must turn to find leaders   11
in the fight for world government?

QUESTIONS ON MEANING AND CONTENT

1. In paragraph 4, Asimov says that a world government would have to be
led by people who wouldn't be petty, selfish, and so forth. Why does he
conclude that scientists come closest to fitting this description? What is

his reasoning? Why doesn't he consider in his argument how scientists think and behave when they are not being scientists—that is, when they are at home with their families or discussing politics and other non-scientific problems such as crime, taxes, human relations, and the like? Or would this factor be unrelated to the issue?

2. In paragraph 8, Asimov says that scientists take "credit for lowering the death rate and for industrializing the world" and they might, therefore, take "the responsibility for the less than desirable side effects that have accompanied those victories." What are some of the "side effects" he refers to?

3. What does Asimov mean in paragraph 6 when he says our experience in living under three levels of tyranny should equip us to live under a fourth?

4. When you finished the essay, were you ready to accept the conclusion drawn by Asimov in the very last sentence of the essay? Why or why not?

QUESTIONS ABOUT RHETORICAL STRATEGIES

1. Asimov sets forth a problem in the essay, proposes a general solution, and then makes a specific recommendation concerning how the general solution can best be carried out. Trace the development of the problem-solution structure by identifying the sections devoted to each step in the development.

2. How does paragraph 6 fit into the development of the essay? Is it essential that Asimov make this argument before going to paragraph 7 where he begins to explain how his general solution should be implemented? Or would the development and effectiveness of the overall argument not be upset if this paragraph were missing?

QUESTIONS ON LANGUAGE AND DICTION

1. The opening sentences of paragraphs 7, 8, 9, and 10 repeat the phrase "who on Earth." This is a phrase very common to speech and one that we use so casually that it has become more of a manner of speech than a phrase to convey meaning. Nevertheless, why is it a good phrase to repeat here and how does it carry meaning for Asimov?

2. In paragraph 4, what does the phrase "pick up our local marbles" mean?

3. What are the meanings of the words *stoically, viable, ardor, harried?*

Universities Must Not Remain Neutral in the Moral Crisis Over Nuclear Weapons

WILLIAM J. REWAK, S.J.

The Reverend William J. Rewak, president of the University of Santa Clara, argues that sometimes universities have to abandon the "objective stance" and become involved in controversial issues. He calls this involvement a "prophetic stance." The arms race and the threat of nuclear war call for such a stance, he argues, if universities are to fulfill their obligation to humanity.

Whatever else a university is, it is primarily a place for reflection and judgment. And I suspect that much of the satisfaction we find in our work—whether we are always aware of it or not—results from the fact that we do lead lives of reflection: We're constantly engaged in evaluating our work as educators and we reflect continually on the worth of the curriculum and of our institution; we discuss and meditate on such crucial issues as peace and faith and justice.   1

Because of the emphasis on reflection, we may appear to others to be living in ivory towers. But anyone who has worked on a university campus knows it is no blessed island surrounded and protected by magic from the harshness of the outside world: Prospero lives only in the imagination.   2

Universities today are centers of research for industry and government; they are harbors for political aspirants (and political refugees); they are active in lobbying and are engaged in business enterprises.   3

Nevertheless, despite its own awareness that it is an integral and active part of society, a university must maintain its autonomy—perhaps even a measure of distance—because reflection, to be valuable, needs to be free of self-interest.   4

That is why it is always dangerous for a university to take a position in a controversy. By its very nature, a university must remain free from pressure and external involvement in order to pursue the truth with objectivity.   5

Such an objective stance is, admittedly, at times difficult for an institution that professes adherence to certain values. A Jesuit university, for example, maintains an allegiance to a tradition that places obligations on administrators and fosters expectations on the part of the students, parents, alumni, and benefactors. But granted that allegiance, even a church-related   6 college or university must honor the peculiar mission of higher education to facilitating dialogue, encouraging research, and searching out all avenues of thought so that the truth may appear and that society may thereby be enriched.

We need never be afraid of such dialogue; we need never worry about 7 exposing students to ideas as long as we avoid propaganda, allow for free discussion and honest investigation, and help students develop the capacity for mature judgment. No one need ever fear the truth.

There are times, however, when an objective stance is not the best way 8 for a university to make a contribution, times when it must—through policy, public pronouncements, and a consistent manner of action—witness to the importance of certain moral values.

There are moments in the life of a university, in other words, when it 9 must take a prophetic stance, precisely because there are moments in the life of society when crises occur that must be addressed. I believe that the present danger of nuclear war is such a crisis.

A university, in fulfillment of its traditional role, has an obligation to 10 meet the issues of war, nuclear-weapons proliferation, and disarmament head on. The resources of our academic institutions—theological, philo-sophical, and humane, as well as scientific—must be put at the disposal of our country, at the service of mankind.

We need to devise institutes, conferences, and special courses to look at 11 the problems from every angle; we should be willing to spend substantial sums on speakers who will lecture, debate—even preach. We should engage in a universitywide exploration of the nature and morality of nuclear war.

Universities have traditionally provided much research for the country's 12 defense program. In recent months, of course, more money has been avail-able from the Department of Defense than from any other government contracting unit. And much of it is intended, directly, for the development, testing, and production of nuclear weaponry.

Should a university be engaged in such activity? I think not. 13

I am not being critical of our country's need for defense—that is another 14 question entirely. Unless there is a major change in the human psyche, individuals and nations will always need to defend themselves against aggression. My point is that a university has a different role to play. It must, through its unique resources, preserve and advance human wisdom, heighten the sensitivity of the human conscience, explore the riches of the imagination, and provide the skills necessary for building a just society.

A university, which is thus dedicated to the preservation and enhance- 15 ment of culture, cannot at the same time be directly engaged in research on weapons of destruction, weapons whose practical result is the obliteration of culture. To carry on both activities at once is schizophrenic.

There are, of course, counterarguments: To work on the instrumenta- 16
tion of a nuclear warhead, for example, is also to improve the possibilities of peaceful planetary research. I would answer, however, that it is the nuclear warhead that is being perfected.

Much ordinary research can, of course, be applied to the weapons 17
industry, and such research seems to me to be acceptable: To devise a more efficient silicon chip is valuable, even though we are aware that computer systems are used in the deployment of weapons. There is a difference between research directly related to weaponry and research applicable to weaponry. That principle may not always be easy to apply in concrete cases, but it is a yardstick against which prudent decisions can be made.

But isn't any research fundamentally neutral? A distinction has to be 18
made here between basic and applied research. Basic research seeks under-standing and does not necessarily lead to an inevitable application, although an eye should always be kept on possible consequences. Applied research, on the other hand, is concerned precisely with application. It is not neutral, for its effect is to change the social or economic or physical environment, and universities, in this area, cannot remain morally aloof.

I am not suggesting that a university be a moral watchdog for society. A 19
university is not infallible; it has no constitutional obligation to tell society how to act. Rather, it hopes to educate young men and women in such a way that they will understand the need to preserve cultural values, that they will be the reflective and compassionate leaders who determine the direction the world will take.

A university has to be objective, I repeat, to preserve its freedom of 20
inquiry and its credibility. It should, indeed, be passionate about human and civil rights, but it should not too readily endorse, as an institution, particular political expressions of such rights. Once a university enters the arena of partisan politics, it forfeits its ability to seek the truth without coercion or compromise.

However, it does have the responsibility to take an institutional stand, 21
even on a politically charged issue, when its life or welfare is threatened by external events—for example, it takes a stand if its students are faced with denial of financial aid—or when its actions, or the results of its actions, affect the external community, such as is the case with conducting weapons research.

We must remember that nuclear war is a new dimension for mankind, 22 and the old arguments don't fit. It is unfortunate but true that when we invent a weapon, we use it: bow and arrow, gunpowder, atomic power. Although any weapon is a deterrent to some degree, no weapon has ever been used as just a deterrent or been confined to self-defense.

It may be easier for private universities than for public to avoid under-   23
taking weapons research, but public universities are, after all, dedicated to the same principles as private and by their charters are committed to the public well-being. Because a private university owes allegiance to no politi- cal organization and can, without detriment to its existence and without compromise, take a stand on such issues. I think it is time to do so.

I think it is time to let our reflection bear fruit in judgment, in the   24
judgment that we can no longer participate in an activity that is so directly inimical to everything a university attempts to achieve. On this issue, there is great danger in putting too great an emphasis on objectivity and in preserving too cool an institutional demeanor. I am reminded that Dante's first message in the *Inferno* is that the hottest place in hell is reserved for those who remain neutral in times of moral crisis.

QUESTIONS ON MEANING AND CONTENT

1. Do people tend to think of universities as ivory towers, as the author suggests in paragraph 2? If so, why? What is your definition of an ivory tower?

2. How does the author describe a university in the first three para- graphs? Would you describe a university in the same way? If not, would you use the characteristics suggested by the author and add to them or would you reject some or all of them before describing?

3. In paragraph 14, the author lists four roles of a university. Univer- sities must (a) "preserve and advance human wisdom," (b) "heighten the sensitivity of the human conscience," (c) "explore the riches of the imagina- tion," and (d) "provide the skills necessary for building a just society." Does your own college or university seem to be dedicated to these four roles? If not, what idealistic principles guide it? How does a university go about fulfilling the kinds of roles listed above? Which of the roles are fulfilled in the classroom? All of them? Any of them? What does the word *wisdom*, men- tioned in the first role, mean? Is that the same as knowledge?

4. Does it seem odd to you that the author doesn't directly talk much about students? Should he? Or would that be digressing from the argument? What parts of the essay show indirectly that students are important to his argument?

5. Why is it easier, according to the author, for a private university to take a stand on issues than it is for a public university?

6. Consider the following statement from paragraph 7: "No one need ever fear the truth." How do you react to such a broad, inclusive statement? Do you accept the statement as it is or would you want to modify it, place bounds on it? Explain.

QUESTIONS ABOUT RHETORICAL STRATEGIES

1. The author says in paragraph 5 that "it is always dangerous for a university to take a position in a controversy" because controversies make it difficult "to pursue the truth with objectivity." What reasoning does the author use to move from this point to urging that universities become involved in the nuclear controversy? Is he convincing?

2. The essay shows that the author is sensitive to opposing points of view. He addresses various points or questions that might be singled out by those who would argue against him. Here are three examples:

a. "I am not being critical of our country's need for defense—. . ." (para. 14)

b. "But isn't any research fundamentally neutral?" (para. 18)

c. "I am not suggesting that a university be a moral watchdog for society." (para. 19)

How does he address each of these points? What is his reasoning as he addresses each one?

3. What reasons can you offer for the author's return to the concept of objectivity in paragraph 20? Early in the essay he devoted considerable attention this topic. Returning to it here also indicates that it is something that has a very strong bearing on what he wants to say. Specifically, why do you think he brings this matter up again? Is he merely reinforcing the earlier argument? Or is he trying to warn readers not to misunderstand or misuse his argument? Remember, he is calling for an exception to the rule against entering controversies. Could someone later use his argument as a reason for entering a lesser controversy by saying, "This case is similar; we have to get involved"?

4. In what places in the essay does the author call for action? What sort of action?

5. What is the assertion the author is arguing from?

QUESTIONS ON LANGUAGE AND DICTION

1. In paragraph 2 the author says, "Prospero lives only in the imagination." This is an allusion to a character in Shakespeare's play *The Tempest*. For many people, Prospero symbolizes a world that is in harmony with itself. Would a reader have to know this—or some other roughly similar interpretation of the allusion—in order to understand the author's point?

2. In paragraph 9, what does "prophetic stance" mean?

3. What are the meaning of the following words: *integral, facilitating, psyche, inimical, Jesuit?*

We Lay Waste Our Powers

DIANA SHAW-McLIN

We have lost sight of what progress should mean, Diana Shaw-McLin argues. We have set the wong goals, measured progress by technological advances and forgotten that progress that ignores people and the planet is a negative kind of progress.

The world is too much with us; late and soon,
Getting and spending, we lay waste our powers;
Little we see in nature that is ours.
　　　　　　　—William Wordsworth, 1807

The terror of these times reminds me of those summer nights during my childhood when the air was so heavy with heat that nothing stirred but my imagination. Sweltering under my sheets, I knew that somewhere in my room, or just outside my window, a monster was waiting to spring upon me and tear me limb from limb. 1

Sometimes I'd whine for my parents who would indulgently check inside the closets and peer behind the blinds, invariably finding nothing to justify my fears. Yet, still, I'd lie cowering, begging God to please, please, please spare me the ordeal which might occur before my next breath and make my worst nightmares seem like sweet, sweet dreams. 2

Since there was never any guarantee that God was listening, I felt relieved only after I'd exhausted myself with worry and fallen asleep. By morning, my fear had vanished, and, while the sun shone, the thought of monsters never crossed my mind. 3

The difference between those nights and these days is that now there is no morning. The sun does not dispel my dread, and no one—not even my mother and father—will tell me that no killers are lurking in the closets or outside the window. The killers are, indeed, in the closets—closets called silos. And they are not only outside my window but surrounding me everywhere. 4

My fear confounds the dignity I ought to feel as a human being, the admiration I should have for the accomplishments of my ancestors and my contemporaries, and the pleasure I should take in the conveniences and luxuries of life in a prosperous and free society. I resent this fear, not only because the burden of terror is hard to bear, but because it derives from an 5 absurdity, a misplacement of priorities which jeopardizes both the point and the fact of human existence.

In my very first history lesson in grade school, I learned that the value of 6 an age depended upon how much progress was made during it. Progress seemed to have to do with the advancement of civilization and included the drafting of rational, equitable laws, the building of useful structures, and the harnessing of natural phenomena to facilitate human survival. It also seemed to involve the development of cultures—ways of interpreting, enhancing, and enriching human experience on this planet.

But now I am confused. My simple notion excludes much of what passes 7 for progress today.

Progress now involves the draining of resources and the impoverish- 8 ment of peoples. It often refers to the expedient exploitation of the earth. Its name has even been lent to the ability to annihilate humanity and shatter the globe. This is clearly a world of divergent values, where progress for some is for others its antithesis: corruption.

The word *progress* implies a goal, and, if the goal is self-destruction, we 9 have made considerable progress toward it. If the goal is a technocracy indifferent to human needs, we have progressed in that way as well. Evidence in both cases is abundant and plain. For example, one billion individuals in the world live without the most basic necessities of life. Nevertheless, in 1982, their governments plied military forces with $600 billion. Our world spends $108 per capita to maintain militaries and only six cents per capita to advance international peacekeeping efforts. And while the fuel efficiency of automobiles manufactured in the United States has merely doubled since World War II, the destructive power of a nuclear weapon has increased three hundred times.

For the sake of a future, and for the assurance of a worthwhile one, we 10 must agree that progress implies the preservation of the planet and the promotion of the well-being of all people, as much as it connotes the advancement of technology. Propitiously understood, progress should involve the acquisition and application of an understanding of science, with reverence for life and regard for human needs.

The brown rim which circles my city like the residue of coffee on a bright 11 blue cup is both symbol and substance of our tendency to co-opt nature rather than cooperate with it. We have been handling the earth as if it were a meal to be polished off at one sitting, ravaging it with a folly comparable to that of the man who slew the goose for its golden eggs. Bombarding it with waste, we treat the planet as if it were a hostile territory rather than a place which spawned us. We pelt it with chemicals, and it retaliates with cancers and mutations which ought to remind us that our fate is tightly bound to that of the atmosphere we relentlessly abuse.

As technology advances, progress must be determined in terms of specific social goals, and ethical guidelines must help us distinguish between an impulse to use a particular device because it exists and an application of that technology which would advance the well-being of individuals and society. With their new technology and techniques, doctors can help their patients defy death. But it is not the ability to prolong life itself which signifies progress in medicine but the judicious application of life-saving measures where vitality and spirit can be restored along with heartbeat and pulse. 12

The technology for exchanging information seems to diversify daily, and the risks the new communications systems involve are well concealed in the convenience and novelty of each new development. While the means of communication are multiplying, the sources of information are not. Repressive governments abroad and commercial conglomerates at home dominate the media. In this country, the editorial priorities of broadcasting companies set the agenda for society and the electorate. Instead of interpreting events for ourselves, we are becoming passive receptors of prepackaged impressions. 13

As we are fed images by programming, we may find ourselves losing the habit of originality and succumbing to collective thought. 14

Progress in communication will depend upon the extent to which the evolving technology succeeds in promoting understanding among peoples of the world and the degree to which it allows us to share knowledge and ideas. Progress will demand universal access to both means of transmission and reception, so no minds will be held captive nor abandoned to ignorance. 15

The dangers we face in this age are new in their specifics. But it takes only a vague familiarity with history and ancient mythology to realize that these hazards derive from the same source which spawned catastrophe in other eras. The Greeks attributed the collapse of mythic kingdoms and the demise of the mightiest of mythic mortals to hubris, the failure to have humility before existence. 16

Out of hubris, we have taken the fate of the world in our hands and we have chosen to flout the laws of nature rather than try to reconcile our desires with them. Out of hubris, we deny ourselves wonder and awe at the world, choosing, instead, to assert ourselves over it, obscuring its splendors with our refuse and threatening it with our arrogance and avarice. 17

Humanity as a species has so much cause to celebrate life. We are strong, spirited, and intelligent, and we have proven ourselves capable of enhancing the beauty and the bounty of the world. If we would only dedicate 18 ourselves to life, instead of bartering it for pieces of earth; if we would only choose to devote our marvelous machinery to the preservation and perpetuation of humanity, instead of to its selective or collective destruction; and if we would only allow ourselves to consider the possibility that the cost of pursuing some of our dreams may exceed the value of attaining them; we will progress to a time when grown men and women no longer live each day with the terror of a small child alone in the dark.

QUESTIONS ON MEANING AND CONTENT

1. If we assume that the author is asking us to revise our concept of progress, how should we alter our behavior to achieve progress? How would we measure progress if we followed the author's definition? Could we still measure with facts, figures, statistics, and the like?

2. How real do you consider the notion of progress that the author encountered in grade school? Does it represent an "ideal" presented in a history book, or does it point to the way people in earlier times actually measured progress?

3. The author says in paragraph 7 that her understanding of progress "excludes much of what passes for progress today." What would not be excluded? Can you think of anything in our recent past that would fit the definition of progress presented in paragraph 6?

4. Paragraph 17 says that we have been flouting the laws of nature rather than moderating our desires to make them work cooperatively with nature's laws. What examples of this does she offer in the essay? Can you think of other examples where we seem to be denying or working against natural laws in order to achieve our own ends?

5. According to the author, how have modern communications systems been misused?

QUESTIONS ABOUT RHETORICAL STRATEGIES

1. What action on our part is the author calling for?

2. How much emotional appeal does this argument contain? Where do you find appeals to our feelings? What does the author achieve with the narrative that begins the essay?

3. In paragraphs 8 and 9, the author establishes that modern progress has goals, as progress should, but that the goals are unworthy ones. How does she support this contention?

4. In paragraph 10, the author establishes the premise that any notion of progress must include preserving the planet and promoting "the well-being of all people" as well as making technological advances. Then, in paragraph 11 she attempts to show that we have not done this. What does she do to convince us of this, and how does she extend this argument through the next several paragraphs?

5. What shift is taking place in paragraph 16? How do paragraphs 16 and 17 function in relation to the essay up to that point? Do they comprise the conclusion to the argument? If so, what is the purpose of paragraph 18, the last one in the essay?

6. How sound is the example in paragraph 9 pointing out that gas mileage for cars has "merely doubled since World War II" but "the destructive power of a nuclear weapon has increased three hundred times"? Forget for the moment that increasing the destructive power of anything is not exactly an admirable pursuit. Consider instead the difficulties involved in each technology and the actual time spent on development. For example, a strong effort to increase fuel economy in cars wasn't begun until more than 20 years after World War II, and the automobile was already a sophisticated mechanism at the time of World War II, with several decades having already been devoted to its development and improvement. Nuclear weapons, on the other hand, were first developed during World War II, and despite their awesome destructiveness at the time, they were, nevertheless, in the early stage of development when the potential to multiply their awesome power was at its greatest. The questions are these: How many readers would be capable of evaluating the example? How meaningful are the phrases "merely doubled" and "increased three hundred times"? Does the contrast in the figures have any emotional appeal?

QUESTIONS ON LANGUAGE AND DICTION

1. In paragraph 16, the author defines hubris as "the failure to have humility before existence." What does the word *before* mean in this context? What does the word *existence* include?

2. Explain the meaning of this sentence from paragraph 13: "Instead of interpreting events for ourselves, we are becoming passive receptors of prepackaged impressions."

3. What are the meanings of the following words: *divergent, antithesis, propitiously, demise?*

Inaugural Address

JOHN F. KENNEDY

John F. Kennedy uses the occasion of his inauguration as President of the United States to speak to all the peoples of the world and to call the American people to action.

My Fellow Citizens:

1   We observe today not a victory of party but a celebration of freedom—symbolizing an end as well as a beginning—signifying renewal as well as change. For I have sworn before you and Almighty God the same solemn oath our forebears prescribed nearly a century and three quarters ago.

2   The world is very different now. For man holds in his mortal hands the power to abolish all forms of human poverty and to abolish all forms of human life. And yet the same revolutionary beliefs for which our forebears fought are still at issue around the globe—the belief that the rights of man come not from the generosity of the state but from the hand of God.

3   We dare not forget today that we are the heirs of that first revolution. Let the word go forth from this time and place, to friend and foe alike, that the torch has been passed to a new generation of Americans—born in this century, tempered by war, disciplined by a cold and bitter peace, proud of our ancient heritage—and unwilling to witness or permit the slow undoing of those human rights to which this nation has always been committed, and to which we are committed today.

4   Let every nation know, whether it wish us well or ill, that we shall pay any price, bear any burden, meet any hardship, support any friend or oppose any foe in order to assure the survival and success of liberty.

5   This much we pledge—and more.

6   To those old allies whose cultural and spiritual origins we share, we pledge the loyalty of faithful friends. United, there is little we cannot do in a host of new cooperative ventures. Divided, there is little we can do—for we dare not meet a powerful challenge at odds and split asunder.

7   To those new states whom we now welcome to the ranks of the free, we pledge our word that one form of colonial control shall not have passed merely to be replaced by a far more iron tyranny. We shall not always expect to find them supporting our every view. But we shall always hope to find them strongly supporting their own freedom—and to remember that, in the

past, those who foolishly sought to find power by riding on the tiger's back inevitably ended up inside.

To those people in the huts and villages of half the globe struggling to break the bonds of mass misery, we pledge our best efforts to help them help themselves, for whatever period is required—not because the communists are doing it, not because we seek their votes, but because it is right. If the free society cannot help the many who are poor, it can never save the few who are rich. 8

To our sister republics south of our border, we offer a special pledge—to convert our good words into good deeds—in a new alliance for progress—to assist free men and free governments in casting off the chains of poverty. But this peaceful revolution of hope cannot become the prey of hostile powers. Let all our neighbors know that we shall join with them to oppose aggression or subversion anywhere in the Americas. And let every other power know that this Hemisphere intends to remain the master of its own house. 9

To that world assembly of sovereign states, the United Nations, our last best hope in an age where the instruments of war have far outpaced the instruments of peace, we renew our pledge of support—to prevent its becoming merely a forum for invective—to strengthen its shield of the new and the weak—and to enlarge the area to which its writ may run. 10

Finally, to those nations who would make themselves our adversary, we offer not a pledge but a request: that both sides begin anew the quest for peace, before the dark powers of destruction unleashed by science engulf all humanity in planned or accidental self-destruction. 11

We dare not tempt them with weakness. For only when our arms are sufficient beyond doubt can we be certain beyond doubt that they will never be employed. 12

But neither can two great and powerful groups of nations take comfort from their present course—both sides overburdened by the cost of modern weapons, both rightly alarmed by the steady spread of the deadly atom, yet both racing to alter that uncertain balance of terror that stays the hand of mankind's final war. 13

So let us begin anew—remembering on both sides that civility is not a sign of weakness, and sincerity is always subject to proof. Let us never negotiate out of fear. But let us never fear to negotiate. 14

Let both sides explore what problems unite us instead of belaboring the problems that divide us. 15

Let both sides, for the first time, formulate serious and precise proposals for the inspection and control of arms—and bring the absolute power to destroy other nations under the absolute control of all nations. 16

Let both sides join to invoke the wonders of science instead of its terrors.   17
Together let us explore the stars, conquer the deserts, eradicate disease, tap
the ocean depths and encourage the arts and commerce.

Let both sides unite to heed in all corners of the earth the command of   18
Isaiah—to "undo the heavy burdens . . . (and) let the oppressed go free."

And if a beach-head of cooperation can be made in the jungles of   19
suspicion, let both sides join in the next task: creating, not a new balance of
power, but a new world of law, where the strong are just and the weak
secure and the peace preserved forever.

All this will not be finished in the first one hundred days. Nor will it be   20
finished in the first one thousand days, nor in the life of this Administration,
nor even perhaps in our lifetime on this planet. But let us begin.

In your hands, my fellow citizens, more than in mine, will rest the final   21
success or failure of our course. Since this country was founded, each
generation has been summoned to give testimony to its national loyalty. The
graves of young Americans who answered that call encircle the globe.

Now the trumpet summons us again—not as a call to bear arms, though   22
arms we need—not as a call to battle, though embattled we are—but a call to
bear the burden of a long twilight struggle, year in and year out, "rejoicing in
hope, patient in tribulation"—a struggle against the common enemies of
man: tyranny, poverty, disease and war itself.

Can we forge against these enemies a grand and global alliance, North   23
and South, East and West, that can assure a more fruitful life for all
mankind? Will you join in that historic effort?

In the long history of the world, only a few generations have been   24
granted the role of defending freedom in its hour of maximum danger. I do
not shrink from this responsibility—I welcome it. I do not believe that any of
us would exchange places with any other people or any other generation.
The energy, the faith and the devotion which we bring to this endeavor will
light our country and all who serve it—and the glow from that fire can truly
light the world.

And so, my fellow Americans: ask not what your country will do for   25
you—ask what you can do for your country.

My fellow citizens of the world: ask not what America will do for you,   26
but what together we can do for the freedom of man.

Finally, whether you are citizens of America or of the world, ask of us the   27
same high standards of strength and sacrifice that we shall ask of you. With a
good conscience our only sure reward, with history the final judge of our
deeds, let us go forth to lead the land we love, asking His blessing and His
help, but knowing that here on earth God's work must truly be our own.

QUESTIONS ON MEANING AND CONTENT

1. President Kennedy is calling American citizens to action. What is he asking of them?

2. The speech also addresses America's enemies. What is the nature of his remarks to them?

3. The speech addresses major problems in the world. What were these at the time Kennedy spoke in January 1961? How much has the list of problems changed since then?

4. In paragraph 25, Kennedy says that American citizens should not ask what their country can do for them but, rather, what they can do for their country. Is he suggesting that Americans tend to ask too much? What do we ordinarily expect of our country? Consider also the other side of his statement. Is he telling Americans to ask the government what they can do for their country or to ask themselves? If you asked yourself this question, how would you answer it? Do you think Kennedy is asking citizens to do something beyond the ordinary (obey laws, pay taxes, and so forth)? If so, what kinds of things could citizens do?

QUESTIONS ABOUT RHETORICAL STRATEGIES

1. Identify the introduction, the body, and the conclusion of the speech. What makes these identifiable? Does the language signal movements to or from each?

2. Does the speech primarily appeal to emotions or to reason? Or to both? Explain, with references to the text to support your answer.

3. One purpose of an inaugural address is to inspire confidence in American citizens. Approximately how much of the speech is devoted to doing this?

QUESTIONS ON LANGUAGE AND DICTION

1. Explain the fear, expressed in paragraph 10, that the United Nations could become "a forum for invective."

2. Many of the words and phrases in this address are more formal and more elegant than those used in ordinary writing or speaking. For example, in paragraph 11, Kennedy asks "that both sides begin anew the quest for peace." Ordinarily we might say something on the order of "begin new peace efforts." How might the following be phrased in less formal situations: "a century and three quarters ago" (paragraph 1), "tap the ocean depths" (paragraph 17), "Now the trumpet summons us again" (paragraph 22).

3. The speech makes much use of antithesis (placing opposites close together for emphasis). "Ask not what your country will do for you—ask what you can do for your country" is an example of antithesis. What other examples can you find?

4. Repeating words and phrases (or repeating them with slight variations) is another device of formal speech meant to stir the feelings of an audience. Kennedy frequently uses this device: "let the word go forth," "Let every nation know," "Let both sides explore," and the like. What are other repetitions or repetitions with slight variations found in the speech?

5. For some reason, repeating the same grammatical unit also has a strong appeal to listeners. Kennedy uses many of these repetitions in which the words differ but the grammatical unit remains constant. Paragraph 4 presents a good example: ". . . we shall pay any price, bear any burden, meet any hardship, support any friend or oppose any foe." What other examples of this technique do you find in the speech?

6. In paragraph 2, why might Kennedy have said "mortal hands" since our hands are, naturally, "mortal." Does he do this just to appeal to the ear or does this add something to the meaning of what is being said in the sentence and paragraph? Is "iron tyranny" (paragraph 7) a similar example?

7. Speeches for occasions such as this often contain allusions and figures of speech. Do you find any here?

8. In the first sentence of paragraph 8, the prepositional phrase "in the huts and villages" could easily be omitted while retaining the essential meaning of the sentence. Why is the phrase there? What does it add?

The Ice Age and the Cauldron

CARL SAGAN

This famous scientist tries to convince us that understanding climatic changes on Earth is extremely important and that exploring outer space is one way to add to this understanding.

On our tiny planet, spinning in an almost circular orbit at a nearly constant distance from our star, the climate varies, sometimes radically, from place to place. The Sahara is different from the Antarctic. The Sun's rays fall directly on the Sahara and obliquely on the Antarctic, producing a sizable temperature difference. Hot air rises near the equator, cold air sinks near the poles—producing atmospheric circulation. The motion of the resulting air current is deflected by Earth's rotation.   1

There is water in the atmosphere, but when it condenses, forming rain or snow, heat is released into the atmosphere, which in turn changes the motion of the air.   2

Ground covered by freshly fallen snow reflects more sunlight back to space than when it is snow-free. The ground becomes colder yet.   3

When more water vapor or carbon dioxide is put into the atmosphere, infrared emission from the surface of the Earth is increasingly blocked. Heat radiation cannot escape from this atmospheric greenhouse, and the Earth's temperature rises.   4

There is topography on Earth. When wind currents flow over mountains or down into valleys, the circulation changes.   5

At one point in time on one tiny planet, the weather, as we all know, is complex. The climate, at least to some degree, is unpredictable. In the past there were more violent climatic fluctuations. Whole species, genera, classes, and families of plants and animals were extinguished, probably because of climatic fluctuations. One of the most likely explanations of the extinction of the dinosaurs is that they were large animals with poor thermoregulatory systems; they were unable to burrow, and, therefore, unable to accommodate to a global decline in temperature.   6

The early evolution of man is closely connected with the emergence of the Earth from the vast Pleistocene glaciation. There is an as yet unexplained connection between reversals of the Earth's magnetic field and the extinction of large numbers of small aquatic animals.   7

The reason for these climatic changes is still under serious debate. It may   8
be that the amount of light and heat put out by the Sun is variable on time
scales of tens of thousands or more years. It may be that climatic change is
caused by the slowly changing direction between the tilt of the Earth's
rotational axis and its orbit. There may be instabilities connected with the
amount of pack ice in the Arctic and Antarctic. It may be that volcanoes,
pumping large amounts of dust into the atmosphere, darken the sky and
cool the Earth. It may be that chemical reactions reduced the amount of
carbon dioxide and other greenhouse molecules in the atmosphere, and the
Earth cooled.

There are, in fact, some fifty or sixty different and, for the most part,   9
mutually exclusive theories of the ice ages and other major climatic changes
on Earth. It is a problem of substantial intellectual interest. But it is more
than that. An understanding of climatic change may have profound practical
consequences—because Man is influencing the environment of the Earth,
often in ways poorly thought-out, ill-understood, and for short-term
economic profit and individual convenience, rather than for the long-term
benefit of the inhabitants of the planet.

Industrial pollution is churning enormous quantities of foreign particu-   10
late matter into the atmosphere, where they are carried around the globe.
The smallest particles, injected into the stratosphere, take years to fall out.
These particles increase the albedo or reflectivity of Earth and diminish the
amount of sunlight that falls on the surface. On the other hand, the burning
of fossil fuels, such as coal and oil and gasoline, increases the amount of
carbon dioxide in the Earth's atmosphere which, because of its significant
infrared absorption, can increase the temperature of the Earth.

There is a range of effects pushing and pulling the climate in opposite   11
directions. No one fully understands these interactions. While it seems
unlikely that the amount of pollution currently deemed acceptable can
produce a major climatic change on Earth, we cannot be absolutely sure. It is
a topic worth serious and concerted international investigation.

Space exploration plays an interesting role in testing out theories of   12
climatic change. On Mars, for example, there are periodic massive injections
of fine dust particles into the atmosphere; they take weeks and sometimes
months to fall out. We know from the *Mariner 9* experience that the temperature structure and climate of Mars are severely changed during such dust
storms. By studying Mars, we may better understand the effects of industrial pollution on Earth.

Likewise for Venus. Here is a planet that appears to have undergone a   13
runaway greenhouse effect. A massive quantity of carbon dioxide and water

vapor has been put into its atmosphere, so cloaking the surface as to permit little infrared thermal emission to escape into space. The greenhouse effect has heated the surface to 900 degrees F or more. How did this greenhouse-overkill happen on Venus? How do we avoid its happening here?

Study of our neighboring planets not only helps us to generalize the 14 study of our own, but it has the most practical hints and cautionary tales for us to read—if only we are wise enough to understand them.

QUESTIONS ON MEANING AND CONTENT

1. The essay makes the case that exploring outer space can be of immense practical value to us? What can it help us understand more clearly? Why is it important that we have this understanding? What can it help us to prevent or correct?

2. When we think of science and outer space, don't we often believe the scientists themselves are mostly interested in expanding pure or theoretical knowledge? Why might a scientist want to argue the practical value of space exploration?

3. Sagan also suggests that we are behaving in ways that could make us victims of forces we don't understand. What are these potentially dangerous things we are doing? What does Sagan conclude about why we are behaving in these ways?

QUESTIONS ABOUT RHETORICAL STRATEGIES

1. Sagan uses cause and effect analysis to show us that it is important to understand how climatic changes take place on Earth. How much space does he devote to this point? Are all the cause and effect situations he discusses equally understood by scientists? Do we often know more about effects than causes? By the time Sagan has presented these cause and effect situations and arrives at paragraph 9, has he convinced you of the importance of learning more about these causes and effects?

2. Sagan's argument that we should explore space and study other planets because they may tell us something important about the earth is a calmly presented, controlled effort to convince readers to agree with him. This effort begins in paragraph 9 and continues until the end of the essay? What does the author try to make us aware of in each of these paragraphs?

3. Do you think Sagan could have begun the essay with the information contained in paragraphs 9–11 and still had a well-structured, convincing essay? Explain. Could he have begun with the information in paragraphs 12 and 13? Why does he use such a long introduction?

QUESTIONS ON LANGUAGE AND DICTION

1. In his cause and effect discussions, Sagan is usually dealing with what we do know and what we can only speculate about, and he qualifies his language when he is talking about unproved or undetermined causes and effects. The phrase "at least to some degree" and the word "likely" in paragraph 6 are examples of this qualifying language. Where else does Sagan's language signal that the information, although based on what we do know, has, nevertheless, not been confirmed?

2. As mentioned earlier, Sagan writes very calmly and even-handedly. He does not make strong emotional appeals. In fact, he works almost gently to show that he is saying something worth our while to agree with. How does the language of the last paragraph reflect this soft approach?

3. Are matters in paragraphs 9 and 10 stated more strongly than anywhere else in the essay? Explain your answer by referring to specific words and phrases in these paragraphs.

4. Check the meanings of any of the following words that you do not already know: *albedo, greenhouse effect, particulates.*

WRITING SCENARIOS

1. You love your older brother Mark very much, but you are constantly irritated by one of his mannerisms: He frequently repeats old adages, unreservedly convinced of the wisdom they contain. You have decided to write him a good-natured essay in which you examine an old saying that has come down to us through literature or history and then argue that the claim it makes or the advice it offers is misleading or often unreliable. The following examples should provide a starting point for your brainstorming:

- Early to bed and early to rise makes a man (or woman) healthy, wealthy, and wise.

- Neither a borrower nor a lender be.

- When in Rome, do as the Romans do.

- Ignorance is bliss.

2. A current controversy in America concerns what rights we should have in defending ourselves and our property. Presently, your state legislature is considering a law that would clearly show what self-defense includes, and has asked for the views of concerned citizens. Propose a law you believe to be workable and present an argument to show why this law would be sound, just, and workable. Your proposal will be sent, along with your cover letter, to your state senator.

3. As a good citizen, you are concerned about any problems in your community that can be rectified easily. Identify a condition in your hometown or near your campus that you think should be corrected, and write a letter to the elected officials who can solve the problem. In the letter, identify the condition, show that it represents a problem that should be corrected, and suggest what action should be taken to correct this condition. The condition may be anything that you believe threatens people in some way, either physically or psychologically. The condition may invite accidents or represent a health hazard or nuisance. One example might be an unlighted place on campus that you fear at night. Another might be an eyesore and health hazard such as a decrepit building, or a junk-filled vacant lot. Or you may complain about the deplorable condition of the streets around your home or of the restrooms in your dorm. Classroom discussions can generate additional topics, and these are meant only to get you started toward identifying a problem. If you are writing about a problem that is campus related, then make your audience the appropriate campus official.

4. The faculty committee in your department has sent a letter to each of its majors indicating that the department is proposing that two additional courses outside of your major field must be taken in order to complete the requirements for your major. These courses may not be ones already required to complete a degree at your school. According to the committee, the extra courses shouldn't add to your technical expertise but should make you more valuable as a person to any organization or community. The committee wants student feedback on the kinds of courses that should be required. The committee asks that your course suggestions be incorporated into a proposal that presents a fully developed argument showing why your proposal will produce the desired results. Write such a proposal to the departmental committee, in which you argue why your course suggestions should be adopted. As an alternative, you may wish to argue that students should *not* be required to take extra courses.

5. The president of your college or university has made a public statement to the effect that college graduates, because they have been privileged to receive an education, owe a special debt to society. The president did not explain what the debt was or how it should be repaid. You have decided to respond to the president in one of the following ways: (a) Agree with the president; make a claim that shows how and why a college graduate is indebted to society and suggest how the debt should be repaid during life after graduation. (b) Disagree with the president and argue that college graduates have no more obligation to society than any other group or citizen. (c) Agree with the president but argue that college graduates as a group have always repaid or more than repaid what they owed society for the privilege of an education. Before beginning to write, you will want to decide about your exact audience. You can make the college president your audience by writing a personal response to him or her. Or you can make all Americans your audience by writing an essay for a publication such as *Newsweek* or *The Chronicle of Higher Education.* Think carefully about your audience before you write. Ask yourself what influence one or another of the audiences would have on the way you might want to present your argument and ask which audience would require the most careful consideration on your part.

6. The journalism department in your college is sponsoring an essay contest with a grand prize of $500.00. The contest rules call for contestants to write an essay arguing why someone should be considered a modern "hero." You have decided to write such an essay. First, you may wish to do some reading, looking for ideas on what constitutes a hero. (Assume that a hero may be a man, woman, or child.) Find two or three characteristics that are generally accepted as ones used to identify heroes. Then name someone and go on to argue that the person you have named is a hero based on the characteristics set forth. Your readers will be members of the journalism department.

7. You have become a very active member of a campus group that monitors the activity of countries around the globe that systematically sanction racism and/or practice terrorism or in some other way officially violate human rights. You have become convinced along with your fellow members that the best way to get these nations to change their policies is to bring political and economic pressure to bear on them. Your group has decided that as a large state university with substantial investments in pension funds and endowments, you have some considerable clout. As a consequence, you have contacted a large number of your state governmental representatives and have been scheduled to present a bill to the state legislature calling for your state government to divest all the university holdings in a particular country notorious for its racial and nonhuman rights policies.

Because you are known to be articulate, you have been chosen to speak on behalf of the proposed bill and argue the case for pulling out the millions of dollars that the university has invested in companies that do business with and support the offending nation. Since you really want to be prepared for this, you compose an essay addressed to the state legislature to convince them of their moral obligation to divest. The essay will be the basis for your presentation.

To research this topic, your best bet would be to search the periodical indexes for articles in magazines and newspapers that deal with divestiture or disinvestment on behalf of conscience and human rights.

8. The CIA has asked to recruit graduating students on your campus. One of the policies at your college is that the student government has to have a say in who is admitted to the campus to recruit. As a student government leader, you feel strongly about this issue and decide to address the student government assembly either speaking for or against letting the CIA recruit on campus. Many students feel that the CIA in its covert activities supports policies and operations that are contrary to the U.S. constitution. Others feel that the secret operations of an agency like the CIA are essential for our security.

You've decided to prepare an essay that will become the basis for your presentation. Most of the students who will be present will be opposed to your viewpoint, so you will need to be especially persuasive. If your presentation is particularly good, it might be printed in the student newspaper. You keep this possibility in the back of your mind. You'll have to do a little research on the CIA's activities and the controversies it's been involved in lately.

GLOSSARY

Abstract and **concrete** are labels based on what a word names. Abstract terms, or *abstractions*, name what we can think about but can't see or touch. *Love, hope, fear,* and *beauty* are abstractions, as are such concepts as *honor, virtue,* and *integrity*. Concrete terms are more readily understood because they name things we can see or touch. Abstract terms *tell* readers how a writer feels about something but often fail to convey much information. To say that someone has *integrity,* for example, tells a reader only how the writer feels about the person. On the other hand, saying that a person has integrity and then illustrating the statement with an example of the person doing something that suggests integrity not only tells the reader something but also provides supporting information.

Alliteration is the repetition of opening consonant sounds on words placed relatively close to each other: "a *f*inely-*f*eatured *f*ace," "*m*orning *m*ists rising from the *m*oor."

Allusions refer to something in the past that the reader or listener is assumed to be familiar with. The reference could be to a person, an event, or almost anything drawn from literature or history. The value of allusions is that they can make a point quickly and in fewer words than it would take to explain the point. However, it is not always easy to determine whether an audience will recognize the reference. Calling someone a "twentieth-century Shakespeare" would be easily recognized by most people and would suggest that the person was not just a good writer but a great writer. On the other hand, to say that someone was "tilting at windmills" would be meaningless to an audience unfamiliar with the escapades of Don Quixote.

Analogy is a comparison that explains something that is not familiar by referring to something that is familiar. For example, someone explaining how writing is structured might compare the writing process to constructing a building. In this case, planning the paper would be similar to designing the building, prewriting and organizing would be similar to bringing the construction materials together, and so on.

Appositives add information about a preceding noun. An appositive works by renaming or defining the noun that precedes it: "Mary Starkowitz, *a social worker,* was the first to volunteer"; "steel gets its temper from quenching, *a sudden cooling process achieved by dipping hot steel into water.*"

Argument and **persuasion** are two closely related forms of convincing people of something. Argument is often defined as the process of convincing people that an idea, proposal, or theory is correct. Argument is also frequently defined as a method for convincing people of something logically by appealing to their reasoning powers. Persuasion is the process of convincing someone to take, or not take, a certain action and often seeks to sway people by appealing to their feelings or emotions.

Assertions are the claims or statements that identify the position taken on an issue being argued.

Audience refers either to listeners or readers. Analyzing an audience is fairly simple for speakers, since people rarely agree to speak to groups without knowing something about the group members. In writing, however, the audience becomes more complex since it can be made up of many different groups, rather than a limited group in a specific setting. Occasionally, reading audiences can be narrowly defined, as when a physician writes an article for a medical journal. Although others may read the article, the primary audience would be fellow physicians. Audiences can sometimes be very broad. Newspapers and popular magazines are frequently read by large groups of people with various interests, educational and work backgrounds, economic circumstances, reading abilities, and so on.

Brainstorming is an activity directed toward gathering necessary information and details before the actual writing begins. Specifically, it refers to jotting down every relevant thought, fact, or idea that may later be used in a piece of prose. Brainstorming helps assure that nothing important has been overlooked and also aids in organizing and developing a piece of writing.

Cause and effect is a method for showing what causes something to happen or to examine the effects springing from causes. Theoretically, either could be used alone, but, in fact, the use of one or the other exclusively is extremely rare since neither causes nor effects can be presented clearly without reference to the other. Quite often, however, an analysis will emphasize either causes or effects. See Chapter 8.

Classification is a method for sorting through a large number of related items, finding those that share important similarities, and placing these into groups. See Chapter 6.

Clauses are grammatical units containing subjects and verbs. A *main* or *independent* or *base* clause can stand alone as a sentence: "For a few minutes, *he was exuberant.*" *Dependent* or *subordinate* clauses do not stand alone as sentences, even though they contain subjects and verbs: "*When I walked down the street*"; "the man *who was here yesterday.*" Clauses appear in so many variations that a good handbook should be consulted in order to get some idea of their range.

Cliché—See *Trite expressions.*

Coherence is achieved when a writing topic is presented and developed so that it is readily understood at every step by readers. Writing that lacks coherence usually fails to present major and minor points in some logical order (first to last, most important to least important, for example) and may contain digressions or lack the words and phrases necessary to show how one idea or point relates to others and to the main idea.

Colloquialisms are words or phrases that are common to casual conversations but are often not appropriate in formal speech and writing. Attitudes vary toward what is colloquial and what is not. Some people, for example, might insist that *center around* is appropriate to conversation but that in writing *center on* should be used. Others would maintain that either expression would be suitable in most writing situations. Colloquialisms are sometimes confused with regional dialect terms (*goober* for *peanut,* for example). See also *Dialects* and *Standard and nonstandard English.*

Comparison and **contrast** are methods of explaining two or more things or ideas. The two can work together in a single piece of writing, but each is really a separate form, with comparison dealing in similarities and contrast with differences. The term *comparing* is frequently used to mean the combination of comparing and contrasting. See Chapter 4.

Concrete Terms—See *Abstract* and *concrete*.

Connotation and **denotation** indicate two different kinds of meaning that a word may have. Denotation is the factual or literal meaning of a word while connotation suggests something beyond the literal meaning. For example, *slim* and *slender* have the same denotation as *skinny*, but each has a more favorable connotation than *skinny*.

Contributing causes, often called *remote causes*, are causes that lead to the more direct causes that make something happen. For example, brake failure may be the direct cause of an auto accident but a quality control inspector's failure to identify a defective brake part at the factory may be a remote cause. See Chapter 8.

Deductive reasoning is a form of logic. It begins with something that is known to be true or accurate and uses that as a base to argue a related issue.

Definitions can take several forms, the most familiar of which is the dictionary definition: it names something, then places it into a general class, and then shows how it differs from other items in the same general class. *Extended definitions* work on the same principle but offer much more information about the item being defined. An extended definition may be a single paragraph or may continue for several pages. See Chapter 5. See also *Operational definitions* and *Stipulative definitions*.

Denotation—See *Connotation and denotation*.

Description has two common forms, objective and subjective. *Objective description* has as its goal a clearly defined, accurately detailed picture of something. *Subjective description,* in addition to describing accurately, also attempts to convey the feeling associated with the subject. See Chapter 3.

Dialects are language variations peculiar to a region or social or ethnic group. The variations may be individual words, expressions, grammatical structures, or pronunciations. In one area of the United States, speakers might refer to soft drinks as *pop;* in another area they might refer to them as *soda*. In New England and the New York City area, a person might *stand on line,* but a midwesterner would *stand in line*. In some areas the word *greasy* is pronounced *greezy* and in other areas with an "s" sound. Language habits can vary just as much among social and ethnic groups—the educated and the uneducated, the rural and the urban, blacks and whites, for example. See also *Standard and nonstandard English*.

Diction refers to the word choices made by a writer. When we use a word, we frequently do so by selecting one from among many. For example, an automobile may be a *vehicle*, a *car*, a *wreck*, a *clunker*, a *set of wheels*, and so on. Diction should be appropriate to the audience, the subject, and the occasion for writing. See *Jargon and slang*.

Distance is the freshness of vision a writer receives from putting a piece of writing aside for a period of time before revising it. Probably all writers have difficulty in judging their own writing just after working on it intensely. The period of time required for distance varies. In actual practice, the time allotted often depends on the time available. Several hours are helpful, a few days even more so, and some writers prefer time spans much longer than that.

Division is a method of analyzing or explaining something by dividing the whole into its parts and showing how they work together. See Chapter 6.

Draft copy refers to any version of a piece of writing except the finished copy. The first more or less complete version is often called the *rough draft,* although this same term can be applied to later draft copies. The number of draft copies for any given piece of writing will vary from writer to writer and writing task to writing task. See Donald Murray's essay, "The Maker's Eye: Revising Your Own Manuscripts," in Chapter 7.

Exposition, or *expository* writing, explains and informs. Chapters 4 through 8 in this book cover various rhetorical modes used in expository writing. The other forms of prose writing are covered in Chapter 2 (Narration), Chapter 3 (Description), and Chapter 9 (Argument and Persuasion).

Figures of speech either directly or indirectly compare one thing with another in order to say something more effectively, more strikingly or in fewer words. Frequently the subjects being compared are not much alike, but one suggests something about the other. The three most commonly recognized figures of speech are *metaphor, simile,* and *personification. Metaphors* frequently use *is, was,* or other forms of the verb *to be* and make the two subjects of comparison seem to be the same thing. In Shakespeare's *King Lear,* when the Duke of Burgundy refuses to marry Cordelia because she has no dowry, the King of France tells Burgundy, "She is herself a dowry," thereby suggesting that her good qualities make her as valuable as the riches making up a dowry. Everyday speech is full of metaphors, many of them worn from overuse: "He's a walking encyclopedia"; "she's an angel," and so on. (See *Trite expressions*.) A *simile* makes comparisons that seem less direct than those made by metaphors, an indirectness achieved through the use of *like* or *as*, two words commonly used to link the subjects of similes: "He swears like a drunken sailor"; "she's about as reliable as a car without an engine." *Personification* gives human qualities to nonliving things: "The trees moaned in the heavy wind"; "the truck behind us was breathing down our necks."

Focus is what a writer achieves by emphasizing some feature of a writing topic. Focusing directs the reader to the purpose of the writing. In narration, focus would determine what events would be included or excluded in order to have the details of the narrative reflect a point. A writer faced with a topic like auto racing might narrow the topic by writing about pit stops and then focus on the importance of time during pit stops.

Formal and informal English are, as the names suggest, varieties of English tailored to situations. A letter written to a friend would likely be written in informal English while a letter to a potential employer would call for more formal language. Formal English uses standard English forms for both speaking and writing. (See *Standard and nonstandard English*.) Informal writing also demands standard English, but nonstandard forms are common enough in some informal speaking situations, depending on the speaker and the audience. Informal language in writing tends to use more contractions, a plainer vocabulary, and more conversational expressions like *of course* and *naturally* than formal writing does.

Freewriting is spontaneous writing, done without lifting the pen or pencil from the paper. It should be done after some thought has been given to a writing topic but before starting on draft copy. Its purpose is to draw forth ideas and information that might have escaped the conscious mind during the information gathering process.

Heuristic, as used in writing, refers to a set of questions designed to generate ideas and information useful to a particular writing assignment. The sets of Prewriting Questions at the end of Chapters 2 through 9 in this text are heuristics.

Inductive reasoning is a method of drawing conclusions after examining details or evidence. The details or evidence should lead logically to the conclusion. Conclusions formed through inductive reasoning are said to have a certain probability of being accurate but are rarely accepted either as truths or facts.

Irony conveys meaning indirectly and sometimes requires the complete reversal of what was said in order to catch the intended meaning. For example, someone might describe a disagreeable person by saying, "Oh, he's a very pleasant person." In speaking, the tone of voice tells the listener to reverse the meaning of statements such as the one above. In writing, other details have to prepare the reader to interpret a statement ironically. Irony can also refer to the unexpected—for example, a champion swimmer who drowns in a backyard pool.

Jargon—See *Slang and jargon*.

Logical fallacies are forms of thinking that have no logical soundness but which may appear sound to people unacquainted with the rules of logic. See Chapter 9.

Metaphor—See *Figures of speech*.

Mobile and stationary (observers) refer to the location or locations from which someone describes something. A stationary observer stands in one place and observes; whereas, the mobile observer moves from point to point while keeping the subject in view. Although the mobile observer sees the subject from several perspectives, the choice of one position over the other is usually dictated by the subject and what the writer wants to convey about it.

Narration is a writing method organized by a sequence of events, usually introduced in the order in which each took place. Storytelling is one form of narration, but many narratives are not stories at all in that they do not lead to some climax or dramatic point. Narration can be used to make a point of most any kind and is frequently used for short stretches in longer pieces of writing in order to support, explain, or illustrate a point. See Chapter 2.

Objective and subjective concern the degree to which a writer's own feelings, judgments, or beliefs influence a piece of writing. Objective writing keeps these to a minimum. Technical and scientific writing are often close to being purely objective, but most other types of writing include at least some subjectivity. Many pieces are intended to be primarily subjective, with the writer working hard to convey his or her impressions of a place, an object, an idea, a theory, and so on. Subjective writing suggests something beyond the factual. In descriptive writing, this may be the writer's feelings about a place or person. In other types of writing, the subjective elements may include the writer's views.

Operational definitions point to what can be observed in order to understand a term. For example, definitions of types of body language often explain what arm, leg, and other body positions to look for in order to understand the particular message being conveyed by the body.

Overstatement—See *Understatement and overstatement*.

Paradox is the name given to statements that seem to contradict what we know or believe, yet we find truth in these statements. "To fear death is to fear life" expresses a paradox.

Paragraphs are the next larger unit of writing beyond the sentence. Paragraphs usually develop one part of the main idea of an essay. Such paragraphs usually have a topic sentence (see *Topic sentences*) which tells the reader what point the paragraph is developing; however, in some paragraphs the idea being developed is so clear that the topic is obvious to readers and is not stated. The essays in this book illustrate a wide variety of paragraph structures and lengths and also demonstrate that paragraphs cannot easily be defined since they can differ from one kind of writing to another, depending on the writer's purpose and the audience. Sometimes paragraphs contain only a single important detail. This is true in much news reporting and in some advertising writing. Generally, however, when a thesis or main idea is to be developed, then paragraphs tend to be organized around topic sentences.

Parallelism requires that similar elements in sentences be written in similar forms: "The old man talked about his experiences when he was a child on the farm, when he was a young apprentice to a master carpenter, and when he organized his own construction firm." In this sentence, everything following the preposition *about* is expressed in a parallel series of adverbial clauses.

Person—See *Point of view*.

Personification—See *Figures of speech*.

Persuasion—See *Argument and persuasion*.

Phrases are units containing at least two words and which have a noticeable beginning and end. Phrases take so many forms that only a rough idea of their nature can be offered here, but the following illustrate a variety of phrases. "A relaxed atmosphere" is one form of noun phrase, a unit made up of a noun and its modifiers. "In the boat," "down the river," and "behind the house" are prepositional phrases. Many phrases contain verb forms ending in *-ed* or *-ing:* "An experience, *remembered in his old age,* carried him back to his college days"; "A raccoon, *clinging to the trunk of an uprooted tree,* looked wet and forlorn as he swept by on the muddy waters." In this last sentence, "wet and forlorn" is an adjective phrase describing the raccoon. In the following sentence, "softly but firmly" is an adverbial phrase: "He told us *softly but firmly* what he expected us to do."

Point of view has several meanings but all relate to the position from which the writer views the subject of the writing. Point of view can be defined grammatically, as in *first person* (use of *I*) or *second person (you)* or *third person (he, she, they, it).* Each of these affects the writer's freedom of expression in some way. First person, for example, allows a writer to register personal reactions more readily, whereas third person permits a writer to be—or appear to be—more objective. Point of view is also defined according to a person's background or interests. For example, a nurse might present a nurse's point of view and a patient a patient's point of view.

Prewriting refers to the activities engaged in to prepare for the writing of the first draft. These activities include gathering information and thinking carefully about the subject. See *Brainstorming* and *Freewriting.*

Process analysis is used to explain how something is or was done. Many processes explain, in step-by-step fashion, how a process takes place. Audiences for this type may wish to repeat the process or have a need to understand the steps very thoroughly. Other processes are presented more generally and appeal to the interests of readers rather than to their needs. See Chapter 7.

Proofreading directs the writer's attention to finding and correcting any small errors that might mar an otherwise sound finished copy. The typical concerns during proofreading are grammar, punctuation, and spelling. See Chapter 1.

Remote causes—See *Contributing causes.*

Revising refers to the additions, deletions, and adjustments made to the first or early drafts of a piece of writing. Revising is a changing, rewriting, touching-up process directed toward the goal of having a clear, well-written, thoroughly developed final copy. See Chapter 1.

Rhetorical modes are strategies for producing particular types of writing. A particular mode may be employed for one or two paragraphs, several paragraphs, or entire essays. Chapters 2 through 9 in this book are devoted to various rhetorical modes.

Rhetorical questions are questions not meant to be answered, since the answer is always obvious. A rhetorical question is usually asked in order to make or illustrate a point or as a lead-in to discussions. "Can a person live without taking risks?" and "Will our highways ever be safe?" are examples of rhetorical questions.

Rough draft—See *Draft copy.*

Simile—See *Figures of speech.*

Slang and jargon are types of language used in day-to-day living and working but much less frequently in writing. Slang is associated with social groups, especially the young or any other cultural group that wishes to identify itself through the language of its members. Slang terms tend to change rapidly, with one expression being replaced with another very quickly, sometimes within a year or two. For example, the following are among a great many other slang terms that have been used over the years in place of the word *leave: Twenty-three skidoo, buzz off, bug out.* Jargon is made up of words and expressions more or less exclusive to a trade or profession. Executives in the auto industry, for example, talk about *outsourcing* (buying parts from an outside supplier) or *just-in-time* inventory systems (having parts arrive close to the time they will be needed on the assembly line). Either slang or jargon can seem absurd or be irritating to readers, especially when the writing should be more formal or when readers are unfamiliar with the terms.

Standard and nonstandard English are two varieties of the language, distinguished from each other by the words, phrases, and grammatical structures preferred by the users of each. Not everyone agrees on how these two types of English should be defined, but generally standard English refers to the conventions of grammar, punctuation, and spelling that educated speakers and writers of the language have agreed through tradition to follow. Except for dialogue in plays, novels, and so on, very little nonstandard English ever passes the scrutiny of an editor and gets published. With some exceptions, standard English is used in formal speaking situations and virtually all serious writing. A good way of thinking of standard English is to consider it the form of English preferred by editors of newspapers, magazines, or editors at publishing houses. Naturally, these are not the only people who prefer standard English, but they exert a strong influence on the writing that gets published and, in effect, help establish and maintain language forms that can serve as standards for comparison. No one can point to the line that separates standard from nonstandard English, but most speakers of standard English would consider the double negative, the use of *ain't*, or constructions such as "He don't" or "She seen" to be nonstandard.

Stationary observers—See *Mobile and stationary observers.*

Stipulative definitions allow writers and speakers to identify a particular meaning for a term. This is often done when a word has several commonly used definitions or when a term is used in a unique or unusual sense, for example, defining an *educated person* as "someone who is aware of how much he or she doesn't know." See Chapter 5.

Style indicates the nature of a writer's habits as they are reflected in words and phrases, sentence structures and sentence lengths, preferred verb forms, and so on. However, many other criteria exist for describing styles, and these vary from reader to reader, depending on the reader's training, attitude toward writing, and so on. Some readers describe styles very generally, based on what they feel as they read. These descriptions might use such terms as *refreshing, pleasing, smooth, irritating,* or *tiring.* Such descriptions carry very little specific meaning. Other readers may refer to *abstract* or *concrete* styles, basing their judgment on word choices or the ratio of general to specific details. Still others may refer to the length of words—*polysyllabic style, plain style*—or sentences (*abrupt style* or *complex style*).

Subjective—See *Objective and subjective.*

Symbols suggest qualities. In essence, a symbol lets one thing represent another in the way that a dollar sign ($) can be used without accompanying numbers to suggest money or wealth. Of course, the dollar sign would be a symbol with or without numbers since it is a figure that stands for *dollar.* The sign itself isn't a dollar, however, anymore than an athletic team is composed of tigers, lions, or bears. These names carry symbolic value and are meant to suggest that the team members have some of the qualities associated with the animals named. Flags, medals, trophies, badges, and uniforms are examples of the countless number of items that serve as symbols.

Thesis statements express the purpose or main idea of a piece of writing.

Tone is a word used to describe how a writer reacts to or has evaluated the subject of the writing. Some pieces of writing are neutral and clearly objective in tone, and the words and phrases offer few clues to what the writer truly feels about the subject. On the other hand, if a writer scorns or admires what he or she is writing about, this scorn or admiration will likely be apparent to readers. Writing can convey a great variety of tones—humorous, lighthearted, somber, condescending, and so on.

Topic sentences serve as controls for paragraphs, expressing in general terms the idea or topic to be developed, explained, or illustrated in the paragraph. Topic sentences commonly begin paragraphs, but they are sometimes located in other places within the paragraph, including the middle or end.

Transitions are words, phrases, and sentences that make writing easier to read and understand because they guide readers from point to point. Words like *but, however, therefore, nevertheless,* and *consequently* are transitions that provide signals to help readers interpret what has been said or to prepare readers for something that follows. Words like *this, that, these,* and *those* frequently serve as transitions. So do repetitions of key words or phrases or the use of synonyms to repeat previously mentioned terms. Narrative writing relies heavily on time transitions like *before* and *that same day,* while descriptive writing needs the assistance of spatial transitions—*in one corner, in another corner, toward the rear of the room.*

Trite expressions are unoriginal expressions too often used in casual talk to be effective in writing or in serious speaking situations. *Busy as a bee, last but not least,* and *better late than never* are examples of trite expressions. The word *cliché* is also used to indicate trite expressions.

Understatement and overstatement are methods of emphasizing. Understatement calls attention to something because readers are looking for a stronger response: "We had been stuck in the elevator for over six hours when we began to smell smoke. That upset us a little." Overstatement, which is sometimes called *hyperbole,* emphasizes by exaggerating: "I support him 1200 percent."

Unity is what a piece of writing has when the introduction, body, and conclusion work effectively together to develop the main idea in a piece of writing. Every paragraph should add support or development to the main idea, and each sentence should contribute to the point being developed in the paragraph.

SUBJECT INDEX

ILLUSION AND REALITY

LANGUAGE AND WRITING

LIFE AND DEATH

MEN AND WOMEN

MORAL ISSUES

OUTSIDE INFLUENCES

RITES OF PASSAGE

SCIENCE AND TECHNOLOGY